Across TIME

LINDA KAY SILVA

Spinsters Ink
2008

Spinsters Ink
P.O. Box 242
Midway, Florida 32343

Printed in the United States of America on acid-free paper
First Edition

Editor: Katherine V. Forrest
Cover designer: LA Callaghan

ISBN-10: 1-883523-91-5
ISBN-13: 978-1-883523-91-6

Acknowledgments

A writer doesn't climb the publishing mountain without a lot of great help along the way. I have had some of the best support anyone could ask for and I'd like to thank those people here.

Katherine V. Forrest—Thank you for fine toning, fine tuning, ah hell, thanks for your professionalism, your patience and your keen eye for detail. You made all the difference in the world.

Spinsters Ink—Thank you for seeing the vision of Across Time. You have been easy to work with and have made this process seamless. Here's to a long-term relationship!

Sandi and Shari—Thank you for being willing to read all of the many rough rough drafts I send your way. You've read them all and still haven't had me committed!

And especially for

Lori—Thank you for giving me the time and the space to live in worlds that don't exist, to be people who aren't real, and to experience adventures without ever having to do the laundry or clean the bathrooms. You are the perfect partner for the writer, the teacher, and the adventurer in me. Let's keep cruising forever!

About the Author

When Linda Kay Silva isn't writing (which is seldom), she teaches various college English courses from American Minority Literature to Introduction to Fiction. Living with her incredibly patient partner of ten years, Linda Kay takes time out to play with Lucy Lui, her cockapoo who loves walks, playing with her favorite toy and blogging. If you want to know more about either Linda Kay or Lucy, you can check either of them out at www.lindakaysilva.com.

When Jessie woke up, they were turning right on Morning Glory Drive. The name suited the street, as there were marigolds all over the hills in front of the old Victorian houses. Cracking a wary eye open, Jessie realized that she had slept through most of the ten hours it had taken to drive from her beloved San Francisco to the sticks of the Oregon Coast.

"Sleepyhead's finally awake!" ten-year-old Daniel announced. Jessie had the feeling it was his intense staring at her profile that awoke her in the first place.

"Hush."

"We're in New Haven, Jess! But I blinked and we almost missed it." Daniel laughed.

"New Haven. What a stupid name."

"If you hate the name, Jess, wait till you see the town." Daniel had his nose pressed up against the window.

Sitting up, Jessie stared at the rugged Oregon coastline and sighed loudly. "That bad?"

Daniel shook his head. "That small. When Dad said small, I think he meant microscopic."

Jessie rolled her window down and smelled the salt air that blew her long red hair about her face. It didn't even smell like the ocean air in San Francisco. Rolling her window back up, Jessie sighed louder. How on earth her parents expected her to *adjust* to Oregon after living her entire seventeen years in the lap of California luxury was so far beyond her, she couldn't even wrap a fraction of her mind around it. It was like eating celery and having someone tell you that someday you'd enjoy it every bit as much as you did hot fudge sundaes.

"Look, hon, Jessie's awake."

Jessie smirked at her mother, whose only response was a grin that bordered on mocking. "Jess, you missed some of the most beautiful scenery. Once you get past Redding and into the state of Oregon, it's so green and lush. There are all sorts of greens here."

Jessie glared at the back of her mother's head and wondered if she had practiced that sing-songy voice while watching too many 1950s sitcoms. She fancied herself a resurrected June Cleaver . . . whoever *that* was.

"The Oregon coast isn't anything like California's," Daniel added, as if he were reading from a travel magazine. He was precocious like that. Everyone loved Daniel. He was the smart kid, the Curious George kid, the kid who could do no wrong. He was the prince, and no matter how mean she was to him, he was seldom ever mean back. There had to be something wrong with him. "It's rocky and jagged and stuff."

As the black SUV climbed higher on Morning Glory, Jessie slunk down in her seat. The Oregon coast could have been littered with gold and it would never compare to Baker's Beach, Santa Cruz or Monterey. How could it? This place was cold and dreary; gray even though it was the middle of June. They had left eighty-five degree weather and entered this fog bank. She had begged and begged her parents to put off their insane notion of restoring an old Victorian into a bed-and-breakfast. How hard would that have been?

"Just one year," Jessie had whined three months ago. "Next year's my *senior* year! Everything happens in your senior year."

Reena, Jessie's mother, leaned across the table and took Jessie's hands. "Honey, it's been such a rough year for you . . . for all of us, really. Your father and I aren't making this decision on a whim. We believe this is the best thing we could do for our family."

"You could have waited."

"We didn't want to wait," Rick interjected. "You're still hanging around the same kids who were busted with you for smoking dope, your grade point average is barely hovering around a two-point. You don't do *anything* except sit around in that room of yours and listen to that God-awful noise you call music."

Yes, it had been a really hard year. Busted behind the bleachers smoking dope, Jessie had had to endure a drug treatment program, community service and restrictions that limited her TV viewing time, her phone time and her after-school time. She hadn't been put on a short leash—she'd been reduced to a choke chain. Her friends weren't allowed to come over, she couldn't go anywhere with any of the kids who had been caught with her, and her weekends consisted of renting videos and eating pizza. She might as well have been in jail.

Her grades suffered because she refused to spend her free time studying. She did not want to be one of *them. They* were the dorks and weirdos who got good grades and sat around talking about important things like politics and education. *Bluck!* She may have been on restriction, but she refused to become boring. She had decided that she would bide her time for a year in Oregon before returning home in time to graduate with her friends in California.

California.

It felt so far away, and Oregon felt so foreign with its hippies and loggers and backwoods mentality. They didn't even pump their own gas! How lame was that?

It would be a very long year, but Jessie was sure she could make it. There was a life back there for her, and she wasn't about to miss out on it because of some stupid pipe dream her parents insisted on carrying out. No, she would bide her time and make her escape at the best possible moment.

A few minutes later, the SUV pulled into the driveway of a lavender four-story Victorian house with white trim. It didn't appear from the outside as if it needed the kind of work her parents had talked about, but then, if there was anything Jessie had learned in her life it was that nothing was ever as it seemed. Her parents rarely told the whole truth about *anything*.

"Here's our own painted lady, kids!" Rick announced, taking his wife's hand. "Isn't she a beaut?"

Daniel was already out the door, excited about scouring the grounds, but it took Jessie everything she had not to ruin her father's moment. Gazing up at the monstrosity before her, Jessie suddenly felt as though she had fallen through the Looking Glass.

"I know it doesn't look like a lot of work yet, but that's because the former owners dropped some pretty pennies on her exterior. It's the inside that needs work."

"The operative word, Dad, is *former*. Ever wonder why someone would drop so many *pretty pennies* on her and then give it all up?"

Rick turned and looked stolidly at his daughter. "The wife of the former owner died suddenly, leaving him with two young kids to raise. I think he moved so he could be closer to his family."

Jessie rolled her eyes. Her father had always been such a sucker for heart-wrenching stories. More than likely, the former owner had run out of dough and decided to cut his losses and get the hell out of Dodge.

"She's prettier than I remember," Reena said wistfully. "Oh look, hon, the wisteria is in bloom." Opening their car doors, Rick and Reena joined Daniel on the stairs of the centuries-old porch, leaving Jessie in her seat.

"I'm in a nightmare," Jessie muttered, folding her arms across her chest. Hundreds of miles from home, perched on a cliff, facing a mountain of manual labor, in a town whose main street was more like a dirt road to nowhere. God, if only she hadn't been busted with that dope. Her parents didn't trust her anymore, and now they were hell-bent on *saving her from herself*. That one incident had been the catalyst that sent Rick and Reena over the edge and in a hurry to get her out of

California, as if doing so would erase all that had happened.

Well, if she was being honest with herself, it wasn't just the dope. It was also the falling asleep in class, the drastic drop in her grades, and the desire to do nothing more than lie on her bed and listen to music. Those were the red flags that sent her parents scurrying off looking for something they could do *as a family*. She never imagined this lavender beast would be their solution.

"How typically boring," Jessie said, shaking her head. "Look at them up there. You'd think they were at Disneyland."

"Come on, Jess! You just gotta see the view of the Pacific." Daniel tugged open Jessie's door and pulled on her sleeve. "You can be depressed later. Right now, get out and look at the view. It's really cool."

Begrudgingly, Jessie got out and walked over to the edge of the lawn. Sure enough, there was a view of the mighty Pacific, in all of its gray glory. Even the beauty of her beloved Pacific was muted in this dreary place.

"Well?" Daniel asked, looking up at her. What was it about little boys that endowed them with such a spirit of adventure? Did they *ever* see things as they truly were?

Shrugging, Jessie plodded toward the house. "Save it, sport. I'm never going to like it here."

Trudging up the creaking stairs, Jessie groaned when she saw her parents sitting on, what else? A porch swing. "I think I've fallen into a giant cliché."

"Come on, Jess, give it a chance. There must be something you can find to like about her."

Jessie sighed. "What is it about calling ships and cars and now, apparently, old decrepit buildings *she*? Can we enter the twenty-first century, *please*, and refrain from genderizing this piece of crap?"

Rick shook his head. "It's a compliment, honey, to call a beautiful thing a she."

"For crying out loud," Reena said. "Enough already. I would like to enjoy our first few moments here in peace. Smell the wisteria? This place feels like a piece of heaven. Surely, even in your bitter state, you can feel some of that, Jess."

Jessie sat at the top of the stairs wanting to bawl; not cry, not sob, but bawl so big, so loud, so hard, she might even puke. She missed her friends, her neighborhood, even her stupid school. Everything she left behind made her heart ache. Like it here? Never.

"Why don't you go and pick out a bedroom?" Rick offered. "The third floor is our floor and there are four bedrooms to choose from."

"Just don't pick the one with the fireplace. That's the master bedroom," added Reena.

Slowly getting up, Jessie was all too happy to leave them to their bliss. They had always been like this, too. When other kids got to have two bedrooms and two parents vying and buying their way into their kids' hearts, Jessie had been cursed with two parents who adored each other and delighted in showing it as often as they could.

Once Jessie saw the error of her ways, she was truly thankful not to have to divide her holidays between parents' homes; not to have to remember whether she left her blue sweater at Mom's or Dad's, and not to have to go to court as a pawn in a game between two people who thought nothing about using their children as clubs to hurt each other. So, even though their frequent, and often, public displays of affection made her roll her eyes and want to gag, it was preferable to what many of her friends had to endure.

"At least we don't have any neighbors around to watch you two go ga-ga over each other. I suppose that could be a bonus." With that, Jessie walked into the old Victorian.

The first floor, it seemed, had just been upgraded, and if there was any work to do on it, it was nothing more than cosmetic. To her left was a grand staircase with dark cherry banisters and a dusty rose stair runner that dripped down the polished staircase like melting pink taffy. The fireplace in the sitting room was one of those ornate, gothic style fireplaces that had a personality like a friendly gargoyle. There were dark wood bookshelves on either side of it, filled with dusty, leather-bound novels. The hardwood floors were in perfect condition, and the walls were a warm tan color. Jessie could already see her parents curled up on the couch in front of the fire in the winter like two bookends reading their books and stroking each other's bare feet.

Yuck.

Moving down the hall on her right, Jessie peered into every room, marveling at how perfect everything was, right down to the paintings hanging on the walls. All of the rooms were already furnished with antiques and cozy bed linens, and Jessie found herself fighting the warmth she felt coming from these rooms.

"I. Am. Not. Going. To. Like. It. Here," she grumbled, trudging upstairs. Deciding she wasn't even going to give this room choice any thought, she took the bedroom farthest from the master bedroom, which looked like something out of a designer magazine. Her room had a corner window that looked out onto the cliffs and over the ocean. The sounds from the miniscule Main Street, some three hundred yards down at the bottom of the hill, could barely be heard through a second window which perched above the stairs. The Victorian did not sit on the cliffs overlooking the beaches, but instead sat tucked in a cubby of the mountain on the other side of Main Street. The Victorian was high enough to look over some of the stores and inns on the opposite side of the street. It sure as hell wasn't Market Street or Van Ness Avenue, and she half-expected to see a stagecoach rolling down Main Street.

"This is it," Jessie said, flopping on her bed.

"This is what?" Daniel asked, standing in her doorway.

"My jail cell for the next ten months, that's what."

Daniel walked over to her window and looked out. "It's a cool house, Jess. You could try giving it a chance."

Jessie put her hands behind her head and closed her eyes. She liked daydreaming about which of her *acceptable* friends she would invite up for a week during the summer. Surely they could find *something* to do in this little backwater town. Shoplift? Graffiti? Steal a horse and ride naked through the streets?

Jessie chuckled at the thought. *That* would sure show them, wouldn't it? After all, she was a city girl, not some hippie-lumberjack-freak. She knew the minute she went to town that she would feel like an outcast—like maybe a girl from the future.

"The first floor is finished, but did you see the second floor? Sheesh.

Lotsa work there, that's for sure."

Jessie opened her eyes and focused on Daniel. "Which room did you pick?"

"The blue one. It's the only one that's not so . . ."

"Girly?"

Daniel grinned. "Yeah. My room's over the garden. It's cool. There are really big flowers down there. Come on, Jess, come exploring with me."

Rising up on one elbow, Jessie inhaled slowly. "Tell you what. You explore and report any other cool things back to me. If something looks interesting, we'll go back and you can share it with me, okay?"

"Okay! But don't bum Mom and Dad out. We all know you don't want to be here, but that doesn't mean you have to ruin it for the rest of us, okay?"

Jessie just stared at him until he turned to go. He'd always been a very bright little boy, but the older he got, the more perceptive he became. His third grade achievement scores were off the charts, but the California public schools had done little to foster his inherent brilliance. Well, she hoped that coming to Oregon would be good for Daniel, but she did not believe there was anything here for her.

Looking around her room, Jessie sighed. It was a nice room, really, done in dark woods that had been polished like a gym floor. Had she been on vacation, she might even like it. With intricate carvings on the four-poster bed matching the legs of the desk sitting under the window, she could see herself journaling at that desk as she gazed out the window and dreamt California dreams. There was an enormous armoire hovering in the corner, probably an antique. The lavender flower wallpaper was a perfect match for the lavender carpet that protruded about three feet from under the bed. It felt like the room of a *good girl* from *Little House on the Prairie* but that wasn't her. That would *never* be her.

Oh, she'd tried to be good, but good hadn't filled that gaping void she'd always felt in her soul; a void she had tried to fill with sex (too one-sided and unfulfilling), drugs (too temporary), and stealing (too risky and unethical). Nothing could warm that cold spot she felt within her deepest recesses. She had always carried within her a frozen dagger she couldn't pull from her heart. She had no idea where it came from or how to get rid of it, but it was there, discoloring her world and adding to the immensity of feeling all the therapy in the world hadn't remedied.

"Jessie seems bitter about life," one therapist had said after their initial meeting. Jessie could only look at her mother and shake her head. She'd never been bitter in her life. Lost, yes. Confused, yes. Even angry, yes, but bitter? She wasn't bitter. Just empty. A piece of her was missing and she didn't quite know where to begin looking.

So, here she was, too far from her comfort zone with only three months between her and a new school filled with kids who probably still worshipped Duran Duran and wore leg warmers. Of course, even those kids probably still had access to their cells, iPods, and MySpace. Those had been the first to go when she'd been busted. She'd have preferred it if her parents had cut off her left arm instead. A teenager without a cell phone might as well not have a heart, either. It was her lifeline and when they took it from her, she was instantly out of the loop. Jason, the boy she had so wanted to hit on just before she left, had lost interest, and her friends had stopped including her in their triangulations.

In effect, she'd become an outcast, and with no technology to keep her informed, she suddenly found herself on the outside looking in.

Sighing loudly, Jessie stared out the window and watched Daniel trek through the flower garden below. Oh, if only she had the adventurous spirit of a ten-year-old boy, maybe this whole thing wouldn't seem like such a nightmare.

What on earth was she going to do?

The first few nights were the worst. There was no phone connected as yet, which meant she couldn't call her best friend, Wendy. No communication made her feel even more isolated and alone. The bones of the house made all sorts of creaking and moaning sounds. If she hadn't been so exhausted from all the work her parents made her do, she might have been scared. Old houses made old noises, but she was simply too exhausted to care. Even poor Daniel had fallen asleep during their third dinner at the house.

Once her funk had settled comfortably inside her chest, Jessie realized that she wasn't the only one having a hard time adjusting. The move had been as hard on him as it had been on her; he just hid it better. Their second night in the house, he'd come into her room well after midnight and just sat on the bed until she woke up. He hadn't done this since he was five.

"Something scare you, Daniel?"

Daniel nodded slowly. "This house is haunted."

The moon shone through the small window and danced across the floor with the shadows from a tall pine tree swaying in the slight breeze. Jessie grinned in the darkness. The night before, she had thought the same thing before realizing how silly that sounded. "I know it sounds like that sometimes, bu—"

"All the time. Even in the day, and especially on the third and fourth floors."

"Really?" Jessie leaned on her elbow. She could only see his outline from the moon.

"Yeah. It's haunted for sure. That's probably the *real* reason why those people sold it to Mom and Dad."

Jessie nodded. "Now there's a thought. Think we should tell them?"

Daniel shook his head. "They wouldn't believe us."

She knew that was true. "What else is bugging you?"

Daniel sighed. "There aren't any kids my age to play with."

"Are you sure? The other day I saw a bunch of kids your age hanging out on the beach."

Shrugging, Daniel scooted closer. "Mom only lets me go to the edge of the driveway as if I was a baby."

"You're kidding me."

"She thinks I'm gonna get lost or something."

"Have you been to town?"

Daniel looked down. Jessie knew that look.

"Did you sneak downtown?"

"Don't tell Mom."

Jessie sat up and mussed up his hair. "You know I'd never tell them. Listen. How about if you get to know your way around and then show me around?"

"Really? You'd really go with me?" His voice rose in excitement.

"You bet. We'll get an early go of it in the morning, before the slave drivers get up. How's that sound?"

"We're not gonna sneak, are we?"

"Nah. I'll leave them a note telling them we've gone exploring."

"Exploring? Cool. Thanks, Jess. You're the best."

She smiled wistfully. "Glad someone thinks so. Now, you go back to bed and wake me in the morning when you get up."

"What about the noises?"

"It's just the house settling. These old maids have boards like bones, and they creak and groan just like grandma's."

Daniel shook his head. "It's not just that. I . . . hear voices or something."

"It's okay. Sometimes the bones can sing. There's nothing to be scared about, Daniel. We're pretty safe in this little burg. Probably way safer than in the city. But if you get scared again, you can always come back in here and wake me up, okay?"

"Thanks, Jess."

"Wake me up early. You know how Reena gets once she's had her second cup of coffee."

"Roger that. You'll be up before the sun. I'll make sure of it."

And he did. Three minutes before six, they both were dressed and out the door, winding their way down Morning Glory Drive to a deserted Main Street. There was a slight fog hovering between buildings like magician's smoke. The occasional gull cawed from a perch on one of the three electric poles in town, and the lighthouse on the Head blew a low note to warn—what? Sailors? Boats? Pirates? Jessie smiled to herself. Pirates. Where on earth did *that* come from? What a moron. Maybe she should have paid more attention in school.

"It's too early," Daniel said as they crossed the empty street. "And cold. The sun here never comes out until noon."

"Let's grab some coffee and hot chocolate at that donut shop over there and watch the town wake up."

"What will I do if I see some kid to play with?"

"You go out there and ask them if they know where you can skateboard or play hoops. You'll know what to say. You always do." Jessie opened the door to Del's Coffee Shop and watched as Daniel walked past her. He had always been such a good little kid and an even better little brother. He was a sweet kid. Finding friends would not be a problem for him. She, on the other hand, was a horse of a different color. Making friends had never been easy for her, and she didn't see why now would be any different.

The donut shop was an old, converted Winchell's, but it smelled better than the paint and turpentine they'd been inhaling the past few days. The shop was clean and warm, and, like so many small town shops, had artwork from local artists for sale on the walls. The paintings were very good, but there were a few photographs that really caught Jessie's eye. One, oddly enough, was of a clipper ship sailing parallel to the horizon. She didn't know why she was drawn to this photo, and before she could put any more thought into it, a large bald man cleared his throat.

"Good mornin' to ya," the man chimed from behind the counter. He wore a white apron and a white baseball cap that said *Donut go gentle.* The same caps were for sale on a shelf above the coffee accoutrements.

"Good morning," Daniel chirped, hoisting himself into a booth.

"What'll ya have this fine morning?"

Jessie walked up to the counter and pointed to the rack behind the baker. "Two of those cinnamon rolls, a glass of milk and your house blend, please."

"Comin' right up. Have a seat and I'll bring it on over. Want those rolls heated up?"

Jessie looked at Daniel, who nodded.

"Sure. Thank you." Jessie turned to Daniel and grinned. It felt good to get away from the inn. They'd been working nonstop since they unpacked, trying to get the last three rooms on the second floor done so they might open it to customers by the winter season. She had painted, sanded, scraped glass clean, and learned how to repair and finish hardwood floors. It was hard work fixing an inn, and even her parents were starting to fall asleep at nine o'clock.

"How'd you sleep last night?"

Daniel shrugged. "I think the noises are coming from upstairs. If I'm really quiet, I can almost hear what they're saying."

"Still heard them last night?"

"Yeah. I try to remember what you said, but it's not creaking, Jess. They're voices. But I don't want to be a baby about it, so I put the pillow over my head and hum."

Jessie grinned. "Good for you."

"How about you? You doin' okay at night?"

"Why do you ask?"

Daniel shrugged. "You talk in your sleep sometimes."

"I do not."

"Yes, you do." Daniel giggled. "I can hear it."

Jessie nodded. "Can you hear what I'm saying?"

Daniel nodded. "Sometimes."

Jessie had never talked in her sleep before. She had been lying there at night, in the dark, trying not to feel the loneliness washing over her. She didn't want to feel the ache of wanting something she couldn't name. Nights were always the worst; when the darkness brought with it all its ugly, sad, empty emotions busy work kept at bay during the day. That's how it had been her whole life; like she was waiting. She just didn't know for what.

"Do you lay there and think about going back home?"

Jessie cocked her head. "Why do you ask?"

Shrugging, Daniel stared out the window. "At night, when you're mumbling, you keep saying *you can't go back*. It's sorta spooky." Daniel sighed. "You're not gonna run away again, are you?"

Jessie winced inside. Running away hadn't been one of her smarter moves. She discovered much too quickly that one can never run away from oneself. "I won't lie to you. The minute I turn eighteen, I'm gone.

I can't live in a place like this. I'm . . . well, I'm a Californian."

"Where will you go?"

"I don't know. Wendy's, maybe. Maybe I'll get a job and find a place of my own."

"No college? Mom and Dad think you're going to college."

Jessie shook her head. "I know it's what the folks want, but I doubt it's going to happen. It's just not in the cards for me."

Daniel kept staring outside. A young couple jogged by as the street slowly came to life. There still was no sun, but the mist or fog or whatever it was that lingered like a lost ghost in the early morning air was finally dissipating.

The baker came over bearing two steaming cinnamon rolls the size of small pizzas and a large, welcoming smile. "You want to know what's in the cards, young lady, you oughtta go see Madame Ceara. She's one of the best in the country."

Jessie grinned back politely, but said nothing.

"Here you go," the baker said, setting the rolls down and retrieving the coffee and milk. "Free refills on your coffee."

Jessie looked up at him. "You're kidding." Nothing in California was free.

The rotund man with the flour on his cheeks nodded. "You must be from California. They all say the same thing when they come in here."

Daniel turned and nodded, staring down at the enormous cinnamon roll. "Cool. And you don't have to pump your own gas, either."

"You're right. Add to those two things my cinnamon rolls, and you'll know why some folks never leave."

Daniel took a bite and nodded, his eyes wide with joy. "You're not kidding."

"You tourists or new to town?"

"New to town," Jessie answered sipping her coffee. It was the best coffee she'd ever had. "We just moved into the inn up on Morning Glory Drive."

"The old Laing place? Then you must be the Fergusons."

"We are!" Daniel cried. "I'm Daniel, and this is my sister, Jessie."

"Nice meetin' you both. I'm Delmar, but folks 'round here call me Del. I own this place. You know, we were all wondering who had bought the inn. It's a beautiful place. I hear your folks are renovating the rest of it."

Jessie nodded. "They're finishing what the Laings started and are turning it into a bed-and-breakfast."

"Excellent. The only other Victorian B and B we have is the bed-and-breakfast over on Cliff Drive, and it's full all year long."

"How long have you been in business here, Del?"

"This'll be my twenty-second year. You want to know something about anything, you ask me. You want to know something about *everything*, you ask Madame Ceara. Either way, one or both of us should be able to answer your questions. The two of us are the oldies in town. Well, you two be sure'n tell your folks about my coffee and cinnamon rolls. They'd make a great addition to any breakfast they might be thinking of serving up on the hill."

Jessie nodded. "We'll do that."

After Del returned to his work, Jessie and Daniel ate in silence, both gazing out the window at the people walking along the quiet Main Street. It was so very different than Market Street in San Francisco, where people hustled and bustled like they were always running late. Here, time seemed to stand still.

Finally seeing a group of boys Daniel's age, Jessie motioned with her chin for him to turn and look behind him. Outside, five boys in jeans and T-shirts were carrying nets and fishing poles and heading toward the marina. "There you go, sport."

Daniel looked over his shoulder before turning to her and wrinkling his nose. "They're going fishing."

"So?"

"I *hate* fishing."

Jessie smiled at the memory of the one and only fishing trip Rick had ever taken them on. Daniel had been mortified that fish were *tortured* in such an inhumane manner.

"Look. They're not *really* going fishing any more than I *really* went to the library all those times I told Mom and Dad I had a study group."

"Really?"

"Really. They're just going to go mess around. Go on and ask them if they'll show you some of the cool fishing spots in town. I'll bet they'd dig that."

Daniel looked unsure. "I don't know . . . there's lots of work Mom is gonna want us to do back at the inn, and—"

"And that dumb inn isn't going anywhere. Go on now and make some friends. It's what Mom and Dad would want you to do."

"You sure?"

Watching Daniel open the door, hesitate, and then jog over to the group of boys, Jessie felt a pang of sadness and envy. She was sad that she hadn't realized how much the move had affected her little brother, and she was slightly envious at how easily boys were able to instantly bond. It did her heart good to see him making friends, and no matter what her parents said, she felt that letting him take the day off to play was far healthier than working him to death in a stuffy old Victorian.

Pulling her leather-bound journal out, Jessie looked up one last time to see Daniel running onto the marina with five other laughing boys. Yes, Daniel would be all right. Daniel had always been all right.

When his blond hair disappeared, Jessie uncapped her fountain pen and began writing.

Every morning, I wake up, surprised and disappointed to find I am still here. Daniel thinks the house is haunted, and I have to admit, this old place groans and moans worse than an old woman. We're almost done with the room preps on 2 to get them ready for painting, but my God, there is so much work to do. I am in hell. I can't wait to have the gang up here. Maybe together we'll be able to see if there's anything worth seeing in this town. I bought a phone card yesterday and used the whole 60 minutes talking to Wendy. Her world now seems so far from mine—like time has stopped for me. I can see how distance makes one distant. I didn't really care who Bailey was dating or that the twins got busted for spraying graffiti. Suddenly, that all seems so . . . useless and dumb. I guess I wanted Wendy to understand my pain, to take more of an interest in what I'm feeling, but she seemed so uninterested. I'm sure I bored her to tears with tales of the inn, but they're all I have. God, isn't that pathetic? If it weren't for Daniel, I'd have taken the bus home, but I don't have the heart to leave him alone on the hill . . . not yet. Maybe when he gets more settled. Maybe when

"Excuse me, got a smoke?"

Jessie glanced up from her journal, surprised. "What?"

"Cigarettes. Do you have any I can bum?" A boy leaned over the chair in the booth. The pierced eyebrow, dyed black hair that hung to his shoulders, a tattered leather jacket, and several silver bracelets screamed *city dweller.*

"Oh. Yeah. Sure." Reaching into her purse, Jessie took her pack out and handed it to the kid. He looked her age at first glance, but he could have been older. It was hard to tell with these Oregon kids. They were so different from the kids she'd known.

Taking a cigarette out, he handed the pack back to her. To her surprise, Jessie waved it off. "Keep 'em." She hadn't smoked since they'd left for Oregon, and she figured now was as good a time as any to quit. It was an expensive and stupid habit she'd picked up in a moment of immature rebellion.

"Nasty habit," the boy said, sticking the cigarette behind his ear.

Jessie shrugged. "It used to work for me. Guess I'm over it."

"Good for you." The boy stuck his hand in Jessie's direction. "I'm Tanner. Tanner Dodds."

"Jessie Ferguson."

"Your parents bought the Money Pit Inn." It wasn't a question.

"God, does everyone know everyone's business in this place?"

"Almost. Gossip is our main course here. Without it, we would wither and die, right Delmar?"

Del shook his head. "Don't go getting that girl into trouble just yet, Tanner. Try to behave yourself this once."

Tanner laughed good-naturedly and Jessie instantly liked him "So, Jessie Ferguson, Mistress of the Great Money Pit, what are you writing?"

A slight blush crawled up Jessie's face and landed on her cheeks as she closed her journal. "Just some thoughts, that's all."

"I've had those on occasion. Nastier habit than smoking." Tanner slid the cigarette from his ear and motioned to her empty mug. "Grab a refill and keep me company while I slowly kill myself. Delmar never lets me smoke in here."

"Ya shouldn't be smoking at all, Tanner," Del returned, not unkindly. "And the refill is for the young lady, Tanner, *not* you."

"Damn it, Delmar, I hate it when you're on to me."

"Which is always."

Tossing a dollar on Jessie's table, Tanner started out the door.

"What's that for?" Jessie asked.

"For the coffee refill I'm going to drink. Just black, if you don't mind."

As Delmar refilled her cup, he nodded toward Tanner. "Be careful of that one, Jessie. He breaks all kinds of laws . . . and hearts."

Outside, Tanner held up the cup to salute Del before taking a sip. "Delmar's not so bad for an old coot. He means well. Most of the other townies don't even let me *in* their shops."

"Why not?"

Tanner flicked a lighter and lit his cigarette. "Look at me. They think I look like a shoplifter, a teen thug, your mama's worst nightmare."

Jessie watched him inhale a lungful of smoke before asking, "Are you?"

Tanner grinned. He had perfect teeth and one small dimple on his right cheek. "I could be, I suppose."

"That didn't answer the question."

Tanner studied Jessie before shaking his head. "I have a bad, yet undeserved reputation. It's the black leather jacket." Tanner inhaled again and blew his smoke away from Jessie. "But no, I'm not a thief. I like my freedom too much to risk doing something stupid like stealing something I can afford to buy."

"You're not from around here, are you?"

"Here, here, as in New Haven? Nope. I was born in Portland and my parents moved down here when my Dad's trust fund kicked in. There are butt loads of trust funders here on the coast."

"Really?"

"Sure. Money goes further here than in California or Portland or

Seattle." Tanner drew a long drag off his cigarette. "So, Jessie Ferguson, enough about me. I'm boring. What's your story? Your parents trust funders who decided to drop their wad in The Pit?"

Jessie shook her head. "Nothing so glamorous, I'm afraid. My parents had a dream of running a Victorian bed-and-breakfast while simultaneously saving their two children from the ravages of the Bay Area. In a nutshell."

Tanner studied her through the smoke he blew out. "Tough nut."

Jessie sighed and ran her hand through her bangs. "It feels like it sometimes. My folks think California has gotten mean and competitive, so they cashed in and dragged us up here."

"Kicking and screaming?"

Jessie sighed. It wouldn't do for her to trash this kid's home turf. "Sort of. It's very . . . different up here."

"That's an understatement and a half. Oregon is about ten years behind the times in education, fashion, music and culture. You must be in shock."

Jessie shrugged. "I don't have time to be in shock. My parents are trying to get the inn ready to open before winter."

"Slave labor?"

Jessie laughed. "Ab-so-lute-ly."

"So, was that your little bro' going off with Chris and them?"

Jessie nodded. "Yeah, why?"

Tanner studied the lit end of the cigarette with eyes the color of caramel. "I'm not the poster child for well-behaved guys, but Chris is bad news. I'd keep an eye out on him."

Jessie straightened up. "Bad news, how?"

"Well, the kid's only eleven, but I think he's following in his brother's footsteps as a doper."

Jessie started toward the marina, but Tanner grabbed her. "It's just gossip at this point. I wouldn't go bustin' in on your little brother's good time just yet. I shouldn't have even brought it up. It was unfair of me."

Jessie pulled her arm away, but kept staring in the direction of the marina. "I'd kill anyone who gets Daniel into drugs."

Tanner lifted his pierced eyebrow.

Jessie turned and stared at him. It was if he could see right through her, and the feeling was disquieting. "Look, it's okay if I do . . . *did* drugs, but woe be it to the asshole who drags my brother down. I've been there, and it ain't pretty."

Tanner nodded slightly. "Ah. I see."

Jessie frowned, avoiding further eye contact. She felt as if he were inside her head, reading her thoughts and knowing more about her than she wanted to let on. "He's a good kid and I want him to stay that way. You can spread *that* around when the gossip train slows down."

"You're a good sister, then."

Jessie shrugged. "Yeah, well, if I am, it's the only thing I'm good at."

"I doubt that. Maybe you just haven't found your niche yet." Tanner inhaled a lungful of smoke and slowly blew it out, where it met with the fog and danced away from them.

"The curse of the teenager, I suppose."

"I think it's the bane of our existence. We spend our lives looking for that one place to belong where we can actually accomplish something with our limited time on this planet. The cosmic joke is that you'll never find it."

Jessie cocked her head. Who *was* this guy? Before she could reply, two boys Tanner's age strolled over from across the street and insinuated themselves on their conversation. Both wore skateboarding T-shirts, jeans and scuffed up 'boarding tennis shoes.

"Gentlemen, and I use that term loosely, this is Jessie Ferguson, future owner of the Money Pit."

"No kidding?"

"Jessie, this is Randy and Brad, two of the town's most notorious dope smokers and car thieves."

"Hi," was all Jessie could think to say after an introduction like that.

"So, your parents are trying to fix up The Pit?" the tall one named Brad asked. He reminded her a bit of Lurch from *The Munsters*.

"Why does everyone keep calling it that?" Jessie asked, suddenly wishing she had one of the cigarettes she'd given away.

"Four families in the last eight years have sunk money into The Pit trying to make the lady into something she obviously doesn't want to become. Every one of them either ran out of money or out of luck before they could complete the job." It was the kid named Randy who answered, pushing his wire-rimmed glasses back up the bridge of his nose.

Jessie glanced over at Tanner, who was studying her intensely. He wasn't handsome or cute, and he was in bad need of a good haircut, but there was something very charming about his demeanor. "Just what does *that* mean?"

Tanner shrugged. "That so far, no one has succeeded in taming her. Painted ladies are like rare and exotic birds. They can only be caught and caged if they want you to catch them."

There was that feminine usage for a thing again. "You're saying the house doesn't *want* to be a beautiful bed-and-breakfast?"

Tanner flicked the cigarette butt to the ground and crushed it out with his heel. Then he did something Jessie had never seen: he bent down, picked the crushed butt up, and flicked it into the garbage can. "You oughtta look up the history of the house. Some really twisted shit happened there."

Jessie thought about the voices Daniel had been hearing. "Like what?"

"Hey guys," Randy said, motioning across the street. "Crazy Ceara is out this morning and heading our way." Randy pointed to an old woman wearing layers of different colored scarves like a Hungarian gypsy. She walked slowly, but very purposefully, her scarves whirling about her like a pinwheel.

"She is such a cuckoo," Brad added, pointing at his temple and drawing circles in the air.

"Leave her alone, guys," Tanner said softly. "I'd hate to have to kick your ass."

"But she's nutso, man, and she's coming straight at us."

"Yeah, Tanner, you don't want her to vex us or anything."

"That would be *hex* you moron, and that's *not* what she does. Now zip your mouths. I told you how I feel about that crap."

Before either of the boys could reply, the old woman walked right past them and straight for Jessie, who backed up until she was against the building. The old woman stared hard into Jessie's face, drilling her with eyes that were the iciest blue Jessie had ever seen. A shock of white hair poked out from under the purple scarf and she blew a puff straight up and off her face. The woman looked just like a gypsy, with fold upon fold of bright silk flowing at the slightest touch from the ocean breeze.

When, at last, the old woman spoke, her voice did not match her aged appearance. "You are *not* in hell, young lady. You are where you're *supposed* to be. Remember that. *Remember*." Her voice was soft and melodic, yet there was a pointedness to it that gave Jessie the chills.

"Excuse me—"

But the old woman turned and kept walking, leaving the small group to stare after her.

"Told you she was crazy," Randy said, shaking his head. "Come on, Tanner, let's get going. I only have the shop until nine."

Tanner waved for his friends to go on without him. "I'll catch up in a minute."

When Randy and Brad took off, Tanner took a step closer to Jessie. "Ceara scare you?"

Jessie started to nod, then shook her head. She couldn't get the image of those blue eyes out of her mind. "I don't frighten easily, but that was way weird. Who *is* she anyway?"

Tanner pointed to a small, intricately carved sign down the road from where the woman had come. The sign read *Madame Ceara* and beneath it, in smaller print, it read *sees all.* There was a palm and four tarot cards beneath it. "She's the local fortune teller. Been here for years and years. No one really remembers when New Haven was without her."

"She's a palm reader?"

"Of sorts. Lots of the old townies swear by her. She has a pretty decent following in Florence and Yachats as well. She goes by Madame, so if you hear people referring to something Madame said or Madame predicted, then that's who they're talking about."

"Why did the guys call her crazy?"

Tanner shrugged. "She sees things. She talks to the air. You know, all that weird stuff that scares little kids."

Jessie studied Tanner. "Does she scare *you*?"

"Not anymore. Personally, I don't think she's crazy any more than you or I. I think it's just part of her gig . . . her mystique. It works for her, too, because she has quite a client base. Can't be a palm reader and be normal. Know what I mean? Look, I really need to get going, but would you mind if I came up to The Pit sometime?"

Jessie stared at this interesting man-boy in his studded leather jacket and eyebrow piercing. Oh sure, he'd be just the ticket to get her sent home, all right. One look at him, and Reena would be sure she was doing drugs again. That sort of prejudgment was on the first page of the Christian Hypocrite's Handbook. *Judge not too slowly, lest ye be judged first.* They'd have a field day with the likes of Tanner, but what more could they do to her? What more could they take away from her? "Sure. I'll be there all summer."

"Great. It was nice meeting you, Jessie Ferguson. Oh, and by the way, you have killer hair."

As Tanner walked away, Jessie could only shake her head and put her hands in her pockets. She wasn't cold as much as she was a little wiggy. She returned to her booth inside and quickly opened her journal. Her hand was shaking as she flipped to the last page. Sure enough, there were her own words jumping off the page and into her face. *I'm in hell.* Slamming the book shut, Jessie stared for a long time at the sign down the street swinging slightly in the breeze.

"Remember . . ." Jessie murmured. "Remember what?"

"I can't believe you'd be so irresponsible to just let him go off with strangers!" Reena yelled as Jessie opened her can of peach paint. Reena had been barking at her since she walked through the front door without Daniel in tow.

"They're kids his own age. He was having a great time, he's learning to adjust to this nightmare you've put us into. What more could you want?" Jessie set the can opener down and carefully pried the lid off.

"What I want is for you to watch your language, be more helpful around here, and try to be more responsible where your brother is concerned. Anything could happen."

Before Jessie could relieve Reena of her worry, Daniel came bouncing past them, whistling some simple tune. He took three steps back and poked his head in the door. "Hi Mom. I'm getting into my work jeans and then I'll be right in, 'kay?"

Jessie waited for him to close his door before she stood and faced her mother. "See? Nothing *did* happen, except maybe he had a good time. He's home, he met some kids who showed him around town, and, in case you *care*, I met a couple of kids my own age as well. So, all-in-all, I'd say it was a good morning." Jessie pulled her paint-splattered bandana out of the pocket of her peach-spotted overalls and tied it around her head.

This stopped Reena cold. Inhaling slowly, she asked, "Where did you meet these . . . kids?"

"At the head shop, mother. They were buying a bong while I waited for my weed to be de-seeded." Jessie shook her head in disgust. "I met them at the coffee shop."

"I don't find that amusing, Jessie, not one bit." Reena stood with her arms akimbo. "And I don't appreciate this fresh mouth from you."

"You can't keep harping on me about the dope stuff, Mom. I'm not interested in it anymore. That doesn't mean I'm going to turn into a librarian and hang out with the geeks. When are you going to get over it?"

Reena returned to stirring her Apricot Fantasy paint. Her light brown hair was streaked with the color. "You can't blame me for worrying. After all you've put us through—"

Jessie groaned. "Will you *ever* let it go or are you going to beat me up with it forever?"

Reena continued stirring her paint, and did not look up. "I'm trying, Jessie, but I'm a mother who trusted her daughter to do the right thing, not to move into the Land of Bad Decisions. That trust has to be rebuilt. All I'm asking is that in the future, could you tell us where you're going? Especially when you're with Daniel."

"I told you. We. Went. Exploring. There's no definitive place when one goes exploring. Don't you ever remember being a kid?"

"Of course I do, but I didn't wind up in juvenile hall when I was sixteen, either. My parents could *trust* me to go where I said I was going and do what I said I was going to do. Jess, I am *trying* to trust you, but you act like you've got a great track record, and you don't. You want trust you haven't earned yet. I know you're not happy being here, and the last time you were unhappy about something, you were smoking pot and getting in trouble. I'm sorry if I can't just *let it go.*"

"So, until then, you're going to be suspicious of everything I do? I did my time, I suffered through community service, and I'm nearly finished with that horribly boring drug rehabilitation program you forced me into. Give me some credit."

Reena looked up at her. "I'm trying."

"Well, try harder. I'd rather eat a bullet than let anything happen to Daniel, and you know why? Because when the rest of the family tossed in the towel, he still believed in me. He's never done anything but like me for who I am. If it weren't for him, I'd have split from here *the second* you turned your back."

"I am happy to hear that you're planning on staying."

"For Daniel. He's made some friends. He's happier than I've seen him since we got here. I am not going to apologize for being a party to that happiness."

Reena nodded, reaching into her pocket and pulling out a ring with three ancient skeleton keys on it. One of the keys was so old it broke off in her hand, so she handed that one to Jessie. "The three rooms at the end of the third floor all need to be taped off. The tape for those rooms is in the supply closet at the end of the hallway."

"What's this key to?"

"I don't know, but one of these other two keys is to the supply room."

Taking the rest of the keys, Jessie started up the stairs. As she walked up each flight, she couldn't stop thinking about the term *Money Pit*. There was still so very much to do before her parents would even come close to starting to recuperate their investment. The floors on the third floor were terribly warped and needed replacing, the bathrooms needed new fixtures, new floors, new tubs, new sinks, and had to be completely gutted before any of those could be installed. The third floor was a mess, and although they could open with four bedrooms on the second floor by the end of July, that meant either halting construction or having four empty rooms until they could finish.

The Money Pit was, indeed, *apropos*.

The first key she tried turned out to be the master key to the bedrooms, so she placed this in her pocket. The second key she used to open the storage room. Holding the third key in her hand, Jessie wondered what it was for. It wasn't shaped like all the others, and felt heavier in her hand. Stepping out of the storage room, she noticed a numberless door perpendicular to the storage room. "That's odd," Jessie mumbled. She hadn't noticed that door when she walked into the storage room. She wondered why it had no number. The other bedroom doors had brass plates with 3A, 3B and 3C on them, but this door had nothing. Just as she started to test her last key, her father's voice drifted upstairs.

"Jess, are you up on the third floor?"

"Yeah, Dad, what do you need?"

"Would you toss me down a package of rollers? I have the wrong size down here."

"Sure, hold on a sec." Setting all the keys down, Jessie grabbed a package of rollers and dropped them over the side railing, watching as her father caught them.

"Thanks, honey."

As Jessie started back to the storage room, she stopped cold. The numberless door was gone. "What in the hell?" Running her hand along the wall, she frowned. Standing back, Jessie saw nothing but wall. For a moment, she felt she were stoned.

"Hey Dad," Jessie called out as she leaned over the railing. "How many rooms are on the third floor?"

"Three bedrooms and the storage room, and the shared bath at the other end of the hall. Why? Aren't you up there?"

"Yeah . . . I just . . . wasn't sure about the keys, that's all." Jessie stood in front of the storage room door for a long time. She *knew* she had seen another door, but the only answer to her question was a blank wall mocking her. As she stared at the wall, she suddenly made out the light blue eyes of Madame Ceara glaring intensely at her.

"I'm not afraid of you," Jessie whispered. Was this a flashback or something? What on earth was going on? "But I know there was a door here, and if I have to bash the wall in to find it, that's what I'll do." Grabbing the tape, Jessie didn't look at the wall as she walked past it . . . but every fiber in her felt as if the wall had somehow looked at her.

Some really weird things are happening here. I thought I saw a door where none exists. This weird house—Daniel thinks it's haunted, but I don't think it is. Then there's Crazy Ceara. She really freaked me out. It was like she could read my mind just by looking in my eyes. She may be crazy, but I think she may have the abilities she professes to have. All in all, and though I am loathe to admit it . . . this sleepy little town has some interesting characters, to say the least. Not nearly the amount of flannel I first expected.

Jessie had been given Saturday off so she could go into town and explore on her own. It had taken Rick almost half an hour to convince Reena that it was time to let Jessie go out on her own, but Jessie didn't care . . . as long as she got to go.

Walking briskly down the driveway, Jessie felt free for the first time in a long time. The Money Pit wasn't just draining her parents' savings, it seemed to deplete her energy as well. She had found herself falling asleep every night well before midnight, weird for someone who prided herself on being such a night owl. There were nights when she could barely lift her arms over her head they were so sore from painting. A part of her was glad she was so tired because she had stopped having that bizarre dream about the woman being chased by a Roman soldier. At last count, she had had that same dream eight times in the last month and it was beginning to bother her.

Daniel had come to her room once more after the first night, and had sat at the end of her bed for a very long time before finally whispering, "Can't you hear it?"

Jessie sat up and listened. "Uh uh. What is it you hear? How about if I come into your room?"

Daniel nodded eagerly. "Would you?"

Jessie slipped out of bed and slid her feet into the Ugg slippers Wendy and Jennifer had given her for her sixteenth birthday. "Let's see what we can find out."

Daniel led the way to a room that was typical of just about any boy. It was filled with car and rocket models, sci-fi posters, tennis shoes, scooters, roller blades, a skateboard, a baseball glove and a lava lamp she had given him last Christmas just to piss off her mother. Reena was a pyrophobe, and she was sure that lava lamp was going to be the death of them all. It had been Daniel's favorite gift.

His bed linen was the X-Men, and a huge poster of Cyclops hung over his bed. Because his room was the furthest from the main area of the house, he was able to escape the Victorian designs throughout the rest of the house. For that, Jessie was glad. No little boy should be forced to live in a room that looked like Martha Stewart lived there.

"Just sit on the bed and listen for a few minutes. You'll hear them pretty soon. They're not shy."

Jessie sat on Storm, of the X-Men, and cocked her head to listen. It didn't take long.

"You *do* hear it, don't you?" Daniel whispered. "They don't come out every night, but they're here a lot."

Jessie nodded, trying to figure out a way to explain to ten-year-old Daniel the sounds he was hearing. "Uh . . . Daniel, I think . . ." Then Jessie realized that it was the shape of his ceiling that enabled the sound to carry directly into his room. "I think, if we move your bed over here, the noises from the house wouldn't be funneled into your room so easily. See the shape of your ceiling? It acts like a conduit, and you're hearing . . . well . . . everything that's going on inside the bedrooms." Jessie had hoped Daniel's intellectual prowess was kicking in. "Do you follow me?"

Daniel frowned as he thought, and the light went on beneath his young eyes. Suddenly, his frown melted away. "Oh. *That*." He wrinkled his nose in disgust. "Them."

"Yeah. *That*. Them" Jessie had nodded and plodded off to bed.

She laughed to herself as she made her way down the hill toward Del's for a cup of coffee and a roll.

"Well, hello again," Del said cheerfully. "Becoming a regular, are you?" He poured coffee for her in a faded green mug that read Save Opal Creek.

Taking her coffee and sipping it, Jessie sighed. "That's great coffee, Del."

Del plucked a cinnamon roll, heated it for a second before taking it over to Jessie. "Lotta great things here, Jessie. Get to know New Haven on its own terms, and you might just find yourself liking it here."

Nodding, Jessie bit into the cinnamon roll she didn't order but was glad he brought over. "Can't get rolls this good in the city, that's for sure."

Del grinned. "Exactly. See? Every place has things that are special just unto it. Find those things and you'll be pleasantly surprised." Returning to his place behind the counter, Del left Jessie staring out the window at the nearly empty streets.

Everything here moved so much slower than in the Bay Area. When she and Reena had first gone to the store, the clerk actually chatted with them as if she was truly interested in what they had to say. Yes, they were the owners of the inn. No, it wasn't ready. Yes, the project was coming along as planned. No, they weren't hiring. Yes, they were enjoying the coast. And on it went. Jessie couldn't believe it, and was surprised at how Reena just answered the questions patiently. Jessie wanted to pull the woman's hair out. Back home, the clerks rang you up, grunted the amount, handed your money back and sent you on your way. There was no idle chit-chat, not even a pretense of niceness. Everyone was too busy, too important, or too self-involved to participate in idle blather.

This place was different, and Del was right . . . comparing was the surest way to alienate herself from the people here. People walked slower, drove slower and even ate slower. Time was different.

Different. Jessie sipped her coffee, remembering what one of her favorite therapists had said to her: *Different isn't better or worse. It's just different.*

Watching the small town slowly come to life, Jessie couldn't take her eyes off the palm reader's sign. How had she known what was in Jessie's journal? Maybe it was just a coincidence. After all, wouldn't any high school kid feel like they were in hell if they'd just moved?

Maybe. Maybe not.

Still, something about that sign kept drawing Jessie's eyes back to it. What would it hurt to poke her head inside the shop? How crazy could Madame Ceara really be if she was able to keep up a place of business?

Del emerged from behind the counter with a fresh pot of coffee.

"Del, is Tanner really as big a troublemaker as you made him out to be?" Jessie asked, surprising herself that the question came out of her mouth. She hadn't even been thinking about him.

"Tanner? Nah, he's an okay kid. His friends are kind of creepy, and they're mostly banned from the shops and stores, but Tanner's harmless. Truth is, he's a pretty smart kid, well-traveled, good manners, nice parents. The problem is, there isn't much for him to do here, so he hangs out with the likes of Brad and Randy, who are punks."

Jessie nodded slightly. "Then, you wouldn't warn me off him?"

Del leaned against the counter, the pot of coffee still in his hand. "I thought I did that already." He chuckled. "I'd take Tanner any day to the likes of Brad and Randy and some of them other boys in town. You get to know Tanner you'll know what I mean. There's more to him than meets the eye." Del started back around the counter.

"And what about Madame Ceara?"

"I suppose those idiots told you she was crazy."

Jessie looked away.

"Depends on your definition, I guess. Most folks would say it's plum crazy pouring good money into that inn of yours."

"Let me put it another way. Do *you* think she's crazy?"

Del shook his head. "Ceara's been here longer than anyone can remember and has always worked that shop. Crazy is all about perception, don't you think? Like perceiving Tanner as a bad kid because he has a piercing and a leather jacket. I'd say the people doing the judging were the crazy ones."

Jessie looked up at Del and watched him clean the counters. Who'd have thought that the local coffee shop owner was a sage in disguise? "I appreciate it, Del, thanks." Jessie half-finished her second cup of coffee, set a dollar on the table and started for the door. Oregon, it was turning out, was a strange place with really nice people. If she wasn't careful, she could actually find something to like about the place, and then where would she put all of her misplaced teenage angst?

Walking down the street, deeply inhaling the salt air, Jessie smiled. There was something freeing about the ocean air, the clanging of bells, and the sounds of the sails flapping against their masts. The fog was thinning enough to allow rays to poke through, and the morning just seemed to get better and better.

There wasn't much to this town, but the seafaring facades were recent additions and were quite quaint, done in royal blue trim with white stucco. Someone had sunk a lot of money into the Main Street shops, she guessed, in order to better attract the tourist dollar.

Strolling down the sidewalk, Jessie noted the different shops. There was a fish food restaurant she could never afford, a five-and-dime filled with all the things beachcombers might want, an art studio with paintings of every sort of sea creature imaginable, an antique shop, a jewelry store, Annie's Ice Cream and Madame Ceara's.

Jessie hadn't realized it, but she had stopped right under the sign and was staring at the front door. "Damn." Quickly turning around, she waited for the cars to pass so she could cross the street. How in the hell had she ended up here? She'd meant to cross the street earlier, but somehow hadn't managed to do so.

"Nothing really is a coincidence," came a voice from behind her.

Slowly turning around, Jessie was face-to-face with those ice blue eyes that impaled her. "Oh—I—uh—"

Madame Ceara lifted an eyebrow. "You ended up here because *here* is where you're supposed to be."

A chill ran down Jessie's forearms. "Is this how you get new clients?"

Madame Ceara grinned, revealing nearly perfect teeth. "It is good to have courage. You are a very brave young woman, and that is good because you are going to need it where you're going."

"The only place I'm going is home to California." Jessie checked the street again, but there was a sudden influx of cars through the green light.

"Perhaps, but then, that's the beauty of the future. We never really know what it holds for us until it becomes the present. By then, our plans have changed."

Jessie smiled politely; deciding that getting hit by a car was preferable to talking to this woman who made her feel as if she had just surgically removed Jessie's soul and was studying it under a microscope.

"Look, Madame—"

Madame Ceara peered closely into Jessie's eyes and then nodded. "You are not alone."

"What are you—"

Madame Ceara held up a heavily braceleted arm that jangled noisily, essentially chopping off Jessie's words. "Trust your own eyes, Jessie. You saw what you saw. Believe in yourself. It just might save her life." Turning so abruptly that her scarves made a swooshing sound, Madame Ceara went back into her shop, leaving Jessie with words still stuck like peanut butter to the roof of her mouth.

By the time she recovered her wits, a customer had followed Madame Ceara into her shop, and the cars miraculously vanished so Jessie could make her way hastily across the street.

Her? Who on earth was she talking about?

"She could not possibly know," Jessie whispered, as she pretended to look at the jewelry in the shop across from the palm reader's shop. That was twice now that the woman had spoken about something Jessie had been thinking or writing about. Was she trying to make a point? Trying to scare her? Maybe it was all like a horoscope, where one size fits all. Say something generic, like a fortune cookie that says, "Something good will happen to you today," and it would fit ninety-nine percent of the population.

Still . . . the woman had been so exact the first time and damn near in her mind this time. What was it she wanted? Suddenly, she felt like going back to the inn. This little burg had more nuts than a Planters mixed can, and flannel or no flannel, it was beginning to appear as if New Haven, Oregon, was a tad bit more bizarre than at first appearance.

Half an hour later, Jessie was going back up the stairs of the inn when found a note taped to the banister which read that the three of them had gone into town to rent a movie and get a pizza.

Jessie grabbed the three keys off the hook and started up the stairs. Had Madame Ceara been talking about the door that was there and then wasn't? Was that what she meant by trust herself? How could she know? If she truly did know, then she was certainly more than the crazy woman everyone believed her to be. And what was it about those eyes? God, it felt like the woman could look right through her. The whole thing was spooky, and Jessie wanted to put an end to it right here.

Slowly retracing her steps that had led to her seeing the numberless door the first time, she opened each of the bedroom doors, and, when she got to the storeroom, there it was! The numberless door! Gazing down at the key in her hand, Jessie felt her palms get all clammy and sweaty. The door *did* exist! But if it did, how come she hadn't been able to see it until now? How come she saw it, it vanished, and now she was seeing it again?

The whole thing made her stomach lurch and bubble, so she opened the storeroom door, set the keys on the shelf, and grabbed a second pack of rollers, just like the ones she had tossed her father. Inhaling deeply, she took three long strides out of the storeroom and turned to the wall.

The door was gone.

"Oh crap," Jessie said, leaning against the banister. Her stomach jumped and gurgled and she felt bile trying to rise in her throat. She wasn't stoned and she wasn't crazy, so what in the hell was going on here? For a moment, she considered running out of the house and down to Madame Ceara's, but then she remembered the old woman's words. She needed courage. She needed to do something she hadn't done in a long time; she needed to believe in herself. She needed to be brave. She *knew* what she'd seen. She could not doubt herself.

Retrieving the solitary key, Jessie dropped the package of rollers back on the shelf before turning the skeleton key over in her hand. It was warm, and by the looks of it, appeared to be the original that came with the house. There was very little wear on the teeth, and no grooves on it from overuse or metal on metal cuts that her ill-fitting house keys had had in California. Maybe this wasn't even the right key. Maybe, when she went back, the door would be gone again, as if the house were playing some sort of game with her. Maybe the voices Daniel kept hearing were really there. Maybe, maybe, maybe. One can't cook with maybes.

Exhaling loudly, gripping the old key as if it, too, might disappear, Jessie stepped outside the storeroom and faced the numberless door.

"It's there," she whispered, taking a step toward the door. The key seemed to be growing warmer in her hand, but that was impossible. Impossible? A door that appears at whim was impossible. A glowing key? Hell, at this point, anything seemed possible.

Turning the key over in the palm of her hand, Jessie felt a rush of adrenaline sweep over her. Her scalp tingled, the bottom of her feet itched, and a cold chill ran up and down her spine. Trying not to be afraid, Jessie decided she had nothing to lose at this point and plunged the key into the lock.

It could have been anything, really; an empty storeroom, an unused bedroom, an old water closet that had been boarded up, or even a clothes closet. Jessie could have accepted any of those. She could have even accepted something as out there as a treasure room or attic that hid some heinous crime of the eighteenth century.

But to open the third story door to find an oak grove doused in the light glow of dusk made Jessie question her sanity and her otherwise tenuous grasp of reality. Her mind screamed at her feet to turn and run and forget that she had ever seen the door, but her heart kept her rooted there, like Madame's stare. She was afraid to move, afraid not to.

"Alrighty then," she said softly, taking a step into the room/forest, for it was, indeed, the forest floor her feet touched. Turning to look back, to make sure that the hallway was still a hallway, Jessie was surprised at how calm she felt. Yes, the hallway was right there, but what would happen if her parents returned home and saw . . . saw what? Could they see this as well? Did they need the key in order to open the door? For that matter, would the door even be there?

Reaching out, as if she were no longer in her own body, Jessie closed the door behind her. And when she turned back to the forest, she looked down at herself and realized she was wearing a white robe, a familiar white robe. Her robe. But how could that be? She owned a bathrobe, but not the kind she wore now. This robe, *her* robe, had a hood, and it fit her perfectly. Glancing up from her robe, she realized that she also knew where she was. This was the edge of McFarlane's property, where the ancient oak trees had managed to escape the saws of the intruders. Yes, this was McFarlane's land, as surely as her robe was the priestess robe she had donned years before. Funny, but for a moment there, she thought . . . what had she thought? What had she come to the edge of the forest to do?

Peering into the distance, she noticed fires burning brightly. Old man McFarlane did not mind the others on his land as long as he knew they were there to preserve, not destroy it. She remembered that much—but why had she forgotten it for a moment?

Shaking her head, she followed the firelight through the trees— walking upon the soft moss that lay like a carpet beneath her feet. Of course! Now she remembered! A ritual was being performed, and she had left it to—to what? Odd, how she had seemed confused, as if the spirits and sprites had been playing tricks on her. Walking through the dense forest, Cate inwardly smiled. She knew every inch of McFarlane's grove even when darkness was beginning to fall and the dryads were out playing pranks on the unsuspecting. The great oaks, a symbol of her strength, nay, her very strength *itself,* towered above her protecting her like a blanket. She loved these woods; loved how alive she felt whenever she was within them.

As Cate slipped through the forest, she could see the orange and yellow blaze of the bonfire as it burned higher and higher. All around the fire were Druid priests and priestesses like her, wearing the white robes and chanting the hymns and prayers intended to see the quester safely home. When she emerged from the forest, all of the Druids turned to stare at her.

"Hold your questions," came a familiar voice that caused Cate to turn to it. The voice belonged to Maeve, her dearest friend and head priestess. Maeve strode over to Cate in such a manner that made her appear as if she were floating on the wind. When she stopped in front of Cate, she smiled softly, her gray eyes filled with deep concern. "Are you all right, Catie?" Maeve whispered, a catch in her throat. "You look . . . unlike yourself."

Cate looked up at her much taller friend and nodded. Something had happened, but she couldn't quite remember what it was. Was this ritual for her? Why could she not remember?

Maeve pulled a torch from the ground and held it close to Cate's face so she could see her better. "You do not remember, do you?"

Cate frowned, then glanced over Maeve's shoulder at the dozen or so other Druids who waited for her to speak. Looking back into Maeve's face, Cate shook her head. "I do not."

Maeve turned and handed the torch to another priest, who wordlessly took it and stepped back. Maeve stepped forward and wrapped her arms around Cate, crushing her to her chest. "It is all right," she whispered, still clutching Cate. "As long as you are returned safely, that is all that matters."

Cate pulled away and peered into those wise, gray eyes that had seen so much and taught her even more in their years together as priestesses of the Art. But for the life of her, Cate could not remember why Maeve would be so desperately relieved to see her.

"Returned? Have I been gone?"

Suddenly, a much taller Druid, perhaps by at least two hands, strode out of the darkness. In his left hand was a large carved stick with the Ogham letters carved neatly onto the handle. Maeve stepped away to allow the priest closer access to Cate. "She does not remember the quest, Lachlan."

The priest known as Lachlan towered over Cate, his clear blue eyes blazing as he studied her. She could not remember a time when she had been able to discern the color of his eyes; so often they had seemed colorless one minute, and fiery orange the next. But right now, they were a clear, light blue, and they were doing more than looking at her—they were probing her. "Do you not remember, Cate?"

Cate wanted to please them. She had always wanted to please them, so she closed her eyes and opened her mind, listening to the crackling of the fire, the leaves as they rubbed against each other on the trees, and the breathing of the two people she loved most in the world.

Remember . . . remember . . . The only thing she could see were two crystal blue eyes telling her to remember. What was it everyone wanted her to remember? And why could she not?

Remembering was most of the Initiate's task during the first ten years of Druidic training. Over twenty-thousand verses were to be memorized; including stories, poems, verses, myths, folklore and prayers. Remembering was of utmost importance to the Druids, for it was they who passed the histories down from generation to generation. And now, it appeared that everyone wanted her to remember—but what was it? Slowly shaking her head, Cate sighed in frustration. "I am sorry, Lachlan, but I do not know what it is you want me to remember."

Lachlan abruptly turned from her and spoke directly to Maeve. "She does not remember. What good does this do us if she cannot even remember why we sent her?"

"Give her time." Maeve's voice was soft yet commanding.

"We do not have the luxury of time! Our destruction is imminent. I thought you said she was the best we have."

Maeve glanced over at Cate, who looked befuddled. "Lachlan," Maeve began, "Cate is exceptional, and you know as much. Please, give her some time to recall. What we have asked her to do is not something we can take for granted or bend to our will. It is the first time we have sent her through. It will get easier each time. Be patient." Maeve reached out and lightly touched Lachlan's broad shoulders.

For a Druid priest, he was incredibly fit and strong. Broad shoulders melted into a tapered waist even the folds of robes couldn't disguise. Beneath the hood lay a shock of curly black hair that hung to his shoulders when not under the hood, which was seldom, since he always had it up to acknowledge when he was working. His body was lean because of the little food he fed himself, but it wasn't just his physical prowess that made people watch him as he walked by, it was his carriage; Lachlan had a royal gait and blue eyes that mesmerized everyone who looked at him. He was well-liked and very well-respected in the village of Fennel, and was known throughout the lands of the Iceni and Ordovices. The Silures were his people, and they were fiercely devoted to him and Maeve, and they deferred to him on almost every communal issue.

So it would have been strange if any of the villagers had witnessed Maeve touching the priest, especially when his hood was up, but Maeve, they all knew, was different. He held something deep for her, and seldom denied her anything. It had been that way between them from the very start.

"I trust I need not remind you how precious every passing moment is, Maeve. If she cannot remember, there are others we can prepare for the journey. Perhaps Angus or Quinn will find what we need, what we must know to survive. If she cannot remember, perhaps they will have better fortune."

Maeve bowed her head, her hood slipping forward to completely cover her face. She showed her deference to Lachlan's words by keeping her head bowed for longer than was necessary. It was for show only. "Thank you, Lachlan, but I believe in Catie's abilities. You have twice seen her use her sight, and you know that her powers get stronger every day. She can and will get us what we need. You must have patience."

Cate could stand it no longer. "Maeve, what is going on? Have I done something?"

"Shh. Come with me." Maeve began to retrace Cate's steps back into the woods, her arm around her waist. When they finally reached the three massive oak trees exactly twelve feet apart and in a perfect triangle, they stopped. They both felt the change in energy as they neared the three trees. The air suddenly came to life, crackling and spitting, as if energized by some unseen force.

"Do you remember walking through these oaks, Catie?"

Cate looked at the triangle, felt the intense energy, and tried to recall the ritual that had Lachlan speaking to her and throwing a fiery liquid at her prior to sending her into these woods. Lachlan was a master of alchemy, but Cate could not remember what it was that he had sprinkled on her.

"I remember Lachlan preparing me for . . . a quest of some sort. It is all so very foggy." Cate's head felt heavy. "I am so sorry if I have disappointed you."

Maeve nodded and rubbed Cate's back. "You never disappoint me, Catie."

"He sent me to the woods to enter the Forbidden Forest so that I could—" Cate thought hard, seeing these icy blue eyes boring into her brain. They weren't just staring at her; they were trying to communicate something to her. "So that . . . so that I could gather the information needed in order to save us. Yes! That is it."

"Yes." Maeve hugged Cate tightly. "I knew you could do it, Catie."

Cate shook her head, and her hood came off, revealing bright red hair. "We sent three of us to find out how to keep the Romans from destroying us. Angus, Quinn and I went through the Sacred Place in the Forbidden Forest hoping to find out . . ."

Maeve swallowed hard. "Find out what?"

Cate sighed. "How to save ourselves from the destruction that is approaching."

"And? What is that destructive power?" Maeve pressed closer, her breath smelling of the mint leaves she so often chewed.

Cate started to pace. "The Romans—Angus saw them coming—crushing us—chasing us, burning and raping us. Quinn saw them utterly destroying all that we know, all that we've built, all that is important to us. So, Lachlan sent three of us through the Sacred Place hoping our spirits would travel ahead."

"Because?"

Cate stopped pacing. "Because of our belief in time."

Maeve nodded. "Tell me, Catie. What have you learned about the concept of time?"

"Lachlan says—"

"No, Catie, what do *you* think? You are the one going forward in time? What did *you* learn about time and our plan to use it to save us?"

Cate inhaled deeply and gazed at the triangle of the Sacred Place. The oak trees were so old, it took five Druids holding hands to be able to encircle one trunk. Mistletoe hung in enormous bunches from the tallest point, and the cracks in the thick bark were deep crevasses—home to other creatures.

Running her hand over the rough bark, she still felt the memories from her trip lingering in the back of her mind. It was frustrating not to be able to recall it wholly. "Time does not exist on a continuum or a single linear line. Multiple times exist at the same moment. My soul was transported into the future so I might be able to gather enough information and historical data to save us from being crushed under the heel of the Romans."

Maeve smiled proudly. "Excellent. Then you remember much of what you were taught."

Cate nodded. "I remember well who I am. I am having a very hard time remembering where I *went* and who I *was* once I got there. It is terribly frustrating."

"I can imagine."

"But I do know my soul went somewhere strange and quite foreign."

"Your eternal soul went to you in another time—a time we know little about."

Cate shook her head, suddenly feeling the same tingling as when she'd first stepped into the center of the triangle. "But Lachlan is right, Maeve. We do not have time. I must remember what I experienced. My soul was transported, indeed, as Lachlan and others before him professed. It is all true. The soul comes and goes—it lives on beyond the body."

"Do you mean—"

Cate nodded. "I *was* someone else. It is as we have always thought. The soul does not die."

"Others have tried what you did Catie, but few returned. There are stories and tales, of course, but no one in our life has successfully gone through and returned. Lachlan will be so thrilled." Maeve walked with her arm around Cate's waist as they slowly made their way back to the middle of the grove. Lachlan met them halfway back.

"Well?"

Maeve kept Cate close to her side. "She is beginning to have vague remembrances, Lachlan, but nothing definitive yet."

Lachlan waited. He was not a patient man, but he knew enough not to press Cate, for fear of Maeve's disapproval. She could be frighteningly protective of the little woman next to her.

Cate inhaled deeply. She was so tired and her head was pounding. "My spirit did, indeed, travel far into the future, but there, I remember nothing of who I am or what my purpose might be. I have no memory of this past, aye, no knowledge of it, either."

"Then how could you know?"

"Because . . . deep down, I was within the shell of the being that now has my soul, but that being . . . she has no concept of time, of history, of the past, of *anything*. What little she knows is fuzzy and unclear. I think that is the reason my head aches. She lives in a haze."

Maeve nodded. "You have a different purpose in the future realm, Catie. The being which houses your soul knows not the import of listening to herself and realizing that the voice she hears is real. She has forgotten who she was. Lachlan believes this is common; the soul is not the mind and remembers quite differently."

Cate shrugged. "I do not know *what* she thinks or feels, Maeve, only that I do not know yet how to master my movement into her. I felt so lost. It was all so very . . . odd. I existed as if I were only able to watch this young woman live her life. I . . . shared the body with my spirit, which has lived well over three thousand years."

Maeve's hand covered her mouth in awe. "Three thousand . . . can that be?"

Cate shrugged. "I can only guess at this point, but she is far far into the future. I was there hiding, as it were, trying to juggle her memory of who we once were. Her spirit did not hear. Her spirit hears little beyond its own thoughts."

"But that spirit is *you*," Lachlan said softly. "You did it, Cate. You went into the future and came back. You have done what no other has."

"But Lachlan, it was a failure. Just as she cannot recall any of *this* past, nor can I, mine. It appears that the spirit chooses to live in the moment, guided by the body and time it inhabits, but brings nothing of a memory with it into its new life. Parts of my soul may come out from time to time, but it is not I. Not anymore."

Maeve looked down at Cate. "But that does not mean that those memories are not there, Cate. It means they are weaker in color, in shape, in form, because there is no body, no senses to remind it of what once was. If you can manage to push your memories through to the being you are in the future, then we can turn this into a success. Catie must return and keep returning until she has opened a door through which to share her memories of this life. The more she is there, the more easily she might be able to help the future Cate remember who she was."

Lachlan gazed off into the distance. An owl screeched as it left its nest in search of food. "It is a possibility I can consider, Maeve, but not without a great deal of thought. I do not know what could happen—"

"We *know* what the Romans have in mind for us," Maeve said, cutting him off. "If we are to save any lives at all, then we must give this a chance. One time through was only a fact-finding quest, Lachlan. If Cate believes she can manage to break through, then I think we need to give it more time."

"Maeve—"

"Time, Lachlan, it is—"

"I wish to return." Cate's announcement caught them both off-guard. "I was not prepared for how I would feel, or the oppression I encountered by a soul that, while my own, is vastly different from the one I currently have. I would appreciate another chance. I have abilities the others do not possess, Lachlan. I can go where others cannot. If our people, nay, if our very existence is threatened with extermination, and my powers can be used to keep that from happening, I have an obligation to use them. I wish to."

Lachlan laid his hand on her shoulder. "Very well then. But not tonight. Tonight, you rest, and let Maeve care for you." Turning on his heel, he left Maeve to watch over Cate.

"It is not as Herodotus believed, Maeve," Cate said, walking slowly back to Fennel. "The portal allows us to move to a place and time not of ours, which means that multiple times do, in fact, exist at once."

Maeve smiled. "Not *us*, Catie, *you*."

Cate sighed. "Indeed. Not everyone can go through, as we have known for quite some time. But I have the sight. I saw the young woman, as clearly as I have seen you in my dreams. My sight has somehow allowed me to venture out—as has Angus's and Quinn's."

"We have not heard from them. Lachlan fears the worst."

Cate felt chills run down her arms. "They have the sight as well. I am sure they will be fine, but Maeve, the idea of multiple times may not be the truth. It is possible that the portal sends me forward . . . that time could still be linear, but there are rifts that allow us to move along it."

Maeve stared at Cate through the rays of moonlight cascading down on her face. The young woman before her was different than the one who walked away from her in order to travel to that part of the forest where people had gone and seldom returned. Everyone in Fennel, as well as in every other village on the east of the isle, knew about the Forbidden Forest and what usually happened to people who were foolish enough to venture into it. Many figured it was haunted with restless shadows; still others thought it was pure evil and many leaders did not allow their Druids to enter it. Only the Silures knew that the Forbidden Forest contained the Sacred Place, and only the Silurian Druids were brave enough to face it.

Cate had been brave. She had had the sight, gone through the portal, and returned unharmed. Changed, yes, but unharmed, nonetheless. Maeve could tell by the look in Cate's eye that she had left here an energetic young lady and returned a weary, if not wary traveler. Cate may not have remembered what it was she saw, but it clung to her like the forest mist, becoming a part of who she was now, in this moment.

"Catie, are you feeling all right?"

Cate pinched the bridge of her nose, tears threatening to escape her closed eyelids. "It's just . . . when I first returned, I . . . I did not even know who I was. I looked down at my robe, and I knew it was my robe, but I did not know who I was yet. It was very disconcerting."

Maeve reached out and gently pushed her hood back, revealing Cate's long red hair. "Perhaps that is the very thing that will save us, Catie. Perhaps when you struggle as you return, that is because you are bringing memories of the future with you; memories we must access to know which way we must turn to save ourselves."

Cate sighed, allowing two small tears to form and drop. "It was very trying, Maeve, and I am so very tired. I understand how important remembering is, but once I crossed over, I became a young woman very much molded by an environment that is more foreign to me than the Land of Chin."

Maeve brushed the tears away with the sleeve of her robe. "Go on."

"Who I am there is shaped by events I know nothing of. Even now, as I try to remember, it feels like trying to remember a hazy dream, and being unable to recall anything but the fog."

Maeve nodded. "The past feels like memories because those events are stamped upon our spirits, but the future is dreamlike because we cannot envision those revelations that time enables us to have. Can you remember any of the dream?"

As they walked, Cate suddenly leaned against one of her favorite trees, drawing strength from it. "I am exhausted, Maeve."

"I understand, sweet one. You need not work so hard. Do not let Lachlan's haste burden you."

Cate nodded. "I know it's important—I shall try. I remember . . . ice blue eyes . . . and the feeling that I was so horribly out of my element, uninvolved, alone, and—this is strange—I was even saddened by something. She is very alone and sad for it."

Maeve sat next to Cate and stroked the side of her head. She could feel the exhaustion drip off Cate like water running down the crevices of the bark. "Go on."

"I remember a curiosity about something, and a willingness to face a fear, though I do not know what fear it was." Cate sighed. "That is all I have." She closed her eyes.

Putting her arm around Cate to let her rest, Maeve whispered, "You are very brave, not only to go, but to wish to go back. You are but three and twenty, yet you are so wise and so courageous. I envy you that courage."

Cate rested her head against Maeve's shoulder. "She's . . . younger," Cate said so softly, Maeve could scarcely hear her. "And . . . not very wise."

Maeve strained to hear Cate's last words before she fell to sleep; "Only wisdom can save us now."

At the very edge of the Sacred Place, where Lachlan and Maeve would stay until one of their questers returned with what they needed, Cate glanced at her hand, at the Egyptian ankh Maeve had given her a lifetime ago. The ankh, in the shape of a gold key, had been hanging around Cate's neck for almost ten years. It was the only thing she possessed and her greatest gift. When she was younger and afraid she would hold it for comfort, so she was surprised when the necklace began growing warmer the closer she got to the portal.

"Remember, Catie," Maeve had whispered to her before sending her off to the portal the day after she had returned. "Remember and return. For if you do not return, I shall go after you. You know I will."

Cate believed her. Maeve always did what she said she would. Cate remembered the very first time she held the necklace in her hand and saw her very first sight.

Lachlan hadn't believed that she had the sight. He thought her too young and inexperienced, as if only aged and gifted priests could see as clearly as she did. But when Maeve had handed her the ankh as a gift that night at the inn, she had seen a world unlike anything she could ever dream. The vision was scary, fiery, and not a place she wanted to be. That was nine years, almost ten years ago, when Cate was a mere three and ten, full of high hopes for obtaining priestess status among the Silurian Druids. Lachlan doubted her then. It was several more years later that he realized the extent of Cate's powers; several years before she saw the same vision Lachlan had seen, and in nearly the same place. She remembered it as if it were yesterday.

Lachlan and Cate had been on a walk. He had been teaching her some alchemy and herbalism along the way. When Cate came to a large rock near the coastal forest, she recoiled so violently from the sight that she fell backward.

"What? What is it you see?"

When Cate rose, she was trembling. "Blood. There was blood on that rock. So much blood, it felt—sacrificial." When Cate saw Lachlan pale, she swallowed back her bile and stated, "You have seen it also." She knew before he answered.

Nodding, Lachlan touched the rock, grimaced, and pulled away. "Blood, yes, but not just anyone's blood."

Cate's eyes grew moist. The most vile, most wretched sight Cate could imagine: it was Maeve's blood on that rock.

"Aye, I have seen the accursed vision, and it haunts me daily." Lachlan then shared his theory about the Sacred Place, about the other visions, and about his fears for Maeve and the others. He admitted his love for Maeve, and the place she held in his heart. This was not news to young Cate, who could tell how he felt by the way he looked at Maeve. He would risk his life for her, for all of them. Cate knew that as well. Then Lachlan told her the one thing that would change her life forever.

"Cate, you have learned how time is circular in nature, and that we live beyond the present time of our bodies. The truly gifted Druids can slip between the fabric of time to discover a future that knows what happened in our own time. Knowing the outcome of our present predicament will enable us to act instead of react. We can plan instead of being caught unprepared. I have known others who have tried to enter the portal, but they were unsuccessful, and it ultimately cost them their lives. But you, Cate, you might just have the powers and the strength to do what the others could not."

"Which is what?"

Lachlan frowned. "Return."

As strange as that conversation was ten years ago, it was beginning to make much more sense now. Grasping the ankh, Cate peered through the darkness, but could no longer see Lachlan, Maeve, or the remains of the fire burning itself out.

She had slept into the afternoon the day before, and risen to eat, bathe, and share stories with some of the other priests, and she was surprised when Lachlan asked if she was ready to go back and try again. Maeve had not been very pleased with Lachlan's suggestion that she go back so quickly, but Maeve did not know what Lachlan and Cate had seen. She could not know the desperation they were feeling now that the portal had become a viable option for them. And if they had their way, she would never know the depth or horror of the subsequent visions they both continued to see long after they had touched the rock.

Now, as she stood at the portal once again, Cate inhaled deeply and released the ankh. She knew the risks involved in slipping through the fabric of time; knew that it was always possible she would never return. Still, she could not allow herself to hesitate like that. She had to be stronger, better than those who went before her. She needed to remain focused on the tasks at hand, because there were plenty of them. She could do it. She knew she could. It was time.

Stepping through the ever-present mist that enveloped the triad of oaks, Cate disappeared into the fog. When she walked to the great white oak with its hollow center, she reverently touched its deep, craggy bark that reminded her of the wrinkles of a very old man. The tree must have been a thousand years old. Once she passed through the trunk, she would be transported to another time, to another place, to another being altogether. If she thought about it for too long, fear would consume her and she would back out. Sending her soul into another time was far more frightening than she had related to Maeve. She did not know what became of her body once her soul was gone. She did not know how far into the future she had gone, and she knew nothing about the person who housed her soul in the future. It was all so much more than her mind could accept, so it was best if she just walked right through the large opening of the trunk and not look back.

And that was precisely what she did for the second day in a row.

When Cate was on the other side, she found herself, once again, looking down at the unfamiliar clothes and the young, slender hand holding a key. A key? Where was her ankh? Reaching for the necklace, she realized she was no longer in the forest, but in a small, apparently unused room in an inn so very far from home.

Home.

This was her new home, and for better or worse, Jessie was going to have to accept it. Staring down at the key in her palm, Jessie wondered how long she had been standing in this dusty, forgotten third-floor bedroom. Looking down at her watch, she was surprised to see that she had been standing there a little over ten minutes. What had she come in here for?

She had come into the room to—to make sure the room existed? Shaking her head, she walked out of the room, closed the door, and locked it again, wondering if, perhaps the stress of moving wasn't getting to her.

Downstairs, she hung the keys on the too-cute kitty key holder in the kitchen, grabbed a bottle of water from the refrigerator, and decided to check out the back porch of the inn. Unlike Daniel, she hadn't shown any curiosity about the inn and its surroundings; he had been over every inch, running all the way up to her room to report news of his findings. One of those findings was the wooden swing on the back porch overlooking those incredible pine trees that hugged the Oregon coastline like a lover. They were the biggest trees she had ever seen next to California redwoods.

The swing wasn't very old, and, to her surprise, was very comfortable. She drank her bottled water and stared out at the wooded forest which was now her backyard. The forests and trees of Oregon were spectacular, and it surprised Jessie how much she had grown to love them in such a short period. She hadn't even given trees, or lack of them, a second thought back in San Francisco. Now she wondered how anyone could live without having them close by. She had always fancied herself an ocean lover, but this feeling she had about the forests and the pines was actually surpassing what she had always felt. How odd to be drawn to something she hadn't given a nanosecond of thought to two weeks ago.

Gently swinging, Jessie closed her eyes and listened to the songs of the red-headed woodpecker and chickadee. She thought she heard the western tanager as well. It had a beautiful little song. As she inhaled deeply the scent of the fir and cedar, her eyes suddenly popped open. "What the hell?" Jessie sat straight up. Jumping off the swing so hard it crashed into the wall, she ran into the house and into the library.

"There it is," she said, pulling a thick book from the shelves and dashing back out to the porch. Standing with one foot on the bottom railing and positioning the dense book on her thigh, she quickly thumbed through the pages of *Sunset Guide to Western Flora and Fauna.* When she came to a picture of the same trees that stood behind the inn, sure enough, they were Douglas firs and western red cedars. Gently closing the book, Jessie stared out into the woods. "How in the hell did I know that?" she whispered, closing her eyes once more. Listening to the many quiet and not-so-quiet noises of the woods, she recognized the call of the gull, the screech of a red-tailed hawk, and the song of the western meadowlark.

Western meadowlark? Chickadee?

She hadn't ever even *heard* of the damn western meadowlark until now. What in the hell was going on with her?

Putting the book back, she headed outside once more.

"This isn't happening," Jessie uttered, her hands trembling slightly. "I can't possibly—no I *don't* know this stuff. I couldn't even pass biology!" At that moment, a shadow flew overhead, and when she glanced up, sure enough, there was a red-tailed hawk. At least it *looked* like one . . . no, it was more than that. She *knew* it was. Somewhere deep within her, she was able to know these things that she had never known before this moment, and it was starting to scare the crap out of her.

"Okay, Ferguson," she said, inhaling deeply and trying to calm her nerves. "Get a grip. There has to be a reasonable explanation for this."

Turning to face the ocean, she hiked a little through the rugged pines swaying from the caress of the slight ocean breeze. Whatever was happening was filling her with a warm, calming feeling that began at the base of her spine. Here, in the woods of Oregon, Jessie felt her first feelings of belonging.

But how could that be? She didn't *want* to be here. This was *not* her home, and yet . . . and yet what?

Something in the back of her mind was poking and prodding her to remember something of great import, but she had no idea what it was or how to reach it. All she knew was that something very strange was happening to her . . . maybe even to Daniel as well. Was it this house? Was it this place? What in the hell was going on?

Sitting against the wide trunk of a cedar, Jessie closed her eyes to bask in the sun's warmth that peeked through the endless clouds that hovered over this coast. She hadn't been stoned in a long time, but her mind was acting as if it were; her thoughts were so disjointed that she could barely keep one train of thought going for very long. Maybe she was just exhausted; drained from the emotional and mental ordeal of adaptation. This felt so much like pot that Jessie wondered if it might be a flashback. Could people flashback on marijuana? She'd never heard of it, but that didn't mean it couldn't happen.

With her eyes still closed, she watched a variety of scenes play out in her head; partying with her friends and relating some old folk tale she'd been reading for class, and having those listening tell her she had a gift; a great gift for storytelling, for holding an audience captive.

She saw herself on the top of the Bank of America building with Wendy just before the junior prom, when she had told Wendy that she always felt like she was looking for something, some deeper meaning than the drug-filled life she was leading. Wendy's advice had been to look deeper into the pot brownies and less into the stupid schoolbooks.

"I just feel like I'm missing a piece," Jessie had said, staring down at the panoramic view of the city. There was no more beautiful skyline than that of San Francisco. "Or maybe I'm just missing peace."

Thinking back on it now, Jessie wondered if they weren't one and the same.

As serenity descended upon her, and the sun's rays caressed her face, Jessie fell into a deep sleep filled with dreams of a celestial blue-eyed man urging her to remember. She dreamt of a young woman with red hair the color of nutmeg, who hovered just beyond the fringes of the dream. And then there was a steel-eyed woman looming grandly like an ancient ghost. Those gray eyes, like the man's, kept imploring her to remember.

Remember what?

When Jessie woke up, the sun had nearly set. The remnants of her latest odd dream tickled her senses so much that she knew she had to do something about it. Too many weird things were going on—from the numberless room, to that weird Madame Ceara, to her dreams and nightmares, and now, to the knowledge she seemed to have dredged up out of thin air.

Well, if there was one person who might be able to make sense of the arcane, it was Madame Ceara, and within fifteen minutes Jessie stood in front of Madame's shop, downhearted that the store was closed for the day. *Of course* Jessie thought, as she heaved a disappointed sigh. Maybe it was for the best. The woman, after all, sort of creeped her out. She was a woman with some bearing, and her carriage bespoke someone who got her way, not some crazy woman who shuffled along scaring little children.

But Jessie *was* scared. Not of Madame Ceara, but of the bizarre things she was experiencing. She had never believed in ghosts or hauntings, or any of that psychic mumbo jumbo, but here she stood, in front of a store that catered to those who *did* believe all that crap. Here she was, wanting the psychic queen of the west coast to bail her out and explain how all of a sudden she *knew* what she was hearing, when she'd never even bothered to listen before. What she needed now was something that resembled an answer, and the only place she could think to go to get one was here and she—

"Isn't in."

Looking over her shoulder, Jessie saw Tanner coming toward her. "Shop's closed."

"Apparently." Didn't this kid have anything else to do other than shadow her? He wore his studded leather jacket about him like a cloak, and she was sure it was an integral part of his identity.

"She's waiting for you down by the marina."

Jessie's eyes widened. "What do you mean, *waiting*?"

Shrugging, Tanner jammed his hands in his pockets and rocked back and forth on his heels. "You think she told *me*? Not hardly. She just asked if I'd tell you she'll be there another fifteen." Tanner shrugged again. "So . . . how ya been?"

Jessie shrugged back and avoided his gaze. What was it about everyone in this town looking right in your face? "Just slaving my life away at the house on the hill."

"I'll bet. You know, if you ever wanna do something fun, you can always give me a shout."

"I don't have your number."

Tanner reached into his back pocket and pulled out a business card. "Gus told me you guys got wired for phones yesterday."

Who the hell was Gus?

Jessie took the card and looked at it. "We did. How come you have a business card?"

Tanner pushed his Seventies-length hair over his shoulders. "I have a business."

Jessie scanned the colorful business card in her hand.

Dirty Dog Design—When you need it now.
Tanner Dodds
Webmaster Extraordinaire/Computer Tech of Outstanding Skill
623-1984
DDog@dirtydogdesign.com

"Don't tell me you're a computer nerd."

"Among other things. I've been called a pothead, a deadhead, a meathead, and any number of other maligning terms."

"Make any money doing it?"

Tanner nodded. "Enough to keep me in fine leather."

Jessie put the card in her back pocket. "Cool card. I'll keep your offer in mind, but I better jam. My folks don't know I'm gone."

"Yeah, and you don't want to keep Ceara waiting."

Just as Jessie looked to cross the street, her parents and Daniel drove right up to her. Her father rolled his window down and stared out, not at Jessie, but at Tanner. "I thought you were staying at the house," Rick said, cutting his eyes over at Jessie before assaulting Tanner with the look only distrusting fathers can give.

Walking over to the car as nonchalantly as she could, Jessie forced a grin. "Just checking things out. It's taken you guys this long to find a movie?"

Daniel shoved his head out the window, oblivious to Rick and Reena's stare down of Tanner's tattered jeans and tough guy jacket. "We ate ice cream at that place at the end of the road. That was the best ice cream I ever had!"

"Who's your friend?" Rick asked.

Before Jessie could answer, Tanner walked over and stuck his outstretched hand in Rick's window. "Tanner, sir. Tanner Dodd."

Rick took in Tanner's jacket as Reena leaned over to get a better look. "We hadn't realized you made any friends," came Reena's tight-lipped reply.

"I've met a few here and there." Jessie felt a flush of anger rise to her cheeks. They were judging Tanner, already leaning toward suspicion of what they might be doing together. She hadn't smoked dope in so long she'd actually forgotten when, but that hadn't kept them from smelling her clothes or her hair whenever she came home from any social event. Even here in Oregon, they threw a dubious eye at her limited social activities. She had even caught Reena smelling her shirts before she did her laundry.

"Well," Reena said, "if you're through visiting, why don't you hop in and we'll give you a ride up the hill?"

Jessie shook her head. "Thanks, but I'm not through visiting."

Rick and Reena exchanged worried glances. "We brought you some ice cream," Daniel piped in.

Jessie grinned at him. "Thanks. I'll have some with you as soon as I get home."

"Which will be when?" Reena asked.

"Half an hour, forty-five minutes, something like that." Jessie wanted to scream at them to either trust her or to leave her alone, but instead she backed away from the car and motioned for them to move on their merry way.

"It was nice meeting you, Tanner," Rick said.

Tanner stepped back up to the car reached into his back pocket and withdrew another business card. "If you need any web page design or other computer-related service for the inn, Mr. Ferguson, I'll cut you a good deal. The other B and B has WiFi, so if you need any help getting yours installed, give me a call."

Rick studied the business card long and hard before looking back up at Tanner. "You designed the card yourself, I take it?"

Tanner nodded. "Yes, sir. I can make something real catchy for the P—the Seaside Inn. A good business card is your first link to a community. The second link these days is your web page, and I can design both at a fraction of what the other guys in town do it for. Check it out. You'll see."

Reena took the card from her husband and studied it as well. "Where did you learn how to do this?"

"I'm a student at the University of Oregon's extension program over in Florence. They offer a couple of decent design programs."

Jessie couldn't stop smiling at Tanner and his poise in the face of danger. What a very interesting person Tanner Dodd was turning out to be.

"We appreciate the offer, Tanner, and if we get that far, we might even give you a call." To Jessie he said, "Don't stay out too long, Jess. There's a load of lumber coming in in the morning, and we're going to need all hands on deck."

"Whew. They're sure wound tighter than a tick," Tanner offered as the Fergusons turned the corner and drove up the hill.

"You're telling me."

"They always been like that?"

Jessie shook her head. "Only about seventeen years."

"Well, Madame waits for no one, so you better get on it. Take it easy."

Halfway across the street, Jessie stopped and whirled back around. "Tanner?"

"Yeah?"

"How'd she—"

He chuckled. "She used her powers, I suppose. Go on, Jess. Don't keep her waiting."

She nearly ran to the marina. Odd how comfortable she was beginning to feel in this place—odd the emotional comfort washing over her.

As she neared the tiny marina, Jessie looked around for the colorful garb worn by the gypsy-like woman, but didn't find her. "Used her powers," Jessie muttered, shaking her head slightly. What had that boring history teacher said last year? *Faith is action based on belief.*

"Just because we cannot see a thing, my dear, does not mean it does not exist."

Jessie whirled around, nearly tripping over a toy poodle on a pink leash. "You scared the hell out of me!"

Madame smiled softly and nodded. "I have a tendency to do that." Madame Ceara's grin broadened. "Now about faith—never mind the details of the picture until you can see the frame. Come. It is time for you to see both the picture *and* the frame." Abruptly turning, Madame Ceara walked down the wooden pier to a smallish houseboat and waited for Jessie to join her.

"You live here?"

"I live everywhere, really. This is just where I keep my things." As Madame Ceara walked down the metal gangplank to her boat, her scarves were whipping around in the wind, nearly snapping Jessie's face as she tried to keep up.

Below deck, Jessie followed Madame Ceara to a comfortable little cabin the size of an RV. Short, fat candles flickered with the sea breeze, illuminating the small area. On the small kitchen table lay several ancient books that appeared well-used. Stacks of tarot cards lined the windowsill, and bright yellow paint gave off an eerie glow that allowed the shadows to dance and leap as if independent of the light. The entire cabin was exactly as Jessie thought Madame Ceara's house would be.

"Would you care for some tea? Soda, perhaps?"

"No, thank you. I'm fine, really."

Madame Ceara sat at the small, beautifully carved oak table. "Are you, now?"

Jessie sat across from her at the table and almost started crying.

Reaching across the table, Madame Ceara patted Jessie's hand. "Now, now, dear, there's no time for that. There's work to be done and we're on a short leash and an even shorter timer." Opening one of her ancient texts, Madame Ceara read quietly for a moment, her lips moving slightly. From where Jessie sat, it appeared as if she was reading Latin or some other foreign language.

"Latin," Madame Ceara mumbled without looking up. "No wonder it's a dead language." The old woman folded her hands on top of the book. "Now, you're here for a lot of reasons, most of which you don't even know, but one of them, I can assure you, is because you are being beckoned to remember, and you simply cannot."

Jessie pinched the bridge of her nose. "I'm going insane. Is that it? The drugs have royally messed me up, right? Because I don't think—"

"Is that why you're here? To have me convince you of your sanity? Oh, my dear, if you were to truly look deep inside yourself, you would *know* why you are really here. However, I can assure you why you are *not* here. You are not here so I can convince you of your insanity, as if sanity were even important."

"It is."

"Is it? Is it even anything you can define? Because I sure can't."

Jessie inhaled deeply. Well, she *did* sort of come here to discuss her sanity, but where to start? Did she start with the door? Her new knowledge? The dreams? Yes, that was it . . . she'd start with the dream.

"I had a dream."

Madame nodded, a satisfied grin on her face. "Ah, a dream. That explains it."

"Explains what?"

Rising, Madame Ceara lit several sticks of incense before pulling out a second ancient text. "The dreams—the memories. So much of our lives could be explained to us if only we listened. But that's not all, is it?" Madame Ceara leaned closer and gazed into Jessie's eyes. "No, no it isn't. You've managed to find your way through the slit, haven't you?" Madame inched closer; her icy eyes grilling Jessie's. "Ah yes, I see it. You have actually been *and* returned." Clapping her hands together, Madame Ceara picked up the book and held it to her chest, singing a song in a foreign tongue. For a moment, Jessie thought the rumors about her might be true.

"You have no idea the gift you have been given, my dear; a gift that not many people of this world or the next will have the chance to experience. You have stepped through a seam in the fabric of time, and you don't remember. That's a common occurrence for first-time travelers."

"Time travelers?" Jessie jumped out of her chair wanting to run for the door, but her feet were rooted. "Are you nuts?"

"Some certainly think so. If I talk about time travel right now, you'll really think those boys might be right about me."

Jessie looked at the door. She wanted to go, but she didn't want to go. "First off, I do *not* believe anything those dorks have to say. Secondly, I'm—I'm not afraid."

"Good. Because we have a lot to work to do."

"Work?"

"Yes. I'd say that our first mission is to get Jessie to remember whatever it is they want you to remember."

"They? Who?" Jessie looked around, as if someone were lurking in the shadows.

Madame Ceara chuckled gleefully and rubbed her wrinkled hands together. "Whoever is imploring you to remember. Someone came *across* to get you. Someone wants you *to do* something. I knew when I saw you—when I'd heard you were the one who moved into the inn."

"That's it, isn't it? The inn is haunted. This is about the inn!"

Madame Ceara waved her off. "Pshaw, Jessie. Haunted? Yes, there are beings gathered about, and they are none too happy, but this—this has nothing to do with *them*."

Jessie grabbed her head in her hands. She was living in a haunted house, but *that* had nothing to do with whatever it was that was happening to her. "Then *who* are you talking about?"

Sitting back down at the table, Madame Ceara leaned over and laid her hand on top of Jessie's arm to still her. Then she slowly pulled her back to the table. "Perhaps it is best if we start from the beginning."

"There's a *beginning*?"

Madame Ceara nodded, her eyes flashing with excitement "Oh yes. If you want to know what is happening to you, you'll sit here and listen. I do not have patience for disbelievers or naysayers. If you truly came here for answers, you will at least hear me out."

Jessie inhaled deeply, and sat down.

"Now, tell me *exactly* why it is you have sought me out. Leave nothing out, no matter how silly or odd it may be."

Jessie looked into those blue eyes and felt a calm wash over her. "I came because all of a sudden, I *know* things I've never known before."

Ceara smiled, her eyes lighting up. "Excellent. Oh, you truly are going to be a quick study. Do go on."

Jessie hesitated about the door. She didn't want to sound like she was completely unhinged.

"Tell me about the door."

Jessie leaned so far back she almost fell over. "You really *can* read minds!"

Ceara shook her head. "Not really. I just know there is a time portal in that house and I think you've gone through it and lived to tell about it; a feat not many accomplish."

"What do you mean, portal?"

"There's a door in the inn that comes and goes, doesn't it?"

"Yes!" Jessie sighed and leaned back.

"That door is the reason you're here right now. It may very well be *the* reason your family has come to Oregon. But that door in your inn has been waiting a long time for someone else to see it. Seeing it is one thing. Stepping through it is another story altogether. One cannot go through it without changing. The question is *what did you see?*"

Jessie closed her eyes and saw the forest, and then quickly opened them. *That* had been no dream.

"My dear, you must suspend your belief in what you believe to be real. You must embrace ideas and notions that others would scoff at. Do not judge your vision or doubt your feelings. Do not doubt *you*. Trust that what you saw was what you saw."

"You said that to me the other day."

"Because so many of us see that which the world denies, and in our fear, we deny it ourselves. We deny that which science cannot explain or even bear witness to. We deny the spiritual realm because not to do so would make others think we were not of sound mind. In this society we are all afraid of that which has not been scientifically proven. Do not be afraid. I will help you through this."

"Help me through *what*?"

"You tell me. What is it you've seen that scared you so?"

Leaning forward, virtually whispering, Jessie proceeded to tell her about the forest she'd seen the moment she opened the numberless door, and how, after that, she seemed to know everything that surrounded her in the woods behind the inn.

Ceara listened attentively, until Jessie said she could have sworn she saw an oak grove in the distance. When Jessie finished with what little else she could remember, Ceara again clapped her hands together.

"That's it. Oh my, dear girl, you've found it!" Jumping up so quickly she knocked one of the candles over, Ceara threw her arms around a stunned, and slightly scared, Jessie.

"Found what?"

Ceara reached across the table and took Jessie's hand in hers. For a long time, she just stared into Jessie's face. "Forgive me, my dear. It's just that I have waited a very long time for someone to be able to do what you did, and I'm just overly excited about it. Forgive an old woman her eccentricities."

"Can I get you some water or something? I mean I don't want you blowing an artery or anything."

"No, I'm fine. I'm better than fine. I feel like today is Christmas."

Jessie shook her head. "Umm—Ceara? I found a forest in the room of a third story, haunted inn. I'm sorry if I don't understand your joy in that, but—"

Ceara waved her off. "I am sorry, my dear. What happened after you opened the door and saw the forest?"

Jessie shook her head. "I looked down and I was wearing a robe. That's all I remember."

"But you *did* go in, and you *do* have a tiny memory of your time over there."

"I was in there about ten minutes, but *where* is there? What *was* that place? I don't understand."

"That's all right, my dear. No one is expecting you to get it all right the first time. I know it's difficult. The whole thing can be disconcerting, especially in *this* time. More will come to you later, but for now, we will work with just what you saw and experienced."

Jessie nodded. "That works for me."

"If that's all you remember for now, then tell me about these dreams of yours?"

"I don't remember much of those, either. The dream I keep having is of this red-haired young woman who is being chased through the forest by a Roman soldier."

Ceara leaned forward. "A *Roman* soldier?"

"Yeah. Wait. I don't know squat about Rome or Roman soldiers. How do I know this?"

"What kind of forest?"

"What?"

"What *kind* of forest? What trees were in the forest?"

Jessie reflected. "It's an oak grove, I think." She shook her head. "See what I mean? I never use the word *grove*. Where is this coming from?"

Ceara motioned for Jessie to continue. "What else?"

"There was a super intense woman with gray eyes telling me to remember."

"Hmm. Interesting. Anyone else?"

Jessie nodded. "A tall, good-looking man who kinda looked like Jesus, and a short red-headed woman."

"What were they wearing?"

"I can't remember. I just remember seeing their faces and hearing them tell me that they wanted me to remember." Jessie sighed. "That's why I came here. I thought if I wasn't crazy, maybe you might know who they are and what they want."

Ceara nodded. "It's possible. Do you remember what the girl was wearing? The one who was being chased?"

Jessie nodded. "A robe. Yeah . . . she was wearing a robe like the gray-eyed woman. A different color, though, I think."

"Well done." Ceara leaned back and sighed. "You have let her in, and that's a great start."

"Who?"

"I can tell you nothing yet, except that you are most certainly *not* crazy, and don't you ever think that about yourself. There are plenty of people who are all too quick to label that which they do not understand as crazy or whacko. I should know. I have lived with the likes of those for too many years to count."

"Then what's happening to me?"

Ceara sighed and licked her lips. "Nothing is happening *to* you, my dear. You are not a victim of any sort of prank or sickness."

"Then what's going on?"

Ceara exhaled and studied Jessie's features. "Promise me you'll sit through the whole explanation, reserving judgment and comments until I am through."

Jessie nodded again, feeling her stomach start the dance of the great butterfly. How could this woman be both so calming and so scary at the same time? "I want to know what's happening."

Ceara nodded and relit the candle she had knocked over. Incense wafted through the small cabin, smelling of lilac and cloves. She inhaled deeply and locked eyes with Jessie. The room became quiet and still. When Ceara finally spoke, her voice was low and soft. "When you opened the door, you stepped through a fold in the fabric of time."

"I went back in time?"

Ceara raised her white eyebrows. "What makes you think it was *back*?"

Jessie frowned. "Because there was this huge bonfire far away."

Ceara grinned. "You *are* remembering. Good."

Jessie sat back and ran her hand through her hair. "I guess I am. I mean it sure *feels* like a memory."

"It is. You see, most cultures who believe like us, know that souls have memory. Eternal memories. They don't just live here with us, die, and then go to heaven or hell, as the Christians believe."

"Is that what this is all about then? Religion and time?"

Ceara shook her head. "Neither. It's about life, and the soul's approach to the living of that life. This is about something far deeper than tripping through the past like some time-traveling tourist. This is about your *soul* . . . your soul and the people who have housed that same soul over the millennia. You have been invited by a past self to a place and time that must want or need something from you. The question is, are you interested in helping?"

Jessie was hooked. Interested? She was coming out of her clothes with excitement, fear and trepidation. She had had a memory of something she had never done, she now knew things she didn't know she knew, and that void in her heart that had been there since birth was suddenly vibrating with life. "Interested is an understatement, Ceara. All my life I've felt like I had no purpose, no reason for being. I've done drugs, alcohol, sex, even shoplifting. I've felt lost my entire life. For the first time in my life, I feel alive, and I don't even know why."

"But you want to know."

"I do."

"And you're willing to listen and leave your preconceived notions outside."

"I'll leave my underwear outside if it helps me understand what is happening."

This made Ceara laugh. "Tell me, what do you know about past lives or the transmigration of souls?"

"You mean, like reincarnation?"

"Well, not exactly, but close enough for now."

"To be honest, I've never really given it any thought."

"I see. Well, we believe—"

"Who's we?"

"Those of us who know. We believe the soul is on eternal time, and that time, as we know it, has a far different rhythm and pace than what we humans measure on a day-to-day basis. Eternal time is a much different idea because it's not linear. Scientists think time runs up and down a line, like a ruler, but the truth is, they don't really know."

Jessie leaned forward, her hair cascading across the table.

"When scientists do not know or cannot prove something, they spend all their time trying to *disprove it*. Any theory that cannot be proven *scientifically* suddenly is not true. So far, no one has been able to measure time accurately or even figure out how it operates."

"I had a teacher once who believed the time line was an inaccurate model for how time operates."

"Indeed. There are hundreds of documented instances when someone knows something they shouldn't be able to know. We believe this knowledge comes from the soul's memory."

Jessie shook her head. "You've lost me."

"Ever read stories about five-year-olds able to play Mozart? Or seven-year-old violinists symphonically superior to people who spent most their lives training? How about the dozens of people who wake up from comas fluent in a language they've never studied?"

Jessie's mouth hung open as she nodded. She remembered Wendy reading something to her out of *People Magazine* once about an eight-year-old chess player who'd beaten a world champion. "Those stories are incredible."

"Incredible yes, and also very true. The question everyone's asking is, *how*. Well, there are many of us who *know* how. It is the soul's memory remembering things it did in another time and another place. What other answer is there for kids who can graduate from college at eleven, or play Beethoven before even having lessons? Or even more incredibly, kids who can give you accurate directions to a place they've never been? The Christians would call it a miracle."

"It does sorta seem that everything we don't understand is either a curse or a miracle."

"Yes. In terms of understanding time, we are in the Dark Ages. Did you know that most of the world's people do not believe the soul lives one life and then goes to heaven or hell? The majority of the world outside Christendom agrees that the soul moves on and takes with it fragments of memories."

"So, you're saying that my soul is remembering something from a past life."

Ceara nodded slightly, her cool blue eyes studying Jessie. "And it's clearly trying to prompt you to remember more. Your soul is not your own, my dear. You have shared it with dozens of others, and someone from your past is trying to get you to remember more."

"How? How can they do that?"

"By coming through time and prodding your soul to remember. You left the seam and went outside of your own time. You went somewhere, Jessie, and returned with fragments of memories from that time. Suddenly, you were remembering things you did not know you knew. You may not have known them, but your soul does. It remembered. Think of all the other thousands of things you know but do not know *how* you know."

"Just thinking about it makes my head spin."

"But there is so much more to it, Jessie. You see, the key isn't just in our eternal souls; the key is also in understanding time and how it moves." Ceara pulled one of her scarves off and set it in a straight line on the table. "We're taught that time is like this. We study time *lines* in school, but we don't really know for a fact that time moves only forward along a straight line. It's a guess. Just like the pre-Renaissance people guessed that the earth was flat. Well, sure, that's how it *appears* when you look into the horizon, but we now know that's not true. Well, time as a straight line is also not true. If it was, it would go against all other defining principles of life."

"Such as?"

"All of the other cycles of life." Taking the scarf, Ceara put it in a circle so that both ends were touching. "Our world operates on cycles. The seasons, our periods, the moon, weather, and life and death are all cyclical. The most fundamental aspects of our culture, of *life itself*, run in cycles. Why wouldn't time?"

Jessie inched forward. "So, if the soul is eternal and is capable of retaining memories of earlier lives, *and* time is not linear, then are you telling me it's possible that we can actually go to another place in time?"

"Not in your body, no, but your soul? Yes, and I believe that is what's happening to you. I believe you've found one of the seams, and your soul slipped back into the body of whoever had it back then. Perhaps you were called, perhaps you merely stumbled upon a memory you did not know you had, but something drew you to that place."

"No way," Jessie whispered softly. "My soul went somewhere without me?"

"Without your body, yes. Without your conscious being, yes. Your soul has been housed in a variety of bodies in a variety of ages. When you step through a portal, your body stays here, and your soul returns to the body it possessed then. In effect, it slips back into itself."

"So you're saying my soul traveled to this other time because someone called to me and invited me."

Ceara nodded. "Jessie, the person who shares your soul is trying to get you to remember something."

"How can you be so sure? How do you know I just haven't fallen through the rabbit hole and *I'm* the one who has started it all?"

Ceara leaned back and steepled her fingers. "Because you had no concept of eternal souls, of time, or time travel. You did not call. You were *beckoned*."

Jessie had *felt* beckoned. She still felt beckoned, as though there were a voice in the back of her head calling her name. It was eerie and exciting all at once. "And I answered. I opened whatever you keep calling it."

"I call it a portal, but those who study time travel refer to it as a seam. Some of them believe the UFOs people have seen are merely beings slipping in and out of these seams."

"It all sounds so science-fiction."

Ceara nodded slightly. "The idea of heart transplants, of artificial insemination, of skin grafting, of stepping onto the moon, of helicopters and missiles, once seemed fantastical, too, didn't they? But they *did* happen. If Michelangelo had been told about digital cameras and color printers, he'd have mocked the notion. Just because the idea seems ludicrous at the time does not mean it cannot happen. You came to Oregon to a house with a seam and a spirit who called your name. Does it have to be so hard to believe?"

Jessie sat quietly gathering her thoughts, questions, and many suppositions as to what to do now. Being called to the past was one thing . . . answering that call was something entirely different.

"I don't want to be a guinea pig here, Ceara, you know, with the press—"

"No! This is not something for anyone else to know, Jessie. You could put your family in great danger. You could find yourself facing a team of doctors wanting to dissect your mind. You could also be putting those people trusting you in danger."

"I get the picture."

"When Da Vinci was trying to make the airplane, many thought he had lost his wits. What's important for you to understand is that whoever is calling you from the past is alive in his or her time. Do not put them in danger by feeling the need to share this."

"Like anyone would believe me."

"You never know."

"I'm supposed to be remembering something and I have no idea what that is. Can't you hypnotize me or something? Do one of those past life regressions?"

"Much of what is brought out during hypnosis comes from selective memories. Many mediums try, and I'm sure many succeed, but I believe there is too much working in the subconscious to know whether or not it is the soul revealing itself, or if the other layers of the mind are at work. It is for that reason that I, myself, do not do past life regressions."

Jessie ran her hand through her hair again and sighed. "Why can't I remember? Am I stupid or something?"

"Can you tell me what you ate on the fourth day of your third year?"

"Of course not."

"Why not?"

"Because it's impossible to remem—oh." Jessie nodded again. "If my soul's been around a long time, there are a hell of a lot of memories to sort through, huh?"

"More than you can imagine. And if your soul has come for a reason, it must first become accustomed and comfortable in this body in this time. It is not easy to go into eternal time where your soul exists and tap into the soul memory."

"Then all of us carry our pasts around inside us?"

Ceara stared into the candle flame and nodded slowly. "And we do not just carry past memories, either. Remember, my dear, time is *not* on a continuum."

"It's not hard to accept the past part, but how can you carry the memory of something that hasn't happened yet?"

Blowing the candle so that it jumped and flickered, Ceara leaned back. "Just because it hasn't happened on this plane, at this time, doesn't mean it hasn't happened yet."

"Whoa, now you've really lost me."

"Take Leonardo Da Vinci again. The man envisioned the airplane four hundred years before it was invented. He actually invented the parachute."

"No way."

Ceara nodded. "Now, can anyone *reasonably* explain how it is that a man would invent the parachute four hundred years before it was needed? Did Da Vinci remember a memory from another life? Because surely, if we believe in past lives, then how can we deny an existence of future ones as well?"

"In for a penny, I guess." Jessie sighed loudly. As bizarre as this conversation was, it all felt so . . . real, and real was important to a person who had spent too much of her youth in an unreal state.

"Look at the pyramids. It took the Egyptians twenty years to build the great pyramid at Giza, yet, even with our advanced technology, we would be hard-pressed to do the same today. How come? What did they know that we still do not know? Did they get their knowledge from somewhere in our future? And what of Galileo and Copernicus,

Shakespeare and Champollion?"

"Champ, who?"

"Champollion. He deciphered the Rosetta Stone after almost twenty years and dozens of other attempts by men far more brilliant than he. Why him, and why then? Was that a miracle? Were his investigative skills better than everyone else's? Or was he just in touch with memories most of us would deny having? The list goes on and on of people who did spectacular things well before they should have been able to. Where do you think their knowledge came from?"

Jessie sat back, pinching the bridge of her nose. "It's mind boggling. That stuff'll really make your head spin if you think about it for too long."

"You said you have been looking for a purpose, Jessie, a reason to do something important that you're passionate about. Answering this call might be the very thing you've been searching for. There are no coincidences in life my dear."

"God, to have a purpose, a reason to get up in the morning . . . what a gift."

"Not a gift, Jessie, but a path, a way. Those of us who are able to find our purpose find a happiness unlike anything the rest of the world experiences. Each one of us has a destiny. If you can unveil yours, you have found your life's path, and you can begin your journey in earnest. Too many of us spend the bulk of our lives on the wrong path going nowhere except wrong turns and dead ends."

Jessie had been on that road. "I'll bet you and your people believe this is one of the reasons why alcohol and drug abuse is so prevalent."

Ceara smiled. "No. We believe it is *the* reason. So many of us are on the wrong path we self-medicate in order to dull the pain and disappointment of where we are."

Running her hands through her hair, Jessie sighed. "I've sure been there. I am so tired of being lost."

"The good news is you don't have to be. Someone is reaching out to you. I can tell you that those people in your dreams must be part of your soul's memory."

"So now what? What do I need to do?"

Ceara stared at the candle for a long time. When she spoke, she did not look up. "You need to go back through the seam."

Jessie inhaled slowly. This didn't surprise her, but her breath caught anyway. "Why?"

"How else are you going to find out what it is they need if you don't go back?"

"What if I never remember?"

Ceara shrugged. "Jessie, whoever is trying to get your attention *believes* you can remember. The very fact that you've been through once already means you have what it takes. You have to believe that you have it as well. *They* do."

Before Jessie could answer, her eyes caught sight of the clock. They'd been talking for over an hour. Her parents were sure to think the worst. "I really appreciate your help, Ceara, but I better get going. My folks will worry. We have some . . . trust issues."

Ceara glanced up at her now. "Aren't you trustworthy?"

Jessie leveled her gaze into those light blue eyes staring back at her. "I am now."

Ceara rose, wrapping her scarf around her again. "Good. When might you return?"

"Here?"

Ceara shook her head. "There."

Jessie stared into those eyes and felt as if she could see hundreds of years into the past. "I'll go back, but don't I need to research or at least know something about where I'll be sending me?"

Ceara shook her head. "The soul knows what needs to be done, if you allow it. That's part of our time's greatest dilemma: we try to solve everything by listening to our minds or our hearts, neither of which are very old or very wise."

Jessie followed Ceara out onto the deck. The air was markedly cooler since she'd come on board.

"Jessie, I realize how scary this must be for you, but somewhere in your past, you were brave enough to slip through the Sacred Place. You are there in your past and you are reaching out to yourself in this time. You were a brave being once. Be brave now."

Jessie sighed. "That's a head-shaker, you know? To think that I used to be someone else and that someone is knocking on my door. Weird."

"Indeed. Weirder than you can imagine."

"This Sacred Place. It exists in all times?"

Ceara nodded. "It is believed by Shamans of many different cultures that the seams in time are everywhere and in every time. Many Native Americans believe it; tribes of the Aborigines believe it; Amazonian people believe it, and many, many more cultures feel that the power of our souls comes from the lives we've led."

Jessie stared up at the moon and sighed loudly. "Who do *you* think I saw in those forests in my dream?"

Ceara stared up at the moon also before returning her gaze to Jessie. The wind whipped her scarves around her neck. "If the forests you saw were oak groves, and the woman was trying to reach them because she thought they would protect her, then I would imagine the people who are trying to contact you are Druids. They were most known for their sacred worship in the oak groves of Britain and Wales."

"Druids?" Jessie pondered this a moment before starting across the plank to the pier. "You mean—like Merlin?"

Ceara nodded as she tried to catch the many colorful layers whipping all about her. "The Druids are certainly not the only ones who can send their souls on a journey, nor are they the only people who have these Sacred Places. Quite a few have been unearthed, all throughout Europe, Africa and Australia."

"Like Stonehenge?"

"Among others. The seams, as you know by now, are not obvious. That is the beauty of them. They are hidden until they're needed, and they can be anywhere and everywhere. They can be in the sacred groves, in the coves on beaches, and in Victorian inns. Just know that you're not alone. If you concentrate really hard, I'll be there. Most questers do not journey by themselves. Nor shall you."

"Quester? Is that what I am?"

"That, and so much more, my dear. You have before you a decision that will alter the direction of your life forever. By returning to find out what it is they want, you are choosing the life of a quester. With that choice comes a great many dangers and responsibilities."

As Jessie started down Main Street, she felt one burden lifting while another settled comfortably on her shoulders. Like a beautiful new jacket, it felt as if it was made just for her.

Suddenly, life in Oregon had taken on a whole new meaning.

The second she saw her parents on the porch swing, Jessie knew she was in for it. Bad enough they had prejudged Tanner, but she was also nearly an hour later than she'd told them she'd be. They were sure to think the worst, and there was little she could do to change that. She wasn't even sure she wanted to try.

"Where have you been?" her mother demanded the moment Jessie's foot hit the bottom step. What could she say? *Gee, Mom, I went to see a fortuneteller who told me I needed to go back in time again to see why I'm needed? What do I mean by again? Well, apparently I've been there before, but am too stupid to remember.*

Yeah. That'd do it. The men in little white suits would come. Well, it wouldn't be the first time they'd shipped her off for repairs. The rehab center she'd been assigned to after the World's Biggest Drug Bust, though not employing white suit wearers, was, nonetheless, the same sort of prison. After two weeks there, if she hadn't mental issues to begin with, she could easily have picked up some. Those kids were whacked. Loonie Tunes. Nutjobs. She had managed to convince her parents to take her out two weeks early, and her Dad had made some arrangement with the judge that let her leave the state.

Well, part of the truth was preferable to none of it, so Jessie sat on the top stair and faced the firing squad. "Tanner introduced me to the town psychic and I was visiting her. Sorry I'm so late, but she's really cool, and not at all like everyone thinks. She knows a lot."

Either she had momentarily stunned them into silence, or they weren't really up to an explanation in the first place. Jessie could hear the rifles load.

"Honestly, Jess, did you intentionally seek out the *exact* kind of boy who got you into all your drug troubles in the first place?"

Jessie stared at her father. He hadn't heard a word she'd said. "I wasn't with Tanner, Dad. I was hanging with Madame Ceara, the psychic."

Reena motioned for Jessie to move closer. Jessie rose, knowing what was coming; another smelling test. God, would they ever tire of hanging on so tightly to their distrust and suspicions? Reena rose and put her face into Jessie's hair. Backing away as if struck, she looked at Rick with so much pain and disappointment, Jessie thought she was going to cry.

"Oh, Jessie."

"What? I didn't *do* anything!"

Rick rose. When he smelled his daughter's head, he crumpled back into the swing, shaking his head and sighing. "We'd really rather you told us the truth, honey."

Oh yeah, now there *was a great idea.*

Reena added, "Remember what the therapist said."

Jessie winced inside. Dr. Dolsby had more loose nuts than a Ford Pinto. "Think what you want. You will anyway. I didn't do anything wrong except visit some people you don't like the looks of. Is that a crime?"

"Honey, we can smell the incense in your hair, on your clothes. As much as you think we are, we're not stupid. We know why people use incense."

Jessie backed away from her mother, but remained standing. "Oh, that's right. Dopers have completely cornered the market on incense burning. Don't you think psychics use them all the time?"

Reena held her hand out to Rick to help him out of the swing. "We're so very disappointed in you, honey. We so wanted Oregon to be a fresh start—"

"But by the looks of it, you've fallen back into the same old patterns of lies and hanging out with—"

"You don't know them and have no right to judge them."

"We're not judging anyone, honey, but we're not going to turn a blind eye to your actions, either. We have a responsibility to both you and your brother, and it would be irresponsible of us to ignore the obvious. We thought you were going to start with a clean slate."

"I'm trying! But what am I supposed to do when you judge my friends before you even get to know them?"

"We met your *friend*, Jessie, and he is obviously not the kind of kid we want you hanging around."

"If you send me to another rehab, I swear to God, you will never see me again."

Rick looked as if she'd slapped him, so Jessie pressed her advantage. "Why can't you believe me? Because Tanner wears black leather and has a piercing, you automatically think he's a stoner? And by talking to him, you think I've fallen back into my old, evil ways? Why can't you just believe me for once? Would that be so hard?"

"Jess, you have to admit, your story is pretty weak."

"Then ask her! Ask Madame Ceara tomorrow if I was with her and if she was burning incense! She'll tell you the truth. Maybe you'll believe *her.*"

Rick and Reena looked at each other and shrugged. Disappointment and frustration hung in the air like smog. "Don't bluff if there's nothing behind it, Jessie, because it will only make matters worse. You know how we feel about lying."

Jessie wanted to pull her hair out. "I'm not bluffing. *Ask* her."

"We'll do that. In the meantime, you're not to leave the grounds. If you think, for one second, that your father and I up and moved our lives so you could bring ruin back into it, you are sadly mistaken."

"I'm clean, Mom. I have been for a really long time. I'll even take a drug test if you want."

Reena folded her arms. "We just might do that. Now, your brother's been waiting and—"

Shaking her head, Jessie opened the front door, leaving the rest of her mother's words to hang limply and unheard in the air. Yes, she'd broken their trust months ago, but she'd spent a lot of time trying to heal those wounds and gain it back again.

Grabbing a pint of ice cream and two spoons, Jessie headed for Daniel's room, where he sat reading a giant *Harry Potter* tome. "Hey, sport."

Daniel did not smile when he looked up from his book. "Mom and Dad are really mad."

Jessie sat on his bed and handed him a spoon. "I know."

"They're worried."

"Are you?"

Daniel shrugged, not looking at her. "Only if you're doing drugs again." Now, he looked up at her. "Are you?"

Jessie squatted down now so she could be eye-to-eye with him. "No, Daniel, I am not."

"Swear?"

Jessie held up the hand with the spoon in it. "I swear. I'm done with drugs forever, Daniel; at least, the illegal kind."

"But where were you then?"

"I was hanging out with this lady who tells people's fortunes."

"What's she like?"

"Well . . . she's very wise. She knows a lot of things about people and places. Oh, and she lives on a boat. We sat and chatted, and because she was burning incense, Mom and Dad think I was smoking dope."

"What does incense have to do with marijuana?"

Jessie took a big spoonful herself and closed her eyes as she savored it. "Not important."

Daniel shrugged. "My friends say everyone in town calls the inn the Haunted Money Pit."

Lowering her spoon, Jessie nodded. "I've heard. Does that bother you?"

"Sort of. I mean, not the money part, but the haunted part. They said if I didn't believe them, I could go to some historical society or something. I forgot. I guess there've been things written about this house because she's a painted lady or something. They say this house has been cursed forever."

"Well, we're here and we need to make the best of it, whether the house is cursed, haunted, or just a stupid old money pit."

Daniel grinned, a drop of ice cream stuck to his chin. "Does that mean you're going to stay? I wake up every morning wondering if you're going to still be here. The whole time you were in *that place*,

Mom and Dad treated me weird. It was a bummer."

That place had always been what Daniel had called the rehab center she'd been sent to. He saw it as some sort of evil entity that took his sister away for a couple of weeks. "Well, there's no rehab for me, and I'm not going anywhere until after school gets out. By that time, you'll have so many new friends, you won't even know I'm gone."

Daniel looked at her and shook his head. "I'd always know."

Jessie dug into the half-empty pint of ice cream. "You know, this place is beginning to grow on me, so don't you worry any more about whether I'm going to stay, okay?"

Nodding, Daniel scraped the bottom of the ice cream pint and finished it all. "Okay. But I think you're wrong about those noises I hear. Do *you* believe in ghosts?"

Jessie sighed. "I'm not sure what I believe in anymore." As she started out the door, Jessie could only think about that gray-eyed woman somewhere across time. "Daniel, what would you do if the voices you hear were asking for your help?"

Daniel swung his feet into the bed and leaned against the wall. "You mean, if I could understand them and they needed me to *do* something for them?"

"Yeah. What would you do?"

Daniel thought about it a moment before shrugging. "I'd help them out, I guess."

"Why?"

"Because it'd be cool to talk to ghosts and because I think we should help people who need us. Don't you?"

It was at that moment, at the urging of an innocent little boy, that Jessie committed herself to doing whatever it was that needed to be done. She would go back through the portal, and this time, when she returned, she would remember.

The next morning, Jessie busied herself with painting and weeding, just waiting for the moment when her parents would have to go into town. She felt a sick delight knowing she'd been restricted to the very place she actually *wanted* to be. Once they were gone, she took the keys off the hook and made her way quickly up to the third floor, where, sure enough, there stood the numberless door.

Jessie stood and stared at it for a moment. Behind that door was a world she knew nothing about, except that someone needed her.

Sliding the big skeleton key in the door, she felt a surge of adrenaline. She was excited and trembling with anticipation. Now, if only she could remember where she was going and what she was seeing, she could understand and appreciate whatever it was she was supposed to be doing.

Opening the door, Jessie was not surprised to see the forest before her. She stepped into the room which immediately transformed from an old, dusty bedroom to the oak grove she had seen before. Glancing down at her clothes, she was no longer surprised to be wearing the white hooded robe. Looking about her, she recognized this as the Sacred Place, but she couldn't remember . . .

Remember.

Cate gathered her robe around her and quickly made her way through the forest. She'd been gone longer than she realized. The dawn was breaking through the trees and there was no bonfire to guide her. Still, she knew these woods better than she knew the paths of Fennel because she had grown up in them. It was here, with her brother, Liam, where she learned how to wield the long sword and to protect herself with a shield. Liam had been such a wonderful brother and she ached for him daily. *He*, more than anyone she knew, would understand why she was doing what had to be done.

No, he hadn't understood her decision to become a Druid priestess, but that was because he'd half-convinced her that she would be a warrior by his side. That women fought battles next to their brothers, sons and husbands, was one of the anomalies that puzzled the Romans occupying much of Britannia; for Roman women had no rights like those of the Silurians, the Ordovices, and the Iceni, not to mention all of the women in Alba. Cate did not wish to think about the oppressive customs of the people who were now governing most of the country. The Romans did not understand them, and they never would. The

Romans were a people who conquered and turned whole societies into Roman culture. It had been their way for hundreds of years, and only Britannia had managed to resist.

But times were changing, and the Roman governor Suetonius Paulinus wanted to make a name for himself by conquering the people who had managed, thus far, to preserve their own traditions and customs even in the midst of Roman occupation. He was a danger to them all, in particular to the Druids, whom he saw as a threat to his power. Liam had paid the ultimate price in protecting Fennel from Roman occupation, as did many other young men who saw themselves as the protectorate of the Silurians. He had died for his beliefs, and oh, how she had grieved his death. Not a day went by that she didn't think about him.

As she came to the clearing, she saw Maeve and Lachlan sitting and leaning against two large boulders which had stood there for hundreds, if not thousands of years. Both were sound asleep, and Cate suddenly felt the exhaustion that had come over her the first time she had slipped through.

Lying next to Maeve, Cate closed her eyes and instantly fell asleep. The dream that came to her was far more than fantasy. In it, a young red-haired girl struggled beneath the weight of a truth that someone older and wiser than she would be able to grasp. In it, she saw herself, at least as a young woman, trying desperately to recall memories from the temple of her soul. But this was such a different world than Cate's world. Dishonesty, distrust, corruption and a complete lack of morals and ethics pervaded this culture. Had it learned nothing from the past? People no longer lived in clans, but were separated from each other with walls and fences, religion and race, money and poverty. It was sad, really, how advanced a people could be and yet, still manage to maintain their barbaric ways. So much had changed and so little had changed, at least from what she could tell from the meager memories of a seventeen-year-old. While the physical environment had certainly changed, people still condemned that which they did not understand, races could not cohabitate peacefully together, and the wealthy still made their own rules. How odd that so much time would go by and there be so little change in the soul of mankind.

With one huge exception.

The many gods and goddesses who guided her and her fellow Druids had been replaced by the God of the Jews and the man some called Jesus. He had been just another victim of Roman persecution, but in the future, he was the only God Cate could see. What had happened to Brigit, Danu and Morgan? What had happened to the Norse gods, to the Romans' own Venus and Apollo? What catastrophe had occurred that people relinquished their deities to one God?

In her sleep, Cate shivered.

It was no wonder then, that the body housing her soul so far into the future should feel so hollow, so disengaged, and so very, very alone. The young girl wasn't even remotely connected to the land. No one was. The land had been used up, annihilated, as it were. It was no wonder the people were so miserable; they had lost their gods and goddesses and had no reverence for the life-giving, life-sustaining land.

Cate could feel Jessie's spirit reaching out to the land, whether it was a conscious act or not. She was beginning to notice the smell of pine, the scent of the salty sea air, and the feel of sand beneath her feet. Somewhere in the back of Jessie's mind, she was beginning to remember who she was. Some of Cate's passions were coming through to Jessie now, whether Jessie knew it or not. The thought delighted Cate. Jessie was beginning to remember. She would be fine. They would connect in the Dreamworld, and Maeve would be saved.

Maeve.

Would Jessie remember? Would she feel within her the eternal love and lasting friendship that had endured all these years? Would Jessie be able to comprehend a time when caring for others was more important than meeting your own needs?

Cate could only hope so.

Sitting up slowly, Cate brushed off the last vestiges of her dream, along with several dry sticks and twigs, only to find Maeve and Lachlan staring at her in anticipation.

"You're back," Maeve said softly. Reaching out, she pulled a dried leaf from Cate's hair.

Cate nodded. "I had to rest. It is very tiring to go through the portal."

"You were talking in your sleep," Maeve explained, cutting a hard look to the impatient Lachlan. No one but Maeve could still the head Druid with a look. "Do you remember your dream?"

Cate sat up a bit more, her robe askew. "It was no dream, Maeve. It was a memory in the form of a dream."

"Are you certain?"

Cate nodded. "I am."

"Was it a dream of Jessie's?"

Cate's eyes grew wide. "Yes!"

"You spoke her name. She *is* a she?"

Cate nodded. "Yes."

Lachlan bit his lip so hard, it nearly bled, but he managed to still his tongue.

Maeve glanced over at Lachlan and shook her head. "We will not pressure her, Lachlan. That was our compromise long ago. If she needs to eat—"

"No, Maeve. I can tell you along the way." Rising, Cate readjusted her robe, but left her hood off. "The future is a hardened place with little joy. The goddesses are all gone, there are no ties to the earth, and people appear to be caught up in this whirlwind of trade and ownership. They seem almost enslaved by things. It is odd to feel Jessie's thoughts of things. She is—she does not quite belong."

Maeve and Lachlan exchanged glances. "So, you are remembering?" Lachlan said, hope in his voice.

Sending forth a successful quester had been his sole purpose these past ten years. He had been searching for a Druid who could go into the future to save them from the destruction that his mother had foreseen. She had known it, had known it for a very long time, but Lachlan had never hoped, never imagined he would find their answer in the likes of Cate. He had always thought it would be Maeve; she was the most powerful of them all, but even she did not have the power that Cate had shown. He had found the one who could do what even his mother had failed to do.

"She is very young, our girl. I do not know that she is—that I am—Oh—but this is all so very confusing."

Lachlan reached out and gingerly took Cate's hand. It was the gentlest gesture he had ever made toward her. "Think of them as memories shared from a friend. The house for your soul is different in every time, during every age, but your memories remain with your eternal soul. This Jessie is you, but there are so many memories your spirit has gathered from the you that exists now to the you that existed then."

Maeve nodded. "Think of her as a sister. Once she remembers you and her destiny, this will not feel so strange or awkward."

Cate studied the sunlight as it streamed through the leaves of the great oaks onto the grove floor. She wondered if Jessie appreciated the beauty of the sun, the peacefulness of the forest, the strength of the eagle's call. She hoped so. She hoped that, somewhere in the far reaches of Jessie's spirit, she could recall a time when the earth was sacred and powerful.

"You do not understand, Lachlan. I am there, inside her, but I am invisible. The people of her time are so completely dispirited, so devoid of any connection to nature and to themselves, that they cannot hear their past memories. Jessie cannot connect, at least not on her own." Cate frowned, thinking about her dream. "But there *is* a sage working with her."

Lachlan and Maeve said in unison, "A sage?"

Cate nodded and shielded her eyes from the sun. Something with ephemeral wings hovered just outside the sunbeam. "I believe that is her role. She is helping Jessie understand. I believe she is a seer."

"This woman—does she know what is happening?"

Shrugging, Cate tried to ignore the growling in her stomach. "I am unsure what she knows, but she is very wise and very patient. Her presence is a strong one."

Lachlan nodded. "The future has lost our goddesses, yet retained seers? Do the villages hold her in high regard?"

"Oh no, not at all. They believe her to be addled, but then, there is little belief in anything of any import."

Maeve draped her arm across Cate's shoulders. "You remember much this day."

Cate nodded. "It was the dream. I believe my spirit opens up to hear and see those things I experience when I go to Jessie's world; a world that values possessions over all else. It is a cold, black void, that future."

They walked through the forest toward the center of town, each wrapped in a cloak of their own thoughts until Maeve quietly asked, "Catie, when you return to the Sacred Place and carry within you your soul's memory those parts of Jessie's life, do you *feel* her within you?"

"You mean, do I bring her back with me?"

Both looked to Lachlan for an explanation of both the question and the answer. He lowered his hood and stared at one and then the other. "Cate's soul exists in this time with her body. It remembers the future because we sent her soul to retrieve information that could save us. Upon return, though, her soul is still housed in this body at this time, with memories from both the present and the future. Just as this Jessie should be able to recall bits and pieces of her past, so, too, do you recall bits and pieces of Jessie's future."

"Then she is not with me."

Lachlan shook his head. "No. Though it may feel that way at times, there is only one soul in one time. She and your soul exist outside of our time."

Maeve turned to Lachlan and asked the question she had wanted to ask many times before, but only now had the courage to hear the answer. "What happens to Cate's body while her soul slips through the portal?"

Lachlan averted his eyes from Maeve's. "It is stagnate. It remains alive but without a conscience guiding it."

Maeve rose on her toes like a mother bear rises in defending her young. "You told me there would be no danger to her! Damn, you, Lachlan, you promised me!"

"And there is not."

Cate touched Maeve's shoulder. "He is right, Maeve. I am not in any danger."

Maeve silenced them both with her glare. "Catie is alone in the forest, unable to protect herself, and you are telling me she is not in any danger? Do I look like a fool, Lachlan?"

Lachlan laid his hand on Maeve's other shoulder. "Cate was well-aware of the risks she made when she volunteered."

Maeve turned on Cate. "You knew?"

Cate looked away and nodded.

"Then why? How could you?"

Cate stole a look to Lachlan, who forced himself to look away. This was between Cate and Maeve; he had no place in this discussion.

"To save the people I love, the land we need, and the deities we speak with," Cate declared. " It is my gift to see, Maeve, and with that gift comes duties. You, of all people know as much. It was *you* who taught me!"

Maeve waved her off. "I did not mean for your duty to be a sacrificial one, Catie. I . . . need you here with me. I did not come all the way from Gaul to find you, only to lose you in what could very well be a pitiful attempt at preserving lives destined to be lost."

"No!" Lachlan's voice was harsh and cutting. "I will not stand here and listen to you talk her out of what may be the most important act of her life."

"To die? Is that what you'd call *an important act*, Lachlan? Have you so easily forgotten that it is our job to preserve and revere life?"

"I have not."

"Then how could you send her to—"

"Maeve," Cate's voice was barely above a whisper, but its stillness got Maeve's attention. "It is *my* choice. It is something *I* want to do. It—it is my destiny." Cate looked up into Maeve's gray eyes. How could she tell her that it was to save her from the ugliness both Lachlan and Cate had foreseen? Maeve was brave to a fault, and would demand they stop this at once, but that was something neither Cate nor Lachlan intended to do.

Maeve stepped far enough away from them both that their hands fell off her shoulders. "If anything happens to her, Lachlan, you and I will enter a dark place the likes of which you have never experienced."

Maeve's voice was cold and exact.

"We shall not lose her, Maeve."

"Do I have your word on that?"

Lachlan glanced over at Cate before shaking his head. "The goddesses shall do what they see fit. I believe Cate is in good hands."

"I would prefer it if she were in *mine*, but since it is apparent the two of you have planned this from the start, I have no other choice but to let her continue. Just mark my words, Lachlan. If Catie ever goes in there and does not return, *both* you and I will go after her. Am I understood?"

Nodding, Lachlan sighed loudly. "Understood."

"Good." Then to Cate, "I have always known when you are keeping something from me, little one. It is not in your best interest to hide yourself from me." Maeve reached out and softly stroked Cate's cheek. "I have found you in many of our lives, Catie, but in *this* life, I would prefer not losing you once more."

Cate's stomach growled loudly. "Do you think it even possible that I could hide anything from you?"

Maeve stared into Cate's eyes and nodded. "It is not *im*possible. You have grown into a very fine priestess. There is much you can do now. Keeping secrets from me, however, is not one of them."

Cate's stomach growled again. "I do understand, and you must rest assured that I would never risk being away from you; not in this life or any other."

Pulling Cate to her, Maeve kissed the top of her head and inhaled her essence. "First, food, then sleep, but after that, Catie, you and I are going to have an understanding."

Nodding, Cate felt Lachlan tighten up next to her, and she knew why. There was only one thing to understand: the Roman governor was coming, and few of the Silurians would live to tell about it.

Lachlan dropped them off at Maeve's cottage just as the village of Fennel was beginning to come to life. These people, the ones the Druids had sworn to protect, were unaware their fate hung in the balance. Like most Britons, they believed they could cohabitate with the Romans who were appearing in alarming numbers; but the Druids knew better. Their Druid brothers and sisters had been nearly wiped out in Gaul by the might of Julius Caesar a hundred years ago on his quest for world domination. The Romans had plundered and pillaged so much of the continent that it had taken them over a hundred years to discover the riches of the island across the channel. Already, their ancient forests had been decimated to build Roman ships, and the Druids knew what this omen portended: a people who would destroy the very earth would not hesitate to destroy the creatures living *on* that land. It had been the pattern of countless leaders before and after Julius Caesar, and there did not appear to be an end in sight. The Romans would conquer, leave their soldiers to plunder, and take as wives the women of the vanquished, so that soon their progeny would be of Roman birth. The Roman leaders would then leave a proxy to head a village, town, or Londinium, as the Romans called it, who would then collect taxes, pilfer goods and ship precious resources back to the Roman Empire. They were an insidious warrior culture preying on the rest of the world.

Their only real hope was knowing that an animal that eats its own kind was bound to fall prey to the same. Julius Caesar killed his own men, and, in turn, his own Senate stabbed him to death on the Senate's steps. These were the men who were threatening to destroy the Druids in an effort to gain power over the Celts. These were the people who believed themselves superior to other peoples in every known part of the world. These were the people against whom Lachlan, Maeve and Cate had vowed to protect Fennel.

Handing Cate half a loaf of bread, Maeve sat across from her at the table, her plate empty, and poured a bowl of stew from a tureen. Pushing it toward Cate, she said softly, "There'll be no talking you out of this, is there?"

Cate shook her head. "You need to trust that you taught me well. Jessie is becoming aware, and she'll be coming back for answers to her questions."

Maeve watched Cate eat her stew. "Tell me about her."

Cate bit into more bread. It was hard and dry. "She has a little brother, whom she cares deeply for, but other than that, she has no clan or any ties to one."

"No family?"

Cate shook her head. "She has family, but they seem to wound her daily. They remind me of Sean's family. I am unsure if they even like her very much."

Maeve pondered this a moment. "Do you?"

Cate had never even considered the notion. While in this time and place, she thought of Jessie as another person in a faraway place, and when she was there, she *was* Jessie, and saw the world through the eyes of a lost young girl. "Like her? I have never thought of it."

Maeve dipped a piece of bread in Cate's stew and tasted it, but said nothing.

"I suppose, if I think of her from here," Cate pointed to her head, "then, yes, I do like her. She is very different, I think, and she perceives herself as not quite—how would she say it? She does not know herself or what she is capable of. She does not feel wanted, I think. She is—out of sorts with herself, her surroundings and her family, and she does not know how to remedy any of them."

"How sad."

"Oh, but I do not think she is sad. I think she is brave. She carries on in spite of it."

Maeve cocked her head and studied Cate. "Then you *do* like her."

Cate blushed. "I do. Hers is not an easy life, nor is it one I would ever want to exchange with my own, but she truly wants to help. She's just so—young."

"And you are so very old?"

Cate giggled. "Not old. Wise. Well, not wise, really, but surely wiser than she."

Maeve smiled. "Of course. Now, what about this sage? Where did she come from?"

"That, I do not know. It feels, at times, as if she knows exactly what is happening to Jessie, but she does not say. Hers is a very old soul with a great deal of wisdom. She has much knowledge to teach Jessie.

I think that is why I do like Jessie: she has allied herself with one who can assist."

Maeve reached across the table and touched Cate's hand. "Are you ever scared?"

Cate swallowed her stew and frowned. "Of what?"

"Of not being able to return?"

Cate stirred the remnants of her stew and sighed. "I am not sure I would even know if that were to happen. To Jessie, my life and I are just fragmented and dim memories, just as she and hers are to me now. She could be in my soul right now, but I do not know, nor do I feel it. She *is* listening to me, though, and that is a good sign. She knows that I have reached out to touch her from far away, and she knows there is a history of her soul that she can learn to listen to. I believe that once I can actually tell her what we need from her, she will help us." Yawning and stretching, Cate patted her belly. "That was delicious. Thank you."

"Why don't you get some rest for now? Lachlan and I are reconvening the others in order to discuss our options when Suetonius Paulinus begins gathering his forces." Taking Cate's hand, Maeve led her to the lumpy straw mattress on the floor and bade her to lay down. Then, taking her own robe, she draped it across Cate's body. "This time, you dream sweet dreams, all right?"

Nodding drowsily, Cate sighed and closed her eyes. She was so tired that already her head felt floaty. "I won't let anything happen to you, Maeve. I promise." With that, Cate fell fast asleep.

When Jessie returned to her body, she was surprised to find herself leaning against the door of the numberless room. Every joint in her body ached, and the cobwebs in the room felt as if they had managed to somehow creep into her head.

Slowly rising, she looked at her faux Rolex watch. She'd been in the room less than an hour, but things were different this time. She remembered walking through the misty forest as the leaves crackled beneath her feet. A mist lingered like the remnants of a dream high atop the farthest reaches of the oaks. It was so clear in her mind, she was sure it was a memory and not the vague residues of a dream. This time, Jessie knew she hadn't been alone. Gray eyes and that tall guy had met up with her on the outskirts of the Sacred Place.

"Sacred Place?" Jessie muttered, shaking her head.

Returning to her room, she listened for the sounds of her parents' return. She wanted to avoid them for as long as she could. They felt like emotional vampires to her, sucking the very essence of her life force with their distrust and suspicious glances.

"Yeah, that's what they are," Jessie said, grabbing her bathrobe off the four-poster bed and heading for the shower. "Emotional vampires. I like that."

After her shower, as she slid her arms through her robe, Jessie stood motionless, staring down at her arm in the sleeve. Her robe was no longer a bathrobe, and she was no longer standing in her bathroom. For a split second, perhaps even a nanosecond, Jessie felt Cate within her.

"A Druid," Jessie uttered, still staring at the robe sleeve. "She was a priestess . . . a Druid priestess." Sitting down hard on the toilet seat, Jessie was jolted back to the here and now. "Oh . . . my . . . God," she said, laying her hand on her heaving chest. It was just as Ceara had said; only this time, Jessie was experiencing someone else's memories. Gray eyes had a name . . . and it was Maeve. And this Maeve was in some sort of danger—a real and present danger which was the impetus that had pushed Cate through the seam.

Cate.

Her name was Cate. And *she* was doing this time travel thing right now, as Jessie stood there naked, except for the robe that had somehow managed to jar her soul's memory of a life lived so very long ago. Cate was with her; *in* her, like a spirit eavesdropping on Jessie's life. But instead of being scary, it was somehow comforting.

"Ceara, help me." Slowly rising, Jessie padded back to her bedroom and grabbed the dusty and cobwebby clothes she had just stepped out of. She needed to get to Ceara, needed her to help make some sense out of what had just happened. Was it the robe that set off the memory, or had Cate just slipped into the future and tugged at Jessie's mind?

Yanking her jacket off the chair, Jessie started for the door, and ran right into her father.

"Going somewhere?"

Jessie's breath caught. "I need to see a friend, that's all."

"Were you not listening to me and your mother, Jess?"

Jessie felt two overriding emotions; one was the now familiar adrenaline surge she had been experiencing lately, and the other was a terrible sense of foreboding. "Dad, I have to go."

"Damn it, why do you have to be like this now? Why can't you just get a grip for a month or two while we all get settled in?"

Jessie stared at him. "I'm trying to like it here, Dad, but I . . ."

Rick sighed and shook his head sadly. "Whether you are or aren't, let's be very clear about one thing; if you leave this house without our permission, you'd better take your suitcase with you because we're not putting up with you breaking the rules without any consequences. We came here to make a fresh start."

Jessie closed her eyes and draped her arm over her face. Without thinking, she suddenly saw one of Cate's memories of a time when *her* father stood over her yelling at her for something she couldn't explain, either. Only, in her memory, Cate was calm—poised even. Cate was sure of herself and the thing she had done. Surely, Jessie could tap into those memories and make them part of her own. It was certainly worth a try.

Opening her eyes and lowering her arm, Jessie willed herself to be composed. "Dad, do you want to listen to me or stand there in judgment?"

Rick's mouth opened and closed like the hinges had suddenly broken.

"I'm not a drug user anymore. I've met a few kids from town who wear leather and have been really nice to me, but I am not about to get involved with *anyone* who uses drugs. I promised Daniel, and I have never broken a promise to him yet."

Rick sat on the bed. "I wish I could believe you."

Before Jessie could reply, Daniel came running to her door. "Jessie, that lady is here to see you!"

Jessie jumped off the bed and sprang past her father. "Ceara came?"

"Who?" Rick asked after his daughter.

Without stopping to answer, Jessie flew down the stairs to the first level where Reena was sitting on the sofa chatting with Madame Ceara.

"Madame Ceara," Jessie said, slowing her gait a little. "I'm so glad you stopped by."

Ceara turned to Jessie and offered her a gentle smile. "I was in the neighborhood and I thought I'd stop by and see how the new place is coming. Just like you said, it's really quite beautiful." Ceara turned back to Reena and held her gaze for half a second. "I do hope Jessie didn't bore you with tales of *my* house. Many of the kids in town go on and on about it."

"Your home?"

Ceara nodded. "The boat, where I live. I'm afraid I kept her chatting with me beyond her curfew. When you get as old as I am, and a young person shows an interest in what you have to say, you have a tendency to drone on a bit. I do apologize for keeping her on the boat so late."

Reena's mouth had the same broken hinge as Rick's; only she managed to find some words. "Oh . . . yes . . . the boat."

"Once she saw how late it was, she scooted off the boat. You have a good girl there, Mrs. Ferguson. She is very respectful, not to mention a wonderful listener. Del said he'd hire her if—"

"Del?"

"From the donut shop. He's always talking about what a breath of fresh air Jessie is. He said he would hire her in a heartbeat if he ever needed the help, but he knows, like we all do, how much time and energy these Victorians take up. I appreciate you giving Jessie some time to rattle around with an old coot like me. It's been a long time since I've had any girls wishing to chat with me."

Rick joined them and stared at Reena, who had lost what few words she had scraped together.

"But look at me rambling on. Please excuse my long-windedness. I appreciate the tour of the inn, Mrs. Ferguson. You've really done some wonderful things with the place. Jess said you had the designer touch, and she's right. You've really prettied up the old gal."

"Thank you. Feel free to come up any time."

"I'll do that." Ceara rose slowly. "Jessie, would you mind at all walking me down the hill? Down is harder on these old bones than up." Turning to Rick and Reena, Ceara asked them if it was okay. Like twin bobble-head dolls, they silently nodded up and down, up and down. "She's a good girl, Mr. Ferguson. I don't let just anyone on my boat, but I knew right off that your daughter is good people."

Not wasting a second of her precious freedom, Jessie hooked her arm through Ceara's and steered her out the door and down the steps. When they were safely out of earshot, Jessie threw her arms around her and hugged her tightly. "Thank you, thank you, thank you. God that was perfect timing."

Ceara held Jessie's arm as they carefully picked their way down the driveway. "I didn't show up coincidentally, my dear. Remember what I said about coincidences."

"Then you—"

"Heard you? Yes, I did."

"You—heard—me."

"Shouldn't I have? You *did* call me, didn't you?"

"Well, yes, I mean, no, I mean, I needed to talk to you, yes, but I had no idea you'd just come."

"Well, here I am. Imagine that. Now what is it that got you so fired up?"

Jessie walked along with her arm through Ceara's, making sure she didn't slip or fall. When they got to the bottom of the drive, Jessie inhaled deeply and took the plunge. "I know who she was."

Ceara came to a dead stop. "What did you say?"

"Her name is, was Cate, and she wore the white robe of the Druids, just like you said. I think—I'm pretty sure she's a priestess."

A knowing smile broke out on Ceara's face, and her eyes came to life with a colorful sparkle Jessie had never seen, making her look years younger. "Oh, my dear, but that is the most wonderful news! I am so very proud of you! Bravo!"

"There's more."

The smile broadened, and Jessie thought she saw a glimmer of a tear, but couldn't tell for sure in the light. "The woman with the gray eyes is named Maeve and she is in some sort of danger. I think, well, I'm not sure about this, but I think that's the reason Cate came through the fold."

Ceara nodded and resumed their walk. "Then you believe this Cate has come on behalf of Maeve?"

Jessie nodded. "I do. I feel how important Maeve is to Cate. She is the reason for all of this traveling about, but I'm just not sure why yet."

"What happened this time?"

"I went through, and remembered nothing, until I started for my bathrobe, and then I had this flash, like a *déjà vu*, and then I saw her— well, saw not as in looked at, but felt her there. It could have been the memory of the trip, but I *felt* something. I was—what's the word?"

"Transported?"

"That's it. I felt transported. When I looked down at my robe, I was *her* looking at *her* robe. It was cool and—disconcerting—and so incredibly real."

"Excellent. The two of you are making progress. You're moving toward a place where you might have a chance to meet. It happens, I'm told, on the dream plane. There have been others who have experience with meeting their old souls. I'll see if I can find some articles about it."

"What do you mean *meet*?"

"Meet. Stand face-to-face and see each other. Anything is possible in the Dreamworld if one knows how to access it."

"Now, *that* would be weird."

"Why? You are not she. You share a soul, but Cate is not you. She has experiences from her own life, feelings wholly different from yours. This will be much easier if you try to see her as a being separate from you."

"Because she is."

Ceara nodded. "How does it feel to have memories your physical being never experienced?"

Jessie looked up through the gray clouds at the stars winking at her. "This must have been how Alice felt when she fell down the rabbit hole. It feels both real and unreal, good and bad, light and dark. It is the perfect dichotomy, the perfect blend of opposites."

Ceara stopped, raising an eyebrow at Jessie, who shrugged.

"Well, *that* sure as hell wasn't me," Jessie said, shaking her head. "I don't even *know* what a dichotomy is."

Nodding, Ceara continued. "She is a strong priestess, this Cate. She has done well."

"She can't, like, take my body over, can she?"

Ceara looked up at the sky, but said nothing.

"Ceara?"

After a short while, Ceara returned her gaze to Jessie. "A body can only be possessed if the original inhabitant allows the possession to take place, so no, you have no worries there. She may be a very strong priestess, but you are equally strong, if not more so, because you have your combined soul's memories. Fear not, Jessie Ferguson, it may feel like you have just fallen into the rabbit hole, but in reality, you have just learned how to do what few people can. You should be proud. It is a privilege to be chosen. Cate was chosen, therefore, so were you."

"Chosen? By whom?"

"By the head Druid priest. Few Druids have the capability to do what Cate has done. It is the mark of greatness, of one with powers beyond those of a simple Druid. Someone has trained her, guided her, and taught her how to use the portal. She was chosen."

Jessie sighed. It felt so complex. "You know what's so weird?"

"What?"

"How *not* weird the memories feel to me. When I looked at the robe, I was *so* not in my bathroom anymore. I've done nothing but think about past life things lately, and what surprises me is how much sense it all makes."

Ceara chuckled. "It is an interesting concept when a society spends millions of dollars trying to make sense of phobias and whatnot that we each carry with us. So much of how we feel about certain things comes not from this world, but from a past one."

Jessie stopped beneath the streetlight at the end of Morning Glory. "You mean like why I have this total aversion to those papiér mache heads at Mardi Gras? Or my dislike of Chinese dragons?"

"Precisely. I have a client who's been phobic about circuses since she was a little girl. When she was eight, her parents had wrestled her into the car to go to the circus, but she would not go. She hates the smell of the circus, the clowns, the center ring, everything that is symbolic of the circus." Ceara paused to look both ways before crossing the street. "Yet, she's never *been* to the circus, never seen one on TV and never read a book or magazine article about them. As a little girl, she knew one thing: she was absolutely not going to go."

"Wow."

"Yes. So, where do such extreme emotions come from, if not from the soul's memory?"

"Why was she seeing you?"

"She wanted a past life reading. Normally, I don't do this, but she really needed some questions answered."

"And did you answer them?"

"Perhaps even more than she wanted. When I told her that she had been a gay man in a circus and her trapeze partner had let her fall to her death, she went white as a ghost. It was then she told me about her circus phobia. And, of course, her fear of bridges and heights. Poor woman had no idea why these things frightened her. She just wanted some understanding."

Chills ran up and down Jessie's arms. "That's some scary stuff."

"Not scary, Jessie. Scary is not knowing. Knowing gives us power, and that power has the ability to change your life."

"Then what you're saying is that everyone is walking around not listening to themselves."

"Exactly, and that is why we are all so lost, so confused, too wrapped up in this sort of therapy or that. We spend thousands of dollars trying to fill a void that would be sated if we only recognized who we really are. The self-help industry is booming because *civilized* man cannot explain his absolute state of misery and emptiness. Once Christianity came along and virtually replaced the notion of the transmigration of souls, western civilization stopped hearing those voices that had been heard from one generation to the next. The Druid practice is about remembering one's ancestors, remembering the past. They knew how important it was to the growth of a soul, but after the Christians plundered the world, they silenced the joy, history and wisdom by accepting the singular notion that we have but one chance to achieve eternal bliss, and only one avenue to travel to get there. Voices silenced, the Christians were free to pursue men's souls."

Jessie sighed. How often had she heard her parents rail on about heaven and the slim chances of getting there. It was exhausting trying to figure out what constituted a sin, or if God was to be feared, loved or both. She had never truly understood her parents' fear of a God who was supposed to love them. "But those of us who *do* remember face so much doubt from others we risk winding up in a rubber room counting the tiles in the ceiling."

"Yes, and therein lies the danger of a religion that so quickly disposed of the others to the point that anything *not* it is viewed as an aberration. You'd have as hard a time convincing the world about the seam as they would convincing you there's no such thing as a soul."

"But I have proof. I've been there and back."

Ceara shook her head. "Jessie, not just anyone can slip through the seams of time. Believe me, people who thought they could simply enter the Sacred Place have disappeared and never returned. It is sacred for a reason. For many reasons."

A notion occurred to Jessie. "Is that what the Bermuda Triangle is? A fold?"

"Perhaps. There certainly have been many start through who did not come back. And those who did, those who have tried sharing their experiences quite often ended up just as you said; in a rubber room counting tiles."

Jessie cocked her head. "What are you saying?"

"I'm saying that you mustn't share this with anyone. The Sacred Place is not a toy, it is not a tourist destination. It is an opening through which only the chosen may slip through and return safely. You must believe me when I say tell no one. To do so would put the very people asking for help in danger."

Jessie shook her head. "Hey, not to worry. I am in no hurry to be thought of as a loon. I have a hard enough time shaking the stoner label." Picking her way carefully through the dark, Jessie held on tightly to Ceara's arm. "But, how do I live with it?"

"Don't just live with it. *Celebrate* it. My soul experiences have so enriched my life here. They're wonderful, really."

"And how many of those lives do you recall?"

"Five are very clear. Two are still somewhat fuzzy along the edges, and seventeen singular memories have come and gone leaving only the barest hint of residue." Ceara released Jessie's arm when they finally came to the sidewalk of Main Street. "Let me ask you this, Jessie: when you remembered Cate in the robe, where did you get the idea she was a Druid?"

"Well, you, I think. You told me some of the Druids' beliefs."

"Really. And you think that's what gave you the idea that she was a priestess?"

"Well, no—I—don't really know."

"Do you know where Druids are from?"

"Mostly England, I think."

"What did they wear?"

"White robes?" Jessie shook her head in frustration. "I don't know a damn thing about them, Ceara. The truth is, I suck in school."

"Perhaps now is the time to unsuck yourself." Ceara waved to a car driving by. "Thank you for a most enjoyable visit."

"No, thank *you*. My parents were getting ready to string me up."

"They long to be able to trust you, Jessie. Whatever bond was broken is slow to mend, but they, too, are trying. Don't be so hard on them. Parenting is the most thankless job in the world."

As Ceara started up the plank, Jessie called out to her. "Are *you* a parent?"

Ceara stopped. Turned. Smiled softly. "A long, long time ago. Goodnight, dear."

"Goodnight, Ceara."

As Jessie made her way back up Main Street, she stopped under the broken street lamp and stared up at the sky. Something about their conversation nagged at her.

"Sacred Place," Jessie murmured, looking over at the boat. As she started toward the inn, Jessie kept wondering the same thing:

How had Ceara known that Cate called the seam the Sacred Place?

Jessie had never seen her parents quite so remorseful. Truth was, they were too hung up on being right to ever feel remotely apologetic or contrite. But there they were, sheepishly drinking their herb tea in what Reena had now dubbed The Parlor.

The transformation that had been slowly taking over her was complete now. She no longer felt like Jessie Ferguson, a teen adrift with no center, no balance and no direction. She carried herself slightly differently than she had a day ago, or even an hour ago. Her previous ultra-boring, entertain-me-now, drug-enhanced life was over, and the present had finally become an interesting place to be.

Walking across the parlor, Jessie sat on the antique yellow and gold settee facing them. As much as she had always wanted to hear them grovel, she was far more interested in examining the outcome of her journey in the privacy of her room.

Reena looked pained. "Jess, please do try to see things from our perspective."

Jessie chuffed a sound of utter disbelief. She could hardly believe it. They weren't going to apologize! They were going to sit here and rationalize their erroneous and judgmental behavior.

Reena said softly, "It's just that—well, your father called around about your friend Tanner, and, quite frankly, he just isn't the kind of kid we want you hanging out with."

Jessie shook her head. "Tanner's not the one you have to trust. I understand if trusting my *judgment* is a bit hard, but trusting *him* isn't even in the equation. Anyway, we've just met. I wouldn't even say we're friends, well, not yet, anyway. And as far as the villagers in this burg go, I could care less what they have to say about anything. They're wrong about Ceara and they're probably wrong about Tanner as well."

Bounding up the stairs, Jessie did not hear any wails of protest.

Poking her head into Daniel's room, where he sat building a model of a 1957 Thunderbird, Jessie cleared her throat. "Hey."

"Hey." Daniel did not look up from his model.

"I'm really sorry about the folks."

Daniel shrugged. He did not look up. "How old were you when you first smoked dope?"

Jessie recoiled at how easily Daniel used drug jargon. Looking at him as if seeing him for the first time, Jessie wondered when he had grown up. "I was twelve. It was the sixth grade at a Christmas party."

Daniel still did not look at her, continuing to glue bumper pieces together. "What made you try it?"

Jessie sat on the corner of his bed with mounting trepidation. She could barely remember. "Peer pressure. Boredom. Curiosity. All of the above, I guess."

"You tried other drugs, too?"

"Why?"

Daniel shrugged. "It must have really been bad for them to be worrying so much about you doing it again."

Jessie weighed her next words carefully as she watched him. "You know, Daniel, drugs aren't necessarily that bad. It's the people who do them who can be bad, and it's the consequences you suffer when you do stupid things under the influence. You remember my friend, Steve?"

Daniel grinned. "The varsity pitcher. He's cool."

"He used drugs."

The grin fell away and Daniel looked up for the first time. "No way."

Jessie nodded sadly. "He started spending more and more time getting high, and less and less practicing his killer curve ball, and before you knew it, the scholarships didn't materialize and he found himself sitting on the bench instead of being a starter. How *cool* is that?"

"How can you say drugs aren't bad then?"

"Because many cultures use drugs to get to a spiritual state of the

Otherworld, and that's when drugs are not bad, nor are the people who use them. But using drugs to escape life is not the right thing to do. *My drug use wasn't the right thing to do.*"

"What were you escaping from?"

Jessie sighed. "Myself, I guess. I didn't like who I was."

"I always liked you."

Jessie mussed up his hair. "I know. And I've always liked you."

"Do they think Tanner uses drugs?"

"Yes."

Daniel blew on the cement glue of the bumper. "Does he?"

"I don't know."

Daniel looked at her dubiously.

"Honestly, Daniel, I do not know. Would that matter?"

Daniel thought about it a moment. "Only if it makes you use drugs again."

"You know, I don't think *anything* could make me use drugs again. I'm just now beginning to like who I am. I'm not going to screw that up with drugs. Why all these questions?"

Daniel turned from her and continued working on his model. "Just curious."

"Bull. Are those boys bugging you about drugs?"

Daniel shook his head.

"Daniel . . ."

"That kid, Chris." The words fairly flew out of Daniel's mouth. "He just thinks he's so cool bragging about drugs and all the cool people he knows who uses them."

"How old is he?"

"Twelve, I think."

"Where did he get it?"

"I didn't say he was using drugs, Jessie, I said . . ."

"Where did he get it?"

Daniel wouldn't look at her, so Jessie crouched down and made eye contact with him. "Daniel," she said softly, "Did he say he got it from Tanner?"

Daniel's eyes filled with tears. "He said if I looked, I could probably find your stash in your room, and he'd give me five bucks if I skimmed some and gave it to him."

Jessie felt a tight band around her chest as she went from a crouch to one knee. Pure red anger flowed through her veins as she looked down at her little brother. A feeling she'd never experienced washed over her, and though she could not name it, she most certainly could feel it.

"What did you say to him?"

He tried to shrug nonchalantly, but Jessie knew better. "Daniel?"

He did not look up. "I told him you didn't do drugs anymore."

Jessie's eyes watered slightly. Even in the face of new friends, Daniel had been loyal to her. "He didn't believe you, did he?"

Daniel shook his head and wiped some glue off his thumb. "Chris said, once a druggie always a druggie, and you hooking up with Tanner was proof you still smoked dope."

Jessie didn't know what bothered her most; that this Chris was impugning her name, or that he had already managed to add so many drug-related words to Daniel's vocabulary. "Daniel, look at me."

Daniel hesitated, then complied.

"Daniel, your friend Chris is wrong. People change all the time. I've changed a lot since I was busted. I've got my act together and I'm so over my stupid drug phase. All it did was mess up my life. If Tanner uses drugs, and I don't know that he does, but *if* he does, then he and I probably won't be able to be friends. But I don't judge people by town rumors and little boy gossip, and you shouldn't either."

Daniel nodded. "And besides, you promised."

Jessie nodded. Those promises meant the world to him. "Yes, I did, and I've never broken a promise to you, have I?"

Daniel shook his head, and Jessie could see the worry and fear slowly leave his eyes.

"And one more thing," Jessie said softly. "I'd stay away from this kid Chris, if I were you. He doesn't sound like a very nice boy if all he does is talk bad about other people."

"I will. He's not very fun, anyway. All he wants to talk about is girls. Yuck."

Mussing up his hair, Jessie said, "Goodnight, sport."

"G'night, Jess."

When Jessie's head hit the pillow, she lay there wide-awake while committee meetings raged on in her head. So much was happening so fast, she could barely catch her breath. In the blink of an eye, she'd gone from not wanting anyone to want or need her, to having people in different worlds thousands of years away needing her. It was all so weird; she didn't quite know what to think.

How it *felt*, however, now *that* surprised her. Need had always implied obligation, but this wasn't how she felt. This felt . . . comforting, as if being needed gave her a sense of belonging, a place to be. This gave her life purpose, and she hadn't had that before. It felt good knowing there was more to life than high school. Exhaling loudly, Jessie rolled over and stared out the window. There were worlds out there where people lived believing they were alone in the universe. But they weren't. She wasn't.

And that felt better than anything she'd ever experienced.

Feeling the beginning of sleep creep around her, Jessie could see the back of a white robe fluttering in the slight breeze.

White robe? Was that Cate?

Cate awoke feeling better than she had in days. After breaking her fast, washing her face and praying, she walked out to a beautiful and glorious morning that wrapped warm arms around her bringing her to life. The village was already bustling with activity as the wine and oil merchants peddled their wares to the market goers, and cooking food wafted through the air. The cobbler waved to her as she stepped out into the rut-lined street. A rare glimpse of sun warmed her back as she watched an aging donkey slowly clip-clop by. Some days, it was just so wonderful to be alive.

Stretching, she saw Maeve buying something from the local weaver. It was difficult for Maeve to complete the transaction because everyone knew and loved her and always stopped to say good morn to her or offer her some fruit or vegetables.

Cate watched her from afar, as she had done so many mornings, and felt more than the warmth from the sun flood her insides. Eight years older than Cate, Maeve had arrived ten years ago on a trade ship from Gaul. The moment she stepped from the boat, the village of Fennel embraced her like a long lost daughter. Wearing long, colorful silk robes that flowed around her like living sea creatures, she appeared to float off the deck of the battered boat. Cate wasn't the only one who thought her a goddess that day. There was something so very different about her that a group of boys scooted off to the woods in search of Lachlan, who was out gathering herbs and working with two of the Vates.

By the time Lachlan made it back to the village, Maeve had already been dubbed priestess from the mysterious land of Gaul, who had come here on a special journey of a spiritual nature. Farmers thought her a good omen. Rumors, stories and myths were quickly abundant that night, as word spread that the woman who walked on water had bought and paid for the house on the hill overlooking the lake.

Those last rumors were true. Cate had seen her pay handsomely for the large four-room house once owned by the miller. Cate had followed her there, and when the transaction was over, Maeve suddenly whirled around and captured thirteen-year-old Cate with those gray cat eyes, riveting her to the very spot where she stood.

"Women on this island," Maeve began, staring into Cate's eyes, "are the most powerful women in the world. Do not *ever*, ever allow anyone to take your power from you."

Wide-eyed, Cate could barely manage a nod as the gray-eyed stranger placed a warm hand on top of Cate's head. "Show me to the one named Lachlan."

Maeve had come to study under Lachlan, a most powerful and influential Druid on the island. He had just completed his twenty years of study under Branwen, and was regarded by other clan leaders as one you wanted as your ally. Lachlan was, by nature, a very stoic young man, with a loyal heart, a sharp eye and a commanding tongue. He had also fallen under Maeve's spell, and broken not a few of the rules by allowing newcomers into the sacred circle. Fortunately for Lachlan,

Maeve was so adored by so many, this never proved to be a problem. The village of Fennel felt grateful and lucky to have a woman so self-possessed and strong among its priests and priestesses. Her healing skills were evident during her first week in Fennel when she aided the healing of a broken bone of a boy who had fallen from a horse. Her gifts were seen early and openly, and the villagers regarded her with awe.

Cate was no different. She had spent much of Maeve's first days just watching her come and go. Maeve spent a great deal of time on the lake, often with her face upturned toward the light. She seemed to revel in the calm, seeking out the quieter areas of the lake in which to meditate and pray. What young Cate did not know was how often Maeve had been watching her.

The second week Maeve was there she had been walking around the lake on the side nearest the falcon's nest when she stopped, glanced up at the sky and sighed. Then, whirling around, a behavior Cate would eventually become accustomed to, Maeve pointed up at Cate, who was wedged between two gigantic branches high in an oak. "Is there a purpose to these observations of yours?"

Cate hastily scrambled down the oak tree. "No. Yes. Well—not really—"

"One can hardly answer no, yes and maybe to one question, unless that question contains a riddle. I do not believe I asked you a riddle, although I could be mistaken. Shall we try again?"

"I mean no intrusion," Cate said, bowing ever so slightly. "I enjoy studying people and wondering what they are thinking."

Maeve raised an eyebrow. The air about her seemed to crackle with energy. "Oh? Then perhaps you can tell me what it was *I* was thinking."

Cate started to answer, but Maeve held up her hand. "Never speak without thinking, never think without feeling, and never feel without trusting."

Cate, big-eyed, nodded and closed her mouth.

"It is always a mistake to blurt out one's malformed thoughts and ideas. Words, and the very act of uttering them, give them power beyond anything you might imagine. So think before you speak."

"I have yet to deduce your thoughts," Cate said quietly.

"Then what is it you think you *might* know, little one?"

Cate felt a blush rise to her cheeks. It wasn't just those gray eyes boring a hole into her that made her nervous, it was everything about her; the way she walked, her tone of voice, the complete command she had of the very air around her. "You were looking deep into yourself for answers. That is all I can tell."

"Tell, or see? Have you the sight, little watcher?"

Cate shook her head. "I do not think so." She pulled herself erect. "I plan to become a warrior."

Maeve's lips turned up slightly. "Oh, do you now?"

Cate nodded and pointed to her dagger. "I have many skills for warrioring. I've learned how to wield a broadsword, a poleax and a dagger."

"To what end?"

Cate appeared perplexed by the question. "For protection, of course."

"And of what are you afraid?"

Cate wondered why it was that every time Maeve asked a question, she became unsure of herself. "I am not."

Maeve raised her eyebrows. "Then why would you need to protect yourself?"

"Aren't there many dangers out in the world?"

Maeve walked toward the water, the direction she'd been heading before she spied Cate. "Perhaps more than many and fewer than none. I believe the true dangers lurk in here." Maeve tapped her temple. "Oftimes, the greatest dangers come from within."

Cate followed her toward the river, not because she wanted to, which she did, but because she felt compelled. At this moment, she knew one thing above all else: she would follow this woman into a spewing volcano.

Stopping suddenly, Maeve turned to face her. "Do you understand my meaning?"

Cate nodded, not at all sure she did. "I think so."

"Explain it to me."

Cate inhaled deeply. This, she knew, was a test. If she failed, Maeve might never speak to her again for fear she was too stupid or weak. That would devastate her for reasons she knew not. Squaring her shoulders, she gave it her best try. "Dangers from within are self-doubt, over-confidence, arrogance, fear and . . . anger."

Maeve's lips turned up slightly, giving Cate her first passing grade. "Very good."

"There are more. Many more." Cate wanted to please.

"Yes, there are. And why would these be more dangerous than, say, a wolf or a Roman soldier?"

Cate was ready. "Those I named could keep you from defeating any opponent, regardless of your physical advantage. One cannot win a battle with a foe if self-doubt exists in one's heart." She had learned this from Liam.

"So then, is it more advantageous to possess a sharp mind or a sharp sword?"

"Both."

Maeve grinned. "Perhaps. However, should you have both, then, might not a moment come when you must choose which to use first? What then, little watcher? How would one make the correct choice?"

Cate thought hard, feeling those gray eyes upon her. "Choose your strongest weapon first. Always first."

"And which weapon would that be?"

"Your mind. Always your mind. And if that does not work, then you can use your sword."

Maeve continued on toward the lake. "Excellent. There is no substitution for being prepared. Only when we are truly prepared can we defeat our enemy." Whirling around so quickly she knocked Cate off balance, Maeve grabbed hold of her and brought her closer. "And to be so prepared, you must *know* who your enemies are. Do you, Catie McEwen, know who your enemies are?"

Cate shook her head slowly, too stunned to speak.

"Then how shall you ever be prepared?"

"I . . . I do not have any."

"No?" Maeve picked up a pebble and tossed it into the calm lake.

"If you are that reed over there, will the ripple from the pebble reach you?"

"Of course. Look now. The reed sways."

"But the pebble landed so far from it. How is it that the reed could be so affected? And, is it affected by the pebble or the ripple? Which one is to blame?"

Cate studied the ripples, the swaying reed, and the spot at which the pebble entered. Maeve's questions created a clarity of vision and thought that enabled Cate to see her answers before she spoke them. "The stone need not touch the reed in order to affect it. The ripple is a result of the pebble's actions, but the swaying of the reed is a result of the ripple. They are intricately connected."

"Exactly. And it is this lesson, above all others, that you must remember, for there will come a day when the ripples reach *you* and you must understand that it is the stone which is ultimately affecting you and not just the ripples. You must always, always, look beyond the ripples for the cause of them."

That day of reckoning was nearing, and Cate had spent the last ten years working with the Vates and Lachlan to prepare them for the moment when the pebble splashed down. The Vates studied the processes of death and regeneration and explored the Druidic relationship with their ancestors by seeking the wisdom of the night, of dreams, and of the moon. They conversed with these ancestors in order to receive knowledge or prophecy of the future. In those ten years, Cate had easily discarded her desire to be a warrior for her chosen craft. At the age of fourteen, she began her training for the craft, but before she could share her joyous news with her family, they were killed by a band of Roman soldiers roaming the countryside looking to cause trouble. Her mother, father and brave Liam had died for the few items not worth stealing at the hands of men who didn't need any of it.

Cate had wanted to hate those men and all things Roman. She had wanted to mount a horse and ride after them, picking them off one-by-one as Liam had shown her how to do. But when her grief subsided, so too, did her anger, and she was left with the hollowness and void only family can fill.

The news of her family's demise would have destroyed Cate when she was younger, but she was no longer alone in the world, and Maeve and Lachlan took tender care of her, even going so far as to make sure Cate could keep her father's house.

Cate owed Maeve and Lachlan so much for the truly wonderful life she had been living for the past ten years, that even if she had not had the horrible vision about Maeve, she would have gladly volunteered to be the one to step through the portal. She owed them that much; perhaps far more than that.

But she *had* had the vision, and others, on that rare, sunny day in the woods. She told Lachlan and Maeve that she dreamt of a young girl who would be able to provide them with the answers they needed in order to escape the ripples that were headed their way.

"You've had a dream, have you?" Lachlan asked, his eyes darting over to Maeve; Maeve, the one woman he wanted but would never have. Her gifts, her powers aided his strength and his hold on Fennel as their spiritual guide, but he would never reach the depths he wanted with her. She was a closed book to him, never to be read, not even a glance.

"She's the one, Lachlan," Maeve had whispered quietly upon the telling of the dream. "I have always known it was so, but I have been waiting for *her* to know it."

And so, Cate did, and it was that knowing that drove them now. It was the knowledge Cate and Lachlan shared that had become the reason for everything they did. It was the last thing they thought about each night and the first thing they thought of when they awoke. It was the chain that bound them, and they had sworn to each other to protect a people who had no idea of the size of the ripple that was heading toward them.

When Maeve finally made her way down the road, Cate waited patiently for the last villager to say her good mornings. It was an inspiring morning, and closing her eyes to the sun, she let her mind wander away to places and corners where she suspected Jessie lurked, listening, learning, and trying to uncover just what it was Cate needed of her. Yes, Jessie was there, or had been; residual spiritual aura could be seen as well as felt if one had the sight. And Cate most assuredly had that. It was odd to think that she now carried within her memories of events that had not yet transpired, but the more she allowed herself to accept them, the more easily they were becoming a part of who she was.

Because Jessie was so young, her thoughts, feelings and memories were tender, if not tenuous. It was Jessie's feelings for the boy that touched Cate the most, and she could practically see his smiling face. Maybe it was because she, too, had once had a brother she adored, but he was older and able to care for himself. This boy in Jessie's life . . . well, there was a bond between them that was stronger than even Cate's bond with Liam.

The other thing that surprised Cate was how much she liked Jessie. There was a courage within her that reminded Cate of herself before she met Maeve and turned away from the sword. Jessie would be the warrior Cate was not. Cate had given up her swords and daggers for verses and craft work, knowledge and mystery. She had turned her back on warrioring and hadn't regretted it for a moment. Still, there was something wonderful about the warrior seed Jessie carried within her. She was a fighter. She didn't know she was a fighter, but buried deep down inside, from pasts Jessie knew nothing about, were warriors from days long gone.

Cate wondered as she traversed the deeper areas of her soul, *How many other lives has my soul lived where the warrior seed sprouted to save others?* Unable to save her family or protect Liam, Cate vowed to herself that, if they lived through the invasion, she would continue her quest into the future as well as the past to keep her people alive. She owed it to herself, and to those who had helped her bring her gift to life. She even owed it to Jessie and the warrior within her.

"So, you do like her."

Cate opened her eyes to find Maeve staring down at her. As she had done dozens of times before, Maeve had been able to tell what she was thinking. Grinning, Cate nodded. "I do."

"I can tell because you visit there more than you have in the past." Maeve tapped Cate's temple with her finger.

Cate eyed her with mock caution. "You are worried. You never attempt to do that unless you are worried. What frightens you so?"

Maeve waved the question off with the flick of her wrist. "What else do you like about her?"

"She has courage, Maeve, and passion. I admire the strength of her energy. She is not afraid of much. I believe she can be of great service."

"I admire *your* courage, my friend. Do you see the spirit you both share is filled with courage and passion? No matter where you go or what you've been, your soul carries with it that which you admire in Jessie." Maeve threaded her arm through Cate's and pulled her closer. "Walk with me."

"Where are we going?"

"You shall see." As Maeve walked, she pulled Cate closer. "William has come to town bearing news that the Roman army is on the move. Suetonius Paulinus is gathering his forces together for a surge."

"But Suetonius is governor, Maeve."

"He is also a general, first and foremost. Remember, in the Roman world, a man gets his political power by the number of enemies he destroys in battle. I am afraid William is correct. Suetonius Paulinus is planning an attack."

"*The* attack?"

"We believe so, yes."

Cate nodded. This was not a surprise to her, but she was a bit taken aback by how quickly the Romans were gearing up. Had they a seer as well? Did they know that the Druids were searching for a means to escape the onslaught?

"You believe in Jessie." It wasn't a question.

"I do. I believe she can do this. She may not be as receptive as Lachlan would wish, but I believe she and I can do this together."

Maeve grinned. "It is odd to hear you referring to yourself in the future and saying *she.*"

Cate shrugged. "You should feel how strange it is to *feel* her inside me. She knows, Maeve. She knows something is happening and she wants to help, but there's that *thing* hovering in her world that prevents her from truly letting herself out of it. It is time to break through and explain to her what we need. I am a Druid. Jessie is not. She does not have the skills I possess. She needs my help."

Maeve sighed, but said nothing.

"How are Angus and Quinn faring?"

"Quinn has established contact and rapport of some sort, but does not know of the time in which she resides."

"She?"

Maeve nodded. "Indeed. Quinn was not prepared to be in the world of a woman. It has made it more difficult for him to concentrate on the task at hand."

"I can well imagine. I suppose this might have been harder if Jessie were a young man. Quinn was aware that the soul has no gender. His surprise is—well—surprising."

"Indeed."

"I should like to speak with him soon."

"Lachlan would prefer it if you did not for now. He believes you stand the greater chance of reaching Jessie than Quinn does his female self, and Lachlan does not want Quinn to interfere in anything you might be thinking or feeling about the future."

"It is a strange future, Maeve."

"It is a strange present, Catie. William spoke to Lachlan and I in private and told us that Boudicca, Queen of the Iceni is raising her own troops in Britannia to rebel against the Roman forces."

Cate stopped walking. This was big news; news she had not foreseen. "She plans to attack?"

Maeve shrugged. "William was unclear, but he said it appeared so. She has sent word to the highlanders and others that anyone wishing to be free is invited to join her." Maeve pulled Cate forward as they stepped closer to the lake. "I have heard great and wondrous things about Queen Boudicca. They say she can best any man and is fiery proud of her heritage. If she does decide to attack first, it will not be without preparation."

"She risks much attacking first, Maeve. If she does not defeat Suetonius Paulinus, he will destroy her."

Maeve swallowed hard and looked away. "They already killed her husband and raped her daughters, Cate. She is beyond that point by now. She lives for vengeance and vengeance alone."

That news chilled Cate to the bone, bringing painful echoes of the deaths of her own family at the hands of the murderous Romans. Maeve wrapped her enormous green cloak around the two of them and leaned closer.

"Maeve, even if she wins, the Romans will only send more troops. What those men want, they have nearly always gotten."

"By blood if not greed, I know. But one does not pluck the reed from the water just because the ripple is coming."

"Maeve, the reed stands not a chance. Time is drawing near. I must break through to her somehow."

Nodding, Maeve walked them to the largest oak tree on the shores of the lake and stood for a long time, basking in their ancient wisdom. "Lachlan and I believe a quest to the Otherworld will enable you to break down the last of Jessie's barriers."

The Otherworld was a place of mystery and wisdom, where one went for guidance and aid. If Lachlan was sending her there, that meant he was afraid the Roman Army would attack before she could find the answers they needed. Time was of the essence now more than ever. She did not know if she was ready for the Otherworld, but she was willing to do anything Maeve and Lachlan asked her to do. There was too much counting on her not to.

Cate slowly turned, surprised. "Will you and Lachlan assist me?"

"Of course we'll help you, silly thing. But we must do so immediately. Herbert says the arming of Suetonius Paulinus' men has been very discreet and he is more prepared than he would lead people to believe." Maeve motioned for Cate to sit with her beneath the oak. "Lachlan is coming shortly." Taking Cate's hands in hers, Maeve asked, "Catie, you must be completely honest with me. Are you scared?"

"Of what?"

"Of all we do not yet know . . . of a world so very far away from the one in which we live . . . of a person who is you, but not you. It is all right, my love, to tell me the truth. Fear is the thing that, if kept hidden, prevents us from seeing clearly, and I need you to see very clearly. I need *you*."

Cate brought Maeve's hands to her lips and kissed each one. "I am not afraid, Maeve. I know what must be done and I am willing to do it."

Maeve smiled softly. "That is good. You will need all of your courage, and certainly all of your wisdom to do this. You have never taught anyone, Catie, and it is not as easy as it may seem. You will have your hands full with her."

"Maeve, I would take a Roman sword through my heart if I thought it would save you from harm. Teaching Jessie sounds much less painful."

Maeve cocked her head and looked at Cate sideways. "I do know that. I do know how much I mean to you, Catie. I have always known."

Cate nodded, two tears dangling precariously for a second before jumping off her lashes. "I can go into the strange future if I know you are waiting for me here."

"Waiting for you? If I could reach through that portal myself and drag you back, I would. You'd best not ever have any plans of leaving and never returning. I may not be the best priestess to go through, but I'll come after you if need be. I would search every hour of every day since the dawn of man to find you again. Do not ever forget."

Cate grinned. "Never."

"Good. Then close your eyes and breathe deeply." Maeve waited for Cate to close her eyes, then produced a green leaf from one of her sleeves and crumbled it beneath Cate's nose so when she inhaled, the sweet aroma entered her nostrils, making all of her muscles relax. "Breathe deeply, my love. Lachlan will come soon, and when he does, you will enter the Otherworld, where you will be given the strength and wisdom you need to complete your task. Breathe deeply . . . and remember."

Jessie felt as if she were caught somewhere between a dream and reality, as if she were hovering in spirit form, observing someone else's life.

Yes . . . yes it was. She was seeing Cate's memories of Maeve when she first arrived from Gaul. How Jessie *knew* this, she didn't know. Cate must have been thinking about Maeve's first appearance from Gaul.

Gaul? Where in the hell was Gaul?

Jessie silently cursed herself for not paying closer attention in history class. God, had she paid attention to *anything* in her life? Now, when Maeve needed her most, she couldn't even remember where Gaul was.

But she *did* remember Cate's feelings about the gray-eyed woman who'd taken her under her wing and opened the world up to her. It was an intense love Jessie had never expected to feel in her life. It was deep, meaningful and intense, and so very important to Cate's emotional well-being. This was the kind of love that carried with it a loyalty that not even death could separate. It was a love that surprised Jessie because it reached right out and touched her even in this spirited state. It caressed her like the wind on a warm summer night, filling her with a sense of belonging and joy. She remembered Cate's memories of the fulfillment of the love, and in doing so, tasted the remnants of a bond that still lingered.

Still lingered. Was that what was drawing her here? Was Cate's bond with Maeve so strong that Jessie was actually remembering it? It had to be. It was the only explanation.

Well, she may not know where Gaul was, but she knew enough to realize it was this bond that sent Cate into an unknown future she knew nothing of; a future as unfamiliar to her as the fortieth century would be to Jessie. It wouldn't have mattered to Cate *which* century she walked into; their love spanned thousands of years, in countless people, and existed in hundreds of ages. One of those ages was where Cate was now. With Maeve.

Rolling over, Jessie opened one eye and looked at the clock. It was a little after six in the morning and her dreams hung in the air like the smell of sleep.

"Maeve," Jessie muttered, rolling back over and staring at the ceiling. Suddenly, both eyes sprang open and Jessie sat straight up. "I remember!" She remembered her dream, her feelings, the thoughts she'd had while discovering Cate's memories. "She's doing it for *you*,"

Jessie said, realizing that her dream may not have been a dream at all. "But what is *it?* What is so important that you'd come to *me*, of all people, and ask for help?" Lying back down, Jessie stared at the ceiling recalling every detail, every phrase, every single piece of information she could about her dream. Once she was able to squeeze as much information out her mind, she rolled over and wrote it in her journal.

So I must keep wondering, why me? Of all the times and all the people Cate could have ventured to, why did she choose me? It's hard feeling worthy of a task (whatever that task is) when I've done nothing but screw up my own life. Now, I'm afraid of doing that to someone else. I'm afraid I might not have what it takes. And then I stop and wonder how can I even impact the past? It's already happened. I can't change any of it. Or can I? There's so much I need to know and I only have a fraction of the information needed. Does Ceara have any of the answers to my questions? Am I even asking the right ones?

All I know so far is that this involves Maeve . . . Maeve, and a fear that hovers near Cate's heart. But what is that fear and what can I do about it from here?

I better go. The more questions I ask that go unanswered, the more confused I become.

Having written down everything she could remember, she took a shower, and started down the stairs, just in time to run into Reena on the landing.

"Going out?" Reena's voice was tight.

Jessie blinked for a second, then opted for the truth. "Yeah. I'm going to see a boy about some drugs."

"Jess . . ."

"I'm messing with you, Mother. I'm going to Del's for some coffee. No offense, but neither you nor Dad can make a decent pot."

"Del's?"

Jessie shook her head. "Ceara mentioned him, remember? The donut shop down the street? You need to get out more. You or Dad want anything while I'm there?"

"When will you be back?"

"Soon. I know there's flooring that needs to come out of three B, and I'll be back to help Dad out with that. I promise."

"Jess . . . about last night . . ."

"Let it go, Mom, really. Just give me the blank slate we came here for, and let's call it a day."

"I'm trying."

"So am I. I'll be right back." Jamming down the stairs, Jessie quickly made her way down Morning Glory Drive and into Del's Donuts.

Del walked over to her and poured her a cup of coffee in a new mug that had the stars and the moon on one side and an oak tree on the other. Her own name was painted down the handle of the mug. "I'm afraid to tell you this, Jessie, but this makes you a regular now."

Jessie stared at the hand-painted mug before looking up at Del. "Where'd you get this?"

"Beats me. Showed up here yesterday. My guess is that Tanner's taken a liking to you." Del walked back behind the counter and pushed a cinnamon roll into the microwave, leaving Jessie to admire the artwork of the mug. By the looks of it, this was not from Tanner. This mug felt more like Ceara.

When the microwave dinged and Del brought the cinnamon roll over, Jessie cleared her throat and asked, "Del, you pretty much know just about everyone in town, don't you?"

"Anyone worth knowing, sure."

"You know a little druggie named Chris?"

Del paused long enough to give away his answer. "Same kid's been hanging out with your little brother?"

Jessie nodded. "Yep."

"He causin' trouble?"

Jessie shook her head. "Not after this morning, he won't be. Where does he hang out?"

"He and the kids like to hang out at the pier—you know, watch the boats come in and see the fish all gutted and cut up for steaks."

"What time do they roll in?"

Del looked at the wall clock. "Near nine. Just about the time you finish your second cup."

Jessie stabbed her cinnamon roll and slid over to the center of the booth so she could watch the town unfold from its sleepiness. Del returned to behind the counter, leaving her to her thoughts. She enjoyed her quiet time in the coffee shop, away from circular saws, jigsaws and paint fumes. Of course, a month ago, if someone had told her she was going to become a regular at a coffee shop, she would have laughed in their faces. But here she was at eight something in the morning, drinking the best coffee in town, eating the best cinnamon roll she had ever had, and waiting to scare the crap out some little boy.

Life was looking up.

"Mind if I give you some advice?"

"Be my guest."

"You and your folks came to town, and the next thing we know, you're hanging out with the two characters who are the most talked about. Now, I've got nothin' against Ceara or Tanner—as a matter of fact, they're both nice as can be, but folks in a small town like this do an awful lot of talking, and they see things one way and one way only. You follow me?"

"Guilt by association."

Del nodded. "Yup. Wish it weren't so, but that's the lay of the land. You can fight it or accept it, but that's life in a small town. So long as you hang out with them, folks are going to talk about it and that talk will eventually reach your folks if it hasn't already."

"Talk is cheap, Del, and so are the opinions of those gossip mongers."

Del grinned. "I had a daughter just like you a while back, and she nearly drove me insane. I'll bet you enjoy making your parents nuts."

Jessie smiled. "I try my best. I just see it as part of my job."

"Well, take it from a man who's been around the block. People's perceptions *are* their reality, no matter how much kids your age like to believe you don't care what anyone thinks, the fact is, some day, you'll realize we all have to care at some time or another."

"I'll take that under advisement. Anything else?"

"Yeah. No matter what anyone tells you, Ceara is not some crazy old lady. She's a quality person, and if she's chosen to befriend you, then you're a lucky gal. Just know that people will talk. But then, people will *always* talk."

"Thanks, Del." Jessie looked out the window and saw three of the boys who had been hanging out with Daniel. "I'll be right back," she said, scooting out of the booth. When she was outside, she called out to the boys to see which one would answer. "Hey Chris!"

A lanky brunet turned around as she jogged up to the group. "You're Danny's sister."

Jessie looked over at the other two boys and jerked her head toward the pier. "I have some business with Chris, so beat it for a sec, will ya?" The two boys took off toward the pier, never even looking back. "Daniel told me about the conversation you two had the other day." Jessie fought to keep the anger from her voice.

"Yeah. So?" Jamming his hands in his pockets, Chris tried for indifference, but was far too affected.

Jessie stepped closer to him so that she towered over him. "I have an instant message for you and your buddies. If you ever go near my little brother again, I'll kick your ass so hard, you'll be a hunchback."

"Wha—?"

Grabbing his sweatshirt so he couldn't run, she pulled him to her face. "Don't screw with me, little *boy*, because I'm crazy. Living and dying are all the same to me, so taking your sorry ass to hell with me is no skin off my nose. And if you think I'm playing around here, then you're dumber than you look. Stay the hell away from my brother."

Chris's eyes bugged, but he managed a nod.

"Repeat what I said, you little creep, so we're very clear what's gonna happen if you mess around with my brother."

"You—you'll kick my ass so hard, I'll be a hunchback."

Jessie released him. "Don't forget it, either, because I'm not bluffing. I'll take you out like that." Jessie snapped her fingers for emphasis. The moment she did, a wave of warm washed over her and she no longer stood near the pier on the Oregon coast, but next to a dock on an ancient island watching a man dressed as a soldier fall to the ground holding his bleeding back. In her hands, she held the bloody dagger that punctured his back, sending him to an early, yet well-deserved grave. Looking across the fallen soldier, she saw Maeve, who had been grabbed by the dying soldier as he struggled to hang onto his life.

"Are you injured?"

Maeve shook her head. Her eyes held no fear—only sadness—a great, great sadness. "Your brother taught you well. Come with me now. We cannot stay here."

"But the fight—"

And suddenly, Jessie was back at the pier, sans dagger, without Maeve, without Roman soldiers. Without . . .

Roman?

Shaking her head, Jessie looked up and saw that Chris had rejoined his friends. "Remember what I said!" she yelled. "Crazy!"

As the boys ran away from her, Jessie walked back to Del's on wobbly legs, feeling as if maybe she'd just spoken the truth.

Suddenly, she wasn't so sure she'd been bluffing at all.

Jessie couldn't finish her coffee or her cinnamon roll. All she could do was sit there and stare at the place she stood when she saw something—no, when she *felt* something from Cate's past. The fight—she could *feel* that memory even now, like the aftertaste of blood after spitting into the bowl at the dentist's office. She could also taste the fear, the incredible fear that he was going to hurt Maeve.

He had wanted to kill her. He would have, too.

But it appeared Cate won that round.

Staring into her now lukewarm coffee, Jessie wondered aloud. "Who were you, Maeve, and why was that soldier after you?" Pushing her cinnamon roll to the edge of the table, Jessie checked her watch. She needed to get back to the inn, but she had to get her wind back. That vision, or whatever it was, had swept the strength from her legs, and she'd practically collapsed when she got back to the booth. Inhaling several deep breaths, she steadied herself. She, or Cate, rather, had *killed* a man. She had stabbed him in the back because she feared he would hurt Maeve—or worse. That fear clung to Jessie now like thistles on her pant legs.

"You gave Chris quite a tongue-lashing."

Glancing up at Del, Jessie shrugged. "I don't care about much, but my little brother means the world to me, and anyone who does anything to try to hurt her, will meet the sharp end of my sword."

The look on Del's face was one of amused confusion. "Her?"

Jessie felt like Del looked. "I meant him, of course."

"Well, I wouldn't want to tick you off, Jessie, especially if you're carrying a sword."

When Del walked away, Jessie stared out the window for a little while longer, wondering what was happening to her. Would she become totally confused about which reality was hers, or was this just a remnant slapping her head to remind her of Cate and what needed to be done? There was only one thing she knew for certain:

It was time to see Ceara.

"See you tomorrow, Del," Jessie said, rising. Five minutes later, she was sitting at the table in the center of Ceara's parlor, replaying what had happened to her when she was out by the pier. When she finished, Ceara patted the hands she'd kept folded up on the table to keep from trembling. "You just sit tight while I go make us some tea. And Jessie?"

"Yes?"

"Try not to be afraid. Nothing can hurt you."

Jessie breathed deeply, leaning back in the large overstuffed chair that matched the one Ceara had just vacated. The parlor looked like something from a movie set. It was far too dark to see much more than directly in front of you; there were incense burners everywhere, most with burning incense in them, and there were bookcases filled with worn leather-bound books. On one of the shelves were crystals, metallic and stone objects, and several worn tarot sets that had "gypsy" written all over it. The only thing missing was a—

"Crystal ball?" Ceara asked, as she returned to her chair. "I discovered a long time ago that people have certain perceptions we must honor if we are ever to truly communicate with each other. When I first opened up, this place was painted light yellow, the window shades were open, and I wore regular clothing. Needless to say, it did not work very well. I made changes based on perceptions, and ever since then, I've managed quite well."

Jessie blushed. "I'm sorry. I didn't really mean—"

Ceara waved her off, as was her manner. "Don't be silly. See? You have the same idea of what you *think* a tarot reader's space should look like. My business quadrupled once I redecorated the room according to what people wanted to see when they walked in here. You can fight some preconceived notions all you want, but there are others that are so ingrained, it's best to just live with them." Ceara rose when the teakettle blew. "But listen to me chattering on. When I return, we'll discuss your vision."

This was now a part of her memory bank, as if Cate had made a deposit Jessie now had to live with. It felt no different than the memory of Jill Britton falling off her bike when they were eight, and cutting her leg open. No different than smoking cigars before the junior prom. Etched into her memory like those she had actually lived, Cate's memories were now every bit as real.

Returning to the table with two steaming cups of cinnamon tea, Ceara set one in front of Jessie. "I figured this would go well with your cinnamon roll."

Jessie's head jerked up. "How did you—"

Ceara chuckled. "Oh, honey, it's nothing as romantic as my powers. I was at Del's this morning and he was making a new batch for his *regular* customers. He likes you." Sitting down, Ceara smiled softly. "But then, you're easy to like."

Jessie shrugged and looked away.

"It would be easier to accept the compliment if you liked yourself. You came here to start fresh, yet you haven't quite forgiven yourself, have you?"

"I royally screwed up, Ceara."

This made her chuckle. "Haven't we all? The key is to learn from it, rub your sore spot for a minute and then let it go. I sense you haven't completed step three."

Jessie sighed. Wasn't that what teen angst was all about? How to get from A to B in the liking your true self game? "If I hadn't messed up so much, Daniel wouldn't be hanging around turds like Chris, and—"

"Did it ever occur to you that *screwing up* is what brought *you* to *Cate?* What if that was the *only* way to get you to Oregon?"

"I hadn't thought of it like that."

"That's what lessons are for: so we can move to the next square in the game, and maybe, just maybe, we can pull a Chance card or get out of jail free."

"I'm just about out of chances."

"Pshaw. Chance is what we make it. Don't you see? You've been chosen for bigger and better things, Jessie Ferguson. Embrace your mistakes. They are what brought you here. Everything in your life is about to change. Don't you find that exciting?" Ceara sipped her tea.

"I imagine I would if my parents could see that change as well."

"Don't you worry. They will. Now then, why don't you tell me about Maeve."

Jessie's face instantly brightened. "Maeve. Cate loves her very much and it goes beyond them just being friends or Druids. She loves her enough to kill a man and feel not a drop of remorse."

"Are you saying they're lovers?"

Jessie nodded. "I think so, but I can't really tell for certain. I don't know anything about the kind of love people had for each other back then. Maybe they just loved better and more deeply than we do today."

Ceara steepled her fingers and rested her elbows on the table. "What does your *soul* tell you they are?"

She didn't have to think or ponder the question. She knew. She just didn't yet trust all she thought she knew. "I'm pretty sure they're lovers."

"Well then, that might explain a lot, don't you think? For Cate to cast herself into the portal two thousand years into the future, there would have to be a damn good reason."

"I think it's to kill that Roman soldier."

"And what makes you think the man was a Roman?"

"I *know* deep within me, deep where Cate lives."

"Excellent. You're learning." Rising, Ceara walked over to one of the jam-packed bookcases and studied them. Running her index across the spines as she walked down the row, she pulled a large tome from the bottom shelf and balanced it on her hip while thumbing through it. "Here it is." Placing the large, dusty book in front of Jessie, Ceara accidentally sloshed some of Jessie's tea. "Did he look like this?"

Jessie stared at the picture. "Yes. That is almost exactly what he was wearing."

Ceara left the book there and returned to her seat. "Cate is reaching you more and more. She must be very strong, indeed."

"Or desperate."

"Perhaps both."

Nodding, Jessie closed the book so she didn't have to look upon the face of the Roman glaring back at her. Just looking at the picture sent a fear to the pit of her stomach she hadn't felt since she was busted for the drugs. Reaching for her tea, Jessie steadied her hand. "Maeve is the key."

"Then it is to these feelings that you must be truly open to hearing. At night, before you sleep, think of Maeve, of those gray eyes, of her demeanor. Focus on Cate's love for and loyalty to her. Open pathways for Cate to continue pouring her memories into. Do this often, my dear, and soon, you will know everything they want. You'll know what it is that brings Cate from her time into this one. Open your mind. Practice doing it when you're painting a room or taking a bath. Be vigilant, Jessie, and Cate will eventually reach you."

Jessie sighed and nodded. "I'm trying."

Ceara grinned. "Jessie, both you and Cate have access to the seam. I think what happened was that she came through it looking for someone, anyone who might feel her. She gave you just enough of a push that you returned to the seam and went through on your own. By going through, you communicated to her you weren't afraid and that you were receptive to her. Your soul was open enough for her to return to it, in *this* time. For whatever reason, you're more open than your soul might have been in seventeen-twelve or eight hundred AD. She tossed herself into the abyss in a desperate search for that piece of her which might, just *might* be open to reception. The only question remaining is: are you going to pull her from that abyss?"

"There's no question about it, Ceara. I'm in this until the bitter end. Maeve needs me, and I have no intention of letting her down. I will do whatever needs to be done."

Ceara studied her a second. "You have a doubt."

Jessie shrugged. "Not really a doubt—just a question. Why Maeve wasn't the one to come through. If she needs me so badly, why didn't *she* come?"

"You're beginning to think like one."

"One what?"

"Druid. Your questions are not as naïve as they were a few days ago."

Jessie reflected back to when Maeve had cautioned Cate about blurting words out. "I'm changing. I'm—different."

Ceara nodded. "Indeed. To answer your question, we have no way of knowing if Maeve has the power to use the portal. Only very powerful Druid priests and priestesses have that kind of power. You must remember that Cate and you share the same soul, not you and Maeve. It was up to Cate to reach you."

Jessie nodded and tried not to look at the book before her. "So, what now?"

Ceara sipped her tea and looked out over the top of the rim. "Well, don't you think it's time for her to know that you're on her side? That you hear her?"

"And how do I do that?"

Ceara set her tea down and smiled softly. "You must go back through the seam with the singular intent of letting her know. You must be stronger and braver than you have ever been. I can help you be both, but once you go across time, you will have to stand on your own two feet. Do you think you're ready for that?"

Jessie nodded. "More than you'll ever know."

The Otherworld.

It was neither heaven nor hell, nor Nirvana, nor Purgatory. It wasn't the Dreamworld, though it often felt like one. It was a special place where Druid priests and priestesses transported themselves in order to gain guidance and wisdom from the inhabitants of that world. To those who had the knowledge and the power, it was an accessible world easily reached, but difficult to truly comprehend. It was not a place for the faint of heart or disbelievers. The Otherworld was a place more real than the very ground they walked upon now, yet that reality was more fluid than the Thames, and just as transforming. It was a special place Lachlan and Maeve were sending Cate to now.

"Do not be frightened," Maeve said as Cate's head bobbed slightly. Leaning closer, Maeve whispered in Cate's ear. "I am *always* with you. I will *always* be by your side." With that, Maeve withdrew and stood next to Lachlan, who lifted a questioning eyebrow.

"I shall never truly understand what it is you see in her, Maeve, to be so frustratingly devoted to her."

Maeve did not take her eyes off the entranced Cate. "Lachlan, have you never met someone and known, with every fiber of your being that your place is with them, no matter where they go or what they do, and in whatever capacity? And that, no matter what happens through the ages, this is how it is supposed to be; how it will *always* be?"

"If I had, Maeve, I most surely would have married her."

Maeve shook her head. "Marriage is merely a legal ceremony, Lachlan, that has little to do with two souls who fit together. My bond with Cate is not a male and female connection that we desire in our society. Ours is a love that spans the centuries, which has no end. I cannot explain, nor would I if I could. But the very first moment I saw her watching me with those wild-girl eyes of hers, I knew she and I had had quite a lengthy sojourn in this world and others. I knew then, but could not act upon any of my feelings until she was old enough to understand who we are to each other; who we always have been and always will be."

"She often tried your patience where that was concerned."

Maeve smiled softly at the memories. "She wanted more than she could have at the time."

Lachlan sighed. "She is still so young."

"We were young, once. I see more in her than you ever will because that is the nature of our relationship. If there is anyone who can save us, it is she."

"There is still so much for her to learn."

"You cannot learn love, Lachlan, and that is one reason your father failed at using the portal. He thought knowledge alone would finally answer the question that haunted him all these years. But love is stronger than knowledge. It is a lesson you must learn if you are ever to lead our people away from the despair that is chasing us. It is Cate's love for me that has helped us succeed where others have failed. She will stop at nothing to ensure my safety; our safety. That love has the power to unlock the doors holding prisoner our answers."

Lachlan looked down at Maeve and shook his head. "You traveled all the way from Gaul because you knew she was here. Have you ever told her that?"

Maeve shook her head. "She believes what everyone else does: that I came here in search of you."

"Why have you not told her? All these years, and you never told her of your vision in Gaul?"

"Deep within, she knows, but I have never told her because I have never wanted her to feel obligated, as if I had given something up in order to come to her. I saw her here, and I came. That is all that matters." Maeve turned to look up at Lachlan. Though they had had this conversation a dozen times, she always got the impression that Lachlan was hoping her feelings for him might change; that somehow, he could overcome ages of love Maeve's and Cate's souls had shared. Even for a Druid priest, Lachlan was still a man—and men, she knew, seldom accepted when a woman chose another woman over them. She wondered if it were still so in Jessie's world.

"That seems a long time ago."

"It was. And now, all of her training and our hard work need come to fruition."

"Well, let us see what happens in the Otherworld. There, she will gather what guidance and wisdom we have not been able to afford her—if she is truly ready."

Maeve knelt down and gently stroked Cate's face. "She's truly ready, aren't you, love?" she whispered. "Seek our answers in the Otherworld, but come back. You belong here and nowhere else."

The Otherworld.

Before Cate knew what was happening to her, she was there. She wasn't sure how, exactly, how she knew, but she did. All those days of training, of learning, of working to this day, and here it was. Maeve and Lachlan had sent her where she had always longed to go.

It was not, however, quite what Cate had expected.

While she was not surprised to be standing within a stone enclosure not unlike that of Stonehenge, she was greatly surprised by the midday sun looming overhead and the mists of a waterfall surrounding water cascading into a calm pool. A fire burned in a fire pit surrounded by level stones for sitting. What surprised Cate was how utterly normal it was. She had expected—

"Mt. Olympus, perhaps?" When a robed figure appeared, Cate turned and bowed. She knew her name to be Blodwin, the Celtic Welsh Maid of Initiation. It was she Cate had prayed to before taking her tests, before learning all the wonders the craft had to offer. Blodwin had come to Cate on many occasions in her Dreamworld, but this was the first time Cate had sought *her* out.

"It is so—regular. I suppose I expected grandeur, yes."

Blodwin nodded and something close to a grin twitched on her lips. "Grandeur has never been our way, Cate. This—" Blodwin stretched her arms wide, her long auburn tresses unmoving as she did so—"is all we ever need."

Cate looked around knowingly. "Indeed. I thank you for allowing me entrance."

"No one allows it. You came because you have the ability to do so. Unfortunately, you come seeking answers I cannot give." Her presence was both peaceful and unsettling. She was, after all, a student of two of the most powerful Druids on the whole of the island. She was prepared for things of this nature, regardless of how unnerving the experience.

"I have not come seeking answers from you. I have come to learn if there is more I can do to help Jessie remember. Surely, you can help me help her."

Blodwin motioned for Cate to sit beside the fire burning brightly at the edge of the forest, before taking her place on a stone next to her. Her energy was powerful, her strength and wisdom tangible. "You believe we can be of assistance."

Cate nodded. "Lachlan and Maeve believe it as well or they would not have sent me." Cate studied the statuesque woman with her aquiline nose and clear blue eyes. She was the embodiment of all Cate ever wanted to be.

"You understand they are using the future to alter the present. They are attempting something only the goddesses should do."

Cate inhaled slowly, breathed out, and then shook her head. "If the goddesses can allow men like Julius Caesar and Suetonius Paulinus to run our people through and violently tear our heritage from our breast, then surely they can give us a chance to save ourselves from certain destruction. Or are they as cruel as the Jewish God, who torments his people in order to test their faith?"

Blodwin grinned. It was not a loving or warm grin, but one of appreciation. "Well-spoken from such a thing of tender years, but insulting the goddesses will not gain you favor."

"Then it is good that I am not searching for favor. I help. It is what I do. It is my purpose here in this time. Oftimes, to be helpful one must *get* help. I shall go where help is offered. If you have none, then I am wasting my time; and time, I am afraid, is not an ally."

Cate started to rise, but Blodwin held out a hand to stop her. "You are as they say, but you do not realize the danger of tampering with time."

"I am always in danger, Blodwin. By my very existence on this planet, I live with death every day. I am trying to save *a way of life* far older than any the Greeks or Romans can even conceive of. The rules of reality, of time, must be twisted to save that which the Romans are bent on destroying. If you cannot or will not aid me in my quest, then I must go elsewhere. But to ask me to fear something I live with daily is a silly request indeed."

Blodwin bristled at this, her erect posture signaling her disapproval.

"The danger you seek to avoid is not directed at you."

Cate shook her head. "Not directly, no. I could live through the Roman onslaught, but I wish to do so with Maeve at my side. I'll stop at nothing to make sure she is."

Blodwin sighed. "Your *anam cara* you carry within you is tangible. It is so strong, you and your Maeve have managed to find each other throughout many, many incarnations. I find it admirable and will not turn you away empty-handed, but you must be aware that time is unforgiving. What you are doing is a dangerous thing for more than just your people."

"I am aware."

"Are you aware that it could destroy your mind? One cannot manipulate their place in time without knowing the extent of the repercussions for doing so. Are you equally aware of those?"

Cate raised an eyebrow. "What do I know not?"

Blodwin reached down and tossed a stick into the flame. "Others before you have attempted to pass from this time to another, many for reasons far better than yours. Many never returned, even more went mad. One's soul is often not strong enough to accept so much new and incredible information, so it closes down completely." Blodwin tossed another stick into the greedy fire. "Be certain of the risks you are willing to take, Cate, and why you are taking them. There is another being across time who deserves that you truly consider the harm you might do her."

Cate sat down. She had never thought about how this was touching Jessie's life. How unfair it was to drag this poor young girl into a time she could not possibly understand.

"I see you had not considered the person who shares your soul."

Cate shook her head. "I had not. I assumed she did not mind since she let me in."

"Are you making assumptions about her letting you in? How much do you know about this one so far in a future you could never imagine? Do you know if she is strong? Is she strong enough, wise enough, sane enough to handle what it means to have *your* memories brought to life within *her*? You've made some very large assumptions, Cate, without ever considering the incredible alteration of her life and what it means to be a quester."

Cate sighed, suddenly very weary. "I hadn't—"

Blodwin eyed her warily. "Perhaps you ought to think more about her as well. Your memories in her life could alter her world forever. You could be entering the mind of someone wholly unprepared for the incredible task you seek to fulfill. Is it fair to do so without telling her all that is involved? Regardless of your intentions, Cate, she ought to know the risks. You can only pursue this course with integrity, or you will find yourself facing a mountain of failure."

Nodding, Cate swallowed hard. She had been so selfish. "She deserves as much, yes."

"Good. As for stopping Paulinus," Blodwin went on, "do you really believe you can stop an entire Roman legion?"

Cate shook her head. "You are assuming that stopping him is my intention."

"Is it not?"

Cate shook her head again. "No, it is not. We are sure that Suetonius Paulinus makes his mark in history somehow. We want to know if we are the ones who pay the price for his fame, and if so, can we save lives and prevent him from completely destroying our way of life? We could kill him, of course, but that would accomplish little. The Romans feel the Druids are a threat to their ability to take over all of Britannia. One evil will be replaced by another; so killing the man might only put us in even greater jeopardy. Our goal is to save lives and our heritage. We wish to preserve our way with as little bloodshed as possible."

"With Paulinus's head on a pike, if it comes to that?"

Cate shrugged. "If it comes to that, but that would only be a temporary solution to the larger issue. The Romans want Britain. They will destroy anyone trying to prevent them from having it."

Blodwin picked up a third twig and snapped it in two. Handing Cate half, Blodwin kept the other. "You are attempting to leap ahead into the person who lives in a time when no one even knows or cares about the recent past, let alone the past of their very own souls. She lives in a time when the one God has taken over many parts of the world, making so many people believe there is but one path for the soul to travel. To reach through to a person with such indoctrination, you must be completely vulnerable to her. You must allow her the opportunity to see you from within yourself. In short, you must pull her deep within you so she can *know*, in the deepest corners of her heart, why she is needed and what the risks are in answering your call. Perhaps only then will you succeed in your quest."

Cate nodded. "And the risks to her? Are they the same as they are for me?"

Blodwin stared into the heart of the fire. "There are those who attempted such as you are attempting, but they did not return. Oft, they became locked, as it were, in the mind and body of the one they sought out. Other times, they became lost in the eternal void of time. Still others simply died because their bodies did not know how to exist without the soul. There are many ways the seam of time can fold up on you, destroying any chance for return. Should that happen to you, your body in this time will be spiritless, and eventually, it will die. And yes, the same risks are involved for Jessie."

Cate inhaled deeply. "Can I keep that from happening?"

Blodwin looked at Cate for a long time before answering. "I cannot say. Just know that it has happened, and it can and will happen again." Blodwin rose and pulled her robe tightly around her. "Being vulnerable, Cate, is the only way to truly understand another being. Open your mind and heart up to her completely, and if she recognizes what she sees, if she knows the truth about what she might be stepping into, then there is a chance you could accomplish your goal."

"And if not?"

Blodwin replaced her hood. "Then anything may happen. Go now. If you return to the portal and do what I have told you to do, you might save the lives you risk so much for. I wish you well."

As Cate rose, Blodwin stopped suddenly and turned around. "Cate?"

"Yes?"

"Be not so careless when next you speak of the goddesses. It is *you* who serve them, and not *they* who serve you."

As Blodwin disappeared into a fog, Cate sighed. If the goddesses cared, then she would be served well. If they did not, and allowed the Romans to succeed, then Cate doubted the goddesses would ever be heard from again.

When Jessie returned home, she found Rick and Reena waiting again for her in the parlor. They did not look pleased.

"What now?" Jessie sighed, sitting across from them on the new sofa they'd purchased a couple of days ago.

"We've had a visit from one of Daniel's new friends' parents. They were very upset, and we can't blame them."

"About what?"

Rick leaned forward, knees on his elbows. "They said you threatened to beat up their son."

Jessie leaned forward in the mirror image of her father. "Did they tell you why?"

"Of course they did." Rick leaned back as if punched. "How could you? He's just a kid, Jess. Doesn't that mean anything to you?"

"Doesn't Daniel mean anything to *you*? That Chris is a troublemaker. I just told him—"

"We know what you told him, Jessie," Reena added. "And now, you've reached a new low. Just when we thought you were sincere about starting fresh, you pull this."

Jessie sat up. "What, exactly, did they say?"

"They said you threatened to beat Chris up if he didn't get you some dope."

"That's a lie!" Jessie was on her feet instantly. "Ask Daniel! That little chickenshit has been pressuring Daniel to try dope and to *find my stash* so he could skim some and sell it. Ask Daniel. He'll tell you the truth. Daniel!" She called.

Reena shook her head sadly. "Your Aunt Sally came to take him to the coast for a couple of days. We—we just can't put him through this again."

Jessie shook her head angrily. "There *is* no *this!* I'm telling the truth!

That Chris kid—"

Rick held up his hand. "Save it and sit down. Your mother and I are tired of being lied to and manipulated by you, but this, this is just about the worst thing you've ever done. Do you have any idea the harm that you could do in a community like this one?"

"Dad, just listen—"

"Sit down!" Rick inhaled deeply and lowered his voice. "I think that's where your mother and I have been making our mistakes with you. We've been listening more than parenting. Well, it's time to parent, and you're not going to like what that means."

Jessie hated psychobabble, but *parent* psychobabble was the worst. "What more can you do to me? You've moved me to the boondocks, where the only kid who could possibly understand me has already been judged by you. You're working me and Daniel to the bone every damn day. What more do you want? What does *parenting* mean this time?"

Rick and Reena stared at each other before Rick slowly turned back to Jessie. "It means fulfilling the rest of the court order from California. You have an appointment with a psychiatrist this afternoon."

Jessie sat down slowly on the couch feeling like she'd been kicked in the stomach. "I thought all that court-ordered crap was over."

Reena shook her head. "It could have been, but after this . . . well . . . we had hoped you might like it here and learn to get along. But it's obvious that two weeks was not long enough. We think—"

"I can't believe this! You're hanging this over my head like a guillotine!"

"We think it's best, Jess, and no matter how mature you believe yourself to be, we're the adults here, and we're making the right decision."

Jessie's heart banged in her chest. "I don't want to see a shrink. I don't *need* to!"

"Honey, you've made it clear you don't like it here, and you won't talk to us about it, so maybe you'll talk to someone else."

Jessie felt dizzy. This was not at all what she had expected when she came home. "Look, this kid—"

"Jess, you need to let that go. Your actions around that little boy are symptomatic of your deeper problems."

"Symp-to-ma-tic?" Jessie slowly shook her head. "You reading Freud or something? Symptomatic of what? Drug use?"

"What we're dealing with now is your anger about moving, and how it's causing you to act out. And if threatening a little boy isn't acting out, we don't know what is."

"Wait. Have you even *met* Chris?"

"No. And we don't need to."

"Honey, you don't even deny threatening him. Don't you see?"

"What I see is that you're taking the word of a little asshole over your own daughter."

She wanted to scream. She wanted to run down the stairs screaming like a madwoman and pulling her hair out. "Look—"

Jessie's words died on her tongue. Suddenly, she realized that everything Del and Ceara had said to her earlier was true. No words could change her parents' opinion about who she was. Their perception was borne of her earlier deceit, her earlier facades and insincerities. Nothing she could say would magically make them trust her. Her mistakes were all they could see. And even though *she* knew that little jerk Chris was lying, her past made that impossible to prove. Suspicious of everything she was and everything she did, they no longer trusted her around the one thing she loved most in the world: Daniel.

If she hadn't wanted to cry so badly, she would have laughed. In trying to protect Daniel, she had driven him away, and returned her parents' well-fed paranoia to its proper place. Could her life get any more ironic?

Taking the slip her mother held out for her, Jessie looked at the two o'clock appointment with Dr. Leslie Uhl. "Fine," she said, stuffing the slip in her pocket. "But you need to call Daniel and ask him what really happened. It's only fair you get the truth from him since you don't want to believe me. He'll tell you what Chris is all about."

Rick's eyes looked even sadder than when she walked in. "We did talk to Daniel, honey."

This rocked her. "And?"

"And he said Chris was okay."

Jessie felt her blood thin. "Did you tell him what Chris said about me?"

"We told you," Reena added, "We're not going to drag your little brother through your mud."

"You didn't ask him about me *at all?*"

"We asked him what he thought of his new friend, Chris, and he told us that Chris was okay."

"Did you even ask him about the whole drug thing?"

Rick shook his head. "It would crush him to know you were still in that sort of life. He believes in you. He believes the promises you made to him."

"How do you know I promised him anything?"

Rick sighed. "Daniel told me a couple of days ago how he thought you were finally better. He told me you'd promised him you were through with drugs."

Reena sniffed back her tears. "How could you, Jess. You know he adores you."

Jessie's spine straightened. "I. Am. Not. In. That. Life. Anymore." Jessie's jaw hurt from gritting her teeth so hard. "I can't believe this." Standing, she paced over to the fireplace. "So, you sent him away without even asking him anything? You just naturally assumed that little doper Chris is an innocent cherub."

"What was there to ask, Jessie? Daniel doesn't seem to think there is anything wrong with that boy. He stood here and told Chris's Dad that he . . ."

Jessie turned on her mother. "You asked him *in front* of the kid's Dad?" Jessie hit her forehead with the heel of her hand. "Are you two nuts? What did you expect him to say in front of the kid's Dad? How about, *Well, gee, Mr. Nimrod, your drug-addled son is pushing dope on me?* Unbelievable." Jessie shook her head. "Absolutely unbelievable."

"That's enough."

Jessie nodded. "It sure is. I'll be in my room." Grabbing the keys from the kitchen, Jessie started up the stairs. "I'll see your shrink at two, but I guaran-damn-tee you, she won't like what she hears."

Jessie ignored her father's pleas to talk to them, choosing, instead, to do the only thing that made any sense to her. At least, on the other side of time, there were people who loved her and cared about her, and *believed* in her. They believed in her so much, they sent her across time to help them. More than ever, Jessie was ready to find a way to let Cate know she would do whatever she could to help her out.

Slipping the key into the numberless door, Jessie took a deep breath before opening it. Whatever was happening somewhere in time was sure as hell better than what she was enduring now. Jessie stepped into the room, closed the door behind her, and entered a world that was becoming more familiar to her with every single day.

When Cate opened her eyes, Lachlan and Maeve were squatting down in front of her, watching her with concern.

"You have returned to us at last," Maeve said softly.

Cate nodded, feeling lightheaded and hungry. She had never been a big eater, but since she started her quest, she discovered that hunger came along shortly after she finished. "I am happy to see you," she said, as Maeve helped her to her feet.

"Well?" Lachlan asked with impatience.

"Hush, Lachlan," Maeve scolded. "Let her return to us completely before you interrogate her."

Cate rose and looked about. It felt as if she were seeing the woods for the first time. It wasn't that they were unfamiliar, as much as they were awe-inspiring. "Jessie is trying," she whispered, realizing that, at this moment, she was not quite alone in her spirit. "She knows about you, Maeve. She knows I have made contact with her. She *knows* she is needed. She *knows*."

"Excellent," Maeve answered, pulling Cate to her in a warm embrace. "I had no doubt you could do it."

"What happened in there, Cate?" Lachlan blurted out at last.

Cate swallowed hard. She had gone from the Otherworld to Jessie's world. Had she intended to do so? She could not remember going to the portal. What had happened after she spoke with Blodwin? "A great many things, Lachlan, but mostly I now know I can do what you are asking me to do, and so can Jessie." Suddenly, Cate's face fell.

"Catie, what is it?"

Cate blinked trying to hold back the tears, but they came anyway. "It's not me. It's Jessie." Cate shook her head sadly. "Like us, Jessie is persecuted at every turn. She tries to be free, but there are chains binding her. She is attempting to throw off these chains to help us, but she is so young, still. She'll need help, but she is telling me she is with us."

"Did you discover this in the Otherworld?"

Maeve tossed Lachlan a look of her own impatience, but Cate lightly touched her arm and shook her head. "No. Jessie was not there. She has come through the portal."

"Do you mean—"

"Yes. She is here with me now, as part of me. Perhaps all of me. I can feel her, and her life's memories—as if I, too, had eaten a—cinnamon roll this morning."

Lachlan and Maeve looked at each other in silence.

"Blodwin visited me in the Otherworld and told me I must allow Jessie to freely see me for who I am, and when I do that, it might embolden her to be stronger and braver in her attempts to contact me. Already, her courage is mounting."

"It must be from Blodwin's help." Lachlan pushed his hood back.

Cate shook her head. "I am afraid Blodwin cares not to assist me, and perhaps I slighted her in a minor digression about the goddesses, but nonetheless, Jessie has already become stronger—without Blodwin's assistance."

Maeve laid her hand on Cate's shoulder. "Is it odd?"

Cate nodded. "To see pictures in your mind that you have never really seen, and trying to make sense of what they all are, well that is *very* strange, indeed. To know that the one I have contacted is so young and not so very wise is also very strange. It might have been easier if she were a priestess of some sort, but she is not. She is just a brave young girl willing to risk her life."

"Risks. I like not the sound of that, Catie. Is there more to what you are saying?"

Cate could feel Lachlan's eyes boring into her, and knew if she told Maeve the truth, she would put an end to her attempts here and now. "Blodwin reminded me of the risks involved, and I do understand them better. Jessie is so far in the future, I cannot conceive of most of what is in her mind. It will be much easier if I allow her access to mine."

Lachlan stared at her. "If Jessie is so far in the future so much so that you cannot understand what you see, she must be much further ahead than we realized. Are you sure she is the one?"

"She is the only one, Lachlan. She is the right choice. I *know* her. I *hear* her."

"What—what does she say?" Maeve whispered.

Cate closed her eyes and listened to her own spirit now embedded with memories of a world she knew nothing about. After several minutes went by, she opened her eyes and grinned. "She wants to know what it is we need from her. She believes she is ready."

"Outstanding!" Lachlan said, rubbing his hands together. "At last. At long last."

Maeve cut her eyes over at him and silenced him immediately. "And what of these *risks* Blodwin shared with you, Catie? What are they?"

Cate did not look at Lachlan when she answered. After all, he *knew*. *They* knew. Clearing her throat, she answered. "Just those we spoke of earlier, Maeve. Blodwin was preparing me for the potential dangers, but she also believes I am strong enough to overcome those risks. If Jessie has slipped through the portal, *now* would be a very good time for me to reach out to her. As one in this body, we cannot communicate. We must go where separate communication is possible."

Nodding, Maeve walked Cate back to the house with Lachlan trailing behind. Once in Maeve's house, she sat Cate down on the bed she had made for herself. "Lay down and relax, Catie. It will be easier for you to reach her in your Dreamworld than on this plane." Maeve picked up a bowl and pestle and ground several herbs up in it. Then she sprinkled the dried herbs on Cate's top lip. "Lay back, breathe deeply, and think of the warmth of the sunlight streaming down upon your face. Inhale softly—slowly—yes, that's it." Lightly stroking Cate's brow with one hand, Maeve held on to the other until she recognized the slight tremors signaling sleep.

Lachlan, who had remained suspiciously silent at the wooden table, rose and paced across the floor. "That did not take long."

"You know how visits to the Otherworld can sap one's strength. She is weary. She has not your training nor my prowess. Can you not see the dark circles around her eyes? This is beginning to take a toll on her. Mind you, Lachlan, and mark my words. Catie shall not come to any harm."

Lachlan sighed. He had to be very careful when speaking with Maeve. She had an uncanny ability to read people. "She knows the risks, Maeve, and is acting accordingly."

Maeve did not take her eyes off Cate. "In her dreams, in the corner of her mind, Catie is about to meet herself from far, far into the future. How does one 'act accordingly' for that?"

"I imagine it must be disconcerting." Lachlan stared out the window, his voice heavy with regret. "It must be—somewhat terrifying."

The tone of his voice made Maeve glance over at him. "She is not your mother, Lachlan, and no matter how gifted you believe her to have been, Catie is a far more powerful Druid than ever your mother was."

Lachlan stiffened. "Speak not of that which you know so little."

"I know enough to know she should never have gone. Malcolm advised her to cease with her obsession, but she could not, she *would* not. She had not the sight Cate has. She was powerful, yes, but not like Cate."

Lachlan's eyes burned as he stepped nearer to Maeve. "Enough." His voice was deep and flat.

"Do not presume to command me, Lachlan. I do not appreciate your tone. Catie is not your mother and I am not your subject. You would do well to remember both."

"I see your fear, Maeve. I know you are not as sure of her as you'd wish me to believe."

"Catie *will* return. Of that, I am sure." Maeve softened her own tone. "I am just sorry your mother was not so fortunate."

Lachlan nodded and sighed loudly. "In all these years, I have yet to know what she went after. I have never known why she went and how it was that she never returned. She just—left us. Sight or no sight, a woman just does not leave her children."

"You treat her memory unkindly, Lachlan. Your mother was a strong and knowledgeable healer, but she should never have entered the Sacred Place alone. She was advised—"

"I *know* what Malcolm told her, Maeve."

"Then perhaps she never went to the Sacred Place at all that night. Did you not tell me her body was never recovered, that not a trace of her was ever found?"

"Nothing." Lachlan sighed heavily again. "Not a single stitch of her clothing. Nothing."

"Then you do not know—"

"I *know*, Maeve, as a Druid priest *would* know. As a *son* would know."

Maeve took Lachlan's hand in hers. "It still hurts, I know."

Lachlan pulled his hand away. "It exists, as she once did, in a place in my heart that will never heal. My only concern now is making sure that Cate does not endure the same fate as my mother." He stared hard into her eyes. "I would spare you what happened to me, Maeve."

As the two of them turned around to look at the sleeping Cate, Maeve nodded. "She will not suffer that fate, Lachlan, nor will I. This time—this time we will succeed."

Jessie wasn't the least bit surprised to find herself roaming through incredibly old forests of—were they oak trees? They were. Yes. Large, handsome, powerful oaks whose trunks were the diameter of picnic tables and whose leaves were the size of dinner plates.

She knew where she was and felt no fear at the thought of being alone in a forest she knew was far, far from home. Ceara had told her fear could be deadly; that fear forced people to make mistakes and see things that didn't exist. Fear had no place in her world right now. As foreign and unfamiliar as all of this was, she could not afford to let fear touch her. She must be brave—willing to go wherever she needed to go to understand what was happening.

As she made her way through the forest, she remembered playing basketball her freshman year, and the coach telling her over and over that fear of your opponent made you hesitate, and all who hesitate are lost. She became a better ballplayer once she learned to listen to herself and not let her opponent dictate what she did. Hesitation, in *this*, wouldn't mean the end of the game, but the end of—

"My people."

Jessie stopped still and looked over at the small figure standing between two enormous oak trees. She was wearing a white robe, a smile, and she carried a contorted staff.

Jessie instantly knew who she was.

"Cate."

The little woman smiled wider as she approached, taking Jessie's hands in her own. They were warm and soft hands, the hands of a healer.

"I am no healer," Cate said softly. "I suppose I could be, but I am a Vate, a seer. It is Maeve who is the healer. She is an incredible healer."

Jessie felt like she knew Cate already, like she was becoming reacquainted with someone who had once been very important to her. It was strange and normal all at the same time. "You knew I'd be here?"

Cate's smile was like the sun. The air around them got brighter and warmer. "I have faith in you."

"I haven't done anything, yet."

"That is where you are wrong, my friend. No one we know of has ever come as far as you and I, and believe me, we have sent many; and those before us sent many as well. You, alone, have enabled me to come across time and revisit the spirit I once was."

"Must be really weird," Jessie said, looking into the light green eyes studying her. She knew so little of Cate, while also knowing so much. The whole thing was weird.

"Weird." Cate tested the word off her tongue like one would a new flavor. "As in strange or odd?"

Jessie laughed. "Yeah. Pretty strange all this, don't you think?"

Cate smiled softly. "Speaking to the one who houses my very spirit is an odd thing, indeed, but *seeing* you, standing here with you is not at all odd. It seems you are an old friend of mine I have not seen in some time."

Jessie nodded. It did feel so real standing here with her. The smell of the grass, the softness of her hands, the warmth of the sun as it touched her face, all felt so real.

"Because it *is* real, Jessie," Cate said, as if knowing Jessie's thoughts. "Come, walk with me. There is much to discuss, yet so little time."

Jessie walked next to Cate, trying to take in every sight, every sound, every smell she possibly could. The scent of the forest was so crisp and clean, and the sounds of crickets far louder than any she had heard at home. She wanted to return with these memories, to remember this place and this time with the woman who came through history for her. "Where, exactly, are we?"

Cate walked out to the middle of the grove where a stone temple stood. She inhaled deeply and began. "You came through the portal this time, and I felt your presence right away. You are wiser than I had thought. You are already making this easier."

"I have help."

This made Cate grin. "I understand that."

"But we're not actually *in* the portal, are we?"

Cate tilted her face up to the sun and closed her eyes. "No, we are not. We are in my Dreamworld."

Jessie stared at her. Not until Cate opened her eyes and smiled, did Jessie say anything. "Dreamworld?"

"Come, sit over here and let me begin at the beginning, and perhaps we can make some sense of this for you."

Jessie nodded, wondering how time was measured in a dream. Would her parents come in to find her near lifeless body in the numberless room, or would mere seconds tick slowly by as she sat in the core of another person's Dreamworld?

Sitting on a square stone next to Cate, Jessie felt the sun at her back. Her own dreams were not nearly as vivid as the one she was sitting in. Why was that, she wondered.

"Some of this you may know already, depending, of course, on how much you remember from our visits together."

"Visits. I like that."

"My people are the Silures, and we live in an area of southwest Britannia. Do you know where that is?"

Jessie nodded. "Britain. But we call it England now."

"England." Again, Cate tried the word on for size. "Well, I live in the sixty-first year, and—"

"Wait." Jessie held her hand up. "You're living in sixty-one AD?"

Cate cocked her head. "I do not know what AD is, but from what I have culled from you, time is measured from the death of Jesus the Christ. If that is true, then yes, we live in the year sixty-one AD."

"Holy crap." Jessie ran her hands through her hair. "You came two *thousand* years into the future to get *me*?"

Cate shook her head. "The portal allows one passage to another time, but whether one goes forward or backward has yet to be controlled. The portal merely opens doors to the time stream. Where one ends up depends on who started the quest. I attempted to go into the future. *Any* future. Once I found you, that door remains ever open."

"Then you weren't looking for me specifically?"

"I had no idea your time was so far into the future." Cate shook her head slowly. "Two thousand years is further than I imagined. It is unbelievable. No wonder your world is so foreign. I recognize nothing of your time, but I *was* searching for *us* in the future."

"Well, you found me. I hope I am not too disappointing."

"Of course not. I was looking for the Silurians, hoping someone had made it through time. I had no idea the portal extended so far into the future."

"Or so far into the past," Jessie added.

Cate reached out and touched Jessie's thigh. "Though I was not looking for you, Jessie, I am certainly very happy it was you I found. You possess the strength of spirit to do the very things we Druids believe in. You have the heart and soul of one, you know?"

Inhaling slowly, Jessie nodded. "Let's hope. So you live in sixty-one AD, which is Latin. *Anno Domini* means in the year of our Lord. Whoa." Jessie shook her head. " I guess I paid more attention in school than I thought."

"Indeed. Do you know what a Druid is?"

Jessie started to nod, then shook her head. "I know it's what *you* are, and I've been meaning to study up on it, but my life back in the twenty-first century is a bitch, and I don't have the time. I'm sorry I don't know more."

Cate nodded. "Druids believe that what you and I are experiencing right now is more than possible. It simply *is*. Soul migration is a vital aspect of my people's beliefs. *We* are who you are trying to save. *You* are one of who we were. You and I have been around a long time as a soul." She paused and bowed her head to hide a slight grin. "It is why we are so wise."

Jessie suppressed a chuckle. "Wise would *not* be a word I would use to describe me."

"Perhaps not at this particular point in your life, but you have a very old, very wise soul. You just have not listened to it. You have only now discovered you have one. Trust me, the wisdom will come. It always does."

"I wish it would get here soon, because I could sure use some."

"It is not coming, Jessie. It is *here*." Cate touched her own temple. "Your world is so fast, it is no wonder you have not the time to stop and listen. But if you did, you would discover aspects of yourself that would astound you. I know not who were we in between my time and yours, but I am confident *we* were someone special."

"What makes you say that?"

Cate leaned over and took Jessie's hand. "You. You are *very* special. There lies within you such greatness if only you would believe."

"I wish I could see it."

"You will. *I* did. I do still."

Jessie looked down at the petite hand holding hers and marveled at how all of this could be. She realized then that she wasn't really holding Cate's hand and that they really weren't two separate beings. Here, they were, of course, but in reality, they were one; one soul, two ages thousands of years apart. It was mind-boggling.

"So here we are, in your Dreamworld as two separate beings. Just how did all of this come about?"

Cate released Jessie's hand and folded both of hers in her lap. "Dreams are where we come to free ourselves from the constraints of life. We come here to see and feel all that we've been and shall become. It is a sacred place that enables those from the past to visit us and impart their wisdom. Has that not ever happened to you?"

Jessie shook her head. "In my world, I mean, in my time, dreams hold no significance except to those society believes to be cuckoo."

"Cuckoo?"

"Insane. Crazy. Mad. People who believe in dreams or visions, that sort of thing are disregarded as looney tunes by the rest of the population. They hold no water anymore."

"How terribly sad. Why would a society choose to deprive its citizens of the wonderful wisdom and peace of the dream world?"

"I don't have a clue."

"Dreams are powerful, Jessie. No matter what the people think in your time, you must *believe* in their power. You must know without any doubt, that this is a special place where souls meet and reflect on the wisdom of the ages. This Dreamworld gives us the means to communicate with each other."

Jessie nodded. "In my time, dreams are nothing. We don't even talk about them."

"Unless you are—looney tooney?"

Jessie laughed. "Looney tunes, yeah. It's hard enough just trying to keep up with real life."

"Your time, Jessie, feels very scary to me."

"It is. It is a very scary place with too many decisions and too many choices, and so few of them are the right ones. It's easy to make mistakes in my time." Jessie looked around and sighed loudly. "I like it here, though. It's very peaceful."

"It is peaceful because I created it this way. Druid magic is powerful magic, Jessie. We are capable of doing a great many fantastic acts with it. Creating our special Dreamworld is just one of those acts." Cate's eyes seemed to change from green to blue.

"Is your real world peaceful like this as well?"

"Not for long. The Romans are going to destroy every Druid they can find. This is the main cause for which I came."

Jessie stared at her. "The Romans, as in Julius Caesar?"

Cate shook her head. "He was killed a hundred years ago."

"I suck at history. Sorry."

Cate managed a small smile. "Well, it is time for you to become good at it, because without your help, thousands of us will be destroyed. Perhaps more."

Jessie ran her hand through her hair once more. "How can I help you from two thousand years away?"

"It will be simpler than you think. We merely need information."

"Information? That's all? You came all this way for some facts?"

Cate nodded. "When Julius Caesar defeated Gaul, he believed in order to destroy and subjugate the people, he need only kill the spirit of his prisoners. That spirit, Jessie, lies within the breast of the Druids. We are the keepers of the way."

"I'm afraid I know absolutely nothing about Caesar or Druids, or anything for that matter. If you came looking for the cavalry, I'm afraid you've ended up with someone riding a donkey."

Lightly touching Jessie's shoulder, Cate continued. "Perhaps you do not know much at the moment, but soon, you shall. Unless—oh my."

"What? Unless what?"

Inhaling deeply, Cate continued. "Our way is of oral tradition. It is largely against our laws to write down our rituals and ceremonies. If the Romans succeed in destroying us, it is quite likely they also erased any evidence as to our existence."

"Could that really happen?"

"More than you know. The victors write history, Jessie, not the vanquished. Ask anyone about the greatest female pharaoh of all time, and you'll see what I mean."

Jessie leaned back, her hands cupped around her knees. "It's just—so sad to think that your people could actually be forgotten, erased from the memory of humankind. And I'm no help at because I'm an idiot from the future who doesn't know a goddamned thing."

Cate leaned closer to Jessie, her red hair falling across one shoulder. "It is not so important what you do *not* know, as it is what you are willing to *learn*. If there is memory of our existence in your time, you may be able to help us save ourselves."

Jessie nodded. "Tell me what I need to do."

Cate fully faced Jessie now. For an instant, she just looked into Jessie's eyes as if probing her. "I am proud that it is you who now carries my soul within you, Jessie. I know it is difficult to see right now, but you carry with you far more wisdom than you could ever imagine. Buried deep within you are visions, dreams, thoughts, experiences of worlds so beautiful, you might someday risk returning to them."

"How?"

"You have the portal, and it allows you to come and go. Someday, if you ever know how to control it, you might even learn how to come and go at will. You could see places that have ceased to exist, visit people who have yet to be born, and learn all there is to learn from the very soul your body houses."

"Whoa. How cool would that be?"

"But you must be careful with this knowledge, Jessie. It is just as easy for an evil soul to step into the portal as it is for a kind soul such as yours. Time is not a power to be harnessed or truly understood. Time is something you can learn from, and respect; it is a tool with endless capabilities. You must not view it as a toy or the Goddess will take it from you."

"Goddess?"

Cate sighed. There was so much Jessie did not understand. "There is not time for me to explain what takes us twenty years to learn, but I *can* tell you that the Goddess chose *you* to slip back and forth along the time stream, and she makes no mistakes. It is an awesome power at your fingertips. Abuse it at your peril."

Jessie nodded. "Understood. I may not know much, Cate, and I might seem pretty damned inadequate right now, but I'm ready to learn. I'm ready to do whatever you need me to do."

Cate inched forward. Her eyes were now a deep emerald and they flickered with intensity. "We need to know *exactly* when the Romans attacked us, and what the final outcome was. What became of the Druids and the clans and tribes we served. Where did we go? How did we get there? What happened *after* they attacked us?"

Jessie studied Cate for a moment. There was that other thing she had seen in her earlier. It was that unspoken thing that hung in the air between them. It was a feeling so deep, so incredibly potent, Jessie recognized it even though she had never experienced it before. "That's not all this is about is it? There's more to this than just the Romans attacking you. This has something to do with Maeve, doesn't it?"

Cate's eyes watered and she quickly looked away. It took a second for her to compose herself before she returned her still-tearful gaze to Jessie. "Do you know what having the sight means?"

Jessie nodded. "Finally, something I *do* know. It means being able to see into the future."

"Close. It means being able to see that which has not yet occurred. I have had a sight—a horrible vision of Maeve being—captured by the Roman guards and—"

"I've seen that!"

Cate went white. "What?"

"I saw that sight. That's how I know Maeve has something to do with it. She was captured and you—well—she was being overtaken by a Roman."

Cate wiped the tears from her eyes. "Lachlan has had the same vision, only in it, Maeve is—tortured by the Romans."

"If we've all seen it, does that mean it happened?"

"Not necessarily. Remember—time is not linear. Just because we see it doesn't mean that it happens or will happen in our time."

"Does she know? Has she had the vision?"

Cate shook her head. "Not that we know of. One's sight usually precludes seeing things about our own lives. That would be too difficult for even the strongest of priestesses. Lachlan and I doubt she has seen this one. If she did, she would get as far away from me as she could in order to protect me, and that has not been the case. This time, it is *our* job to protect *her*."

Jessie nodded. Suddenly, she felt much older than seventeen, and, for once, somewhat wiser. "Your feelings for Maeve are what touch me the deepest, Cate. I know there's nothing you wouldn't do to protect her."

"Nothing," Cate said softly, staring into Jessie's eyes.

Jessie gazed deeply into Cate's emerald eyes and asked a question she hadn't even known she was thinking. "Are you two—lovers?"

Cate cocked her head sideways. "Lovers. That word is too bound up in the physical connection between two people. Maeve and I mean far more to each other than what that singular word can convey."

Jessie tilted her head to match Cate's. "Is that a yes or a no?"

"If you are asking if Maeve and I share our bodies with each other, the answer is yes, but that is such a tiny thing compared to her being my *anam cara*." She waited to see if recognition registered in Jessie's eyes. When it didn't, she continued. "We believe that our *anam cara* always sees our light, our beauty, our very best traits. Our *anam cara* accepts us for who we truly are. The *anam cara* love awakens the fullness and mystery of life. We are joined in an ancient and eternal union that moves across all barriers of time, convention, philosophy and form. In this life, Maeve and I are both women and Druids. That may not be so in the next life, but that does not mean we won't still find each other."

Jessie was silent for a moment before barely uttering, "Wow."

Cate nodded. "It is quite special."

"I'll say. Then I say we keep you guys together at any cost."

Cate rose and wrapped her arms around Jessie. "Thank you so much."

Jessie pulled away and wiped Cate's face. "Cate, I *am* you, and the depth of your feelings for Maeve resounds through every cell in my body. Every day, I feel it more and more. She lives in me as surely as she does in you."

Cate rose. "I am not surprised you are capable of sensing her importance to me and my life. After all, you have residual memories and emotions from me."

"Even time can't overcome love, can it?"

Cate shook her head. "Not in my world, no. Perhaps, not in yours as well. Without Maeve and Lachlan, I would be so alone. When my parents died, they stepped in and helped me learn how to handle being alone in the world. But I wasn't alone for long, because Maeve never left my side. My grief was immeasurable, but she gave me a place to call home." Cate smiled softly. "I'll never be alone as long as she lives. She and I have spent lifetimes together, and, the Goddess willing, will continue to do so."

"You're really lucky."

"Luck is not something we put any faith in, Jessie. The world is full of magic, of alchemy, of transformations the human mind can only marvel at. Lachlan has shown me much about the laws of attraction and the way the world can be. He is a brilliant teacher."

"Tell me about him. Who is this guy?"

"Lachlan is the chief Druid of the Silurians. He is the one who allowed me to join when Maeve requested it of him. He is a very powerful Druid, with many influential friends to the east. He and the Druids of the Iceni have a communication system that keeps us apprised of what is happening in Londinium. We know when boats come and go, and we know that the governor has been building up his troops."

Jessie nodded sadly. "So, Lachlan is your spiritual leader."

"Yes."

"Okay. So far, so good. What I'm wondering is this: if I tell you what the outcome was, won't you change history by *not* doing what history says you did?" Her head starting hurting again.

Cate frowned, her brows nearly touching. "This is where it becomes a bit more difficult to understand from your side. What you read about *has* happened. We cannot change what has already occurred. However, and this is the tricky part, it happened that way *because* of what transpired here."

"I don't follow."

Cate looked around and picked up a stick. With the wave of her other hand, she created a fire at the end of the stick. Jessie sat up and started to say something, but Cate cut her off. "We are in a dream state, Jessie. It is not magic."

"Oh." Jessie felt her face flush.

"See how this is flaming? In the future, if you write about it, you will say that the stick burned to this last knot. Now, if I go into the future and see what you wrote, I can come here and put the fire out when it reaches its last knot."

Jessie nodded, remembering Cate's and Ceara's words. "Time isn't linear."

"No, it is not. The portal has always existed, and people have always been able to slip in and out. The future often happens the way it happens because *we* mean for it to be that way. If I could change what happens in your time, then that would mean time is on a line, and it is not. I cannot change what your time says happened, but I can work around it in mine."

Jessie's head was really beginning to pound. "So if you know what happens during the invasion—"

"We may be able to save many more lives by going where the Romans are not. People will die, lives will be lost just as your history may record. How *many* lives lost is entirely up to the people in my time."

"Okay, I think I get it. We can't change what *has* happened . . . because we may actually *be* the cause of what has happened. Is that right?"

Cate appeared relieved. "Yes. Lachlan wants to save as many lives as he can, and I, well, the Goddess may not be too pleased with me at the moment, but I am trying to prevent Maeve from suffering."

"Absolutely." Rising, Jessie picked up a stick and waved her hand at it but nothing happened, so she tossed it in the fire. "I'll do my best, Cate. You know I will."

"Time is our enemy, Jessie, and I will answer all your questions in time. Suetonius Paulinus, the governor, is mounting his men for an attack, and we fear that he is following along the lines of Caesar, and will attempt, not only to drive us out, but to destroy us entirely. He fears the people of this land, especially our leaders; the Druids."

Jessie inhaled deeply, puffing her chest out and feeling big. "Then let's save as many as we can."

Cate reached out and took Jessie's hand in hers. "Thank you. Thank you so very much, and remember, *you* are not alone. I am with you. Always. If you need answers, you need not always come through the portal for them. I am you. You are I. We are within each other now and always."

"I'll keep that in the front of my mind, Cate. I swear."

"Good. And remember . . . time is of the essence. We have it not to waste."

"Then we won't. You take care of Maeve. I'll do what I can on my end." With that, Jessie turned from Cate, and suddenly found herself back in her own time.

Unfortunately for Jessie, that time consisted of a two-o'clock appointment with a shrink she had no desire to see. Already, Jessie could feel the grains of sand running through the hourglass as she entered Dr. Leslie Uhl's office for the first, and hopefully, the last time.

"Hi, Jessie, have a seat." Dr. Uhl, a tall, fortyish woman with long, straight brown hair out of the seventies, motioned for Jessie to sit in an aging brown leather chair across from her. "Your parents have told me that this is a court-ordered appointment due to an arrest you had around drug use in California."

Jessie shrugged. "Then I guess it is." She hated shrinks. "That bust happened almost a year ago. I did a half a stint at a drug rehab and haven't needed therapy since. I don't need rehab or therapy now."

"Really?" Dr. Uhl asked, writing something down on her pad.

Jessie nodded. "I'm not using drugs, I haven't been in trouble with the cops and I'm finally starting to get my life together. I don't need therapy." Jessie shrugged. "That just about sums it up."

"Well, that's a good place to start. Your parents tell me they're worried about the friends you've chosen for yourself here."

"My parents worry too much."

"Why do you suppose?"

Jessie glanced at the clock. "My parents worry so much, they don't see how I have changed. I've grown up, and to be honest, I think that scares the crap out of them. So they hang on to my past transgressions as a way of hanging on to the little girl who did them." Jessie lay back and folded her arms across her chest. Let Dr. Uhl psychoanalyze *that*.

"Changed in what way?" Dr. Uhl had thin lips beneath a silly putty nose that looked like it was about to slide off her face. Her eyes, a hazelish-brown, were hawk-like in the way they narrowed whenever she asked a question. Like most folks in town, she was underdressed in khaki dockers, a white collared shirt and a blue blazer. J. Jill all the way down to her black Simple loafers.

Jessie thought she would scream. "Do you know who I hang out with? Madam Ceara."

Dr. Uhl gave nothing away. "Oh?"

"Yeah. Look, I'm seventeen, in a new town, in a new state working my ass off in a house the locals call the Money Pit. Ceara reached out to me and I reached back. There are *no drugs*. I don't do drugs, my new friends don't do drugs. There. Are. No. Drugs."

"And you think drugs are the only reason they're worried about you?"

"My parents sent my little brother away because they believed the story of a kid I threatened to kick the shit out of."

"Why did you do that?"

"Because the little prick was hassling Daniel about *drugs*." Jessie leaned forward in her chair. "I let him know what would happen if he did it again. End of story."

"So, what happened?"

"The kid beat me to the punch and told my folks a bunch of bullshit. Hence, they shipped Daniel out of town thinking I was using again when all I was trying to do was protect him. It's so unfair."

"Is fair important to you?"

Jessie rolled her eyes at the tediousness of the question. God, an hour ago, she was in the first century talking to a Druid about saving lives, and now here she sat answering inane questions about fairness.

"The truth is what's important to me, Dr. Uhl, and the fact that no one believes it when it comes out of me."

"Trust has to be earned."

Jessie groaned. "Right. And as long as the dog is on a leash, we trust that it won't run away. That's not trust, is it, Doctor? No, it isn't. Real trust is letting the dog off the leash and knowing it won't bolt in front of a car." Rising, Jessie sighed. "The difference between me and a dog is that, unlike the dog, *I* can take off my own leash."

"What are you doing?"

Jessie turned back to her. "The only important thing here is that *I* know I'm clean. I can't waste my time running around trying to prove my innocence to anyone; not my parents, and not you. A few weeks ago, I would have stayed till the end to humor everyone, but frankly, I have more important things to do than sit here dissecting what's been, up to now, a pretty unremarkable life." On that, Jessie started for the door.

"Why up to now, Jessie? What has happened to make your life more interesting?"

Grabbing the doorknob, Jessie said over her shoulder, "If I told you that, I'd be in padded cell so fast, I wouldn't have time to unhook this leash." With that, Jessie walked out of the building.

Madam Ceara had just finished with a customer when Jessie burst through the door all out of breath. She was talking so fast, Ceara had to stop her several times and ask her to slow down.

Inhaling deeply, Jessie started over. "I met Cate."

Ceara headed for the kitchen with Jessie close on her heels. "Where?"

"In her dreams. Her Dreamworld. She felt my presence when I went through so she induced sleep or something so we could meet. Why didn't you tell me we could do that?"

Ceara turned on the faucet and watched as the water entered her teakettle. "*We* can't. *She* apparently can. She is very good, my dear, to be able to make something of that magnitude happen. She knows the craft well." Setting the kettle on the stove, Ceara turned up the flame.

"Go on."

Jessie told her all about their conversation, and Ceara stopped her only a few times for clarification. When Jessie began describing Lachlan, Ceara's eyes grew wide and she held her hands up. "Are you certain she said *Lachlan?*"

Jessie nodded. "Are you okay? You don't look so hot."

Ceara nodded slowly and motioned for Jessie to continue, the color completely gone from her cheeks. "I'm—fine. Please—continue."

"Cate saw what horrific thing might happen to Maeve and the others, so she and Lachlan decided Cate would go through, although I don't know why he made her go and not himself. Cate made it sound like he was the bomb."

"They need him to lead the people. If the Romans are going to attack, they need their chief Druid to assemble everyone together and devise a plan."

Jessie watched the flame lick the bottom on the teakettle. "Anyway, my job is to find out as much as I can about Druids and Romans, England and all that history I never paid much attention to. If they have a general idea of what happened—"

"They can work around that, yes. It's a brilliant notion, really." Ceara nodded as she watched the steam rise from the mouth of the teapot. "Fortunately, my dear, you have friends who are well-connected. I have studied a bit about the Celts and their society, and I should be a great deal of help to you. Add my Internet connection on the boat, and we will provide you with more than enough reading material." Ceara checked her watch when the kettle blew. "I do have several appointments this afternoon. Can you meet me at my boat tonight around eight?"

"You bet."

Ceara smiled and patted Jessie's hand. "Don't panic my dear, or go off half-cocked. There's a method to compiling the evidence we need to help. At least now you know what is required of you. Now, we have a direction in which to travel."

Jessie couldn't stop thinking about her conversation with Cate. "It's as weird as it is incredible."

"What is? Soul travel?"

"That, too, but I was thinking about *them*. Cate's so connected to her. It makes me feel—"

Ceara leaned closer to Jessie and looked intently at her. "Are you telling me you can *feel* Cate's feelings for this Maeve?"

Nodding, Jessie was surprised by her own answer. "Yeah, I think I do."

"Oh—my. That must be something then."

"Is it a problem?"

Ceara stared out the window and sighed loudly. "Love should never be a problem, dear girl, but what you're feeling between them goes far beyond our meager definition of love."

Jessie barely nodded and felt as if she were hardly there at all. Deep inside her, she experienced that life-giving kind of love they held for each other. She felt it as if *she* had someone in this time that she loved with just as much intensity and power. It was real, it was potent, and it filled Jessie with an unexpected joy.

Ceara cupped Jessie's chin in the palm of her hand. "What you're feeling is *your* soul mate."

"*My*—soul mate? You mean—Maeve?"

Ceara nodded. "Yes. Has it not occurred to you yet that she or he is out there now?"

Jessie had to sit down for this one. "I never—I never thought of it. I mean, for the last couple of years, I felt like I was missing something—like there was a puzzle out there with a missing piece and I was it."

"And now?"

Inhaling deeply, Jessie said very softly, "Now, I don't feel that way at all. Ever since I went through I've felt more at peace, more whole than I ever have. Is that—"

"Because of Maeve? It very well could be. It could also be because you are finally on the right path. When we are where we're supposed to be, life just becomes so much easier."

"Well, all this history and time travel isn't really easy, Ceara. It's damn scary and super confusing."

"And yet?"

Jessie looked up at her and grinned. "I wouldn't trade it for the world."

Ceara nodded and pulled out two mugs. "Good for you."

"You know, as weird as it is to find myself constantly thinking about Maeve, there's something about Cate that's irresistibly adorable. She is just filled with goodness."

"And love?"

"Oh yes."

"If you can *feel* Cate's emotions for Maeve, then she is a far stronger priestess than I ever thought existed."

"Then you think we can do this? Can we really help them?"

Nodding, Ceara poured the steaming water into two small teacups. "Can, my dear, and will."

"And then, she just disappeared, as one would expect one to leave a dream."

Maeve brushed a stray hair from Cate's face. "You have done well. I am so proud of you."

Cate started to smile, but was prevented by a huge yawn and stretch. "It was so very weird."

Maeve tilted her face. "Weird?" She said it as if it were a foreign word.

Cate yawned again and nodded. "Yes. Strange. Odd. To stand there and speak to the person who will have your soul in two thousand years defies logic. It is . . . an odd experience mere words just can't convey."

Lachlan rose and strode over to the door. He stood there staring at Cate for a moment before speaking. "I, too, am proud of you, Cate. You have done well on your quest."

"It is easier since Jessie is also a quester."

This caught Lachlan by surprise. "A quester? Are you certain?"

"As certain as I can be about anything in the twenty-first century, yes. She has my soul, after all; the soul of a quester cannot stay silent long, Lachlan."

"What does she know of us?"

Cate shook her head. "As to history, she knows virtually nothing, but she is willing to learn—to find out."

Lachlan nodded. "Excellent. I must go. The Chieftain needs to see me this morning. I will see you both in the grove this eve."

Cate watched Lachlan leave, wondering if he had ever experienced any joy in his life. She could not remember the last time she saw him laugh.

"How do you feel?" Maeve asked, helping Cate off the bed.

"Fine." Cate straightened her robe when she stood. "Do you know the strangest thing? I was thinking about your question the other day; the one about Jessie. I like her. I truly do like her."

"Of course you do. Why do you think so many of us like *you*?" Maeve stroked Cate's cheek with the back of her hand. "She is not so very different from you, is she?"

"She is young, but willful. I was clear with her about what to do and she understands our need and the urgency of our request. Without complications, I believe Jessie will do what must be done."

Just then, the door swung open and Lachlan rushed back in. "Governor Paulinus's men are on the move and marching this way. It is said they are leaving Londinium in the morning and will be coming south."

Maeve quickly moved to his side. "What must we do?"

"Pack only what you can carry, hide anything that would show you are a Druid, and spread word we will be meeting in the grove within the hour to discuss what the Chieftain wants to do."

"So. It has begun."

Cate joined them at the door. "How long do we have?"

Lachlan rubbed his face. "Days. Perhaps less than a week. Not long. Paulinus has set his sights on bringing the island to its knees." Lachlan looked down at Cate. "Let us hope she moves quickly, else we may be the last of our people."

"How could you?"

Jessie locked eyes with her mother, but refused to respond.

"Dr. Uhl said you were combative and rude. Rude, Jess. You just can't seem to get out of your own way, can you?"

"Is that a rhetorical question?"

"Don't get fresh mouth with me, young lady. I've had enough of your antics. If we didn't feel that sending you back to San Francisco was a reward instead of a punishment, you'd be packing your bags right now."

"But we don't want to foist our problem on someone else," Rick added, entering the parlor. He sat next to Reena and held her hand.

"Is that what I've been reduced to? A problem?" Leaning back, Jessie swallowed the anger rising in her throat.

"Don't act the victim here. You left your appointment early, you were disrespectful, and now, you have earned a restriction."

Jessie shot forward. "Are you kidding me? I'm seventeen. Who puts a seventeen-year-old on restriction?"

"Maybe if you started acting more mature and less rebellious, we wouldn't have to."

"Look, Jess, we have a lot of work to get done here. Every day that goes by without guests is a day we get deeper and deeper in debt. We can't afford to be chasing after you and worrying that your— activities—are casting a gray cloud over the inn."

"And you think putting me in lockdown is the answer?" Jessie crossed her arms and shook her head sadly. "Then bring Daniel home. It's not fair that you've sent him to the hinterlands because of your dark and, if I might add, erroneous suspicions about me. I'll stay home, but I want him to come home."

Rick chuffed and shook his head. "This is not a negotiation, Jessie. Daniel will come home when we feel it is best."

Jessie rose. "Fine. Anything else?"

"Yes. Finish painting room five. Your mother and I have some errands to run and I want it to be done by the time we get back."

When Rick and Reena finally drove down Morning Glory, Jessie was already ten minutes late to meet Ceara at her boat. Time was already taking on a new meaning now that she had a destiny to fulfill.

Destiny.

What an interesting word, she thought. People her age didn't usually think about destiny or purpose. We just go through life expecting tomorrow to be there like a gift waiting to be unwrapped. With little planning or preparation until our senior year, and then *BLAM*, everyone expects us to know what we want to be for the rest of our lives. Even then, most people still don't really *know* what their purpose is. What's worse, they don't even care until it's too late, and then they're stuck doing something they never saw themselves doing when they were younger.

But *she* cared. She cared very much. The more time passed, the deeper her feelings were for a woman she would never meet. And those emotions were becoming stranger now, because they were no longer Cate's emotions, nor were the visions Cate's alone. They were her own now, borne of an ancient spirit that had raised its head and whispered to her to remember the ancient ways.

And to remember her love.

How perfectly natural it felt that it was the love of another woman that touched her so deeply. She'd never been attracted to girls, herself, but she'd had a lesbian friend her sophomore year who was one of the coolest kids she'd ever met. Unlike Jessie, the girl didn't do drugs, so their friendship was short-lived. Still, she had always wondered what it would feel like to love a girl. It was something she and Wendy had talked about one super-stoned moment.

Jessie had tried her best to love guys, to plug that void she'd felt her whole life, but love in high school was a pseudonym for sex, and she'd had her fill of that. After the first six guys, she had wondered what all the fuss was about. It was no big deal, and in the end, she decided it was more of a hassle than it was worth.

But now . . . now that she could *feel* what love truly felt like, she could understand how sex with someone she really loved might be more meaningful. That kind of love was eternal and binding, and yes—void-filling. It had already managed to soothe that hollow feeling that had been such an intrinsic part of her being. Jessie heard, and she was remembering. It wasn't a coincidence her parents had dragged her to Oregon and the Money Pit. It was her destiny, and it was now her *job*, her *responsibility* to keep Maeve from harm and to protect a way of life.

Jessie thought back to when she saw Cate stab that soldier in the back. When had that happened? Was that before Cate and Lachlan's vision, or after?

Desperate to know more, Jessie had waited for her parents to leave and immediately ran down the backstairs and into the night. "Restriction, my ass," she muttered, careful to avoid the motion-sensor lights on the porch. Destiny would not be slowed down by parental restrictions. The clock was ticking.

Five minutes later, Jessie stood on the deck of the boat, out of breath from running the entire way.

"Come in, come in, my dear," Ceara said from her cabin below.

Jessie ducked as she entered the cabin and was surprised to find several large books strewn about the table, and a laptop plugged in on the counter.

"There is a great deal for you to know before you go back there, Jessie."

Jessie nodded. "I know. I don't think I have ever felt this stupid. Why didn't I ever pay attention?"

Ceara batted the question away. "Believe me when I say this, Jessie Ferguson. What you were, you shall *never* be again. Who you are *now*, and who you are *going* to be, was never fully your own decision. Trust that you have already begun to change. You must learn to understand these changes. Without understanding, you will be lost."

Jessie nodded. "I have been lost, Ceara. Here—now, is the first time I've felt—found."

"Good. Your eagerness to complete your quest will make the learning easier. Come. Sit."

Jessie sat at the table and stared down at the open book. It was an encyclopedia of ancient religions, and it smelled as old as God, himself.

"First, you must remember what *they* are, because what *they* believe is vital to your understanding of what it is they need to know. Without knowing them, you can only guess at how to help them."

Jessie shook her head. "I don't understand. Why can't I just open a history book and see what happened and then tell them that?"

Ceara sat across from Jessie and as she pulled the encyclopedia to her a Celtic cross fell from the folds of her silk scarves and swayed about an inch above the table like a pendulum. Jessie didn't remember ever seeing it before. "You cannot read a single history book and then run to tell them what happened."

"Why not?"

"First off, there is always more than one account of a historical incident. Actually, there are always several different accounts of any one single event."

Jessie frowned, thinking back to a time when she and Wendy had seen a man run out of a mini-mart. He had just robbed the store, they both saw him, and yet, their "eyewitness" accounts of his appearance were vastly different.

"Many historians claim there were six million Jews killed during the Holocaust in Europe, while other historians dispute that by saying there were not even six million Jews in the whole of Europe. If you only read the latter account, you would be accepting a revisionist's point of view. To get the facts, you will have to research, and research well. You will have to consider the subjectivity of the author, how much research he or she did, etcetera, etcetera."

Jessie sighed. "I hadn't thought of that. I guess I would have just gone forward and maybe even given them incorrect information."

Ceara nodded. "Without knowing precisely what they are up against, you could inadvertently send them all prematurely to their graves. Life, my dear, isn't just good and evil. It is layered and textured, and if you do not understand each layer, you cannot make the right decision as to what to tell them."

Jessie nodded slowly. She was just now beginning to see the scope of her involvement.

"So, we shall start at the beginning with a crash course in Druids and Druidry. Ask any questions you may have, but pay close attention."

"Can't I just tap into Cate for all of this?"

"Normally, you might be able to, if you were experienced at astral projection or other phenomena, but after two thousand years, think about how many other lives your soul has lived. It would be like going into a haystack and expecting to retrieve hay straws that were cut in August of nineteen sixty-one. It cannot reasonably be done, especially by an untrained individual. You must re-learn what your soul knows . . . in essence, you must remember, and in remembering, you will find yourself wondering, *how do I know this?*"

Jessie nodded. "Soul memory."

Ceara nodded. "Yes. When one wonders why they are afraid of bridges, you will know it is because of something the soul remembers but can't quite bring to light. So, we suffer with our phobias, our neuroses, even our love of things, and yet, we do not know why they exist for us."

"How sad. No wonder Cate thinks we, in our time, are so disconnected from ourselves. We are."

Ceara rose and opened the small window above the sink. "Once the Romans embraced Christianity, and it spread, it all but destroyed other ways of thought in the western world. As you will see, when the one God replaced the many, the world never recovered. Religions were forced to go underground, to hide, to live in fear of being tortured into false confessions and equally false conversions. As you'll see, the Romans accomplished a great deal on their move toward world domination."

"What finally brought them down?"

Ceara chuckled beneath her breath. "Barbarians, if you can believe it. Barbarians and Romans themselves brought down the great Roman power. But that's another tale. Right now, you must understand who you were, what motivated you to become a Druid and to find yourself in the future."

"But I *know* what motivated me. Maeve."

Ceara cocked her head in question for a mere second, before a slight smile pushed her lips up. "Yes. You *anam cara*, for whom we would do anything. There is but one connection that neither man nor time can sever, and that is when two souls commit to each other for all of time. If, of all the soul memories you remember, Cate's feelings about Maeve come through the strongest, then it is clear that saving Maeve is why she came through."

Jessie nodded and rose. Pacing across the small cabin, she jammed her hands in her pockets. "Okay, about this soul mate thing. It's clear they're lovers and all—but I'm not gay."

Ceara shrugged. "The soul is genderless, my dear. In this life, Maeve could be your brother, a friend you haven't met, one of your parents, or anyone you have already come across but were too young to understand what you were feeling."

"Oh—I get it. So a soul mate doesn't have anything to do with sex?"

Ceara shook her head. "Absolutely nothing. In Cate's life, Maeve is her soul mate. They took that love to a physical plane which may or may not happen in your own life. Who knows what you both were in the life after that or the ones before it."

"You mean, like, we could have been pilgrims or pirates or something?"

"Yes. You could have been lovers, friends, siblings, or, you may never have connected in the life after that one. You may have missed each other in certain ages."

Jessie shook her head. "No way. Maeve would have found me."

Ceara cocked her head and stared at Jessie. "Oh?"

She did not know how to explain it. She had not been able to put words to it, but ever since she knew Maeve existed, her life was brighter, somehow, more full of light. She was no longer empty and seeking, but content and not alone. And wasn't that silly, since Maeve had been gone for nearly two thousand years?

"My dear, do not hope to understand that which needs no explanation. Go to the bookstore in Eugene, and you will find shelf after shelf of books about finding your soul mate. We are born and we live with two shadows following us; one is the ever-present specter of death, and the other is the shadow of our soul mate, without whom we are not as fulfilled as when they are within us. Maeve is within you because of Cate's eternal bond with her."

Jessie sighed and sat down hard in the chair. To be understood was better than any drug she had ever had. "That's exactly what it is, Ceara. It's like I finally found what I've been looking for—but—I haven't. Not really. At least, not here in my own time."

Ceara patted Jessie's hand. "Does it matter so that the soul you seek is not here with you right now, when you have access to her in your past?"

Jessie's eyes brightened. "Not really."

"You are young yet, my dear. You have plenty of time to find her or him again. Just know she could be in any form. She could be a child playing in the park. She could be the man who sells newspapers. She could be a professor, a homeless person, or someone you pass on the street. That is one reason why the Druids believed everyone should be treated with respect, because you never knew whose soul resided in the being you were speaking with."

"Wow."

Ceara nodded. "The world would be a nicer place if we all thought that, eh?"

Jessie nodded, and suddenly her chest was warm and full as she realized that she loved this old woman sitting across from her, this woman, whom her parents had judged and deemed somehow unfit; a woman whom the town made fun of, whom the world had forgotten. She reached out to Jessie when Jessie didn't know how to reach.

"I'm ready, Ceara. Teach me what I need to know."

Ceara nodded and pulled out a second large tome. She opened up the old book, which crackled from age and disuse to a picture of a Druid. The robe, staff and bonfire in the background brought a feeling of knowing to Jessie. "It took up to twenty years to become a Druid. I am going to give you twenty minutes worth of those twenty years. The rest, you'll have to get on your own."

"But wait. Cate's not that old. I mean, she'd have had to start her training when she was like, four or five."

"She has obviously shown exceptional abilities. Lachlan and Maeve must be good teachers." Ceara took quick sip of water and continued. "Druids are not the people your generation have transformed into role-playing pieces. They were not wizards or soothsayers, magicians or dragon-slayers. In Celtic society, they were the intellectual class, the philosophers, historians, doctors, judges, teachers, seers, astronomers and mathematicians. They gathered deep in the woods to learn, to share and to tell stories. It is believed they were capable of divination and prophesy, healing, levitation and shape-shifting into animals."

"Shape-shifting? Like metamorphosis?"

"A little. They were brilliant men and women who memorized nearly thirty thousand verses. They were the best of the best, and after Caesar and others tried to destroy them, they went deeper into the woods. They sought security and comfort in the oak groves they so loved. The word itself, *Dru-wyd,* supposedly combines two words that mean oak knowledge or oak wisdom."

"What do you mean supposedly? How can we not know any of this for sure?"

Ceara shook her head sadly. "The Druid way was an oral tradition, so very little was ever recorded. In many areas, the act of writing down the rituals was illegal. Then, the Catholics came along and converted the islands of Britain and Ireland, destroying hundreds if not thousands of ancient texts that had been written down when the Druids saw their end was near. Saint Patrick himself is recorded as having burned over one hundred and eighty Druid texts in an attempt to convert Ireland to Christianity.

"The Druids, who roamed what is now known as the United Kingdom and parts of France, left us very little information about themselves, so what we do know of them is an incredibly Roman-biased point of view. What we *do* have recorded—and remember, that does not mean that it is the gospel truth—is that the Druids were persecuted by the Romans, the Norse, the Normans and the Saxons. And once Christianity made its bid to be number one, the Celtic religions were nearly wiped out. Pockets here and there managed to survive, and even make a comeback, but for a thousand years, their ways were practically lost."

Jessie felt an incredible sadness in her chest. "Then it doesn't really matter what Cate does because eventually, they lose."

Ceara shook her head and frowned. "Again, my dear, I caution you against swallowing all the information historians feed us. Do you not think that Japan's history books tell a much different tale about the dropping of the bomb on Hiroshima? Do you not think that some Germans have a different side to the telling of the war? History is a man-made convention with plenty of flaws and inconsistencies. You are in the singular position to actually see it for yourself."

Jessie shuddered. "I don't know if I want to if all it is is one destruction after another."

Ceara patted Jessie's hand. "I've painted a bleak picture, and I apologize. Certainly, there are wondrous things from history that have been recorded, it's just, we aren't discussing the good things that happened to the Druids, because that would not help."

"True."

"The Celts were a strong and brave people who believed that your soul lives on, and since they truly believed this, they fought with a ferocity that scared even the well-trained Roman soldiers. Would you ever go to war against someone who had nothing to lose? Would you battle someone who did not fear death?"

"No way."

"Exactly. The Celtic warriors were unafraid of death because they knew they would see each other again in another life."

"Scary if you were an opponent."

"Very. Julius Caesar felt that, without the Druids, the Celtic people would not be as strong, and so, if you cut the head from the beast, you could then conquer the beast itself."

"And did he?"

"Not quite, but certainly not for lack of trying. He managed to deal some very heavy blows, but after Gaul, he—well, let's just say he had other things on his mind."

"What happened in Gaul?"

"Around sixty BC, Caesar went to Gaul, which is France now. There, he served as governor and was a brilliant general of over fifty-thousand loyal men. Caesar directed his army in conquering the rest of Gaul, which consisted of the remainder of current France and Belgium and parts of Germany, Holland and Switzerland. He nearly wiped out all Druids in Gaul." Ceara sipped her water and continued. "The problem for the Celts in England was they were not unified. The separated tribes and clans made it easier for the Romans to conquer. In fifty-five BC, after only two summers of fighting, Caesar went back to Rome, but he still managed to gain a toehold in England. Still, it was enough to start a turn of events that leads us right to sixty-one AD, where Cate and Maeve face a tenuous and not-so-pretty outcome."

Jessie was on the edge of her seat. Finally, she would find out just what had happened to those Cate and Maeve were set on protecting.

As if sensing Jessie's excitement, Ceara held up her hand. "Oh, no my dear, not quite yet. First, you must gather as much information as you can about the Roman occupation of England in the first century. Then, you'll need information on the Druids on the Isle of Mona, and then—"

"But there isn't time."

Ceara shook her head. "There isn't time to make a mistake, either, Jessie. Whatever information you gather will be used to move as many of their people as they can out of harm's way. If you have incorrect information or biased sources, you could send them right into the line of fire." Ceara softened her voice as she reached out to touch Jessie's hand. "Youth is impetuous. It rushes headlong into the fray before assessing the dangers. They cannot afford for you to act rashly. I understand you want to make a difference, and you will, but only if you act wisely and not like a naïf."

"Okay, okay, I get it. Slow down."

Ceara visibly relaxed. Reaching across Jessie, she touched the mouse pad and clicked on her browser. "Now, would I be assuming too much if I thought you knew how to use the Internet?"

"I'm a teenager, Ceara. We *live* on the Internet."

"Good. You will need to narrow down the specific information we need. Of course, you are welcome to come aboard anytime in order to use the laptop. I keep it locked in here, and the key is in the butter dish in the refrigerator. There are chat rooms listed in my favorites section, but don't spend too much time there. We need accurate information, not people's opinions."

"Got it."

"And don't forget to take notes. When you go home, read everything you've written and memorize as much information as your brain can contain. You'll need to recall as much of it as possible later, when you go back. Whatever skills you acquired in our disappointing school system will need to be at their peak."

Jessie nodded, and then she saw the clock on the desktop. It was getting late, and she wasn't even supposed to be out. "I'll give it my best."

Ceara put her fingers to Jessie's lips. "Remember, it matters not what you once were or what you once knew. Cate believes in you, so it is now time for you to believe in yourself."

Nodding, Jessie realized that she did, indeed, *feel* differently since the last slip through; differently enough to actually walk out of a shrink's office in the middle of the session. While not a real smart thing to do considering her parents' reaction, it had somehow marked a change in how she saw herself. This was her chance to turn her whole world around—to experience something few people believed in and even fewer had tasted. She wasn't about to let her parents' misperceptions of her keep her from her destiny. Not anymore.

"I'm getting there," Jessie said, as Ceara clicked open her mailbox. Jessie grinned when she saw Ceara's address. It was Cearaseesall@seesall.com.

Ceara typed in her password and then opened a letter from someone from the University of Oregon. "I took the liberty of writing to a professor friend of mine at the U of O. He's in the history department and has written two textbooks about Roman history. He's done much of the research we need."

"I don't know what to say, Ceara. You've been working really hard at this."

"We all have our reasons, don't we?" She pushed her glasses up the bridge of her nose. "He tells me he has a friend in London who is an authority on the Romano-British age, and he has another friend in Rome who wrote a book on the Roman governors of Roman provinces and that we ought to be able to get something from both of them quite soon." Ceara turned and held Jessie's chin. "Now, here's what you need to find out first. You must make sure their village is called Fennel, and if it is in the area we call Wales. The name of the people once inhabiting that area was the Silures. If you can get the true date on your next visit, that is even better. The more information you can get from Cate, the better. Ask for specifics."

"I'll go back tonight."

"Look for things that will help you remember. It will be much better if you can pinpoint their exact location and date, otherwise, we could give them information that isn't what they need."

"Maybe it's still called Fennel?"

Ceara shook her head. "Already checked. There is no Fennel. Like so many villages and towns of the time, the name was probably Latinized after the Romans came."

Nodding, Jessie glanced over at the clock one more time. "Okay, but I really have to get moving. If my parents know I skipped out on them, who knows what they'll do?"

The villagers met in the deepest part of the groves, *No Man's Land* to the villagers and *Haunted Forest* to outsiders. They came carrying little save their ceremonial devices such as herbs, cauldrons, swords and staffs. They left behind everything of world value in homes that were, as they spoke, being set afire so as to conceal any possible evidence of who had lived there.

All told, there were fifty-eight Druids from Fennel and the two surrounding villages of Gaston and Maubrey. They had come seeking refuge and advice; for the Romans had moved from the north where they had already killed, tortured and run off many of the northern Druids. The last message Lachlan had received from his Chieftain was that the Romans were headed toward the people of the rock. They were safe for the time being, but Lachlan did not know for how long.

Stepping into the circle, Lachlan pulled his hood down and addressed the waiting group. "The time is upon us, my friends, when we must choose to fight or flee. Our warriors are gathered together to prepare for the battle Rome is forcing on us. But we cannot rely solely on swords to protect us from the enemy. It is not the warriors Paulinus seeks to destroy, but us. Another warrior can replace a warrior, but we cannot be so easily replaced. We must continue on—our people rely on us to protect them from these invaders, and we cannot do so if we cease to exist. So—the question all of you are thinking is *do we fight?* Do we fight with our warriors or do we flee so we can lead from afar once the dust has settled and we can try to rebuild our world? Do we take better care of our people by remaining alive and saving our secrets for another day when we rise again to the seat of power, or do we use those very secrets in an attempt to destroy an enemy that, like a lizard that grows its tail back, appears to be invulnerable?" Lachlan waited while the group murmured among themselves. Maeve took Cate's hand and held it firmly in her own. Cate could not look at her friend for fear Maeve would see how utterly afraid she was.

Lachlan held up his hand for silence. "The Druids who were able to escape Caesar in Gaul knew the true treachery of the Roman people. Though they have called us barbarians, we are not the ones raping women and killing children. We are not the ones invading their lands and taking over their farms and villages. While we honor all life, they destroy it to suit their greed, they desire to create a world where Rome is the center and we are nothing but support."

The crowd murmured again. They did not know that this very speech was being replicated in the mountains where the Chieftain addressed his men in preparation for the coming battles to be fought.

Again, Lachlan waited for silence before continuing. "There are other even more powerful people, the people of the Iceni and the Ordovices who can aid us should we choose to fight rather than flee. But whatever route we take, we must take it together. To faction off as our tribes have historically done will surely mean the death of us all. We cannot remain divided and hope to win."

"What of Cate McEwen?" one asked from the crowd. "Has she not been successful?"

Lachlan slowly nodded. "Indeed, more so than we could have hoped. We are so very close to having answers, but the Romans are very close as well. That is why we must make a decision so that we may be prepared in the event that Cate's information is received too late."

"What shall you have us do, then?"

Lachlan addressed the speaker. "I ask that we spend this eve discussing our limited options. In the morning, we shall return to the fire to see what message I will take to the Chieftain. Speak your mind this evening, question each other, and search your hearts for what you truly believe would be best for all of us."

"What say you, Maeve?"

"Yeah. What does Maeve think we should do?"

Everyone stopped and turned to Maeve. Since her arrival from Gaul, the Silures regarded her as far more powerful than most Druids. She had been able to rise to her power in a country that had been crushed by Caesar, and already, there were legends and stories of her, some exaggerated, some not, and all looked upon her as a strong, guiding force. Her word meant everything.

Inhaling slowly, Maeve released Cate's hand. "I believe in Catie and the work she has accomplished thus far. She needs a little more time; time we may not have, in order to retrieve all of the information we need. Still, we must be prepared for the eventuality that the Romans will attack before we have what is required. We must be prepared for everything."

"And foresight, Cate?" one woman asked. "Have ye seen anything?"

Cate shook her head. "None different than what I shared with you weeks ago."

"Do you still believe you can do what Maeve believes you can do?"

Cate looked over at Maeve and held her gaze for a very long time. No words needed to be said; each knew what the answer was.

"I have gone further than the others and returned safely. It is a new quest and if I had time, I believe we could change the course of events. Still, there is help, and I am seeking it. It—is the best I can do."

"Is it true Quinn has not returned from the portal in over two days?"

Maeve and Cate stared at Lachlan, who nodded sadly. "Quinn has yet to return, it is true, but that does not mean we shall never see him again."

The crowd groaned in unison, memories of past failures looming over them like a group of circling vultures.

Maeve held her hand up and the crowd silenced immediately. "Quinn has exceptional abilities. I have faith in him as well. Do not give up hope."

"Until tomorrow, then," Lachlan said, effectively cutting off any more questions. "Ian will take our decision to the mountains where the Chieftain will announce to the warriors what needs be done. Be well this night."

As the members of the order wandered over to the fire to sit and converse about the decision facing them, Maeve turned to Cate and stared down into her face. "There is not much more time, my love."

Cate stood erect, unblinking. "I know."

Lightly touching her cheek, Maeve gently pulled her into an embrace. "We *will* get through this."

Nodding, Cate felt the mounting pressure of her task and a small window of fear open up inside her. Would Jessie come through for them? Cate could only pray she would.

The first message from the Chieftain was not good. The Romans were already burning through the northern villages. He would wait until he heard from Lachlan before making a move, but there was little time.

"What will you do?" Maeve asked Lachlan the next morning before the discussion was put to a vote.

"We need to talk to the Chieftain. We will take him our decision, but I do not believe flight is in our best interest."

"You do not?"

Lachlan shook his head. "The Romans have always just taken. Flight will only enable them to take without cost. If they are to take anything from us, there must be a high price."

Maeve sighed. "Shall we go, or do we send a messenger?"

"I think that we must go. We must bless the warriors, of course, and the Chieftain will want to see us before it begins. It is crucial the warriors know we stand beside them."

"Agreed. I sensed their unease at the start of the march. It is never easy leaving one's home."

"What of Cate?"

Maeve shook her head. "She needs to be near the portal. I do not believe it best if she goes with us."

Lachlan turned and studied Maeve. "Are you trying to keep her from harm?"

Maeve nodded, surprised she was so easy to read. "Yes. Would you expect any less of me?"

Lachlan shrugged. "I wonder that you could leave her at all when she is so close."

"Lachlan, I have spent the last nine years training her, tutoring, mentoring and loving her. It is time for her to show her teacher what she has learned. I cannot protect Cate from the inevitable sadness that will befall our kind, but I can certainly give her the chance to show us the true extent of her powers. She is a powerful priestess, and I believe she may save many lives. To do so, I must cut her loose from me."

Lachlan reached out and touched Maeve's cheek. It was the most intimate touch they had ever shared. "That is difficult for you, is it not?"

Maeve looked up at Lachlan, her eyes filling with tears. "You have no idea."

"Your faith in her is boundless."

"As it ought."

"Faith misplaced can cause ruin, Maeve."

Maeve reached out and took his hand away from her cheek. "Your mother was a very wise woman, Lachlan, with skills few could match and even fewer could replicate, but Catie has her own attributes, not the least of which is her courage. It is easy to believe in one who is so brave."

Lachlan nodded. "Indeed, she is brave, as are you. I know it is not an easy thing to leave her during this time, and I admire you doing so."

"We must all make sacrifices, Lachlan, for the greater good. Now, I will take my leave to see Cate. She has been making the rounds discussing our options with everyone."

"Is that Birch she is speaking with now?"

Maeve glanced over, shielded her eyes from the sun, and nodded. "Indeed. Birch has been asking a great many questions about Quinn's disappearance."

Lachlan cast his eyes down and shook his head. Lachlan, more than anyone else, knew what happened after the third day of absence into the portal. Quinn could be anywhere in time, as anybody. He could be lost in the spaces between times, in the dark, black void his mother had referred to as the Great Nothingness. His absence was felt strongly by each and every one of them. "He was too young. I should not have let him go."

"He has the sight, Lachlan. You *had* to."

"His gift should not have become a curse."

"Stop berating yourself. I would have done the same thing in your place."

Lachlan raised an eyebrow at Maeve. "Truly?"

"Truly." Maeve turned back toward Cate, who was in an animated discussion with Birch, a curmudgeon of an old man who was adored by all. For a moment, Maeve paused to watch Cate as she tried vainly to prove her point to the old man. Maeve's heart swelled with pride. She had grown so very much. How had time slipped by so quickly? Just yesterday Cate was a young woman questioning everything Maeve taught her; pushing to make a place in a world that wasn't sure it knew what to do with the likes of her. She had been eager to please, quick to learn, and even faster at challenging Maeve and Lachlan. It had taken them less than a year to discover that she had the sight, and it had happened quite by accident.

Maeve and Cate had been taking a walk when a man on a horse passed them. Cate called out to him to check the riggings of his saddle, but the man paid her no mind. Two hours later, when they came across the man, he was sitting on the ground with his ankle twisted from having slid off his horse. The rigging was broken, and his saddle had fallen right off the horse. He gazed at Cate with awe and respect as she helped him to his feet.

When Maeve fixed his ankle and sent him on his way, she turned to Cate and gazed deeply into her eyes. "You have it, don't you?"

"Have what?"

"The sight. You knew that man was going to get hurt."

"I knew his saddle was off, but—I am unsure how I knew."

Time and time again Cate had shown them instances of her powers, and each time, Maeve begged Lachlan to take her into the grove to teach her what it meant to have such powerful magic. When he finally acquiesced, Cate's abilities proved to be far more than just sight. Cate had seen something of the future, and although she had been unsure of what it was she saw, she knew one thing: she had been there, somehow, someway, to a time she could not comprehend.

Thus began her two years of training to prepare her for the journey that might ultimately save those she loved most. Cate had proven to be an excellent student and paid very close attention to the lessons Maeve and Lachlan delivered on a daily basis. Every week for two years, Cate had visited the portal and been transported across time, only to discover there was no viable recipient prepared to receive her.

Until Jessie.

Cate had actually seen Jessie a year and a half earlier, but there had been something wrong, something that fogged up her mind so much, she could barely remember what she had thought a second ago, let alone remember what her soul had been doing nearly twenty centuries ago. Jessie had not been receptive then, and even if she had been, that fog kept Cate from probing into her mind. It appeared, at that time, to be a wasted trip.

But then something happened, and not only did the fog lift, but Jessie had been brought to a portal herself; she now had the means to transport herself across time, and she had done so with remarkable skill and ease. She was so good at it, Maeve did not doubt that Jessie had somehow accessed Cate's soul memory and had managed to use that information to do what no others from the future had ever been capable of; she had left her time and returned with her sanity intact.

And now, as Maeve watched her in animated conversation, she wondered how Cate had managed the feat as well. Was there a bond between past and present that allowed those two young women to connect to each other almost without effort? Or was there some other driving force that tied them to each other, as if two separate beings were connected by a common thread? Maeve wondered if she would live to find out.

She did not doubt, of course, that it was Cate's love of her that pushed her beyond her limits, but did that love extend to Jessie as well? After all, Jessie was not a Druid, but did she not have the soul of one? Just like Cate had the mind of a Druid, but her heart—her heart was pure warrior, and it beat with a courage Maeve was sure came from another time and another place. For that, she was glad, because it was going to take more than Druid magic to prevent bloodshed; It was going to take the kind of bravery both Cate and Jessie possessed.

Now, if only Jessie came through in time.

Jessie stared up at the ceiling listening to her parents' voices droning on from Daniel's room. They had been discussing what to do about her for the last two hours. Little did they know that Daniel's room acted like a conduit and that she could hear them as easily as if they were standing in the room.

They were discussing whether or not they ought to send her back to California.

California.

A week ago, she would have leapt at the chance. Now, the very thought panicked her. How could she ever face herself if she let Maeve down? Didn't Maeve deserve a true heroine, and could Jessie actually be that for her?

Rolling over, Jessie covered her ears with the pillow. Why now, of all times, was she feeling these feelings toward Maeve? Was Fate that cruel? Had she been delivered a gift and not allowed to open it? It was clear how Cate felt about Maeve, how connected they were, but how was it possible that Jessie could also feel *so strongly* about a woman dead nearly twenty centuries? Was the soul's memory *that* powerful? Could two people actually be so bound to each other, so cosmically connected that even the residue from their thousands-of-years-old emotion could be felt as strongly as Jessie felt it? All of the love and devotion Cate held in her heart for Maeve was now within Jessie as well, and she was determined to be as strong, as brave, and as successful as Cate.

If not for Maeve, then for herself.

She was done being a loser; done wandering about aimlessly with that ugly black teenage chip on her shoulder. She was almost embarrassed to have become such a cliché, a caricature of the brooding teenage girl. There was so much of life to live, and she was done squandering it as if she could always get that time back.

She couldn't.

Time wasn't something you could just put in a bank and retrieve when you needed it. It wasn't replaceable at all, and she had certainly wasted her fair share of it, but not anymore. No, she was through traipsing aimlessly through life not being accountable to anyone or anything. She *was* responsible. She was accountable to two people in her past life she was beginning to truly love. She had failed at a lot of things in her life, but not this time. This time, she would succeed, no matter what the cost.

As sleep finally, mercifully tickled the edges of Jessie's consciousness, she slowly fell into fragmented dreams that came fast and disjointedly, most of them about Maeve and of a time when there was little fear of Roman attack. In this dream, Maeve sat on a stone, her long, auburn hair reflecting the sun's rays as she pulled a brush through it.

"You can do this," Maeve said. To whom she was speaking, Jessie could not see. "You have never let me down. Not now, and not in the past. I doubt you ever will."

Jessie peered into the dream, wondering to whom Maeve was talking. Was it Cate? It had to be, but Jessie did not see her.

"She thinks I do not know . . . thinks I have not seen the vision Lachlan and she have seen of my fate at the hands of the Roman soldiers. She does not know it was that very sight over a dozen years ago that made me step foot onto that boat and out of Gaul. That bloody vision did not just show me a possible end to my existence, it also showed me a brave, wonderful soul mate who would stop at nothing to save me from that very fate. I knew I needed to find her, not just for myself, but for a part of our Celtic culture that would be utterly destroyed if we cannot stop them. This is not about me, although Catie would make it her life mission to save me from that horrid fate. This is about a beautiful people few understand and even fewer will get the chance to know. You are our only hope now. Be strong. No matter what you face, no matter how afraid you become, remember that there is a people who rely on you to act wisely and bravely."

The dream (was it a dream?) dissolved like a film fade out, and this time, Jessie saw tens of thousands of Roman troops lined up and moving across green woodland valleys. Their sheer numbers were astounding, the sound of their death march deafening. How could Maeve ask her to be brave and then show her what they were up against?

The scene shifted to burning buildings, fiery huts and villages aflame. Wooden houses burned high, their flames licking the bottom branches of the huge oaks standing guard against the wind. Babies cried, women speared in the back as they ran, and the dead bodies strewn about were crushed beneath the horses' hooves. The village and everyone in it were destroyed as Roman soldiers crushed bodies, life and memories beneath their sandals.

Was this a dream, a memory, or neither? Jessie had no idea. What she did know was that it was vivid and very, very real. There was even the dream about Ceara, who had walked up to the Pit to inquire about Jessie. Even that dream felt within her reach. In this dream that wasn't a dream, Daniel was standing behind her folks.

Daniel!

Jessie tried calling to him at first, but this was a dream where you could scream your head off and no one could hear you. Jessie wondered if everyone had those kinds of dreams. She'd had too many to remember, and she hated them. Screaming but not screaming. She wanted to yell and wave her arms to get Daniel's attention.

But then . . . Daniel did the most amazing thing. As Jessie's parents told Ceara about possibly sending Jessie back to California, Daniel stood right behind them, his eyes locked onto Ceara's, and he was vehemently shaking his head. He knew the truth, didn't he? Somehow, some way, Daniel was telling her that it was going to be all right—that she wasn't going back to California.

But how could he know?

Waving to her, Daniel smiled and then pointed to the ceiling. Jessie looked up at it and saw his X-Men poster. Cyclops was blasting a bad guy and Wolverine was slashing some big guy in red. When she looked back, Daniel was gone. Jessie sighed. Cyclops and Wolverine were Daniel's heroes. He was telling her that she was one as well.

Thank you, sport. It's easier to believe in yourself when others do as well.

And, for the first time in her life, she truly did.

Lachlan and Maeve were picking their way through the woods when Maeve stopped to rest. It had been a long night of travel, and she was weary from the pace of the journey.

When they had drunk their share of water from the skin, Lachlan sat next to Maeve and said, "I am sorry we had to leave Cate behind."

"You need not apologize any more, Lachlan. We were right to. The grove's decision to fight instead of flee means that now, more than ever, we must know the information she can retrieve from Jessie."

"Had you hoped for fleeing to be their response?"

Maeve shook her head. "Not at all. We are a proud people, Lachlan, and fight is something we do quite well. I am only surprised at how lopsided the vote was."

"We have much to hate about the Romans."

"Hate is such a dark word."

"So is death."

Maeve looked at him and saw the same sorrow she felt. "Lachlan, are you ever afraid?"

Lachlan opened the skin once more and drew a deep draught. "I stopped feeling fear when my mother died. I made a promise that I would never allow fear to control any part of my world. Fear did not stop her and it will not stop me."

"But she died in the pursuit of truth. Where truth is, there is no room for fear."

Lachlan nodded. "I like to believe she found what she was looking for. Can I do less than that?"

No one could remember when, exactly, the portal had been discovered, but many marked its existence occurring when the old deities, the Tuatha De Danaan, went to the Underworld for the final time. They caused such a tear in the opening of this world that it could not quite close, and lest someone attempt to follow them, they created a portal that would send any quester across time, unbidden, and completely out of control, so as to never disturb the Tuatha again.

Finding the portal was one thing; knowing what to do with it, how to harness its potential was another task all together; a task that had begun long since anyone could remember, carried forth by Lachlan's mother and her apprentices, and now, by Lachlan himself, though he had vowed never to set foot into the portal himself, he was the overseer of the Sacred Place, and it was his decision who would go. Maeve knew why he pushed so hard; partly because of what they knew was coming, and partly because of the loss of his mother so many years ago.

When he was younger and not as wise as he was now, he had boasted that *he* would be the one to enter the portal and learn its secrets. When his mother died, and he went charging into the forest after her, Birch had barely managed to stop him and tell him his mother's last wish:

"Promise never to allow my son to follow me," she had said to Birch just before going through. "He does not have what is needed to be a successful quester." Those were the last words ever spoken by the great Druid priestess.

Birch had kept his promise, and Lachlan had searched for the right individual who had what his mother possessed. He'd found Quinn, who had yet to come back. Maeve had found Cate, and in time, they had feverishly trained her.

And now, time was running out.

• • •

"When was the last time you bought or smoked?" Dr. Dunbar asked. He wore those goofy black-rimmed glasses that were back in style and they sat upon a bulbous nose that was pink at the end.

Jessie counted back on her fingers. "Five months ago."

Dr. Dunbar looked up from his file. His face registered disbelief. No surprise there. He cleared his throat and ran a hand through jet black hair that looked as if he had cut it himself. "Then why are you here now?"

"I jumped bail on another psych visit."

"Because?"

"Because I don't need therapy and I had better things to do."

"Such as?"

Gee . . . like traveling through time. "Meeting new people. Of course, my folks don't approve of my new friends, even though one of them is seventy-something."

"Really? Why do you suppose that is?"

"Honestly? Because Tanner wears a studded leather jacket, which makes him a stoner in their judgmental Christian eyes, and Ceara wears gypsy clothes and reads palms and tarot cards for a living." Jessie shrugged. "I suppose being hell-bound disturbs them a bit."

"You don't agree with your parents' religion?"

"I don't believe in being so goddamned judgmental, no. Ceara is one of the most fascinating people I have ever met. So what if she reads tarot cards for a living?"

"And what does that make her in your parents' eyes?"

"A cuckoo. Look, Dr. Dunbar, I'm here because I'm a victim of my parents' misconceptions and erroneous prejudgments of people they do not know. I haven't smoked weed in five months because I am through with that phase of my life. It's a go-nowhere, do-nothing place that is a draino. The only problem I'm having is finding someone who will *believe* me."

And so the session went. When it ended, Dr. Dunbar said, "I know it's hard to believe at times like these, Jessie, but your parents really are on your side."

"Oh really? Is that why they believed an eleven-year-old stoner over me?" Jessie held her hand up. "Rhetorical. I already know the answer." How long would she would have to play these games with her parents and these shrinks? After all, time was of the essence, and she had so little of it to waste.

"Let me ask you this, Doctor: if someone you loved was in danger and you knew it was within your power to save them, would you let anyone stand in your way?" Before he could answer, Jessie held up her hand to stop him. "No questions, no shrink response. Just give me your honest person-to-person answer."

Dr. Dunbar set his chin on his hands. "I doubt that I would, no."

Jessie nodded. "Thank you for that."

"Is someone you love in danger?"

The question grabbed hold of Jessie's heart and she realized what she had said when she posed the question. Someone *was* in danger, and yes—yes, she *loved* them both.

She leaned forward on his desk, her brow furrowed. "Okay, since I'm here, let's make the most of this, shall we? I want to talk about self-love."

Dr. Dunbar removed his elbows from the desk and leaned back. "That's a good place to start."

Smiling, Jessie nodded. "Yes it is."

Watching Maeve and Lachlan walk away was one of the hardest things Cate had ever done. For the last nine years, she and Maeve had been inseparable, and though most people believed their relationship was one-sided, Cate knew better. Maeve had come for her, yes; for her and no one else, and once she had found her, she had never let her go.

Until now.

Now, when the time of reckoning was so near, Cate understood why she needed to stay behind, but that hadn't made it any easier to let Maeve go. Even though she was with Lachlan, he was a man of peace, with very little warrior within him. He could not wield a sword like she could; he did not have it in him to kill another man, and that worried her.

Still, after the vote, Lachlan and Maeve left for the hills, leaving Birch in charge of the necessary ceremonies and rituals. Birch was a good man, a strong priest, and a loyal friend. He would make sure all that was needed was met, and that their people were properly protected by the Goddess.

"Watch over them," Cate murmured as she turned and started for the portal.

"Cate McEwen!" Birch called out to her.

Cate turned. "Sir?"

"Before you go, I'd like a word or two with you if you don't mind."

Cate walked over to Birch. In the last year, his hair and beard had turned completely white, but his blue eyes sparkled from beneath his furry white eyebrows. "Did you know that I'd give anything to be going with you?"

Cate nodded. Birch had been in love with Lachlan's mother many, many moons ago, and though he had lost her, he had never stopped loving her and had been a chaste man since her death. "I do, Birch."

"We need what Maeve and Lachlan are sending you for, that much I do know, lass, but we also need you to return. We canna keep losing our folks to that thing."

Cate put her arms around him and hugged him tightly. "You won't lose me, Birch, I'll be back."

"Well, I do not rightly know what transpires in that portal of yours, but I do know there are dangers involved—deadly ones. You must be ever-vigilant, ever-cautious and ever-mindful that you are *never* the one in control. Do not forget, not even for a second, that the Tuatha created the portal. They control it, and they will do whatever they please with those arrogant enough to enter it."

Cate nodded. She had always known how afraid Birch was of the portal, but he had never deigned to speak of it until now. What did he know that he wasn't sharing with her?

"I shall be very careful, Birch. I have no desire to leave this life sooner than I ought."

"Good. Then think with a clear head, do not push the goddesses to act, and, most importantly, know your limitations. It was Lachlan's mother's greatest mistake not knowing her own weaknesses. Do not follow suit."

"I won't. I swear."

Birch leaned upon his walking staff, a gnarled old oak branch with Ogham carved on one side. "Tell me then, what weakness of yours could bring harm to you?"

Cate inhaled deeply. She knew the answer to that question as easily as her own name, but how could she put it into words? "You know the answer to that, as surely as you knew why you did not follow *her* into the void."

"I did not follow because she bade me not to. She was not a woman a man wished to anger."

"You stayed to care for her son, which you have done well. She risked all she had to find answers to save those she loved. I can do no less. The Goddess has chosen me and I will not shirk my duty out of fear."

"Then the answer to my question would be what?"

Birch never, ever let you escape without naming a thing. "Love, Birch. My greatest weakness is love. Love sends me into a place that could take me away forever."

"And what, do you suppose brings you back?"

"That same love."

"Then it is both your greatest weakness and your greatest strength."

Cate thought about this before nodding. "It is a double-edged sword, yes."

"Good. Perhaps that is why the gods have chosen you. When one understands both sides of a sharp sword, one is less likely to be killed by it. Go now, and Godspeed. I shall guard the entrance as I once did so many years ago, but Cate McEwen, you must swear to return. I do not think my heart could stand to lose another to that accursed portal."

Cate stood on tiptoe and kissed the old man's cheek. "I promise."

With that promise on her lips Cate entered a world that had changed since her last visit. The murky mist that typically enveloped her was gone, replaced by something more ominous. Something had happened to Jessie since their last visit.

Stepping back out of the portal, Cate shook her head and tried to collect her thoughts. What was happening to Jessie? Was she in some kind of danger? As Cate stepped further away from the portal, she watched it shimmer like a liquid mirror until it congealed again and ceased its movement. Her head hurt. This was new.

Had Birch known? Why was Jessie so hard to reach? Why did everything feel so closed up and dungeon-like? What was happening on the other side of time?

Cate sat next to the portal and considered going back and trying again. Perhaps . . . if she could go when Jessie was asleep . . . perhaps they could manage another conversation. She had not ever considered the possibility of something happening to Jessie.

Cate rose and she began pacing. She realized with complete clarity what was happening to her, and it was slightly alarming: Cate McEwen *cared* about the life of Jessie Ferguson. If Jessie was in trouble and needed help . . . then Cate was going to give it.

And it appeared she was just in time to do so.

They heard the hooves pounding long before they saw them. Too late, Lachlan and Maeve tried to make it back into the embrace of the forest, but they were cut off by a squad of Roman sentries patrolling the marshes.

"Should we split up?" Maeve yelled at Lachlan as they ran through the woods. Branches lashed at their faces, but did little to slow them down.

"I'll not leave you to face them alone," Lachlan shouted back.

"Then stop running."

"What?"

"We cannot outrun them, Lachlan. It would be better to turn and face them."

Lachlan immediately stopped, and turned to take Maeve's hand. Together, they stood waiting for the sentry commander to ride up to them. It felt as if the forest itself were waiting to see the outcome.

"Shall I weave a mist?"

Lachlan shook his head. "If they know what we are, they will surely kill us."

"They may do so any way."

"I do not want you to risk it, Maeve. We must act like we are not what we are."

A guard astride an enormous silver beast brought his steed to a stop and glared down at them. "Only Druids could run through a forest this dense without stumbling or falling. Who be you?"

Lachlan and Maeve said nothing.

"Speak!" he commanded in an awkward, unfamiliar Latin tongue.

"We may, indeed, be as you say," Maeve answered, "But we'll not discuss this with an underling."

The guard glared at Lachlan as if Maeve had not even spoken. "What kind of man allows a woman to speak for him?"

"It would depend on how wise the woman was," came Maeve's retort. To Lachlan's surprise, she spoke the Roman's language. Was there no end to the things this woman could do?

The other seven sentries behind him chuckled at this. The commander motioned to one of the men, who hopped off his horse and tied Maeve's and Lachlan's hands behind their backs, and slipped a noose around Lachlan's neck.

"If you are very powerful Druids, you should be able to escape ties such as those that bind you now. If not, then it appears your powers are waning even as we speak." The commander jerked his horse's reins away. "You are now the prisoners of the Governor. Your very lives, whether they be Druid ones or not, are in his hands, so you ought to pray to your cannibalistic gods for mercy."

Lachlan and Maeve looked at each other as they began walking behind the sentry on the white horse. "Maeve . . ."

"Shh, Lachlan."

"I . . . do not know how to get us out of this," he said in Gaelic.

Maeve glanced over at him. His face was scratched from the rope, and his neck was already burned from it being too tight. "It is all right, Lachlan. You may not know what to do, but I do. Be patient. And for once in your life, let *me* do the talking."

"But—"

"Lachlan?"

"Yes, Maeve?"

"Be still. We shall not be harmed."

After reporting back to her parents that she had stayed for the entire session with Dr. Dunbar, Jessie asked them, once again, to trust her. She wanted Daniel to be able to come home and be with them, but they waved this off. They felt she was just too volatile and unstable to be around him. It broke Jessie's heart to know she was the cause of her little brother being uprooted from their new home.

Exhausted, Jessie barely had time to say goodnight before falling into a deep sleep. Again, her dreams came to her strangely disjointed. She saw Ceara looking out the window of her boat as if searching for her, and the Roman soldiers were back, only this time Jessie watched seven or eight of them making their way through the forest on horseback.

Next, she saw herself as Cate, reaching into the portal and then stepping away, as if there was something scary in there. She did this over and over again, as if confused about whether to come or go. Then, a statue of Julius Caesar came to life and picked up a Merlin-esque creature, crushing it in his hand. These were the dreams that poked at Jessie's subconscious, challenging her to choose the memories from the fictions. In her dream, she did not know what to do, until . . .

The next scene took her breath away. She saw Maeve standing defiantly before a large Roman soldier, a commander of some sort. Suddenly, this dream took on a quality unlike any of the others. There was a texture to it, a nearly tangible feel to it that let her know this was not a dream, but a memory. She was sure of it, but she could not figure out how it could be a memory when Cate wasn't there. This was Maeve's memory, wasn't it? Was that possible? Could it be that this was

Cate's memory of a *tale* told her by Maeve?

"Oh, my God! Maeve!" Jessie could hear herself, but she couldn't be heard in the memory. Of course she couldn't. *She* didn't exist in this memory. *She* was just an onlooker now, watching the cataclysm of events unfold before her. What she saw chilled the marrow of her bones.

The soldier turned to Lachlan and asked him if Maeve was his woman. They stood in the middle of a large circle of soldiers next to a bonfire, and Lachlan's bare back was sweating from the heat. He looked at Maeve for an answer, for the right response, and he heard her answer in his head.

"She is not."

The commander walked toward Maeve, studying her like one might when purchasing a horse. "Would you *like* her to be?" His accent was thick and he struggled with their native tongue, but Lachlan knew exactly what was being said.

This time, Lachlan stared straight ahead. These were the "civilized" people who pitted man against man for amusement in large arenas, who used little boys as one might a common prostitute, and who allowed corrupt politicians to lead them around by the nose. Forcing Lachlan to rape Maeve for their evening entertainment was certainly not beneath the likes of them, and Lachlan knew it.

Lachlan chose his next words carefully. "*We* do not force our women to submit to us as you do, Commander. *We* prefer they come to us of their own accord."

"Oh, do you now? Is that why they are allowed to divorce you as well, dishonoring you and disgracing your family name?" The commander stood in front of Lachlan, inches away from his face, yet Lachlan did not flinch.

"There is no dishonor in divorce, Commander. Only the truth, and *we* are not afraid of the truth."

"Then isn't it *true* that you'd like to bed her? Look at her. She is a beautiful specimen for your kind." The soldier grabbed Lachlan's face and forced him to turn and look at her. "Look at her. Is she not becoming?"

Lachlan ripped his face out of the soldier's grasp and glared hard into his eyes. "She is, indeed, but it is not true that I wish to be with her."

"You do not find her stunning? Are you not that kind of man?" the commander glanced over at his men, who laughed too loudly. "We have plenty of men like you back in Rome. Perhaps you prefer the company of someone—younger."

"I prefer no man's company to that."

"No man, yes, but what of a woman?" Before Lachlan could answer, the commander wheeled around and ripped off her dress down to her waist.

"Maeve!" Jessie sat up in bed, trembling and sweating. Frantically looking around, she was surprised she wasn't in Wales staring at Roman soldiers who were humiliating Maeve and Lachlan. Jessie's heart was racing so fast, she had to take a few deep breaths to calm herself. How could everything feel so real? Jessie shuddered as she recalled the dream that wasn't a dream. She knew that from its distinctive character, its rhythm and pace. It had the feel of Cate's other memories, but how could that be? Cate hadn't been there.

Or had she?

Jessie lay back down and pulled the covers up to her neck. She felt vulnerable and afraid for her friends. Occasional goose bumps popped out on her arms as she recalled her dream. Was Cate trying to tell her something? What in the world was going on?

Closing her eyes once again, Jessie inhaled deeply and willed the dreams to come.

And come they did.

The next dream was definitely not a memory, and Jessie was sure of it. She was back in the forest when she called out to a befuddled Cate who was quickly making her way across the grove. Cate did not pause, but kept moving rapidly through the undergrowth.

"Cate!" Jessie yelled, sprinting through the grove. She knew where she was going this time; she was running for the stones she and Cate had sat on. How she knew where they were, she did not stop to question. She just knew. And she hoped to find Cate sitting there waiting for her.

Maybe there was even a fire still burning, and—"Cate!" Jessie called louder, pushing herself harder. When, at last, she came to the sitting stones, no one was there.

"But *I'm* here," Jessie said aloud. "And the last time *I* was here, Cate was asleep and I had come through the portal and entered her dream." She sat down and shook her head. This was *her* dream and maybe Cate would appear in it.

"Cate!" Jessie yelled. "Cate McEwen!" She stood, yelled once more and then sat again, not even pausing to wonder how she knew Cate's last name. She knew things. It was enough now to know she knew them. And she knew that if she waited long enough, Cate would show.

She didn't have to wait long. Out of the mist hurried Cate, head covered by her robe, staff in hand, light blue mist whirling about her. The air crackled with energy all about her.

She had changed.

"Oh, Cate," Jessie was on her feet in an instant, her arms encircling the smaller woman. She did not have time to think about the fact that she was hugging herself. "Maeve's in trouble, Cate. Awful, horrible trouble."

Cate lowered her hood, revealing a perplexed expression. "Trouble? Why she and Lachlan left just this—"

"They have been captured by Romans—and they—"

"They what?" Cate's voice was thin and tense.

Jessie felt tears roll down her cheeks. "They're trying to force Lachlan to—to—"

Cate stepped away from Jessie as if Jessie were diseased. "How can this be? Moreover, how is it *you* would know this? They left this morning, and there were no sentries near the highlands, no one has seen any Roman soldiers."

Jessie wiped her eyes and shrugged. "I don't know. It—it couldn't have just been a dream, could it?"

Cate stepped forward and took Jessie's hand. "Did it feel like a dream?"

She shook her head. "It felt like a memory, but if *you* weren't there, how can that be? Oh, God, this is all so confusing."

Cate studied Jessie a second before asking, "What was Maeve wearing in your dream?"

"Wearing? Well—it was the first time I saw her not in her robe. She was wearing a green dress with a crème-colored bl—"

Cate's eyes widened and she dropped her staff to take Jessie by the shoulders. "Lachlan! What was he wearing?"

"A blue peasant shirt with—"

"It *is* a memory, Jessie. That's precisely what they were both wearing when they left. Where are they? Think! Where did you see them?"

Jessie swallowed hard and tried to focus on the contents of her dream-memory. Her heart pounded so hard, she could feel it in her temples. "They were in the woods just south of the swampy mist area. Maeve and Lachlan had taken a path outside of the forest in order to avoid the marshes." Jessie paused, blinked twice, and inhaled. It was a freaky thing to know the terminology of a place she had never visited or even known about. "The sentries came from the east. There were seven, no eight of them. They took them back to their camp."

"Which is where?" Cate gripped Jessie's shoulders tighter.

"I'm not sure."

"Be sure!"

Jessie closed her eyes, allowing her mind to paint the whole picture. Her grandmother had always said it was hard to see the picture if you're standing in the frame, and she had been in the frame in her dream trying to see all that which she hadn't really looked at was difficult. "By—wait a minute—it's coming." Jessie frowned, her eyes still closed. "By Finnegan's Farm. They're in the foothills behind the stables of a place called Finnegan's."

Cate hugged Jessie. "Good girl! I knew you could do it." Cate bent down and picked up her staff and quickly started back toward the mist. "If I hurry, I can prevent the worst from happening." Cate stopped just before the mist and turned back around. "Did you see an ending to this memory?"

Jessie shook her head. "I did not."

"Good. Then perhaps it ends well. Thank you, Jessie. Thank you for possibly saving our soul mate." With that, Cate vanished into the mist.

Cate and a dozen other Druids rode all through the night, pushing their steeds harder than a soldier might because of their particular relationship with the animals and the animal world. They would cover twice as much distance with less superior horses than any Roman could, and Cate was determined to do so. None of the others questioned Cate's drive of the horses, and each one, to a man, stood solidly behind her decision to leave the safety of the woods in order to save their friends.

The fingers of fear kept curling around Cate's neck, but she refused to feel them or to even acknowledge their existence. Instead, she thought about Jessie's words and what she had said the soldiers would attempt to do to Lachlan and Maeve.

She knew how far it was to Finnegan's, and, unless the soldiers had hoisted Maeve and Lachlan upon a horse, they were walking to the farm and not riding. This would give Cate the extra time she needed; time to formulate some kind of plan that would enable all of them to leave without harm. Now, she needed to think like her brother had taught her to—like a warrior. She needed her fighter's mind now, and though Maeve had done her best to tame the beast in Cate, what Maeve had not known, what she might never know, was that Cate had seen a part of herself in the past, and she had been a true hunter, a man who was capable of staring a lion in the face and not be afraid.

She was staring at a den of lions now, and she was determined not to be afraid.

As the day broke, Cate could see Finnegan's Farm in the distance. Through the morning's mist, the smoking chimney could barely be seen. It was at that very moment that Cate knew what she was going to do.

When she went to get the keys to the numberless room, they were gone. So were her parents, and though Jessie tore all through the house looking for the keys, she couldn't find them.

"Damn them!" she cursed, pounding her fist on the wall. "They'll ruin everything!" She needed to get to the seam as soon as possible. She *had* to know if Maeve was all right. She had even taken a nap, hoping Cate would come through, but there was nothing. The answer about Maeve's safety would only come when Jessie stepped through the portal and back into Cate's world.

Cate's world.

Since being restricted, all Jessie had wanted to do was return to Cate's world and learn more about her life. She hungered for knowledge about the Celts, the Roman invasion of England, a life and time she knew so very little about except in the deepest recesses of her soul memory. Yes, she had had flashes here and there of swords, of thatched-roof houses, of peasants in fields, but those were like the single bright burst of a camera flash that blinded you for a mere second and then was gone. She understood that the more she knew, the more help she would be, but that knowledge just ate at her now, since she had no way of accessing it.

After searching again and again for the keys, Jessie closed her eyes before dinner, falling asleep almost instantly. Her first few dreams were mere snapshots—stills as it were, of a battlefield filled with corpses and wounded horses. On and on the pictures continued until a huge red-haired woman rode a chariot over the peak of a mountain to survey the death and destruction before her. Her green eyes narrowed suddenly as she glared at Jessie from her chariot. Raising her spear, the woman yelled one single word that echoed throughout Jessie's soul.

"Boudicca!"

Lachlan stared deeply into Maeve's eyes as if willing her to hear his thoughts. He could hardly believe how calm and unafraid she was. The fate glaring harshly at her was every woman's greatest nightmare, and yet, here stood Maeve, poised, self-confident, proud. He should have been prepared for her next words, but he wasn't, and when she spoke them to him in her soft, yet cutting voice, he nearly recoiled.

"Do as they wish," she said in their native tongue. "It is merely a body, Lachlan."

Lachlan stepped back, away from the slash of the harsh words, only to feel the tip of a sword in his back urging him forward. "No, Maeve," he said in ancient Gaelic. "I would rather die than harm you."

"Oh look," the commander said, bemused. "They're barking those ugly sounds they call language. Well then, Druid priestess, when he thrusts his magic wand into you, I want to hear your pleasure as well as your pain in the *only* civilized tongue. Do you understand?"

Maeve turned from an anguished Lachlan toward the commander. "*Civilized* men do not pervert their souls with the likes of this *entertainment.*"

The commander sneered at her. "Get on with it, priestess, or your man will feel the bite of a sword before he can feel the bite of your womanness."

Lachlan's eyes pleaded with her. "I—can—not."

Maeve stepped up to him and slapped his face. This brought a resounding cheer from the soldiers. As they filled the air with their roaring sounds, Maeve gritted her teeth and said, "Catie needs more time, Lachlan. Please, do as they command. We *will* live through this if you do as I say."

Lachlan's sorrow was replaced by surprise. "Cate? Oh, Maeve, she is so far away. Too far that even she cannot help us now."

Maeve's hand suddenly reached out and grabbed his neck. This, too, was well-received by the soldiers as they beat their swords against their shields. "Then, do as I command."

"Maeve—" Lachlan murmured. "I beg you."

She grabbed his face and pulled him to her. "Listen," she hissed in an even more ancient language only Druids spoke. "Can't you hear?" She whispered loud enough to be heard over the shouting men. "Listen carefully. Listen with your nature spirit."

All Lachlan could hear was the sound of metal on metal and the blood rushing through his body.

"She's out there," she said, violently pushing him away, as if he disgusted her. The soldiers booed and hissed as Lachlan stumbled backward, nearly falling into the fire. Again, the sword prodded him forward. With a look of utter helplessness, he took an aggressive step toward Maeve, who nodded. "Trust me," she mouthed. "You'll not do me any harm."

"Maeve, do not be a fool," he said, digging his fingers into her shoulders. "It is *not* Cate. You delude yourself." For years, he had dreamt of being with Maeve, but this—this was nothing like his dreams. This was a nightmare. To force Maeve into accepting something from him that should be freely given and equally received was more than he could bear, and a small part of him knew it would irrevocably change their relationship if they were to live through this.

"You are a good man, my friend. This charade is almost over." Once again, she slapped him, sending him reeling backward.

"I'll not allow this one to touch me, Commander. Perhaps you would rather in his stead."

Before Lachlan could do anything more, a low rumble could be heard and the ground began to shake. The soldiers paused their metallic banging long enough to hear the first hooves of the approaching stampede. Glancing about, they immediately formed a blockade against the onslaught of whatever was coming.

Out of the lifting mist charged one hundred rampaging cows and bulls, knocking soldiers to the ground and crushing them beneath their hooves. This way and that, the cows charged, crushing shields and breaking dropped swords. In the center of the maelstrom, Maeve and Lachlan stood erect calmly watching as the soldiers, one-by-one, fell to the onrush of cattle that seemed to have no end. The Commander made a dash for his horse, stepping over his fallen soldiers, but when he reached the hitching post, all the horses were gone. Turning, he glared at Lachlan and Maeve, who went unharmed among the huge beasts as they rushed by them.

"Why do they not kill you?" he cried, shaking his sword at the two of them.

Lachlan stood tall. "We are Druids. Nature harms us not."

"We shall beat your kind event—" His final word was lost as the next dozen bulls knocked him over, and trampled him with their sharp hooves.

When the dust settled and the cattle had completely destroyed the makeshift camp, only Lachlan and Maeve stood alive among the eight corpses littering the woods. "She is here," Maeve whispered, smiling softly at Lachlan.

"Maeve, she is nearly a day's walk from here."

Maeve ignored him and started in the direction the cattle had come. "You're wrong. She's here. I know it."

And out of the mist she came, riding a small dappled mare that was breathing hard and sweating profusely. Sitting next to her on a tall amber-colored horse was Sean Finnegan who beamed broadly at the damage his beasts had done.

"Maeve!" Jumping off her horse, Cate ran to Maeve and embraced her so hard they nearly toppled over.

"Oh, Catie, I knew you'd come."

"Are you all right? Did they hurt you?" Cate looked at Maeve's torn dress and then pulled Maeve to her before she could respond. She wept, out of fear, out of a sense of relief, out of all the emotions that had been swimming inside her since she spoke with Jessie. She could not find any words, any at all, to express how she felt, so she just cried.

Finally, when Maeve could no longer breathe, she gently pulled away and brushed the tears from her face. "It's all right, now, Catie. We're all right."

Nodding, Cate tried to compose herself. "I—it—Jessie—"

Maeve nodded slowly. "Ah, I see."

"In a dream, one of my memories of this awful event forced its way to her. She told me what was happening, so we grabbed what horses we could and rode all night."

Lachlan walked over and patted Cate on the back. "And thank the Goddess you did. That was very brave of you to come through the forest at night, Cate McEwen. You continue to surprise me. Thank you for reaching us in time."

Cate blushed. Lachlan handed out very few compliments, so when he did, it was cherished. "You're welcome, Lachlan, but it wasn't me. Well, it wasn't me acting alone. I had help. Without Jessie—"

Lachlan stared at her. "Jessie?"

Cate nodded. "She warned me. She saw this memory."

"But how could she have a memory of something you were not a part of?"

Maeve smiled knowingly. "It was not *her* memory. It was mine. Do not forget, Lachlan, that Cate and I are soul mates. I will tell Catie what happened to us here and thus, it will become part of her memory. It was that 'memory' Jessie saw."

Lachlan shuddered. "And thank the goddesses she did."

Maeve quickly repaired her torn dress as best she could and glanced up to ask, "Were you able to get any of the information we need?"

Cate shook her head. "We were more concerned with saving you both from these Romans butchers." With a look of disdain, Cate glared at the crushed and bloody bodies on the ground. "We had no other choice but to tend to this first."

"It was a good choice, Cate," Lachlan said. Then, he turned to Sean and shook his hand. "Well met, Sean. If any of your animals are missing or injured, we will gladly pay you for them. Thank you, my friend."

Sean sat straighter in his saddle. "The bloody Romans will want to feast on the meat of my cows, but not if they are loose and run free. I had planned on letting them go when I heard the soldiers were near, but this was a far better use for them."

"We appreciate your sacrifice."

"It was my pleasure watching these pigs get trampled by cows. Thank me not."

"How on earth did the two of you manage to stampede so many cattle?"

"I am not alone, Lachlan." On that note, twelve other Druids appeared as if by magic from various parts of the forest. "We herded them here with help from Sean. Once they were gathered, we prayed and I led a protection ritual. I knew you would be safe from harm."

"You performed a ceremony?" Lachlan asked.

Cate nodded. "I had to. It was my duty to protect you. I asked the Goddess Boann of the sacred white cow to protect you."

Lachlan turned to Maeve. "But how did *you* know she was here?"

"I found Cate all the way from Gaul. It was nothing to know she was near. It is how we are. It is how we shall always be."

Lachlan shook his head. "There is more."

"Indeed. Do you think, of all Cate's memories housed within Jessie's soul, that it was pure coincidence that *this* memory pushed its way through?" Maeve asked.

Lachlan's face registered surprise. "You did it?"

Maeve smiled. "Cate's soul is connected to mine, whether she is in the future and I'm in her past. Jessie was able to access that memory because I supplied it for her."

"You were able to send a memory? How can that be?"

Maeve nodded. "Forget not my powers, Lachlan. You have only seen what little I have chosen to show you."

Lachlan bowed his head. "Indeed, madam. I shan't forget again." He bowed low, not merely for a show of respect, but to let Maeve know whatever nearly transpired between them did not lessen his deep respect and admiration for her. She returned the bow to him to repair any damage their experience might have wrought.

"Are we to head back to the grove?" one of the Druids asked Lachlan.

"Not until we have spoken to the Chieftain. He awaits our decision."

Maeve raised an eyebrow at him. "What about Catie?"

"She is here now. We shall not send her back. If she and Jessie are as connected as you believe them to be, perhaps it is best if we return her to the Otherworld or to her own Dreamworld where they may reconnect."

The Druids prayed together, performed a short ceremony to thank the goddesses for bringing them all here safely, and, finally, headed off to the highlands, for what could very well be the last time.

Jessie woke up exactly at six in the morning. Sadly, it had been a dreamless night, and she figured it was because Cate was doing what she could to save Lachlan and Maeve. Not knowing what had happened to Maeve and Lachlan was driving her nuts. As hard as she tried to access her soul's memory within her, she could not. Jessie decided that that was one of the first things she was going to learn when she got her life back. She was going to learn *how to remember*. She knew Ceara could help her learn how to hear her past when it whispered to her. It was there. It was only a matter of being able to retrieve it.

She had just finished breakfast when the doorbell rang. To her surprise, it was Tanner.

"Hey. I brought some samples of my work for your Dad to look at. Mind if I drop them off?"

Jessie opened the door, glad for the company. "Come on in. What have you been up to?"

"I've been trying to straighten out that mess Chris got us into by spreading those damn rumors. What a little asshole." Tanner sat on one of the sofas in the parlor and set his work on the coffee table. "Heard you're restricted. That totally sucks."

Jessie nodded. "You have no idea."

"What do you do all day? Work?"

"I've had plenty of thinking time."

"About what?"

Jessie studied him a moment, weighing whether or not she could or should trust him. "Have you ever just *known* that doing something in particular would change your life? That you were stepping onto a path you *knew* was right?"

Tanner shook his head. "Nope. Well, maybe. This may sound weird, but I kinda have that feeling about you."

Jessie sat up. "Really?"

"Yeah. I've never really hung around someone who had their act together like you do. Your folks are whacked if they think you're a screw up. Whacked and way off base."

Jessie didn't know what to say. No one had ever really believed in her before, and now, suddenly, it seemed as if everyone around her was beginning to. It felt good. No, it felt great. "Thanks."

"You're good people, Jess. You deserve a better break than the one you got when you came here."

Jessie grinned broadly. "Thank you, Tanner. I'm glad you think so because you're good people, too. You just have to believe that no matter what anybody else says."

"Who I believe, is Ceara, and she said you might need some help getting out of here in order to—how did she put it? Get the job done? Does that sound about right?"

Hope filled Jessie's chest. "You're here to bust me out?"

He nodded. "I'm here to help you do whatever it is that has Ceara's panties in a wad. She's been like a panther in a cage pacing back and forth. The least I can do is see if I can help you guys. You need a ride somewhere, I've got wheels."

"But my parents would kill me if they knew I left."

"Ceara told me to tell you to let her worry about them. You game to get out of here or not?"

Grabbing her jacket, Jessie raced for the door. "Let's go."

Cate felt the quiet desperation in the air as they made their way to the Chieftain. She felt it from the trees, from the animals and from the birds taking flight. The air was filled with bad energy; like the kind one feels just before lightning strikes or the earth trembles. The world knew what was coming and it was sad for it.

"Can you feel it?" Cate whispered when her horse sidled up to Maeve's.

"Aye. It is thick and pervasive. There is so very little time. The land is preparing to drink in the blood that will be spilt from here to the coast."

"They mean to take the whole of the island."

Maeve nodded. "The Romans have always believed in conquests and expansion. We are merely another bauble for Rome's collection."

"What of Eire? Shall they conquer that as well?"

Maeve shook her head. "I have seen nothing of a Roman invasion of the islands to the west, but that does not mean it is not so. And you? Have you seen anything?"

Cate shook her head. "Nothing of the sort. Rome does not land on the emerald isle during our lifetime."

"Let us hope that is a long life, my love."

Cate nodded. "Would that we could see that as well. You know, I will never understand how a culture so rich with artisans and philosophers could so crudely demean those they conquer. They do not understand our way of life."

"Nor do they wish to. To them, *we* are the barbarians, uncultured, unworthy to lead ourselves."

"But Maeve, so much of what they do is unnatural."

"Indeed."

"Can it truly be that they will be the ones to dominate the world?"

Maeve reached over and patted Cate's leg. "Perhaps you can have that answer tonight."

"Tonight? I cannot make it back to Fennel this eve."

"Nor shall you try. Lachlan and I shall put you in another deep sleep. From there, you must reach Jessie and learn what the Romans are going to do. Perhaps then, you can discover what becomes of such a people."

"It has never occurred to me to ask."

"Because you are a kind and gentle soul. You would never use Jessie or her information for personal gain. It is the reason the Goddess has given you the ability to go and return from the portal. You are more than worthy."

Cate had to look away. Maeve could not be more wrong. Oh yes, preventing the Druid population from being annihilated was the original reason for sending her through, but saving Maeve's life was her primary concern. It *was* for personal gain, and there was no way around that. Perhaps Blodwin might know. Maybe the Goddess was well-aware of her true intentions and was allowing her to proceed anyway.

They rode for quite awhile without speaking, and Cate sat astride her mount wondering about Jessie and the life she was leading so incredibly far away. Was she happy? Did she have goals and desires? Was she loved? There were so many things Cate wanted to know about the young woman she would become, yet there was so little time to devote to those matters.

She was beginning to understand the inner workings of the sight, and how the portals contributed to the strength of it. She was experiencing the eternality of the soul and seeing firsthand that it does not die, but learns its lessons and moves on to another life in another time. What lesson, Cate mused, could she learn in this life that would help her soul have a better, happier life in the next world? The Silures believed in the transmigration of souls to such a degree that it enabled them to live life more fully than so many of the other peoples the Romans had conquered. Silurian warriors, like most of the Celts, were not afraid to die, not afraid to whoop and holler and go berserk during battle because they understood that death, like life, was only temporary. This, ultimately, was what the Roman emperors had always been most afraid of. How can you rule a people who despise you if they do not, in fact, fear you as well? Roman domination resulted because people feared them, feared their slavery, their destructiveness. But the Celts felt no such fear of the Romans or anyone else. They were a proud and fearless society that felt pity for the Roman people who allowed the elite to rule them with such an iron fist. It would not be so easy to wrestle from the Celtic people their homes, their religion, their way of life.

That was going to be a very difficult fight, Cate knew. She needed no sight to know that thousands from both sides would give their lives in battle. Thus far, no one had been able to stop Rome, but that didn't keep the Druids from doing everything in their power to keep their people's culture intact. They would do everything they could to preserve the memory, traditions and rituals of a people too proud to surrender and too brave to quit.

Otherwise, what good were the Druids to their people?

Closing her eyes, Cate sighed. How odd that the fate of her kind rested on the shoulders of a young woman two thousand years away. How much odder was it, still, that Cate believed in her.

When Jessie got to the car, she was surprised and delighted to find Ceara sitting in the passenger seat.

"I have been worried half to death," Ceara said, taking out a handkerchief and wiping her eyes. "When I hadn't heard anything—"

"We don't have the Internet here, and the phone lines are sporadic at best. I can't get to the place—" Jessie said, cutting her eyes over to Tanner. She didn't want to sound like a complete loon in front of him.

"Tanner can be trusted, my dear. He is well-aware of what we're about."

Tanner slowed as they came to a light. "I'm just the driver today, Jess, but if you ever needed anything else—"

Jessie's mouth was hanging open. "Wait. You two are *friends?*"

Ceara chuckled. "Good friends, actually, though, to make Tanner's life easier, we don't generally let it get around. He has it tough enough as it is, and I—well—you know what the folks say about me."

"People have told me about your parents asking around. Your dad thinks I'm some kind of hoodlum."

"They came here to start fresh and they don't feel as if I have because of some of the choices I've made. The truth is, I don't think they'd be happy if I hung out with nuns." Jessie glanced out the window. "Where are we going, anyway?"

Tanner shook his head and tossed a quick glance over to Ceara. "Ceara wants to go to the U of O and talk to her professor friend and I have to drop something off for my dad."

"What about my parents?"

"They've gone to pick up your brother. Do not worry about them. What we have to do is far more important. Don't you worry, though. The Goddess is with us."

An hour and a half later, they pulled up to a large brick building in the center of town.

"I'll be back in about an hour," Tanner said, pulling into a parking space. As Jessie and Ceara got out, Tanner grabbed Jessie's wrist and gently pulled her back into the car. "I just wanted you to know—for your own peace of mind—that I haven't done drugs in over a year. I'm clean and I plan on staying that way."

Jessie reached up and laid her palm on his cheek. It was bristly and rough from his unshaven face, and she realized, for the first time, what a man he really was. "Tanner, that doesn't matter to me."

"It does to me, Jess. I'd hate to think that being friends with me would cause you so much pain. I just wanted you to know. I guess—"

"That you're worth it?" Without stopping to think about it, Jessie leaned over and kissed him softly on the cheek. "I think you're wonderful. Thank you for being my friend."

A deep blush rose to his temples. "Hell, Jess, that's easy."

"The mutual admiration society needs to come to a close, kids. We have things to do." Ceara squinted at a group of young women playing hackey-sack in the quad. "Professor Rosenbaum is just the man to help us find out what we need to know as quickly as possible."

"You called him for help?" Jessie started through the parking lot.

"Of course, dear. After all, it's been a few days since you've made contact with Cate."

"Um—not quite." Jessie explained about her memory and how Cate had managed to get into her dream. The entire time she spoke, Ceara stood there, wide-eyed, nodding slowly, as if in a trance. "But I don't know what happened before Cate got in. She said something about having a hard time reaching me because I was in a dark and evil place. Does that make any sense to you?"

Ceara nodded. "Ofttimes, when the body is imprisoned or constrained, the soul's power is somewhat diminished. It is one of the phenomena of the concentration camps that psychologists spent years researching. They wanted to know why some people who appeared physically stronger than others died long before the physically weaker survivors. They have always searched for a way to measure one's emotional strength. Of course, there is no known way to gauge the strength of the human spirit, but it does not take a rocket scientist to figure out that once your spirit quits, your body is soon to follow regardless of how strong it is."

"What you're saying is that Cate could feel my spirit being broken?"

"Not broken. You're too strong for that. But she may have known you were not okay. Your parents' lack of trust has created a prison within you. I imagine that's what Cate means. We must be moving, my dear. Professor Rosenbaum is a busy man."

"What does he do?"

"His field is ancient civilizations. I asked him to abbreviate his normal lecture about what transpired in England and Wales in sixty-one AD. I want you just to sit there and listen until he is finished and then you can ask questions."

"Gotcha."

"He is doing this as a favor to me, so please pay close attention. He abhors dull-witted people and simpletons who cannot focus."

"I'm all over it."

"Good. I have pulled tons off the Internet that should be able to fill in any information you miss today, but you need a crash course since time is of the essence."

Jessie nodded and inhaled the musky scent of the building. It was a familiar scent from somewhere in her past, and she smiled to herself, knowing it was a memory she had just experienced. She didn't know from what era or what part of the world, but it was familiar nonetheless. The aroma of old leather books beckoned her like a magnet drawing metal slivers; it was a force she could not ignore.

"When we're done here, Ceara, would you mind if we dropped by the admissions office?"

"Of course I wouldn't mind, but whatever for?"

Jessie looked around at the dark oak doors and the bookshelves filled with knowledge she had never cared to know, and said, "Because I belong here. I'm going to apply."

Ceara clapped her hands together. "What a wonderful idea! What will you major in, my dear?"

Jessie grinned as Professor Rosenbaum's office door opened. "What else? History."

The Silures' Chieftain was a large block of a man with big barrel arms and logs for legs. His reddish hair met a beard that was beginning to streak with gray. On his left thigh he sported a scar the length of

Cate's forearm, and his right bicep looked as if a large animal had taken a bite out of it. He was, it was rumored, a warrior who had cheated death nearly a dozen times, and by the looks of his body, Cate believed it.

Sitting in front of a fire and a makeshift camp, the Chieftain beckoned them to come forward. "I understand you had a bit of trouble along the way. I am pleased to see you are well."

Lachlan nodded. "Fortunately for me, sir, the women were more than capable of felling the eight soldiers who had captured us."

The Chieftain laughed at this. "I do so love tales of Celtic female warriors destroying the enemy. Are these they?" The large man peered through the dark at Cate and Maeve. "Maeve, is that you? Come forward, lass. Are you the tigress who saved our head priest?"

Maeve shook her head. "Cate McEwen is the one who saved us, sir."

"McEwen, ah yes, your father was a great man cut down in the prime of his life. You have your father's fighting skills then. I honor thee." The Chieftain bowed low to Cate. "You must be very brave, little one."

Cate bowed her head and backed away to allow Lachlan and Maeve to conduct this matter. "I am merely one of us trying to save as many lives as we can."

"Indeed. What say you, Lachlan?" The Chieftain motioned his man to retrieve three goblets of wine and waited for Lachlan and Maeve to have a sip before answering.

"The Silures' Druids have chosen to stand fast and fight."

The Chieftain smiled briefly. "I expected as much. Do you believe it best to fight here in the highlands or further west? There are stories that the Romans are moving northwest. I do not want to move on hearsay. What do you see?"

"Death, mighty one. There is no escape from it, only a lessening of the damage done."

"And what will my Druids do during this devastation?"

Lachlan shrugged. "We await your command."

The Chieftain stroked his great beard. "The Iceni and Ordovices are also planning to rebel, but they are far too slow in rallying their people. If you fight here with us, then our might is more concentrated, but if I send you off to the Isle of Mona, we can split their forces and weaken their numbers, as they shall surely come after you."

Lachlan looked at Maeve, who shrugged. This was when they needed Jessie's information the most. "If that is what you believe best."

Looking at Maeve, the Chieftain asked, "Think you we ought to send warriors to Mona to fight alongside our priests and priestesses?"

"I cannot say. My only sight reveals blood and death, misery and ruin. Whether we are on Mona or here with you, our people will suffer horrible losses."

"Aye. My reports indicate that the Governor's soldiers double daily. I would think you might be safer here with me and my men."

Maeve glanced over to Cate, who spoke very softly. "We might have different answers for you in the morn."

The Chieftain stared into the fire. For a long time he sat motionless, just looking into the flames. When he finally spoke, his voice was soft yet cold. "Then my men will continue to prepare. We will be ready no matter where the Romans attack."

"We have not much time," Maeve added. "At all. Suetonius Paulinus's men will be here shortly."

He nodded. "I shall await your instructions regarding your people and the Isle of Mona and will send a message to the Ordovices to hold off on any attack until they hear from us. I will await your wisdom on the matter, Maeve, until it becomes too dangerous not to act. I trust in your guidance for you have never led me astray. Let us hope and pray that we continue in that manner."

When the Chieftain left them, the three of them sat at the fire thinking their own thoughts, searching any unthought-of options, and when one of them finally spoke, it was Cate's quiet voice they heard over the crackling fire.

"I am ready. Tonight. Now."

Maeve touched her shoulder lightly. "Are you sure?"

"Jessie fully understands our dire need. Wherever she was, I am sure she is no longer in its grasp. She, too is a fighter. We must do this

Maeve, tonight. This may be our final opportunity."

Maeve took Cate's hand in hers. "There is so little time left."

"I know."

"Then we shall proceed." Maeve motioned to Lachlan to rise.

"And if nothing happens? If Jessie cannot be of help to us?" Lachlan asked.

"Then we will have stepped through into another world in vain."

"Suetonius Paulinus wanted to subdue the mutinous spirit of the Britons, so he resolved to attack them and drive them to the Isle of Mona, called Anglesey today." Dr. Rosenbaum was in the middle of his lecture to two rapt listeners. True to Ceara's instructions, Jessie had asked no questions nor interrupted his flow of speech, relying, instead, on her limited note-taking experience and her newly awakened mind.

"He ordered a number of flat-bottomed boats, new in that time period, to be constructed so that he could send men across with their horses. He knew how familiar the Celts were with their woods, and without horses he would never catch them. Many of those boats arrived with infantry as well. It seems to us like overkill, but Paulinus wasn't kidding around. He was trying to earn his own bragging rights, and to do so, he needed a high body count, especially of the Druids that even Julius Caesar had failed to eradicate.

"On the shore, the Britons were prepared to meet their attackers. Tacitus writes a subjective piece about women pulling out their own hair and acting insane, but his point of view, like so many other Roman entries, is biased. Clearly, the women fought alongside the men as well, and were equally as prepared to die, but the hair pulling and screaming were Tacitus' paint- by-numbers rendition of the scene. Anyway, when the Romans finally arrived, the Druids called forth their gods and goddesses, and initially, this so scared the Roman soldiers that they failed to act. It wasn't until one of the leaders struck down a Druid that the soldiers realized they could, in fact, be killed. That's when—"

Jessie's sharp intake of breath made the professor stop. "Are you all right?"

"I'm fine. It's just such a waste of life, that's all. I'm sorry. I didn't mean to interrupt."

"Human life meant nothing to the Romans if that life wasn't of taxpaying Roman citizenship." The professor pushed his glasses back up the bridge of his long nose. He was a short, bald man with a graying tincture surrounding his head like a halo. Like a throwback to the Sixties, he wore a brown tweed smoking jacket with patches on the elbows and buttoned at the waist. The faint scent of pipe tobacco lingered in the air.

"Tacitus goes on to say that the island and the oak groves they so cherished perished in the very flames the Druids had set themselves. Much of Mona was destroyed by fires that burned out of control, and though Tacitus would like to blame the Druids for starting fires, many historians today believe that the Romans sent flaming arrows into the woods to prevent the Druids from fleeing there. They were too afraid to give chase, but not to fire flaming arrows. Anyway, the island was eventually conquered and the army was garrisoned there in order to kill any uprisings and destroy any future Druidic activity. Paulinus concentrated his attack in South Wales and Snowdonia, where he managed to drive the Druid population further into the mountains of Scotland and across the water to Ireland. Druidry survived there and in the Welsh mountains for decades, but did not make a revival until the Middle Ages when the stories of King Arthur and Merlin abounded." Here, the professor stopped and looked at them both for questions. "Is that what you were wanting to know, Ceara?"

Ceara nodded and lightly touched a tense Jessie. "It is very good, thank you."

"Questions, Jessie?"

Jessie looked up from her notes. She took a deep breath. It felt like she hadn't been breathing. "So the Silures were not *completely* destroyed?"

"Can anything be completely destroyed? Remember, ninety-five percent of our information about the Druids comes from *Roman* sources, so it's not likely to be one hundred percent accurate. In history, we tend to give historical data an eighty to twenty ratio of correctness.

Given how little information there is on this particular subject, one would have to lower that to an easy seventy to thirty."

"What do *you* think, Professor? What has all your research shown you about the Silures?"

Professor Rosenbaum took off his glasses, leaving two red indentations on either side of his nose. "I believe the Britons had the means and the manpower to fend off the Roman invasion, but since they were so factioned off into tribes and clans, they did not have the central leadership needed to push back tens of thousands of Roman soldiers Paulinus sent into the forests."

"But you think some survived."

The professor looked down at Jessie and nodded. "Oh, of course. There are tales, mind you, not historical data, proclaiming how they were driven deep into their beloved woods, where they managed to remain for centuries, hiding in burrows and underground caverns. They continued their illegal practices under cloak of darkness. Up until the myth of Merlin, Druidry remained an underground operation, so to speak."

"So these tales say some did escape," Jessie said insistently.

"Yes, but there is little evidence supporting it. Documentation of the Druids is as elusive as a unicorn, I'm afraid, and so much of what we know about them is pure conjecture."

Jessie inhaled deeply in prelude to her final question. "How many died on Mona?"

The professor shrugged. "Thousands. The Druids had been sent to Mona because they'd been given faulty information from one of the other tribes. I do not believe the Silures would have left their people on Mona had they known Paulinus was going to put both man and horse on boats. That was a new strategy even to the Romans, but it paid off. Going to Mona was a huge and costly mistake for the Silures."

Jessie swallowed hard, feeling almost claustrophobic in his cramped office.

"I hope this hasn't been too confusing. It is difficult to cram a college quarter's worth of information into a half hour. Is there anything else I can answer for you?"

Jessie rose and nodded. "One last thing. Let's say you could step back in time and *you* were on the island. What would be the best way to get as many people as you could off of it before the Romans came to shore?"

The professor cast a curious look to Ceara before replying. "The only way to save yourself during that particular attack would be by boat, of course. Without a boat, you'd be pinned by the Roman soldiers. If, of course, you survived the fiery forests, there would still be no place to go unless you had the foresight to station boats on the opposite side of where they attacked."

Jessie nodded. "Thanks. And thank you so much for your time. I was mostly interested in the possibility of escape."

As Jessie and Ceara turned to go, the professor opened the door for them. "Oh, and one last thing in case you're interested. If you *were* to escape the island, you could have gone to the east side of the island, because the Romans launched their attack from the southwestern part of the country and did not even bother surrounding the isle. If that helps any."

Jessie smiled. "It does. Thank you."

"I do hope I've been of some help. It's not every day someone is interested in what happened to another people from history. Even my students find it boring at times."

As Jessie stepped out of his office, she turned to him one final time. "Can I ask you a personal question, Professor?"

Dr. Rosenbaum put his glasses back on. "You can try."

"Do *you* believe the Druids had powers outside our scope of our comprehension?"

Professor Rosenbaum looked over at Ceara, shook his head, and smiled. "What I wouldn't give to have her for a student." To Jessie, he answered, "I'll deny saying this, Jessie, but I believe the Druids, along with the Native Americans and the Aborigines, were the only individuals capable of keeping mankind from destroying the planet and himself along with it. You can call it a craft, voodoo, magic, or miracles if you want, but those cultures had something we lost a long time ago."

"Do you think we can ever get that back? Is it possible we can find it again?"

Professor Rosenbaum shook his head. "Not unless we could turn the clocks back, Jessie. I'm afraid our time on this planet is going to be rather limited."

With that, Jessie and Ceara hustled down the hall feeling the hands of time slowly wrapping around their necks.

When Tanner dropped Jessie and Ceara off at Ceara's shop, he handed Jessie another business card. "In case you lost the last one. I'm always just a phone call away."

Taking the card, Jessie smiled at him. "Thanks for everything. I don't know how to thank you."

"Be my friend, Jess. Good friends are hard to come by in this world. I'd be mighty pleased to be one of yours."

"Done."

"I better get going and get the car back to my dad."

Jessie waved to Tanner as he drove away, feeling like she had really made a good friend.

"He is." Came Ceara's soft voice from the doorway. "He's one of the best. You could do far worse than have a friend like Tanner Dodds on your side."

"Been there already, Ceara."

"Yes, I believe you have. Come on, girl, we have work to do."

Once in the shop, Ceara left Jessie to read more Internet historical pieces to fill in any gaps from their history lesson, while Ceara returned to the boat to pick up the rest of her printouts.

Sitting at the table where Ceara did her tarot readings, Jessie laid her head down on the table and tried to absorb all the information. She wondered if Cate had any desire to know what had happened to the once powerful Roman Empire. Wouldn't she be surprised to learn that Latin was a long dead language and that Rome was now only the capital of a single European nation? Would Cate want to know? Would she even care? Jessie's head felt thick and she needed a nap.

Rubbing her burning eyes, she sighed loudly. So much had happened since Cate's time. Would Cate want to know about the plague, or that man could fly? Would she just fall over backward to learn that man had actually walked on the moon they so valued? Would any of *that* knowledge change Cate's life or make it better? Would knowing that man could teleport his molecules as a means of travel ten thousand years from now do anything to improve the quality of *her own* life?

She didn't think so. Sometimes, people were so transfixed on the future that the moment slipped quietly away without ever being noticed. She didn't want to live her life like that. She wanted to experience all life had to offer in *this* moment, whether it was good or bad, pretty or ugly, light or dark. She wanted to live *now*.

And suddenly, Jessie understood that that was all Cate wanted, too. She wanted Maeve and Lachlan to live through their *now* together. Nothing else really mattered. All this time, Jessie had only thought about saving Maeve and helping the Druids to live beyond sixty-one AD, but she had never even considered the possibility that *Cate* might not live through the massacre on Mona.

Jumping to her feet, Jessie paced back and forth across the room. The idea of Cate dying was like a bone caught in her throat. While failure wasn't an option, death was even less of one. She knew Cate would eventually die, but to die because Jessie couldn't come up with a few important facts, well, that was more than she could bear.

"Maybe she doesn't die for a long, long time," Jessie said aloud. As she paced, Ceara returned bearing file folders filled with computer printouts.

"Ceara, what if Cate dies at Mona?"

"What?"

Pulling Ceara into the shop, Jessie took the files from her and set them on the table. "I've never even considered that *she* could die at the hands of Paulinus's men."

Ceara sat in her chair and motioned for Jessie to sit in the chair next to her. "First of all, Cate is *already dead.* Secondly, death is always a possibility and something you can *always* count on. I thought you understood that."

"I always thought that Cate would live a long time. It never dawned on me that she might not make it—that we might be too late."

Ceara looked out over the top of her glasses. "The odds are not in her favor, my dear. You heard Dr. Rosenbaum."

"But if Cate dies—"

"Then you will never know what happens to Maeve and Lachlan. That's what's really bothering you, isn't it. The possible disconnect from the one being you know is your soul mate." Ceara tapped her chin as she thought. "Unless—"

"Unless what?"

"Unless your souls meet in another life beyond that one and the soul you tap into remembers what happened to Maeve. Remember, you have Cate's soul inside you. It is always within your grasp to retrieve memories; and not just hers, either, but *all* of them. Those before Maeve and after. You just don't know how quite yet. But don't you worry. That's what I'm here for. There is so much for you to learn about the portal, the soul, your lives. You have been handed a great privilege and an even greater responsibility; you must learn as much as you can in your life about how it works and what it all means."

"And you're going to help me do that?"

"Indeed. There is much to know, but you must be patient."

"I'm trying, but all I can think about is saving Maeve."

Ceara sighed and shook her head. "No, all *Cate* wants to do is save Maeve, but you, you have a far greater purpose. You, my friend, must save *the Druids*. Do not forget that."

Jessie held her head in her hands. "But we already know the outcome, don't we? The professor has it all right there on his desk. I can't change the past."

Ceara waved the words away like she was swatting a fly. "Oh Jessie, there is so much about time you still do not understand. Their future has not happened yet. *This* is what you must understand. In *our* past, we know the Romans drove the Druids into the hills, but do we know why? Why did they go to Mona? Do we have any account about how they escaped their attackers on Mona?"

"I don't know. It didn't sound like it."

Ceara nodded. "All the records we have of the historical events, and we still do not know how they managed to escape the well-trained Roman army? Don't you find that odd?"

Jessie tilted her head in question. "I hadn't thought about it."

"Well, *think* about it. The Druids escaped. We know that. They managed to flee and stay hidden for the next eight hundred years. We know that as well. How do you think they knew where to go, where to hide, where to run to escape an army that nearly owned the world at one point? How did they *know*?"

Jessie stared hard into those light-blue eyes, feeling not only illumination at last, but a familiarity as well. "Because of *me*."

A smile lit up Ceara's face. "Yes. Because of you. There was no one to write about it because who knew about it then? Who would believe it? To explain *you* would be to uncover information about a portal that had been hidden all those years. To uncover *you* as their source of information would be opening themselves up to disaster. The portal and all its knowledge is not for the common man, my dear. It is for the likes of you."

Jessie sat back and shook her head. "Wait a minute. *I* play a role in the turn of events of an entire culture?"

"I know it's difficult to comprehend, especially when we live in a time when most don't believe one person can make a difference. You save them from complete annihilation, allowing them to live in relative peace for nearly a millennium. Maybe they were regrouping, maybe something else happened in history, but we know one thing for certain: *something* saved the Druids on that island, and that something could very well be you."

Jessie's head started pounding. "But what if I did nothing? What if I just sat here for the next week and let them die. How could history explain that?"

Ceara grinned. "Because you are not the only time traveler in existence, are you?"

Jessie's face fell. She remembered strange names mentioned before . . . was it Angus and . . . Quinn? "Quinn has yet to return to the portal. They think he's dead."

"But he *could* be alive. Anything is possible when you're dealing with time. You ought to know that by now."

Jessie nodded, a tiny ray of light shining into her numbed mind. "So, I tell them about Mona, and they . . ."

"They fight the good fight. You will not change the past, Jessie. You will become *part* of it. Do you understand now?"

Before Jessie could respond, Tanner burst through the door. "Her parents have left and were last seen on one twenty-eight. The coast is clear to get her back to the Pit."

Jessie looked at Tanner as if he were nuts. He, in turn, winked at her and reached to help Ceara up. "I'd say you have a good three hours before they return."

Jessie rose and helped Ceara gather all the files. "Do you have spies watching the house?"

Tanner laughed. "Nothing as mundane as that. One of my hobbies is fiddling with electronic surveillance gadgets. Once they left the house, it triggered one of my ladybug devices and I hopped in the car and followed them until they got to the freeway. Now, you gonna stand here yakking or are you going to the Pit to finish whatever it is you started?"

Jessie looked at Ceara, who smiled. "Well, my dear? Is it time to be off to see the wizard?"

Jessie nodded. "Absolutely."

As Jessie and Ceara approached the wall where the numberless door materialized, Jessie took the keys out of her pocket and looked at Ceara as the door slowly materialized.

"Oh—my," Ceara uttered. "It's been—it's so—how very odd."

Jessie turned to Ceara. "Why don't you come with me?"

Ceara shook her head. "No, Jessie. This is a journey for the young."

"But Ceara—"

"No."

Jessie's forehead furrowed as she gazed at the old woman. Never before had she heard her sound so harsh. "Ceara? What is it? Are you afraid of the seam?"

"It is nothing. Now stop all this nonsense and get going. You are wasting valuable time. Remember everything the professor told you, and do not leave until Cate has picked your brains clean. If you do not know, say so. Don't guess. Don't make anything up."

Jessie nodded. "I could really use you in there."

Ceara waved her off. "Go now."

Jessie hesitated a moment before hugging her. It felt like she might not ever return. "Thank you, Ceara, for all you've done." Jessie opened the door, stepped in, and closed it. Once again she found herself in Cate's world, where mist hung in the air and clung to the trees, and where she knew, if she walked just past this clearing, Cate would be waiting.

And she was.

"Jessie!" Cate cried, jumping to her feet and running over to her. Emotions overwhelming them both, they drew each other into a tight embrace. "I am so very happy to see you!"

Jessie pulled away, nodding. "Me, too. Did you save Maeve from the soldiers?"

"Just barely. She sends you her gratitude and appreciation from the bottom of her heart, as do I."

"And Lachlan?"

"He is well, also, though I believe the very nature of what the Romans were wanting him to do has upset him quite a bit. He does so respect Maeve."

"Where are they now?"

"He and Maeve are watching me as we speak."

"This is your dream then." It was a statement of fact. The feelings of a dream state were far different from those of actually being *inside* Cate. Jessie was becoming more familiar with the tastes and textures of a true quester.

Cate nodded. "I am too far from the portal so they induced me into a very deep slumber to enable you to reach me. I take it this means you have extricated yourself from that dark place you were in?"

"Hell, yes. I'm fine now. I've retrieved the information you need, but I'm afraid it doesn't look good."

Cate motioned for Jessie to sit down on the stone next to her, which she did. "We are prepared for the inevitable, Jessie, so please, go ahead. I am not afraid."

Jessie ran her hands through her hair, and inhaled a deep, painful breath. "Paulinus has amassed troops in excess of sixty thousand. He is turning his attention to the Silures and plans to push you off the coast toward the Isle of Mona, where there will be little place to run."

Cate stared down at her folded hands. "What—what happens on the Isle of Mona?"

Jessie felt older than her years and younger than her soul. It was the question she knew was coming but didn't want to answer. Taking a deep breath, she very quietly said, "The Druids . . . are defeated."

Cate did not look at her, but stared into the fire before them. "Defeated or destroyed?"

"Nearly destroyed. Some of you survive, but not many. Those who do, end up in Ireland and the Scottish Highland." Jessie paused as Cate looked confused. "It's the island west of Britain and . . . what do you call the area up north?"

"Alba. We escape to Alba?"

Jessie nodded. "Apparently, the Romans never got that far north nor to the islands in the west."

Cate inhaled a long, sharp breath. "Eire. The island is called Eire."

"Well, those of you who make it there remain in hiding for over a thousand years. But it's Mona that's going to be the Druid burial ground. If you can stay away from there, you three could live through this."

"The Chieftain has already sent word that the Isle was the safest haven for our people. He has sent most of his strongest Druids there believing the Romans would not attempt an assault upon the water. They do not like the water very much. Are you *certain* the Romans attack Mona?"

Jessie ran her hands through her hair once more. "Paulinus has flat-bottomed boats built to be able to hold his horses. Your Chieftain was given faulty information, most likely from someone who is supplying Paulinus with information."

"Flat . . . bottomed . . . boats . . ."

"Yes. He didn't want your people to be able to run into the woods, so he made sure they have horses to run you down. If your people are moving from the coast to Mona, they'll be killed there."

"But most are Druids."

"Exactly. Paulinus isn't out to destroy the Silures. He's out to destroy the Druids because your people rely on them so much for leadership. Destroy you and your people will fall in line."

"And our Chieftain has stranded them now upon that very isle." Cate held her head in her hands. "This cannot be. In trying to preserve us, he has sent us to our doom."

Jessie looked at Cate's profile. She appeared so small and fragile that she made Jessie's heart hurt. "The Silurian leaders had no idea how deep Paulinus's campaign against you was. It is not your Chieftain's fault."

"Is there anything that can be done?"

"Other than keeping Maeve away from Mona?"

Cate sighed and fought back tears. "When I tell her what you have just told me, the Isle of Mona will be exactly where she will want to head. She will want to save as many of us as she can. It is how she is, and I would expect no less from her."

"And Lachlan?"

"He goes where Maeve goes."

"Where are you now?"

"Nearly two days' ride from the coast."

"Then you still have time to have the Chieftain stop sending Druids to Mona."

"Jessie, it is possible that the Chieftain may not even believe my report."

"Why not?"

"I am supposed to tell the greatest warrior of the Silurian people that there are sixty thousand soldiers preparing to run us all through, and that those sent to a sanctuary will be run down like wild boars by men on horses? He will be disgraced. Disgraced men do not often act in the best interest of their people."

"Then forget him. You take Maeve and Lachlan to Mona if you must. If you're going to save lives, it will only be from there. That's what the historical information reports."

Cate looked up at her for the first time. "What historical information?"

"Your people's written history, what little there was of it, will be largely destroyed by the new religion called Christianity. The Catholics will do everything they can to eradicate your people's philosophies from history."

For a long time Cate said nothing, she just stared at Jessie. "I have so many questions, but I am afraid my heart would break in the knowing."

Jessie sighed. "I apologize I don't have more for you, but there isn't much. Believe it or not, the first mention of Druids that we can find comes from Julius Caesar."

Cate held up her hand signaling Jessie to stop. "Please. I can bear it not. I wish I would be able to hear it, but it is too hard to think that my people have nearly been forgotten, remembered only by a man who reviled us. It is as if all the work we have done has been for naught."

"But that's not true. The Druids who *do* survive Mona keep your religion alive. It is during a time now called the Dark Ages that Druids make a comeback and actually have kings consulting them."

Cate's dark expression brightened. "For truth?"

Jessie nodded; glad she could offer *some, any* positive news to Cate. "For truth. A guy named Merlin comes along, and there are great tales told about his powers and his love of a king called Arthur."

"Then why are the times considered dark?"

"Well, I don't know much about history, a fact I intend to rectify, but Christianity and religious fervor took over for rational thought and people stopped learning."

"Stopped learning? How can that be so?"

"You'd be amazed. Like I said, I don't really know much about history, or I could tell you more. I just know your people *and* the

Druids make a big comeback."

"It does my heart good to know that we are not entirely extinguished by the blood-thirsty Roman army."

"The Roman Empire will extend quite a ways, Cate, and for hundreds of years longer. They do not get their comeuppance until the fifth century."

Cate once again held up her hand. "No more. Maeve tells me that too much information from you will cloud my true vision—but—it is good to know they do not go unpunished."

"Let's just say they lost it all except for a country now known as Italy."

"No!"

"Yep."

"Oh—my." Cate leaned forward and gazed into the fire. There was so much she wanted to know, so many things she wanted to ask, but there just wasn't time, and she needed to heed Maeve's words because—

"Because I would be disappointed in you if you did not."

Both Cate and Jessie wheeled around toward the mist, where the third voice had come from. Out of the fog that swirled around her head walked a tall, auburn-haired woman wearing the same robe Cate most often wore.

Jessie immediately knew who it was. "Maeve."

Maeve glided across the surface of Cate's Dreamworld to where they now stood.

"You've come," Cate whispered greeting Maeve. "It has been a very long time since you visited my dream self."

Maeve lightly brushed Cate's cheek before turning to Jessie and greeting her. "It would be rude of me not to come and thank the woman who helped save my life. Hello, Jessie."

Jessie walked up to Maeve and, oddly enough, bowed. "It feels like I have known you forever."

Maeve smiled and repeated her gesture on Jessie's cheek. "You have."

Cate agreed. "You just did not know it."

Jessie looked up at Maeve, amazed at how tall she was, at how beautiful and regal she was. "How—"

"How is it that I am here in Catie's Dreamworld?" Maeve smiled. "You need more information about the nature of the creatures we are. There are many other worlds one can visit if one knows how. Normally, I would never presume to come uninvited, as it is a very invasive act, but under the circumstances, I knew Catie wouldn't mind."

Cate shook her head. "I learned long ago, Maeve, that you come and go where and when you please."

Maeve's eyes softened as she looked at Cate. "Indeed." To Jessie, Maeve said, "If, as I suspect, your world no longer honors the true soul of the earth, then the very fact that you listened to the warning regarding myself and Lachlan says a great deal about the power of the craft residing within you."

"The craft? You mean . . . Druidry?"

Maeve nodded. "Even if the last Druid were destroyed, Druidry will exist forever because we are in the souls of the trees, of the animals, of the ground and the sky. While we may not roam the earth, the earth carries us within her. We may perish in this life, but the soul of a Druid goes on into others. It is a marvelous thing, really."

"And *I* have powers?"

"Do you think it is a coincidence that you were the person chosen to unlock the secrets of the portal?"

Jessie shook her head. "I no longer believe in coincidences, Maeve. I know better."

Maeve smiled as a teacher would at a student who finally fully understands the answer to a problem. "Yes, you do. Do you now understand why you could never embrace your family's religion?"

Jessie's eyebrows shot up. "How did you know?"

Maeve held up a hand to silence her. "There is a place in your heart that is closed off from their belief system for a reason. At the time, you believed that you were making a conscious choice, but it was so much more than that. Your spirit, that of you and Cate, and countless other individuals before and after her, has deep Celtic roots . . . Celtic and Druidic, for our people have existed far longer than the great historians have thought. Your spirit, Jessie, will never accept the idea of one God commanding all, because it knows better. You never made a *conscious* choice not to follow their path—your soul made it for you long before you were even born."

So much of her own life was beginning to make sense to Jessie now. The Celtic crosses she always looked at, the Celtic violins and music she listened to when no one was looking; her new attention to nature, were all part of who she was, now and eternally.

"So, Cate's spirit still strives to be heard even two thousand years away."

Maeve nodded. "Catie is to become a very powerful Druid in her life, and not even death will be able to diminish her powers. You see, Jessie, it will fall upon Cate's shoulders to keep our memory alive. I came to Britannia to teach her how to do that, and how to become one of the greatest priestesses of her time. Catie will be talked about long after her corporeal form has vanished."

"That's a heavy burden and a gift wrapped in one package."

Maeve grinned slightly. "Is it?"

Staring at Cate, Jessie realized how intertwined their destinies were.

"Knowledge, Jessie, must always pre-empt action." Maeve's gray eyes were so mesmerizing, Jessie wondered if one could be hypnotized in a dream. "There is much for you to know . . . much more for you to learn in order to remember the vast amount of knowledge within you. But you must be patient, for some of those lessons will take years. You must be open to all sorts of people, all different kinds of ideas, no matter how foreign or unfamiliar to you, because you may never know if the people you meet are questers seeking knowledge you possess."

Jessie nodded almost mechanically. "In California, I probably never would have given Madam Ceara a chance. I mean she—"

Maeve and Cate both looked so stricken, so pale, that Jessie stopped in mid-sentence. "What?"

"Who did you just say?" Maeve's eyes changed from gray to a bright blue in such a flash, Jessie wasn't sure she saw what she thought she saw. "What was that name? That name you just said."

"Madam Ceara? She's the woman who has been helping me understand all of this." Jessie glanced over at Cate, whose mouth hung open and whose eyes were wide with surprise.

Maeve turned to Cate and they locked eyes, sharing words that need not be spoken. "Pray to the Goddess. Can it be? She—she made it."

Cate murmured, "Unbelievable. We thought—"

"We obviously thought incorrectly. Something must have happened."

Jessie rose and jammed her hands on her hips. "What are you two talking about? Who made what? What happened?"

Maeve rose and stood closer to the fire. For a moment, Jessie thought she might be praying. When at last Maeve turned, tears brimmed in her eyes. "Of all the news you have brought to us this day, Jessie, that news will stun Lachlan the most."

"What news?"

Maeve looked down at Cate before turning her now gray eyes back to Jessie. "The news that his mother is alive and living in the twenty-first century."

Jessie's hand went up to her mouth as all of the innuendo, dropped sentences, and mysterious lines uttered by Ceara came at her all at once. Could it be? Could the woman she had trusted with her greatest secret truly have come from this age? "You don't mean—"

Maeve nodded. "Your Madam Ceara is Lachlan's mother."

When she came out of the room, she had no idea how much time had passed, nor did she care. All she could think about was talking to Ceara.

"Why didn't you tell me?" Jessie asked the second she saw Ceara sitting on a small stepping stool outside the supply room. "How could you have kept something like that from me?"

Ceara rose and took Jessie by the arm. "It's been hours. We must be off."

"How could you not tell me?"

"We can talk about it at the beach house. A friend of mine is off visiting her mother and I am house-sitting. Let's go there and talk. According to Tanner, your parents are still out of town, so you're safe for the time being. Tanner will let us know when they're on the way back."

"Tanner again? Who's he? Merlin?"

Ceara grinned softly. "Not quite, but I advise you never to underestimate him or his abilities."

"Abilities?" Jessie groaned. "Do I want to hear this?"

"Hush yourself, my dear. Hurry along now."

Jessie managed to keep quiet during the ride to the beach house owned by Ceara's friend. It was a high-ceiling palatial estate overlooking the ocean. Jessie surveyed the home and marveled at how beautiful it was. The great room overlooked the coast and had a cathedral ceiling giving the room an open-air feel.

"Would you like some tea?"

"Actually, Ceara, I'd like some answers first."

Ceara took off three of her colorful wraps and stood with her back to Jessie looking out the expansive window at the water crashing on the rocks below. It was quite a few beats before she spoke. "I wondered how long it would take her to figure it out."

"She didn't figure anything out. I mentioned your name, and she and Cate nearly fell over from surprise."

"What did they say?"

"What else? That you are—were—are—Lachlan's *mother*." Jessie stared at her. "It's true, isn't it?"

Ceara imperceptibly nodded. "Aye. Lachlan is my son."

Jessie blew out a loud breath. "How could you have gone all this time holding that kind of a secret? Didn't you trust me *at all*?"

Ceara watched the waves and sighed. "It wasn't about trusting you, my dear. You want a simple answer, and there isn't one."

"Sure there is. You were once a powerful Druid priestess who went through the portal and didn't return. How's that for a start?"

Ceara shook her head. "You call that simple?"

"But something happened, didn't it? What happened, Ceara? What went wrong that trapped you here? You *are* trapped here, aren't you?"

Ceara did not take her eyes off the ocean, and when it became clear to Jessie that she wasn't going to answer, Jessie continued. "You were in the portal when something happened, and somehow you found yourself stranded in this time. Is that it?"

Ceara bowed her head. Suddenly, she looked very old and frail. "I wasn't just trapped outside of my own time, my dear." Ceara slowly turned to face Jessie. "I found myself trapped in the body of a crazy, drunken, homeless woman."

Jessie slowly reached out and put her hand on Ceara's shoulder. "And that's why you were so adamant about not going with me."

Ceara nodded. "There was no *there* to go to in sixty-one AD, unless I had already been reborn, and I could not take the chance that I hadn't been yet." Ceara's voice was barely above a whisper. "I no longer lived. I do not know what happened the last time I entered the Forbidden Forest, but I ceased to exist there. My body did not make it. Instead—I was here, in an insane woman's body, trapped in a time I could not fathom in a shell I could not stand."

"But—you're not a crazy, homeless person."

Sighing loudly, Ceara shook her head. "Not anymore, but I was for a long time. Edith, that's whose body I have been in all these years, was the town entertainer. She was not entirely crazy, but insane enough to be unemployable. She lived on the streets, ate out of dumpsters, and found herself beaten and raped enough for two dozen lifetimes."

Jessie's hands rose impulsively to her mouth. "Oh. How awful."

"Her existence was joyless, her life void of meaning."

"What changed that? What happened?"

"*I* happened. I did what a Druid priestess should never *ever* do. I possessed her body."

Jessie swallowed hard. "Possessed? I didn't know that was really possible."

"You didn't think time slipping was possible, either."

"True."

"It was so easy, Jessie, so very easy. She fought me not at all, preferring a quieter, more peaceful and far less painful existence deep in our soul."

"She went away willingly?"

Ceara nodded. "Yes, I played the role of Goddess that day, and sent her deep within the bosom of our being so that I could take her body over and live out my life here in sober peace."

"It didn't frighten you?"

Ceara shook her head. "Not at all. I was just another voice she kept hearing, and, in the end, she nearly begged me to stop her pain. She was considering drinking herself to death, and, quite frankly, I had just died in one world, I wasn't ready to do so again so soon after."

Jessie inhaled a deep breath. "So, you took over her body and have been forced to live it all in this time."

"Yes. I wish to apologize. I have been wanting to tell you, but so much has happened and we've been working so hard to free you, to free Maeve, to keep everyone alive so we can do what needs to be done, that my own issues seem so insignificant. You have no idea how incredibly happy you made me the day you told me Lachlan lived. I have done nothing but sit and wonder daily at his fate since the day I became trapped."

"Why wouldn't Lachlan have been alive? Wasn't he just a little boy when you left?"

Ceara nodded. "I had no idea how much time had gone by. Lachlan could have been just six, or he could have been sixty when you returned."

"Right. You didn't want to get your hopes up."

"Precisely."

"He's a very handsome man."

"So was his father." Ceara let out another deep breath. "Leaving that world and coming to this one was so hard. I was so lonely for such a very long time, and there was much I did not know or understand. Even accessing Edith's memories was difficult because she was nearly pickled when I was first trapped. Eventually, when she sobered up, I made the decision to live, and accessed as many of her memories as I could. Eventually, I learned how to live in this time, acting as if I belonged here and understand your ways, but it wasn't easy. It has never been easy."

Jessie patted her shoulder. "I can't even imagine."

"I'm afraid no one can. Still, time slipping was a choice I made. It was not foisted upon me. We all must learn to live with the consequences of our decisions even if that means two thousand years into the future."

"What did you do after you took over?"

"Sobered up, which, I must say, was one of the ugliest experiences I've ever had. Nauseating, really. Then I went out and got a job. It became apparent early on that money had replaced religious values in this time, so I worked as a maid during the week and a tarot reader on the weekends. The maid job enabled me to get off the street, and the tarot reading allowed me to keep my Druid skills in order."

"Do you still have your powers?"

Ceara finally looked away from the ocean at Jessie. "You mean my sorcery? My witchcraft? My pagan ways? Yes. But I learned long ago that while this society no longer burns, tortures, or drowns heretics, they have found *other* ways to ostracize and condemn those who are different from the norm."

"So, you only use them to do your readings."

Ceara nodded. "This is not a society that casts a favorable eye on the craft."

"How did you go from maid to entrepreneur?"

"When I realized that money is the true God here, I had two wealthy women as clients who became much wealthier when I told them it would be in their best interest to divorce their philandering husbands. Two divorces later, they rewarded me by buying me my shop outright with some of the money from their lucrative divorce settlements. Then, I gave them a bit of stock information, which netted both of them nearly a million dollars apiece. They bought the boat as a write-off and gave it to me as a thank you. Once on my feet, I stopped abusing my gifts, but until then, I needed to use everything at my disposal to clean up poor Edith's life."

"Yeah, sounds like she had pretty much dug herself a hole." She could well understand—she'd nearly dug a similar hole herself.

"Not her. This wretched society. Her doctors had overprescribed medication that was addictive. Her life soon became one drug after another until she had no money, no means for support and no place to run to. She eventually turned to alcohol to ease her troubles, and by that time, her life was lost. It was so sad, really. She never had a chance."

"Until you."

"Don't confuse the two, Jessie. I am still in her body, which, thank the Goddess, she relinquished without a fight."

"But still, you never told me. If you didn't want me to tell Lachlan, I wouldn't have."

"I did not want him knowing, Jessie because I was sure the boy would have come through the portal to see for himself. We were quite close when he was a lad."

"Why can't he? What would be wrong with that?"

"As strong as Lachlan believes he is, he is not a quester. I was a far stronger Druid than he will ever be, yet the portal closed on me, leaving my body defenseless. It was then I knew one simply did not step across time because the portal existed. The portal can only be entered by someone incredibly powerful *and invited*. I came unbidden, and was stranded here. You—well, my dear, the truth is, you were beckoned and you answered the call. You have the strength to do that which Lachlan can only dream of."

Jessie stared deep into Ceara's blue eyes. They were blue much like Lachlan's, but then, how could that be? This was not the body that bore him. How weird to think that Edith was in there somewhere, listening, watching Ceara control their destiny.

Destiny.

Is this what destiny truly was? To be called upon and to answer? To heed the sound of an inner voice that said, *Come, do this thing and reach your highest potential.* Was it her destiny now to go through time helping others?

"I have waited what feels like eternity for one such as you. I knew the second I saw you, but I needed you to *remember.* I could not force you, nor could I supply you with all of the answers. I needed to see that you were strong—that you were *chosen*. So many individuals came and went at the inn, that I began to doubt if it would happen in my lifetime."

"And then I bumbled along."

Ceara grinned. "You did not *bumble* into anything. You and your parents were called. If you truly look back on all of the steps that led your family here, you'd see for yourself that this path, this journey you are now on started long before you came to Oregon." Ceara headed for the kitchen. "All this chatter has parched me. I think I'll make us some tea. Come."

As Jessie followed, she thought back to the events that brought her family here from San Francisco. Hadn't her father received a brochure or letter or something alluding to having his own business in Oregon for a quarter of the cost of having one in California? At first, her parents discussed that they'd do it once Daniel was grown, but suddenly, her parents were e-mailing someone about the inn, and the next thing they knew, they were in Oregon.

But hadn't they kept saying they were coming here for a fresh start? They'd always made it sound as if they had done it for her and Daniel, but she couldn't help but wonder if her father hadn't known on a subconscious level the real reason behind their journey.

"But why didn't you tell me? I mean, after all this got started, I would have understood."

"You were already so overloaded with information." The kettle whistled and Ceara dropped two tea bags into the mugs. "There were more important things to worry about. You had the fate of an entire civilization on your shoulders. I couldn't add to that. I couldn't and I wouldn't, especially once I realized that one of those lives was my son's."

Jessie stared through the kitchen window at the cliffs below. "That secret must have eaten you up inside, Ceara."

"It could have, but when there's a greater good, we must follow our conscience and do the right thing. There never was a right time to tell you, so I took that as the Goddess's way of telling me to keep my mouth shut."

Looking back at her, Jessie nodded. "I can't believe you got stuck in this century. How horrible."

"You have no idea. This is a sad, sad time. A time that will make the Dark Ages appear happier and brighter. They had the plague, you have AIDS, cancer and even consumption has not been eradicated."

"Consumption?"

"Tuberculosis. The Dark Ages were filled with religious zealots who wanted to take care of your soul, this age has religious zealots who want to take your money from you. In the Dark Ages, heretics burned; here, anyone who is not a true believer is going to burn in Hell. My dear, a thousand years from now, this age will be called something far worse than what the present historians might call the Age of Technology. Historians a thousand years from now will see this age as the spiritual and moral wasteland it is and name it accordingly."

"It must have been really hard at first."

"Very, very hard. But remember: I chose to come here."

"Why here and now?"

Pouring the hot water over the tea bags, Ceara continued. "The portal was nothing we used frivolously, mind you, and few of us even knew it existed. But in fifty-two AD, the Romans came after the Silures as a people, and defeated us. I came here in fifty AD hoping to find a way to keep them from destroying our people entirely. I never made it back in time to help. In the end, we were forced to surrender and had to allow the Roman militia to occupy our home, bed our women and change our culture."

"What prevented you from returning?"

Ceara shook her head. "I don't know what truly happened, only that I dreamt one night of a Roman soldier, afraid for his life, and scared of the near lifeless Druid before him. He struck my body down with one slash of his blade. I awoke, in a sweat, crying, sobbing actually, because I knew I could never return."

"Did you try?"

Ceara handed Jessie a steaming mug. "What do you suppose would happen to a soul who steps through the portal and there is no host to receive it?"

Jessie shook her head. "I have no idea."

"Neither do I, but it can't be good."

"So you never tried."

"And I never will. I know that I no longer exist in sixty-one AD, and I have no desire to return to a decaying corpse."

"So you came to save the Silures, but Rome did not destroy them."

"There were many more questers than just I, just as there are more portals to more times. Still, in fifty-seven AD Emperor Nero passed a law prohibiting the practice of our craft. Many of us were persecuted in an attempt to frighten the people away from the belief. I was chosen by our priest to come through because I was a very powerful and wise priestess, and the best choice at the time."

"But you left only nine years ago."

Ceara grinned softly. "Time is not linear, remember? When you're in the portal ten minutes, it's quite possible that ten years could go by."

Jessie remembered the second time she came out of the portal, and a wall she thought Daniel had already painted hadn't been as yet. She'd figured she'd made a mistake. Now she knew the truth.

Ceara walked over to the couch near the large plate-glass window and sat down. "It was almost good enough knowing that he lived to manhood."

Jessie joined Ceara on the couch and balanced her mug on her thigh. "I wish I had more to tell you about him, but he remains pretty much a mystery to Cate."

Ceara nodded, sipping her tea. "That was always his way. I'm not surprised. Even as a little boy, he was always within himself. How did your conversation with them end?"

"You mean in the Dreamworld?"

Ceara nodded and patted Jessie's thigh. "You're going to make a splendid Druid."

Leaning back with her tea in her hand, Jessie grinned and finished the story.

• • •

"She's what?" Jessie felt like someone had kicked her in the stomach. "She's Lachlan's *mother?*"

Cate stared at Maeve, who did not take those haunting eyes off Jessie.

"Apparently she has not told you. What do you know of this Ceara woman, Jessie?"

Jessie told Maeve everything she knew about Ceara; from the first moment they met to her refusal to enter the portal. When she was done, Maeve finally looked away, leaving Jessie feeling slightly dizzy.

"It is she," Maeve whispered, sitting on one of the rocks. The bonfire leapt and crackled. "No wonder you have had such an easier time of it, Catie. You two have the help of a woman who was once one of the greatest healers on the island. People came from as far as Gaul to be healed by Ceara."

"She's a healer?"

Maeve nodded and motioned for Cate and Jessie to sit. "Not just a healer, but a very powerful priestess who loved those in her village so much, she would let none other than herself pass through the portal. Lachlan, I've heard, howled for days after her death, and all of Fennel mourned her loss and saw it as an ill omen that they ought to leave the portal be."

"Will you tell him?" Cate asked, reaching for Maeve's hand.

Maeve stared into the fire and sighed. "I do not know that it is my business to tell him. Perhaps, Jessie, when the great battle is over and life begins anew, you can return one last time and let Catie know what Ceara would like done. It is, after all, her decision."

Jessie's eyebrows knitted together. "One more time? You make it sound as if this is the last time I'll see you."

Maeve glanced over at Cate before replying. "Slipping through the thin fabric of time, as Ceara has shown, is truly very dangerous. We were not meant to leave our realm in search of a better future or more interesting past. The portal is a tool—and as with all tools, it could also be used as a weapon to be used against tyrants, against injustices, against those who would persecute and deny a people the right to exist. When the war is over, Catie must go on with her studies. She will live out her life in this realm, for better or worse, until her last breath sends her elsewhere. She has a life to live and that does not include risking it traveling to other ages." Maeve paused and turned back to Jessie. "And you, you have a life to live in *your* time. There is so much for you to learn, for you to do, for you to *be*. You cannot, you *will* not spend it going in and out of time, risking what Ceara risked, taking your present life for granted. You must swear that when this is done, you will return to your life and forget the portal exists unless called again."

"Forget? How can I forget something as huge as this?"

Maeve smiled softly and took Jessie's hand so the three of them created a circle. "Perhaps forget is the wrong term. Ignore would be better. Jessie, you have done so well, but you must live. You must return to a life and learn the lessons Ceara can teach you. Do you understand?"

Jessie felt her eyes well up with tears. They were her friends and yet—she had to let them go? Never to see them again? It didn't seem fair.

"Have you made plans for getting off the island?"

Maeve nodded. "Even as we speak, we are moving boats to the east side of the isle as you suggested. We may not save everyone, but with your help, we will save many more than without it."

"I just wish I could know how it all turns out."

"You have the ability to access Cate's memories, as well as all of those who have come after. If you learn how to hear those voices, there is nothing you won't be able to do or know. You have Ceara. What you will *not* have is a good life in your time if you are not *present* in it. I am asking you to be present in your own life and let Cate be present in hers."

"I—understand, but—"

"Your life will forever be changed by this experience with us, as will ours, but you must be wise now beyond your years and *stay in your time*."

Jessie had no idea what to say. Was this how her destiny began or how it ended? Was her purpose over so soon?

"No, Jessie, your purpose has only just begun, but it is not to linger in the Dreamworld with Cate. Your destiny, the path you are on, is just the beginning of your life. Your mind is now open, your body young, and your spirit forever changed. Do not be sad at this passing. Instead, rejoice that we have shared and that you now know Catie is within you."

"But how will I ever know if you survived Mona?"

"You may never know. Perhaps it is better that way. You carry within your breast the heart of a warrior, the spirit of a Druid and the mind of a bard. Call on them when you need them. For if you reach down deep enough, you will touch Catie's light and she will always show you the way." Reaching up, Maeve touched Jessie's cheek with her palm. It was hot; Jessie felt the heat all over her. "And remember, no matter where you go, you will find me, or I, as I did in our time, will find you."

"You mean—"

Maeve grinned and nodded. "I *am* out there, Jessie. We just have not met yet." With that, Maeve touched her shoulder before standing at the edge of the mist. "We *will* meet again, Jessie Ferguson. This, I promise you." Turning, Maeve disappeared into the mist. For a long time, both women stared at the misty opening as it slowly closed around her.

"Will I know?" Jessie asked softly.

Cate nodded. "I did. The moment I saw her, something happened within me. I knew."

"Immediately?"

Cate shook her head. "In a heartbeat or two, but you'll know. *We'll* know. I'll help you know."

Sighing, Jessie walked over to Cate and hugged her tightly. "You've become a good friend to me. I'm not very good at goodbyes and I wish this wasn't one."

"You have done a great thing, Jessie. Tomorrow, we will head to Mona to see how many lives we can save. I will do my best to make you proud."

Jessie nodded. "And Maeve? Will you be able to save her?"

"I shall or I will die trying."

As Jessie stepped away, she could barely believe the hollow emptiness inside; the pain of a goodbye far more excruciating than when she left San Francisco. "Then I guess I have to just walk away believing the two of you die a very old age. It's the only way I can leave and live my life without wondering every day if you made it—if you're safe and happy."

Cate nodded, but then her face changed, like one who just got a great idea. "Do you know where Mona is in your time?"

Jessie nodded. "It's called Anglesey now."

"Close your eyes."

Jessie did and immediately saw a stone structure much like Stonehenge.

"See it?"

"Yes."

"Do you see a very large, white rock about the size of two horses off to the side of the henge beneath a large oak tree?"

Jessie nodded.

"Open your eyes."

When she did, Cate was removing the ankh from around her neck. "If we live through this, *both* of us, then I will bury this ankh an arm's length beneath that rock on the western side. I do not know if it will be there two thousand years from now, but if it is, then you will know."

Jessie realized, for the first time, that Cate had made the assumption that Jessie was in England or Wales, and it was no wonder. In Cate's time, there *was* no America. Columbus and the New World were a good fourteen hundred years away.

"I'll find it."

"Thank you, Jessie, for answering my call. I promise I will live my life befitting one who has shown such courage. You are a wonderful person, and I am proud to know that you are who I become so far into the future."

"I'll miss you, Cate." Jessie shook her head and wiped her eyes. "More than you will ever know. You, my little priestess friend, are the very best of me." With that, Jessie found herself back in the inn.

• • •

"Oh, my dear," Ceara said, patting Jessie's thigh. "That must have been very difficult for you."

"Like someone had ripped my heart out and squashed it into the ground." Jessie turned to fully face her friend. "But you know how that feels, don't you?"

Ceara nodded. "And then some."

For a long, silent passing, as the sun set, and dusk sprinkled new colors on the horizon, Jessie and Ceara sat sipping their tea, both feeling a unique sense of loss that happens when you're beyond the point of no return.

"Do you think the ankh could still be there after all these years?"

Ceara's face lit up. "I have a great picture book of Wales. Why don't I go get it and we can see if the stones still stand?"

Jessie's exuberance matched Ceara's. "Would you? God, if I could *know* that they made it, it wouldn't hurt so much having to say goodbye. I can't stand the thought of not knowing, of wondering if I made a difference at all."

"Of course you made a difference. You mustn't ever believe otherwise."

Jessie sighed loudly. "I guess it's done then. I mean, there's nothing else we can do, right?"

Ceara patted Jessie's shoulder. "What will you do now?"

"Go home and face the music, I guess."

"Do you think they'll keep distrusting you?"

Jessie shrugged. "You know what they say about actions speaking louder than words? Well, I'm going to show them how much I've changed by going to the university and doing everything I'm supposed to do."

"That's a great idea. Your parents truly do only want what's best for you."

Jessie sipped her tea. "I do know that. The truth is, I *have* been sneaking around. They're suspicious for a reason and I can't really blame them for being paranoid."

"Good for you. Accountability is going to be important in your life. You'll be asked to do a lot more than what you did this time."

"What do you mean? I thought this was it for me."

Ceara grinned. "You are a quester, Jessie Ferguson. That means others are likely to call on you in similar situations. You may never see Cate or Maeve again, but that doesn't mean your days of serving are over."

Jessie perked right up. "Really? You mean this isn't the end?"

Chuckling, Ceara patted her shoulder. "My dear, this is just the beginning."

Getting to the Isle of Mona took less time than they thought because the Chieftain had given them his swifter horses, and because Druid magic was, after all, magic. Once they were back in Fennel, they collected all the remaining Druids and headed desperately for the coast.

"He ought to have followed us," Lachlan argued. He had done everything but beg the Chieftain to turn his troops toward the coast, but the Chieftain had other plans. He did not wish to fight on the water, choosing, instead, to come at the Romans from behind.

"I do not think he believed the whole notion of flat-bottom boats," Cate said.

Maeve nodded. "Just the thought of a boat having a flat bottom was too foreign to him, but he is surely not to blame. It is as strange to him as the idea of man in flight."

"In all the years, we have never led him astray. He should have believed us. He should have faith." Lachlan shook his head angrily and pounded his fist into his palm.

"It is his job to do what he thinks best for our people, Lachlan. You must respect his position."

"That he would let us go to Mona to fend for ourselves while he does what? Wait to battle? The battle is to be on Mona! He believed us not, or he would be acting along with us. Does he truly believe we can push the Romans out of Britannia? According to Cate, we are to suffer huge losses, and yet, he does not follow? The Chieftain is a dolt."

"Lachlan!"

"Spare me your platitudes, Maeve. The man is short-sighted and he's led us straight into a trap."

"He may be short-sighted, but *we* are not. If anyone can save those sent to Mona, it is we. Stop your fretting. It does us no good."

They rode a few more hours before finally reaching the coast. Lachlan went to the small fishing villages of Ness to see about arranging a boat to the Isle of Mona. No longer wearing his Druidic robe, he had difficulty convincing the fishermen he was who he said he was. The people were justifiably suspicious of everyone claiming to be a Druid since the practice had been outlawed four years ago.

When he returned, he told Cate and Maeve they could cross in the morning, and would be able to leave their horses in the stables overnight.

"Have they seen any boats at all?" Maeve asked.

Lachlan shook his head. "Nothing. I did ask him about flat-bottom boats and he laughed outright. Apparently, he does not believe they would float." Lachlan cut his eyes to Cate, as if beginning to doubt the possibility of flat-bottom boats.

"Our job, Lachlan," Maeve lectured, "is not to doubt the information we have received, but to put it into action. If Catie says the Romans are going to walk across the water with camels on their backs, then our job would be to stop them before they got there."

Lachlan sighed. "I apologize, Maeve. Twelve hours in the saddle has made me somewhat irritable."

"We shall bed here tonight under the stars and leave for Mona at first light. Maybe then your intolerance will diffuse a bit."

It didn't take Cate longer than four deep breaths before she fell fast asleep. She dreamt of many things—of deer running through the forest mist, of digging beneath a large round rock, of an eagle soaring, and something—something that ripped her from her sleep.

As she stood looking into the hills, at the eagle, at the deer, at the thing coming directly at her, Cate's breath caught in her throat. A large red and gray chariot pulled by two broad-chested mares rode out of the sunset at such a speed it was all too quickly upon her. Driving the chariot with the reins in one hand and a spear in the other was a tall, broad-shouldered woman with long flaming locks trailing behind her. She held the spear high above her head and let out a huge war cry before slowing down long enough to stare into Cate's face. The woman grinned conspiratorially, slapped the reins against the horses, and took off—but not before looking over her shoulder at Cate and yelling one word that reverberated through the air.

"Boudicca!"

Jessie slept better than she had in many nights. The large four-poster bed engulfed her like the feather comforter lying at the end of the bed. When she finally woke from a dreamless sleep, it was twelve hours later.

Slowly rolling out of the big bed, Jessie started downstairs and was met by the delicious aroma of bacon frying and coffee dripping. "Ceara?"

When there was no answer, Jessie poked her head into the kitchen and was surprised to find Tanner standing at the stove. Jessie immediately tried to straighten up her hair, but she knew it was to no avail. She had bed head and there was no turning back.

"Hey," Tanner said, flipping the bacon over. It was the first time she'd seen him without his black leather jacket and she was somewhat surprised by how fit he was.

"Hey yourself. How'd you get in here?"

"Ceara called me this morning and asked if I'd make you breakfast. She was worried you weren't eating."

Jessie looked over at the stove. There were scrambled eggs, bacon, hash browns and coffee, all of which smelled divine. "Coffee would be great."

Tanner poured the coffee into one of the whale mugs and handed it to her.

"Where did you learn how to cook?"

Tanner poured himself a cup. "I was a short-order cook at Denny's on Main Street for a summer. It sucked, but I learned a thing or two."

Jessie wrapped her hands around the mug and watched Tanner

finish cooking. "Are you always so nice?"

Tanner laughed. "Hardly. I just know what it's like to be in distress—to feel so out of whack you don't know which way is up. A little kindness is often enough to get your balance."

"Well, I appreciate it. I'm afraid I owe you big time."

"Nah. Call it celestial payback. Ceara helped me when I was at my lowest point. She came out of nowhere, yanked me to my feet, dusted my ass off and helped me get my act together. She believed in me, and sometimes, that's all any of us need to get back on track."

"What was wrong? I mean . . . was it drugs?"

Tanner turned the gas off and dished up two plates of food. "It was everything. The drugs were just a symptom." Taking both plates into the dining room, Tanner set them both on the table that already had fresh flowers in a glass vase and table settings for two.

"Did you bring the flowers, too?"

Tanner nodded. "Madame loves fresh flowers. She believes they still have a certain energy that changes the ambiance of every room."

Jessie yawned and stretched. "I never would have guessed you and Ceara were so close."

Tanner sat down opposite her and took a bite of bacon. "No one would. She knew I'd have no friends if people thought I hung out with the town looney, so it's not like we broadcast it." Tanner held his hand up. "And before you get all self-righteous on me, it was *her* plan, not mine."

Jessie tasted a forkful and nodded. "It's good."

"Thanks."

"But if it wasn't the drugs, what was it that took you to such a dark place?"

Tanner moved his hash browns around his plate before looking up and exhaling loudly. "Madame says you can be trusted. With anything."

"I can."

"She assured me you would never betray my trust."

Jessie set her fork down. This was something very important he wanted her to know. "On my word of honor, Tanner, whatever you tell me stays with me."

He grinned sheepishly. "It first started when I was about six. I thought it was fun to pick up on people's feelings, to know their state of mind or emotional state before they even spoke it. But as I got older, I could not control it, and the emotions I was receiving became overwhelming, nearly driving me insane. What was fun at the beginning quickly became a curse."

"What is *it*?"

Inhaling deeply, Tanner looked out to the ocean for a moment before turning his eyes to Jessie's. "I am an empath."

"A what?"

"An empath. It is the emotional equivalent of a mind reader, only I get vibrations from people and these vibrations translate in my mind as emotional energy."

"You mean, you can tell how people feel?"

Tanner nodded. "Yes."

"Wow."

"But the problem was, the older I got, the less control I had. I was going crazy hearing everyone's vibrations. The only thing that blocked them out was dope. So, at the age of ten, I was smoking dope as a means of escaping the power I'd been born with."

Jessie leaned back, speechless.

Tanner shrugged. "I know. It's sorta hard to believe, but you know how it is. Any supernatural or preternatural abilities are either magic tricks or outright frauds. We may not kill people with extra senses, or burn them as witches, but we do everything we can to break their spirit."

Jessie could only stare at him. She thought *she* was different. "So, you smoked dope to escape these vibrations."

Tanner nodded and finished his bacon. "When I was fourteen, I ran, literally *ran* into Madam. I'd just stolen a watch from the store to sell so I could buy more dope, and I ran right into her. Knocked her down. She grabbed me and gazed right in my eyes with a look I swear to God, went right through me. And all she said was, "I can help you. You don't need to do this anymore. When you are ready to understand what it is that is happening to you, come see me."

"And you did."

"Well, it was a week when I couldn't get any dope and emotions were, like, overloading my circuits. She took me in and taught me how to build psychic walls to keep the vibrations out unless I chose to hear them."

"She taught you how to use your senses?"

"Yeah. That's when my whole world opened up. She taught me that we're all mammals, you know? And mammals in the animal kingdom rely on senses we call instincts, the deer that suddenly raises its head because it *feels* a hunter nearby. A male animal of nearly any species knows when it's the right time to mate. Jessie, we're just mammals who wear clothes and who pay bills. We claim to be the smartest animals on the planet, but we choose to ignore the other senses that would truly enhance our lives."

Jessie remembered her conversation with Ceara about women's intuition. So much of what she and Tanner said made perfect sense.

"We can't escape the scientific fact that we are mammals, but we do everything in our power to deny ourselves the unproven scientific issue of natural instinct."

"What do you mean, *unproven?*"

"No one can prove instincts in animals. We call it that, but we could just as easily call it extrasensory perception. Whatever we call it, it's just science guessing at the strange and wonderful phenomena animals use to communicate with each other. Look at all the work we do trying to understand dolphin-speak. It bothers us that we don't know how they talk to each other. We're wasting all this time and money studying their clicks and whistles, when they probably communicate via telepathy of some sort."

"Are there many like you?"

Tanner shrugged. "I don't really know. Madame says there are plenty of psychics who are really clairvoyant. The problem is, there are three times as many phonies who just want to make a buck, thereby invalidating those who truly have the sight."

The sight. Jessie shuddered at the term, hearing Maeve's voice in her head. "Are you?"

"Clairvoyant? Hell no. I'm just an empath." Tanner chuckled. "Anything more than that, and I'd have to slit my wrists." He finished his breakfast and set his fork down. "Speaking of which, you better call your folks."

Jessie groaned. "They're at the inn, aren't they?"

Tanner shook his head. "Actually, no. They never came back or I would have woken you up. They must have decided to go after your little brother after all."

Jessie lightly touched his wrist. "Thank you. You're a really good friend, Tanner, and your secret is safe with me."

Tanner grinned. "Good. And your secret, Jessie, is still a secret. Whatever it is."

Nodding, Jessie stared out at the waves below. Her secret: a life she'd never lived but was drawn to; a love she'd never experienced but deeply felt, and a crisis she'd known nothing of but had the power to change her world, those were her secrets.

Those secrets gnawed at her now, after seeing Ceara's beautiful photo books of Wales, of Mona, and of the large monoliths Cate had placed into Jessie's head that were, as of the publication of the book, still standing.

Still standing . . . after all these years.

The questions were, had Cate, Maeve and Lachlan lived through the disaster at Mona? If they did, where did they go after that? Would Cate have made it to the huge gray monolith standing watch over the hallowed grounds in Wales? If so, was it possible that she would ever make it to Wales to find out?

She could only wonder.

There were thousands of Druids on the Isle of Mona; so many, Cate could not believe it. There were others as well, but the vast majority were Silures and Druids, with a few dozen Iceni Druids tossed in for good measure. A handful of island warriors were scattered here and there, but most of them were awaiting word from the Chieftain.

When Cate's boat landed on the east side of the islands, dozens of Druids were there to greet them. "They look glad to see us," Cate said, pulling the three boats they had towed up to the shore.

"We bring news, and any news is better than guessing," Lachlan said, surveying the crowd and helping her with the thick ropes attached to the empty boats. "But where are the other boats? How can we get them off without boats?"

"Perhaps they are on the other side," Maeve offered, feeling the first pangs of worry.

As they disembarked, an old man carrying an oaken staff approached them. "Greetings my brethren and sisters. I am Doald, high priest of the Druids of the Isle. Have you come bearing news or are you, too, seeking sanctuary on this, our beautiful homeland?"

Sanctuary, Cate thought, shaking her head. They were in the direct line of the Roman attack, yet believed themselves to be safely ensconced on the island. "This island is—"

"Greeting, Doald," Maeve interrupted. "Is there a private place where we might talk?"

When Doald saw Maeve's gray eyes, he nearly fell prostrate upon the ground. "You are she, from Gaul. I—I had no idea it was you. It is most certainly a great pleasure to have you here on our island. The others will fill with joy and hope upon seeing that you have come. My humble abode is just across the river. Come."

They followed Doald for a bit until they came to a small village nestled next to the river at the opening of a great oak forest. Maeve understood why the Chieftain thought this a safe place to be; the woods offered protection while the river enabled quick escape to the ocean. It had its merits, if the Roman Army did, in fact, come by boat. While Maeve was informing Doald of the Roman battle plan, she was also considering the possibility that Eire would be the safest place to send these Druids, since Jessie had mentioned that the Romans had never been able to attack that island. But, would they be welcome, and for how long? Maeve sighed. They would send many to Alba, where clans were still strong and the Romans had yet to conquer them at all.

If only there was time.

There was not. Paulinus's fleets could be seen making their way along the coast. Dozens and dozens of flat-bottomed boats swimming ever closer to Mona. Following Doald's instructions, the Druids did not panic. Instead, they followed Maeve, Lachlan and Doald to the other side of the island in order to send as many as they could to Eire and Alba. There were not many boats, not nearly enough to save even a fraction of the people who either lived here or had come here for sanctuary, but they did their best. Maeve requested a boat or two be left behind should anyone survive the attack and need to get off quickly.

Those left behind to fight—men, women and children—collected spears, swords, daggers and even rocks and lined the shores with these weapons to use in defense. Others built fires all around the island, doing rituals, praying, preparing traps, and making means to attack the Romans from the spiritual realm.

They spent the entire day and into the evening readying the island. Every now and then, someone would climb down from the highest cliff to announce the closeness of the Roman fleet. As darkness finally fell over the island, the Druids and their loved ones gathered around the big bonfires sharing tales, myths, legends and prayers. This was not a morose sharing, for these people believed they would be together again. Doald, himself, shared a tale or two, even eliciting laughter from those who shared his bonfire. It was a remarkable end for a remarkable people who knew in their hearts their time in this life would soon be over. Proud, merry and brave, even as the specter of death hovered over them, they stayed together deep into the night, relishing every precious moment.

Except for Cate.

She felt saddened that for all her powers and her travels through the portal, she hadn't been able to do more. These people were a special breed, misunderstood and even feared by the mightiest beings on the planet, who sought to destroy those it did not understand. If a people did not speak that ugly Latin tongue, then they were an enemy of the arrogant Roman Senate, who, all too often, turned its sword upon its own. What kind of people were these Romans who could so easily take the lives of some of its greatest heroes?

Who were they that they could come so close to destroying the beautiful people gathered around these fires?

Closing her eyes, Cate leaned against a tree far from the light of the bonfire, and rested. She just needed a little nap—a moment's respite.

It was a sleep that would change history.

After Tanner left, Jessie spent the rest of the morning flipping through the numerous books Ceara had left for her. She had known nothing about the British Isles; she hadn't even known that Ireland was an island. God, how had she managed to pass *any* grade in school with such limited knowledge? How could she not know how beautifully green England was? If it weren't for Princess Diana, she'd know nothing about England or its people. It was a wondrous place filled with monoliths, burial grounds and myths that blurred folklore and reality.

The more she looked at it, the more familiar it became, and though she had studied hundreds of pictures, she kept coming back to the big white stone where Cate was to have left the ankh.

"Someday, Cate," Jessie whispered, tracing the rock with her finger, "I'll go there. I'll not rest again until I know for sure."

She opened one of the newer history books and idly leafed through it until she came across a picture that made her blood run cold. It was a painting of a woman in a chariot with a lion's mane flowing behind her as she urged her steeds onward into battle. One look at the caption, and Jessie knew. It was the woman from her dream.

It was Boudicca.

"Who in the hell *are* you?" Jessie whispered, leaning over to turn on the lamp. "Boudicca, Queen of the Iceni." She knew the Iceni. They were the group that lived to the east of the Silures.

Reading on, Jessie felt her muscles begin to tighten and her stomach fold in on itself.

Boudicca became Queen of the Iceni after her husband, Prasutagus, was murdered and her two daughters raped by soldiers of the Roman Army. She raised an army of close to 100,000 and, upon the advice of her administrators, attacked the Roman Army as it was in the midst of its final and complete destruction of the Druids and Silurians.

Jessie stared at the word *advice*. Someone had told Boudicca when to attack, causing Suetonius Paulinus to withdraw from Mona and Wales before he could complete what he had come there for. *That* was why she'd seen Boudicca in her dream. It was *the Queen's* intervention that saved the Silurians, not just knowing that the Isle of Mona was going to be attacked.

"Shit." Jessie spat, running for the phone and calling Ceara's shop. "Ceara?"

"Jess? Are you all right?"

"I have to go back."

"Oh, my dear, I thought Maeve had made it clear—"

"They still don't have all the information they need. I've had—I don't know what you'd call it, but I think I've had a vision of some sort."

"What are you talking about?"

"Can you meet me at the Pit in ten minutes?"

"Let me close up shop and I'm on my way."

When Jessie got to the top of Morning Glory, Ceara was already waiting for her behind one of the tall cedars.

"What is going on, my dear?"

"Boudicca."

Ceara's face fell. "Oh—my."

Jessie nodded. "I think *she's* the one who ultimately saves the remaining Druids and Silurians by entering the fray early and forcing Paulinus to turn his troops away from Wales and toward the Iceni. I read about it in one of your books. The book said someone *advised* her to attack sooner than she'd wanted to."

Ceara nodded slowly. "You believe you might be the one who advises her?"

Jessie nodded. "She changed her plans at the last minute."

Ceara's eyes narrowed as they walked toward the house. "What do you have in mind?"

"What if Boudicca *isn't* advised to start her attack early? The reports say she was advised. If Boudicca isn't warned, if I do nothing, is it possible that *everyone* on Mona could be killed?"

Ceara sighed. "If there is no event in history, there can be no memory of it."

"What does that mean?"

"If you do what is *not* recorded by anyone, if no one sees it or hears of it, if it just happens, there will be an effect that no one will truly know *why* it occurred."

"Like why she attacked early. All it says is advised."

"You keep forgetting that you are not merely changing history, but you are becoming *a part* of it. She will attack early because *you* advise her to do so. Is that what you're asking?"

Jessie nodded. "Yes, I am. And if the history books can't say why or who advised her . . ."

"It is because they do not know."

Jessie grinned. "I get it now. It's like that Buddhist line *If a tree falls in a forest and no one is around to see it, does it make a sound?*"

Ceara nodded. "Precisely. If you are going in to advise Boudicca, I suggest we get going before your parents return." She started for the house. "Just keep in mind you might not be welcome, nor might you be in time."

"I still have to try."

Ceara reached out and touched Jessie's shoulder. "You are not understanding me, my dear. It is quite possible that Cate is already dead."

Jessie felt like Ceara had punched her.

"You must consider all the consequences of going back Jessie, because if you go and Cate is—dead, wounded, not able to receive you—there are any number of things that could happen to you, and none of them good."

Jessie nodded, but her mind was made up. She would not be afraid. She would not let fear control her. "This is my destiny, Ceara. It's not just that. I couldn't live with myself if I didn't do more."

"For Maeve?"

Jessie nodded again. "She'd go back for *me*." Jessie started up the stairs and reached into her pocket for the key. "I won't be back until I am certain Cate hears me."

"Jessie—"

Turning to her, Jessie nodded. "I can think of worse fates than being trapped in the first century."

Ceara nodded. "Indeed. Please be careful, my dear. Who knows what could happen? I shall be here waiting, hoping, praying that you are not too late."

"See you soon, Ceara. And thank you. Thank you for everything." Slipping the key into the lock, Jessie was not the least bit prepared for what she was about to encounter.

All along the shores, Druids cast prayers, spells and spears at a befuddled and fearful Roman Army as it slowly, methodically, disembarked from the many, many, flat-bottomed boats arriving like waves upon the shore. The Roman soldiers, who had heard plenty of myths and legends about these strange people, were staring statues, afraid of the mythical might of the Druids of lore.

Silurian men and women alike screamed and ran back and forth along the shore, hurling curses against the soldiers, who were surprised by the preparedness of the Druids of Mona. They had been told not to heed the magic of the priests, but no one had told them the Druids would be standing on the shore waiting for them, unafraid, unfettered by the fear of death. The Romans had believed what Caesar had written about them; that they were aged and weak, slightly off-center and without bloodlust.

It was disconcerting to see none of that was true. Horses stamped on the ground, officers yelled and bullied the men to move forward, but it was to no avail. The Romans were clearly afraid. Even their horses seemed unsure as to what to do.

Suddenly, a Druid spear flew through the air striking a mounted Roman square in the chest, knocking him off his horse, impaling him to the ground. That act, that singular aggressive move seemed to chase the fear and trepidation from the soldiers. Instantly, they began responding to their commanders' orders.

In that moment, Cate knew all was lost. The Roman soldiers, swords swinging, arrows flying, began cutting down the first line of Druidic defense. Blood was everywhere as the soldiers compensated for their earlier hesitation by killing everything and everybody in sight. Old women and young children alike felt the bite of Roman metal swung by massively muscular arms. Horses trampled the dead beneath their feet as they pursued the retreating Druids.

Some soldiers died beside their feared and hated prey, but it became clear to everyone that Paulinus's order had been not to capture, but to destroy them. There would be no surrender, no prisoners and no survivors. These soldiers were a death squad sent to clean up the island of Mona and eradicate the leaders of a people too proud to bow to the Roman Senate.

The Chieftain, in his limited wisdom, had trapped his own priests on an island that was quickly turning into a burial site.

"Maeve," Cate whispered, watching the death and destruction from a hill by the river.

"I know, Catie. We cannot fight them or even hope to hold them off much longer."

"Flight?"

Maeve nodded. "If we wish to live another day. Thank the Goddess we were able to ship many away."

"The boats cannot make it back in time."

"I know."

"We must retreat into the woods. The Romans are afraid of our woods."

Maeve agreed. "The Druids from Mona wish to fight to defend their home, even unto death. Collect as many others as you can. Get them to build up the fires and tell them to escape into the groves. They ought to go in as far as they can."

"But the fires—Jessie said—"

"I know what Jessie said, my love, but without the cover of fire, we shall die much sooner."

"What of you? What are you going to do?"

"I am a Druid priestess, Catie. It is my job to call forth the spirits of the Otherworld to ask their assistance in this, our darkest hour."

"I will not leave you."

Maeve barely grinned. "Of course you won't. Come back here once you have sent word."

"Must I be the one to go?"

Maeve reached out and touched Cate's cheek. "Fear not. I shall be safe, as will you. Go quickly and return as fast."

"Have you seen it? Our safety? You know the outcome of this?"

"I know that you and I have much to do in this life yet. Go now, and be swift afoot."

Cate nodded and left, wishing she did not have to leave Maeve alone at all. This was not how she thought it would go. Something was terribly wrong. Had she misunderstood Jessie, or was Jessie's message too late? In trying to save Maeve, had Cate, in fact, damned them all? Those questions died on her lips because after she told their leaders of the retreat plan, she saw the one image before her she had gone across time to prevent: Roman soldiers were quickly bearing down on Maeve, who was so deep within herself and the Otherworld, she was not aware of the great threat approaching her.

"Maeve!" Cate cried out, plucking a dagger from the neck of a dead Druid, raised it high in the air and without another thought plunged it between the soldier's shoulders preventing him from swinging his sword in an attempt to cleave Maeve's head from her body.

"Maeve!"

This time, Maeve opened her eyes in time to see the flat end of a sword hit Cate on the side of the head, sending her to the ground like a dropped rock. In an instant, everything went black for Cate, and she did not see Maeve rise from her kneeling position, remove the dagger from between the dead soldier's shoulders, and ram it into the armpit of the soldier who had struck Cate.

All Cate saw was blackness. All she heard was a familiar voice trying to bring her to life.

"Cate? Wake up. It's *me*. You've got to wake up or we're going to die."

"Jessie?" Cate asked, feeling woozy, but able to get to her feet. "Oh.

We're in the Dreamworld, aren't we?"

Jessie started toward the mist and pulled Cate through it.

"Am I dead, then?" Cate asked when Jessie did not answer her.

"Well, if you are, so am I, and since I have no idea what dead feels like, I think we ought to just assume we're both still alive."

Cate shook her head, as if trying to gather her wits. "But—what are you doing here?"

Jessie helped Cate sit on the same stone she always sat on. Kneeling in front of her, Jessie held Cate's hands. "I haven't given you the most important piece to this puzzle. I came back because without it, you'll all die on Mona. There is one who can save you if you can reach her in time."

"Her?"

Jessie nodded. "Queen Boudicca."

"Boudicca of the Iceni? Why would she help us?"

"She has nearly one hundred thousand warriors ready to attack the flank of the Roman Army. If you can get word to her that Paulinus's men are on Mona, she'll know it would be a good time for her to strike. Paulinus will have to pull his men off Mona in order to face the greater threat of the Queen and her army."

"How does that save us?"

"It will keep Paulinus from destroying you outright. He will be forced to withdraw to face Boudicca, and when he does, you and the others can escape to Iona and Snowdonia, where your people will be safe."

Cate's eyes lit up with hope. "Then we must reach her at all cost."

Jessie nodded. "In the history books, she is *advised* by someone to attack Paulinus just as he invades Wales. That someone, my little Druid priestess, is *you*. You absolutely *must* get off this island and find your way to Boudicca."

Cate inhaled deeply and shook her head. "Queen of the Iceni will have no audience with the likes of a Silurian priestess."

"She will if you tell her that you know she has a scar the shape of an X over the inner right thigh she received in a battle earlier this year."

Cate stared at Jessie.

"It's in the books, Cate, that she carried many battle scars on her body. If you prove yourself to be a powerful enough priestess, she might grant you an audience."

Cate nodded. "I *am* a powerful priestess, Jessie. But what about Maeve? I will not leave her."

"Maeve must lead the remaining Druids to safety until Boudicca does her part. We have to leave her th—"

"No."

"Cate, you *must*. Now is the time to do the *right* thing. You have to see the Iceni Queen, and Maeve *must* lead the people to safety. It is the *only* way."

"Lachlan can lead," Cate said stubbornly.

Jessie shook her head. "No, he can't. Lachlan is doing what he does best, and that's heal people. He can heal those with minor injuries and let Maeve take to the woods. Surely, in the woods, we are at an advantage."

Cate thought about this and ever so imperceptibly nodded. "'Tis true."

"Then you just have to suck it up and go."

Cate cocked her head. "Suck. It. Up?"

"Be tough. Come on, Cate. For every minute you sit here, more die. You take a boat, get the hell off the island, grab a Roman horse and ride until you can't ride any more. Trust me on this. Boudicca can save you."

Cate looked into Jessie's face and nodded. "It will be done as you say."

Jessie sighed loudly. "Good. Be strong, and Cate—"

"I know. Suck. It. Up."

Jessie nodded. "Yeah. Something like that."

Rising, Cate inhaled deeply, straightened her spine, and looked like a woman getting ready for war. Taking Jessie's hands in hers, Cate leaned her forehead against hers. "You're a great woman, Jessie. Goodbye one last time. Perhaps, some day in the future, we shall be lucky enough to meet in our dreams."

"I hope so, Cate. Good luck, and Godspeed."

In that moment, Jessie found herself back in the bedroom, surrounded by dust and cobwebs with Ceara waiting for her out in the hall.

"Thank goodness," Ceara said. "Were you in time?"

Jessie felt so sick to her stomach that she sat on the hall floor. She had never imagined so much death and destruction as she was remembering now. "That was—awful. It was a bloodbath, Ceara."

"What of Cate and Maeve?"

Jessie sighed loudly. "I've done all I can for them."

"Then—"

Jessie nodded. "They were still alive. Barely. Cate got knocked in the head and so there we were, trying to figure out what to do from her dream world. She didn't want to leave Maeve, but I think I convinced her that was best."

"But there was still time?"

Jessie shrugged. "Too close to call. Cate is going to have to bust a gut to get there, and even then, she has to convince Boudicca to see her."

"Not great odds. Boudicca was not known for her patience or kindness."

"I think Cate can do it. It's what she's been trained for."

Ceara turned for the stairs. "Ah, the hopefulness of youth. I hope you're right, my dear. For all of their sakes."

"Where we going?"

Ceara stopped on the third step of the backstairs and turned to Jessie. "*I* am going to work to make money and pay my bills, as mundane as that is, and you—well, you need to figure out what you're going to do with the rest of your life. *This* life."

Jessie nodded. It was time to face the music and—well—do the right thing. "I need to talk to my folks, huh?"

Ceara nodded. "Our lives are here now, Jess, no matter how much we may both want them back there. Let your parents know who you are even as you go about finding *out* who that is. If you remember nothing else from this experience, remember that wisdom comes where you find it. And, somewhere in the future, your soul may very well need the wisdom you're gathering in this life."

Nodding, Jessie hugged Ceara and helped her down the steps. "Thank you so much. My life has changed so much because you are in it."

"Oh, my dear, there will be many more people who will change your life if you just let them."

"Like Tanner?"

"Perhaps."

"He told me."

"Did he now?"

"Do you always take in those society would just as soon straitjacket and toss in hell?"

Ceara's light blue eyes sparkled. "Nah. Only the good ones, and you, my dear, are most assuredly that."

When Ceara left, Jessie inhaled deeply, walked over to the front porch stairs, and sat on the top stair to wait for her parents. Jumbled emotions zinged about her heart as she tried to settle into the notion that she would never see Cate or Maeve again unless she, too, learned the craft. That was on her list of top ten things to do, the first of which was to get straight with her parents.

When they arrived, Reena charged up the stairs and hugged Jessie tightly even as she sniffed her hair.

"You're choking me, Mom."

Releasing her, Reena stepped back to allow Daniel through.

"Hey there, sport!" Jessie threw her arms around him and hugged him as tightly as Reena had hugged her. "Miss me?"

He laughed as he pulled away. "Like bad gas!"

Releasing him, Jessie shook her head as she studied him. "You okay?"

He nodded. "I just wanted to come home. Auntie's got really boring without ghosts and fishing and—you." Daniel turned to Rick, who waited at the bottom of the stairs. "There's something Mom and Dad need to tell you."

"Can I have some tea first? And then, can we all sit down and discuss where to go from here?"

Rick and Reena looked at each other as if to ask *What happened to our daughter?*

"Uh—sure, honey," Rick said, going to the kitchen to start the water.

Sitting next to Jessie on the top stair, Reena and Daniel replayed Daniel's version of Chris and the marijuana story.

"We were wrong, Jess. Totally wrong. I guess that Chris kid really is bad news. Daniel was adamant that we clear everything up with you the second we got home."

When she finished, Jessie mussed up Daniel's hair. "Thanks for finally getting that out in the open."

Reena put her arm around her shoulder. "We should have asked Daniel when you said. We never really gave you the chance to explain and we're really sorry. We jumped to conclusions based on your past behavior."

Jessie nodded. "It's not like my past behavior didn't merit present suspicion, Mom. Maybe we're all a little to blame."

"Jessie *promised* me two things, Mom: one, she wasn't doing drugs, and two, she wouldn't leave me here alone. She kept both promises."

"Circumstantial evidence is hard to ignore but I haven't smoked dope once in Oregon, and I'm not hanging out with bad influences. Regardless of what you think of Tanner, *he's* not the one you have to trust. I am. Give me the chance to be trustworthy. Others have."

Reena nodded. "We are so very sorry we doubted you."

Rick returned to the porch and handed Jessie a cup of tea before kissing the top of her head. "We haven't really given you much of a chance to start over, have we? I guess we thought you'd eventually try to go home—"

"Dad, this *is* my home. That's what you weren't hearing. I *love* it here."

Rick and Reena stared at their daughter.

"Look, I know I was a pain in the ass about moving here, but I've fallen in love with this crusty old place. It has lots of character, and I'm even beginning to like the inn. I'd like to show you how serious I am about changing, I want to strike a deal with you."

"A deal?"

"What kind of a deal?"

"I want to cash in some of the bonds Grandma left me so I can go to Wales."

"You want to go see the humpback whales? They're right here on the coast."

Jessie shook her head. "To *Wales*. The country in Great Britain. I'd like to go for two weeks before school starts."

Reena leaned forward, spilling some of her tea. "School? School starts September sixth. That's in less than two weeks."

"High school starts then. I'm talking about college. I've applied to the University of Oregon, and since I've taken so many honors courses, I'm only three credits shy of my diploma. I can take those cre—"

"You've what?" her parents said simultaneously. They looked dumbfounded.

"I want to go to college. I've grown up a lot since we got here, and if you'd just give me a chance, you'd see that I am *not* the girl who left California. I want to attend the university. I applied."

Rick looked at Reena, who was speechless. "Is this a joke? Is there a punch line?" He shook his head in exasperation. "Have I been in a coma?"

"Look at her, Dad," Daniel suggested. "*Really* look at her. You don't even *see* her anymore."

Rick stared at his son, then at Jessie, then back to Daniel. "Apparently, Jess isn't the only one who's grown up."

Jessie winked at Daniel. "You're my hero, but I still have to pay my dues. I'll even finish out rehab if it'll make you guys feel better, but I *really* want to go to Wales."

"And then you're going to go to college?" Rick asked. Reena just sat there with her mouth agape.

"Ceara's sparked my interest in history. I want to learn more. I've spoken with a professor, I got an application, and then I met with an advisor. I can late-register if you'll let me go."

Reena shook her head. "Let you go? Honey, *of course* we'll let you go."

"Then it's a deal?"

Rick answered for his stunned wife. "You really will finish out at the rehab center?"

Jessie nodded. "Part of being grown up is doing the right thing. If it will make you see how I really mean to stay straight, I'll go. Once I finish, it's done and in the past. I can move forward with my life, drug-free, debt-free, obligation-free. That's what I want. I want the clean slate we came here for."

Reena started crying silently and threw her arms around her daughter's neck. "Oh Jess—"

"Will you let me go to Wales if I can get Ceara to come with me?"

"Of course it's a yes."

Hugging her mother, Jessie closed her eyes and thought about Cate trying to convince the Iceni guards to allow her an audience with Boudicca. What happened, how it all turned out, would remain a mystery until she could get herself to Wales. More than once she'd stood with the key to the room in her hand, tempting herself to enter, begging for a sign that told her it was safe to go.

But it wasn't. She knew as much.

Instead, she and Ceara had concocted a plan that would take them to the only place on the planet that held the answer: Wales.

"What happened?" Reena asked. "I mean, really. What happened to change you so much?"

"Life, Mom. Life happened."

And life kept happening.

Two weeks later, Ceara and Jessie were on a tourist boat to the Isle of Anglesey. Rick and Reena had been so thrilled Jessie wanted to go to college they'd decided not to press her into finishing out her rehab stint, and instead paid her for the work she'd been doing at the inn.

In Wales, Ceara had cried for happiness, sadness, for memories of a time that had no resemblance to her own. It took her a day just to ride the rollercoaster of emotions that went with a homecoming such as this. When she was finally over the emotional tilt of it all, she changed into her tour guide hat and explained all of the landmarks and history she knew by heart. If it were possible, she was even more animated than ever, and she and Jessie grew closer than either had ever imagined.

Together, they had traveled to where the village of Fennel had once stood. Now, of course, it was a growing urban area. Still, seeing the land through Ceara's eyes was uplifting and exciting. Jessie had never had a better time, and had been frequented by a number of Cate's memories within her. Every night, Jessie had gone to bed hoping that Cate would visit her in the Dreamworld. She went to sleep longing for any vision that would tell her they'd made it out safely. Every morning, Jessie was disappointed not to have seen her. She so wanted to know that Cate had made it.

Through it all, it was this trip to the Isle that Jessie had waited for, and as the boat neared shore, her heart beat faster. She remembered Cate's fear when they first came to Mona; how everyone on the island was preparing for a most devastating attack. She remembered the pain, the anguish, the overall desperation of the Druids, as the Romans poured off the boats and onto the shores. She remembered, just as everyone had asked, and many memories continued to flow into her; yet the one she most wished to see wasn't one of them.

After freshening up in their hotel room on the Isle, Ceara ordered a taxi, and soon they were on their way to the Standing Stones. Jessie had tried to prepare herself for the distinct possibility that they had not made it out, or that Cate had forgotten to bury the ankh. There were more reasons why the ankh *wouldn't* be there than why it would. It was such a long shot, and yet, long shots were something Jessie was only now beginning to believe in.

"Nervous?" Ceara asked, patting Jessie's leg. "If it is not there—"

"A part of me just *knows* they survived. I feel it in my bones."

"Or soul."

Jessie grinned. "Yeah. There, too."

"You've not been able to access *anything* that would let you know they made it?"

Jessie shook her head. "Not a damn thing, and it's not for lack of trying. I can't find her no matter how hard I look."

"That happens sometimes, my dear. Memories aren't always accessible or available just because we want them to be."

"I wish they were. I *need* to know."

When they finally reached the Standing Stones, it was nearly dusk, but Jessie could easily distinguish the rock Cate had pointed out to her. After two thousand years, there it stood, just like the image in Jessie's mind. "That's the one."

"You sure?"

Jessie nodded. "I've memorized every single feature of it. I could see it blindfolded." Taking out her backpack, Jessie waited for Ceara to pay the cab. Then they walked across the length of two football fields to the Standing Stones.

When they came into view, Jessie stopped. "I can't believe they're still standing. After all these years—it's unreal."

Ceara sighed and brushed a tear away. "Some things just don't change." She reached out a trembling hand and touched the stone. "My God, it feels alive, like it contains all the memories of the ages." She knelt down and began a chant in a language Jessie had never heard.

When she finished, Jessie pulled a folded military shovel from her backpack and unfolded it. "You keep watch. She said it was an arm's length, so it'll take awhile."

Jessie dug for almost an hour, each shovelful weighing heavily on her heart. Just before darkness set in, she struck something solid. Dropping to their hands and knees, they both used their bare hands.

"What? What is it?" Ceara asked, tossing handfuls of dirt to the side of the hole.

"It feels like a box." Jessie strained to pull the small box from the hole. "Ceara, it's here! Something's here!"

"You're not fooling with an old woman's ticker, are you?"

Jessie shook her head. "It's made of some kind of metal. Thank God, she had the foresight to use metal." Slowly pulling the box out, Jessie held it up for Ceara to see.

It was a small metal box, no more than four inches to a side, and nondescript except for the latch holding it closed. "She did it," Jessie whispered, lightly touching the box. "My God, she did it."

"If you don't open that box in the next five seconds, my heart is going to burst."

With trembling hands, Jessie lifted the latch. Inside, lay the ankh Cate had shown her in the Dreamworld. Gently cradling it in her palm, she started crying. "They made it. They really made it."

Ceara stared down into Jessie's hand. "It is beautiful."

"We did it, Ceara."

"*You* did it, my dear." When Ceara reached out to touch the ankh, she, too, started crying.

"Wait. There's more," Jessie said, as she pulled out a necklace in the shape of a Celtic knot.

A small yelp escaped from Ceara's mouth. "That's—that's—"

Jessie gently took Ceara's palm and placed the knot inside it. "It's yours, isn't it?"

"It's the necklace I gave to Lachlan not long before I left." Ceara stroked the necklace softly, tears falling from her cheeks.

"They must have told him."

Ceara held the necklace to her chest and wept. "Oh, Jessie, he made it. My son made it. You saved his life."

"I had lots of help, Ceara."

For a long time, both women quietly cried, until finally they stopped long enough to take one last look inside the box. There was one more item. Someone had written a letter on a piece of vellum and wrapped it carefully in leather. Jessie's hands trembled as she carefully untied the leather strap and opened the leather piece to reveal the vellum.

"She wrote a letter." Jessie stared down at the parchment. "But the language is unfamiliar to me."

Ceara adjusted her glasses as she stared at the letter. "Not to me." She smiled softly. "It's written in my native tongue." Looking over Jessie's shoulder, Ceara inhaled deeply and read the letter aloud.

Jessie and Ceara—

We all made it off Mona, thanks to Boudicca's precious sacrifice. We are traveling to Eire where it will be somewhat safer to live out our lives as who we are. There are not words enough to thank you for all you have done for our people and us. Yes, Lachlan knows, and has included his own note. Know that you are always in our thoughts, and Jessie, I am a better person for having known you. You will not hear from me again, so please do not seek me out. You must live in your time and I must live in mine, but no matter where we are or what we do, we shall forever be one. Blessed be.

Cate

My dearest mother—

Ceara had to stop reading. The address was simply more than she could bear. "My son," she said to Jessie as she wiped her eyes. "He—called me mother. You have no idea how I longed to hear from him just one more time." Wiping her eyes, Ceara read on.

Remember this? You gave it to me with these words: "Grow up with the intention of changing the world. Everyone has within them the power to make a difference. Go, and make a difference in the world." I shall, mother, as you will see from where you now live. I can be happy now, knowing you still live, and always will inside my heart. I will do you proud.

Your loving son,

Lachlan

Jessie put her arm around Ceara and hugged her. "What a wonderful gift."

"Indeed. It fills my heart more than I ever thought this old heart could take. But there's one more note, my dear. To you."

Jessie—

Remember . . . I am still out there, looking for you, as I have since the dawn of humankind. Close no doors, for you shall never know which one I may be behind. Ours is a love time cannot conquer . . . You will know the moment you see me. Trust that. Trust yourself.

I am now, and shall always be yours.

Maeve

Ceara stepped away from Jessie, who was smiling through tear-filled eyes. "Oh, my dear, there could be nothing more precious than the gifts in this box."

Taking Ceara's hand, Jessie held it long into the dark of night as they sat together recalling a love so strong it had traveled across time to touch their hearts and change their lives forever.

Afterward

Although the historical events in this book actually did take place, I have taken some creative liberties along the way for the sake of the story. Any potential mistakes whether intentional or accidental, in regard to timelines or place are solely my own.

According to Tacitus, the Druids were attacked on the Isle of Mona and their groves burnt down. Did any of them escape? I like to think so. Did Boudicca really turn her chariot around for no apparent reason? I believe great leaders always have a reason. Are past lives possible?

You tell me.

Those who do not remember history are doomed to repeat it (Santayana). When a certain group of people have their rights violated, for whatever reason, it is up to the rest of us to stop it and demand justice. There are oak groves burning all over the world…groups like the Druids targeted every day. People who are "different" from the majority.

Let's not be doomed.
Let's remember.

Publications from Spinsters Ink

P.O. Box 242
Midway, Florida 32343
Phone: 800-301-6860
www.spinstersink.com

MERMAID by Michelene Esposito. When May unearths a box in her missing sister's closet she is taken on a journey through her mother's past that leads her not only to Kate but to the choices and compromises, emptiness and fullness, the beauty and jagged pain of love that all women must face.

ISBN 978-1-883523-85-5 $14.95

ASSISTED LIVING by Sheila Ortiz-Taylor. Violet March, an eighty-two-year-old resident of Casa de los Sueños, finally has the opportunity to put years of mystery reading to practical use. One by one her comrades, the Bingos, are dying. Is this natural attrition, or is there a sinister plot afoot?   ISBN 978-1-883523-84-2 $14.95

NIGHT DIVING by Michelene Esposito. *Night Diving* is both a young woman's coming-out story and a 30-something coming-of-age journey that proves you can go home again.

ISBN 978-1-883523-52-7 $14.95

FURTHEST FROM THE GATE by Ann Roberts. *Furthest from the Gate* is a humorous chronicle of a woman's coming of age, her complicated relationship with her mother and the responsibilities to family that last a lifetime.   ISBN 978-1-883523-81-7 $14.95

EYES OF GRAY by Dani O'Connor. Grayson Thomas was the typical college senior with typical friends, a typical job and typical insecurities about her future. One Sunday morning, Gray's life became a little less typical, she saw a man clad in black, and started doubting her own sanity.　　　　　ISBN 978-1-883523-82-4　　$14.95

ORDINARY FURIES by Linda Morgenstein. Tired of hiding, exhausted by her grief after her husband's death, Alexis Pope plunges into the refreshingly frantic world of restaurant resort cooking and dining in the funky chic town of Guerneville, California.
ISBN　978-1-883523-83-1　　$14.95

A POEM FOR WHAT'S HER NAME by Dani O'Connor. Professor Dani O'Connor had pretty much resigned herself to the fact that there was no such thing as a complete woman. Then out of nowhere, along comes a woman who blows Dani's theory right out of the water.
ISBN 1-883523-78-8　　$14.95

WOMEN'S STUDIES by Julia Watts. With humor and heart, *Women's Studies* follows one school year in the lives of three young women and shows that in college, one's extracurricular activities are often much more educational than what goes on in the classroom.
ISBN 1-883523-75-3　　$14.95

THE SECRET KEEPING by Francine Saint Marie. *The Secret Keeping* is a high-stakes, girl-gets-girl romance, where the moral of the story is that money can buy you love if it's invested wisely.
ISBN 1-883523-77-X　　$14.95

DISORDERLY ATTACHMENTS by Jennifer L. Jordan. The fifth Kristin Ashe Mystery. Kris investigates whether a mansion someone wants to convert into condos is haunted.
ISBN 1-883523-74-5　　$14.95

VERA'S STILL POINT by Ruth Perkinson. Vera is reminded of exactly what it is that she has been missing in life.
ISBN 1-883523-73-7 $14.95

OUTRAGEOUS by Sheila Ortiz-Taylor. Arden Benbow, a motorcycle riding, lesbian Latina poet from LA is hired to teach poetry in a small liberal arts college in Northwest Florida.
ISBN 1-883523-72-9 $14.95

UNBREAKABLE by Blayne Cooper. The bonds of love and friendship can be as strong as steel. But are they unbreakable?
ISBN 1-883523-76-1 $14.95

ALL BETS OFF by Jaime Clevenger. Bette Lawrence is about to find out how hard life can be for someone of low society standing in the 1900s.
ISBN 1-883523-71-0 $14.95

UNBEARABLE LOSSES by Jennifer L. Jordan. The fourth Kristin Ashe Mystery. Two elderly sisters have hired Kris to discover who is pilfering from their award-winning holiday display.
ISBN 1-883523-68-0 $14.95

FRENCH POSTCARDS by Jane Merchant. When Elinor moves to France with her husband and two children, she never expects that her life is about to be changed forever.   ISBN 1-883523-67-2 $14.95

EXISTING SOLUTIONS by Jennifer L. Jordan. The second Kristin Ashe Mystery. When Kris is hired to find an activist's biological father, things get complicated when she finds herself falling for her client.
ISBN 1-883523-69-9 $14.95

A SAFE PLACE TO SLEEP by Jennifer L. Jordan. The first Kristin Ashe Mystery. Kris is approached by well-known lesbian Destiny Greaves with an unusual request. One that will lead Kris to hunt for her own missing childhood pieces.
ISBN 1-883523-70-2 $14.95

Visit

Spinsters Ink

at

SpinstersInk.com

or call our toll-free number

1-800-301-6860